ANCIENT ONES

Also by Kirk Mitchell

Procurator
New Barbarians
Cry Republic
Never the Twain
Black Dragon
With Siberia Comes a Chill
Shadow on the Valley
Fredericksburg
High Desert Malice
Deep Valley Malice
Cry Dance
Spirit Sickness

ANCIENT
ONES

KIRK
MITCHELL

BANTAM BOOKS
NEW YORK / TORONTO
LONDON / SYDNEY / AUCKLAND

ANCIENT ONES
A Bantam Book / May 2001
All rights reserved.
Copyright © 2001 by Kirk Mitchell.

Book design by O'Lanso Gabbidon

Map by Jeffrey L. Ward

Library of Congress Cataloging-in-Publication Data
Mitchell, Kirk.
Ancient ones / Kirk Mitchell
p.   cm.
ISBN 0-553-10914-6
1. *Parker, Emmett (Fictitious character)—Fiction.* 2. *Turnipseed, Anna (Fictitious character)—Fiction.* 3. *Indians of North America—Fiction.* 4. *Government investigators—Fiction.* 5. *Warm Springs Indian Reservation (Or.)—Fiction.* 6. *Oregon—Fiction.* I. Title
PS3563.I7675   A84   2001   00-052920

Published simultaneously in the United States and Canada

Bantam Books are published by Bantam Books, a division of Random House, Inc. Its trademark, consisting of the words "Bantam Books" and the portrayal of a rooster, is Registered in U.S. Patent and Trademark Office and in other countries. Marca Registrada. Bantam Books, 1540 Broadway, New York, New York 10036.

PRINTED IN THE UNITED STATES OF AMERICA
BVG   10   9   8   7   6   5   4   3   2   1

ANCIENT ONES

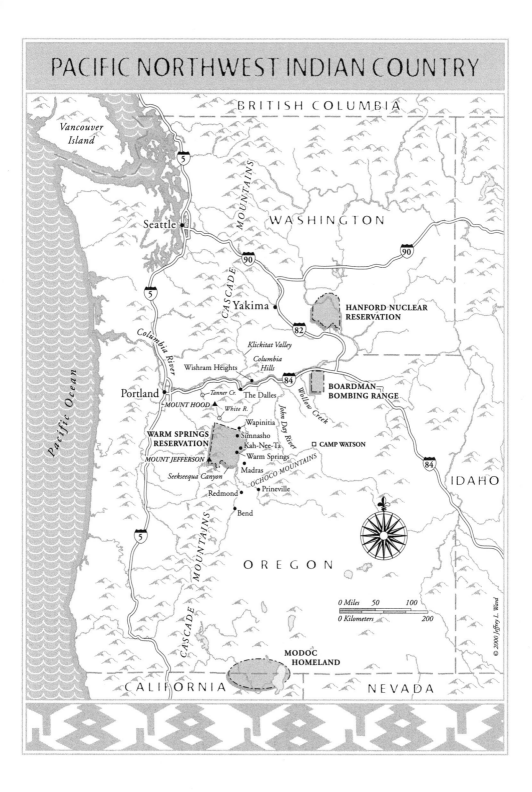

PACIFIC NORTHWEST INDIAN COUNTRY

BRITISH COLUMBIA

Vancouver
Island

WASHINGTON

Seattle

CASCADE MOUNTAINS

Yakima

HANFORD NUCLEAR
RESERVATION

Columbia River

Klickitat Valley

Columbia
Hills

Wishram Heights

BOARDMAN
BOMBING RANGE

Portland

Tanner Cr. The Dalles

MOUNT HOOD

White R.

John Day River

Wallow Creek

Pacific Ocean

Wapinitia

WARM SPRINGS
RESERVATION

Simnasho
Kah-Nee-Ta
Warm Springs

☐ CAMP WATSON

MOUNT JEFFERSON

Madras

Seekseequa Canyon

OCHOCO MOUNTAINS

Redmond

Prineville

IDAHO

Bend

CASCADE MOUNTAINS

O R E G O N

0 Miles   50   100
0 Kilometers   200

© 2000 Jeffrey L. Ward

MODOC
HOMELAND

CALIFORNIA

NEVADA

1

For years, Gorka Bilbao drove sheep back and forth across the hills of north central Oregon. Each day began anew the search for fresh grass and tender green herbs. He baked his bread in a Dutch oven over a sagebrush fire. He slept alone in a coffinlike travel trailer. That is how his father and his grandfather had earned their living, and Bilbao never dreamed of doing anything else. But when he was forty-two, the federal government cut back the number of sheep it allowed to graze on public lands. The conservationists said sheep were overgrazing the range. Most of the herds went to the slaughterhouses, and Bilbao's old way of life passed away.

What to do?

For a while, he washed dishes at his cousin's restaurant in Portland. But cities were his downfall. They tempted him to do bad things. A woman would get inside his head and not let go of him until he had her. He was completely helpless against this desire. And it eventually cost him his freedom. Released from prison, he returned to the badlands east of the Cascade Mountains. He could find no way to earn his bread there, so he drank up his welfare money and waited to get sick and die. All things without purpose on the desert get sick and die.

Yet the badlands wouldn't let him slide off into oblivion.

Each winter, the rains washed a new crop of fossils and old bones out of the volcanic ash that jacketed the barren hills. For as long as he could remember, Bilbao had stumbled across weathered bones and flat rocks with the imprints of leaves and strange creatures in them. He never gave these oddities much of a thought. But then, while waiting for his next welfare check, he came upon a man in a floppy straw hat and short pants who was scratching at the banks of the John Day River with a pick. A college man, it turned out. On that day, Bilbao heard the word *fossil* for the first time. The college man showed him a fossilized three-toe hoof, explaining that it came from a dog-sized horse that had once roamed this country. Bilbao asked if it had been an Indian pony. Smirking, the college man said no, this was long before there were any men in Oregon, long before there was such a place called Oregon. All this was of mild interest to Bilbao.

But what the college man said next made the unemployed shepherd's ears perk up.

The professor would pay good money for fossils. Others, although not he, would pay even more for human bones that weren't quite fossils. As much as their weight in gold. That astonished Bilbao. It also made him grimace as he recalled all the skeletal remains he'd passed by through the years. The college man said that fossils and bones, once exposed to the elements, quickly crumbled and lost their value.

No more would Gorka Bilbao pass them by, and on that afternoon he became a fossil hunter.

Ten years later now, he was back along the John Day River. His shoulders were hunched and burly from a decade of hacking at the ground with a pick, and his tangled beard was flecked with seeds from the thickets that lined the river. It was the last week of September. Mist hid the canyon walls, although a pale sun kept trying to break through. The unseasonable chill had made Bilbao take out his moth-eaten army overcoat and mittens with the fingertips cut off so he could still pick up fine bones. Soon it would be winter. This was a cold desert. Blizzards howled down the canyons. Ice fogs stole in during the night and left diamonds on the brush when the heatless sun came out at dawn. It'd be nice to hole up in his cabin in the Ochoco Mountains during the bad months, to do nothing but drink, but he always seemed to need the cash from more fossils and bones.

Bilbao suddenly halted. "Here we go," he whispered to himself. "Here we go now . . ."

At the foot of the bank lay a fossil fragment shaped like an oyster cracker. He recognized it right off: a scale from the shell of a giant turtle that had swum the vast, inland lake that had once covered this now parched country.

Bilbao looked over his shoulder for the U.S. Bureau of Land Management ranger who patrolled the area. The cop knew him, knew what he did for a living, and tried to keep an eye on Bilbao. But the desert was a big place.

Seeing no one, Bilbao pocketed the piece of turtle shell. The turtle was an animal with a backbone, and the fossils of animals with backbones were off-limits. Much of what Bilbao collected was against the law to possess, and nothing more so than the remains of human beings. But oh so valuable. Yet, they had to be ancient. Very, very ancient. Once, on a moonless night, Bilbao had dug up a skeleton from the graveyard outside the old Bureau of Indian Affairs hospital in Warm Springs, then soaked the bones in potassium bichromate, hoping to pass them off as being thirteen thousand years old. That was the magic number to the college men; they didn't figure Indians had been in this country much longer than that. He tried to sell the remains to a professor, but the man knew at once they were fakes and refused to do further business with Bilbao. After that, the fossil hunter became more careful.

College men knew bones like shepherds knew sheep.

Still, there were ways to find the genuine article.

Last autumn, the Army Corps of Engineers had finished the Clarno Reservoir—Bilbao could see the sweeping concrete face of the dam from where he stood. And three weeks ago, the spillway gates had been opened, disgorging a man-made flood. This was to help the Chinook salmon make their way up the canyon and over the dam's fish ladder to their spawning places. The torrent had chewed at the banks of the John Day, hopefully scouring out old bones like nuggets of gold. Last night, the gates had been shut, and the river had dropped again. These fluctuations were posted by the Army Corps of Engineers in the local newspaper, and Bilbao was usually first to search any canyon after a water release.

A loud splash turned him around—a slab of bank had just peeled off into a muddy pool.

Bilbao scurried over to this hump of dissolving earth and ran his practiced eye over the debris of centuries. There were flakes of stone left by Indian arrowhead makers. Charcoal from a brush fire that may have swept this way a thousand years ago. Black pellets of sheep dung from a herd he himself might have run when he was younger.

By noon, Bilbao had found the vertebra of an oreodont, a stubby-legged, plant-eating creature.

But nothing else.

He waded across the shallow river. The water slopped into his boots and soaked his socks. He must get used to the cold again. He couldn't let the weather stop his searching, just as he'd never let it make him neglect his herd.

At dusk, a chip of darkly soiled bone caught Bilbao's attention along the east side of the John Day. It was resting on top of another slab of earth that had sloughed off the bank. Anyone but Bilbao, who saw bone fragments in his dreams, would have missed it.

"Slow down, slow down," Bilbao reminded himself. Haste had no purpose here.

Just to the left of the chip was a knee joint. Carefully, he pried the thigh bone out of the silt and examined it. Human. It was definitely human. But how old? Bilbao sucked on his lower lip, studying the bone. By nature, he was suspicious of good fortune, for he'd had almost none in his life, but his heart was beating fast. This was good, so very good.

He peered down.

Strewn around his boots were a jumble of rib, finger and toe bones.

"Jesus!" he cried out loud.

Most of a skeleton, maybe. Rare, so very rare, for with time the Earth scattered her dead children far and wide. But this specimen still might be in one place.

All of a sudden, the hair on the back of his neck prickled. As if he'd blundered into a rattlesnake den. Something rattled angrily all around him, but when he held his breath to listen over his pounding heart, he heard only the murmur of the river. Something was rising from the mud. He could feel it swirling in the air, almost see it spinning into shape. The fog blew back from the mound, and the brush topping the bank shivered as if trying to yank free of its roots and bolt away.

Bilbao shut his eyes.

The nearby Warm Springs Indians claimed that there was bad power in old bones. This power was easy to awaken but almost impossible to put to rest again. He didn't want to see anymore. He was chilled by his find. Evil surrounded it, just as evil surrounded him when the city got hold of his soul and made him do things against his nature.

But there was also pleasure in evil—and profit. As if on that thought, the air went still. Dead still.

Slowly, Bilbao opened his eyes.

There was no sign of the strange restlessness that had just sprung from the ground. Calming down, he began searching for the other bones of the skeleton.

He located the sternum several yards upstream. Grinning, he was reaching for it when the same blustery evil seemed to explode out of the silt. It gave the breastbone life, made it appear to be a gigantic centipede scuttling through the ooze.

Bilbao staggered back on his heels.

This had happened before. In the detoxification tank of the Portland city jail. Things had wriggled out of the lime green walls to molest him, a gushing mass of cockroaches, worms and spiders that vanished only when the jailer answered Bilbao's hysterical screams.

He forced himself to approach the breastbone again. It lay completely still now. Just a sternum. But one stained dark with age. He made up his mind that nothing was going to spoil his good fortune.

Then his breath seized in his throat—jutting from a sand bar was the domed curvature of a human skull.

Splashing over to the bar, he lifted the cranium free. Only the upper portion of the skull. The lower jaw was probably buried nearby. Bilbao studied the specimen. A narrow face and a slightly projecting upper jaw. Not the round face and flat upper jaw of other skulls he'd found. He'd found no Indian skulls like this, but he'd been told to keep an eye out for this very thing—a different-looking skull of great age.

"My God, this is one of them! *This is one!*"

Through the gaping eye sockets, he saw himself sitting in front of his cabin in the shade of his pine tree, sipping Thunderbird wine, planning his next trip to the listless but complying women who walked Portland's streets.

Bundling the bones up in his coat, Bilbao laughed giddily to himself. "Son of a bitch, yes—I'm on a roll! Nothin' can stop me now!"

• • •

Out of an awkward silence—and there'd been several awkward silences so far—Anna Turnipseed's gently smiling, white-haired therapist said, "Well, you're both Native American. That should make communication a snap. And you both have the same job, FBI agents . . ." Anna expected Emmett Parker, her yet unconsummated lover of three months, to correct Dr. Tischler. Anna was the FBI agent; Emmett was a criminal investigator for the Bureau of Indian Affairs.

But he didn't.

He looked like a POW under interrogation. One who'd resolved to give nothing more than name, rank and serial number.

"How's communication been flowing lately, Emmett?" Dr. Tischler asked.

Parker shifted his tall, muscular frame on the sofa as if the simple act of sitting had begun to torture him. "Okay," he finally replied.

Less than a ringing endorsement for Anna's and his progress since their last session three weeks ago in this office.

Dr. Tischler pressed, "Has Anna continued to share things about her childhood with you?"

"This and that," Emmett said indifferently, avoiding Anna's eyes. That stung. She'd told him more than "this and that." Dredging up those malignant memories had nearly killed her. It had amounted to an extraordinary act of trust, running her soul over the cutting edge of the past. For an adult survivor of child abuse, the past was not a stroll down memory lane. She wanted to smack Emmett, but relaxed her fists for fear Dr. Tischler would scope on this hint of aggression.

"Do you appreciate how hard it is for Anna to discuss these memories, Emmett?"

"Of course I do." He slowly ran his hand over his close-cropped black hair. Hair with the lustrous sheen of raven feathers, but for the recently sprouted touches of gray. "I've investigated dozens of cases just like hers, and I can't imagine a worse nightmare for a child than being molested by a parent. But what's past is past. Why can't Anna accept that?"

"Good question," Dr. Tischler said. "People who were sexually traumatized by their caregivers have recurring experiences long after the abuse. Such as flashbacks. The past is very much part of their daily lives." The psychiatrist folded her hands in her lap. Her one concession to Emmett's presence was not to break out the knitting she worked at when alone with Anna. "Last time, Emmett, you promised to be patient with Anna while she develops a perspective toward her late father."

Anna blurted, "Emmett's been more than patient, Myra." Then, too late, she realized that she was rushing to defend Emmett just as her mother had her father. All at once, she wanted nothing more than to get out of this office, even if it was out into the glaring, wide-eyed Las Vegas evening.

"I'm pleased, Anna," Dr. Tischler said. "So you two continue to lay the groundwork for healthy sexual expression . . ." She took a sip of mineral water, the loose skin of her underarm jiggling as she set the glass back on the coffee table. The psychiatrist was pushing seventy, and Anna dreaded the day the woman would retire. She didn't want to go through all this with somebody new. "And I sense a strong desire for commitment here. Anna, didn't you just turn down a promotion so you could remain relatively close to Emmett?"

"The assistant directorship of the Indian Desk at FBI headquarters in Washington."

"What's that, dear?"

"A special department that oversees cases in Indian Country."

"So at this time in your life you consider your relationship with Emmett to be more important than career advancement?"

"Yes." But Anna's quick reply made her feel nauseatingly compliant, so she echoed, "At this point."

Dr. Tischler brightly shifted gears. "Okay, let's try to figure out what went wrong this time and adjust our tactics. Any ideas, Emmett?"

"None."

Anna had to unclench her hands again. In private to her, Emmett had accused the psychiatrist of showing "survivor bias," aligning with Anna. Now he was apparently out to prove it.

Dr. Tischler said, "Our goal is to create a good sexual experience for the two of you. Right?" Anna nodded, but Emmett's face remained deadpan. "Of all the techniques I suggested, which has come closest to achieving that?"

Silence.

"What about hand-holding?" Dr. Tischler checked the mantel clock over her gas-fed fireplace. Blue teardrops of flame flickered up from the grill. It was the middle of October, and the north winds were just starting to abate southern Nevada's furnacelike heat, enough so for the Boston-bred doctor to celebrate the seasonal change by lighting the burners. Yet she seemed to be one of those easterners who'd been captivated against her will by the desert. The stark and haunting quality of its sunlight, she'd once explained. "Did you enjoy the hand-holding, Anna?"

"Very much so."

"Emmett?"

He sighed.

Dr. Tischler smiled coolly. "Meaning you didn't enjoy it?"

"No, I did," he answered. "It just felt a little funny to me."

"How?"

"Well, sitting in Anna's living room in the dark, holding hands half the night like a couple of teenagers."

"How old are you, Emmett?"

"Forty," he replied as Dr. Tischler scribbled a note on her pad. "Thirteen years older than Anna," he added pointedly.

The psychiatrist asked, "Is hand-holding a traditional way of expressing affection in Comanche and Modoc cultures?"

Anna shrugged, then saw Emmett do the same. Her mother and father had never held hands in her presence. Nor shown any tenderness to each other, which told Anna that deep down her mother had known what was going on.

"All right," Dr. Tischler said, "how else did you two try to build a foundation of comfort? Any imagery rehearsal?"

Anna replied, "I think we're a little too old-fashioned to talk . . . you know, Myra . . . so explicitly about the act."

"Are the Comanche a prudish people, Emmett?"

He sat up, obviously provoked. "Not at all."

Anna swiftly inserted, "Emmett also shampooed my hair."

"And how'd you find that, dear?"

"It was sweet. He kept asking if he was hurting me."

"Was he?"

"No, he was very gentle. And we laughed a lot."

"Excellent, Emmett," Dr. Tischler said. "So I take it you enjoyed the experience as well?"

"Kind of."

"Kind of . . . *what?*"

"Well, I got this crazy urge to do her nails too." Emmett laid his Oklahoma drawl on thick. "And I dang near asked Anna if I was too old for beauty school."

Dr. Tischler chuckled after a moment. "All right, you character—so you both worked up to taking a shower together. Tell me how you prepared yourselves."

Emmett clammed up again, so Anna volunteered, "The week before, we talked about it over the phone."

"And how'd that make you feel?"

"I don't know," Anna said. "Silly. But safe."

"That's right. Things don't strike us as being silly unless we feel safe," the psychiatrist observed. "In this case, Anna, your sense of safety came from distance. You live here and Emmett lives in Santa Fe."

"Phoenix," he corrected.

Anna could tell that he was smarting from her "safe" remark. She now regretted having uttered it. Regretted everything she'd ever contaminated with her sordid problem. In every other regard of her life, she was strong and in control. But as soon as she stepped inside this office . . .

"Go on, Anna," Dr. Tischler coached. "You're doing fine."

Anna suddenly choked up.

Emmett took over. "She flew down to Phoenix last Friday night. Dinner was great. The drive to my apartment was great. She thought my idea of putting candles in the bathroom was great. Everything was great till I turned on the taps and dropped my Levi's. Then she freaked on me."

"I did *not* freak." Anna raised her voice enough for Dr. Tischler to jump a little.

"Could've fooled me," Emmett went on. "When a woman buries her face in her hands, I call that freaking."

Dr. Tischler turned to Anna. "Flashback?"

Anna nodded vehemently.

"Just because I took off my goddamn trousers?" Emmett said. "I don't know how you Modoc are raised, but everybody in my family showers in the nude. Now, I don't want to be culturally insensitive, but there are a helluva lot more Comanche than Modoc, and I'm beginning to see a pattern that might explain—"

"Thank you, Emmett," the psychiatrist cut him off. "Anna, did your father wear Levi's back in those . . . ?" The woman didn't have to finish.

Her stomach churning, Anna confessed, "Old faded pairs. Like Emmett was wearing Friday night."

"How was I supposed to know that?" he complained. "I always put on my old Levi's as soon as I can get out of that monkey suit and tie the BIA makes me wear."

"Anna tells me you have a scientific degree."

"Criminology major, anthropology minor," he said sullenly.

"Then you'll understand—we're dealing with conditioned stimuli that inhibit Anna's arousal. It isn't you. And this is a trial-and-error process. Now you both know the effect a pair of old jeans can have on your attempts at intimacy." Dr. Tischler checked the clock again. "What's really important—how'd Emmett's disrobing make you feel, Anna?"

"Small," she said quietly.

"Made *you* feel small!"

Anna gave his hand a squeeze. "Don't be mad, Em. It's just that some things you do take me back to how I used to feel. Not all the time. I like the way you make me feel when we're detailed together on a case."

"Good point," Dr. Tischler interjected. "You learned to bond as professional partners over these past months. Now you must learn to do the same as lovers. In either case, it's seldom easy."

Emmett's look softened, and Anna let go of his hand. No one said anything, and the ticking of the clock became audible.

Dr. Tischler was first to break another extended silence. "Anna, did you look forward to the shower or dread it? Be honest with us."

Anna felt the heat of a blush on her cheeks. "Looked forward. There were moments when the thought of it really seemed sexy. That's what so disappointed me Friday night, Myra. I'd really looked forward to being with Emmett like that."

"All right, dear. We have to design a different kind of situation. Another stepping-stone on the path to full intimacy. One that assures you that you're not expected to go all the way, but gives you a taste of sensual pleasure under controlled conditions. Emmett, take Anna somewhere public and show her how much fun heavy petting can be. The only condition—it has to be a place where intercourse is completely out of the question."

Emmett's jaw had dropped. "We're federal law enforcement officers."

"So?"

"We've got conduct codes hanging over our heads."

Dr. Tischler smiled impishly. "Then you'll have to be sneaky, won't you?"

• • •

On the drive across Las Vegas, Emmett came within a breath of asking Anna how long this delay would go on. Previously, he'd been married and divorced in less time than the nine months he'd known Turnipseed. But as he cooled down after another profitless and embarrassing session with her shrink, he realized that any sign of his growing exasperation would devastate her. He was tired, yet suggesting that they just go back to her condo and relax—before she retired to her bed upstairs and he to her couch downstairs—would be taken as his throwing in the towel.

"You hungry?" she asked. Strange how swiftly after the turmoil of these sessions her self-confidence returned. As if there were two halves of her self that never intersected.

He shook his head at her offer to eat.

She was so damned pretty. Petite, pert bobbed brown hair, big and expressive eyes, a light cinnamon complexion, great legs. But how much more simple and less convulsive his life would be today if that prettiness had left him cold last December when they were teamed up in Las Vegas to investigate the homicide of a U.S. Bureau of Land Management bureaucrat. Long hours together in the field had led to his infatuation with her, and that infatuation had deepened into love over the months of her convalescence. She, an innocent and a rookie at the time, had been tortured and nearly beaten to death by a sociopath who'd been after Emmett, and that made him wonder if his inexplicable patience with her had as much to do with guilt as passion. Endless patience from an impatient man who was used to sensual gratification. For Anna Turnipseed was apparently untouchable. As much as she obviously cared for him, she would not be touched.

Maybe this troubled relationship was Emmett's personal purgatory. The dead were the last to realize that they were dead. He'd been shot on duty out on some lonely reservation and had yet to comprehend this otherworldly reality. Anna was a tantalizing object lesson, and now he had to confront the rampant desires of his youth before moving on to a higher spiritual plane. Or maybe he was doomed forever to try to draw the waters of lust with a sieve. *But what have I done wrong?* Sex was like food to a Comanche, essential for healthy life.

"Any ideas where we can go?" Anna asked.

"Not without getting both of us dragged before a review board," he replied. He'd considered the airport, but just the notion of necking in a phone booth among hordes of potbellied, camera-toting tourists was enough to turn his stomach. "You mind just driving out into the desert?"

"Myra said someplace *public*," Anna sharply reminded him.

"How about the nuclear test site? It's monitored around the clock by Department of Defense police. That safe enough?" Emmett turned right on Tropicana Avenue around the New York, New York casino. Manhattan, Venice, Paris, imperial Rome—not one of the mega-resorts had a motif to remind the tourist that he was in Great Basin Nevada. Maybe it was a blessing. Emmett couldn't imagine all this chintz invested in a desert-Indian ambiance. The Southern Paiutes who'd lost these lands preferred their landscape unadorned.

Emmett had powered down his car window, and a mix of squeals and screams drifted from the top of the false New York skyline that overspread the hotel.

On an impulse, he veered into the valet parking entrance.

Within minutes, Anna and he were gliding up an escalator out of the casino hubbub to the arcade level. Without looking at him, she touched the back of her hand against his. Again. Then she took his hand. It was done with such silken grace, Emmett felt his pulse quicken. Was she trying to drive him out of his mind? If so, she was close to succeeding. "When I want you . . ." he started, then stopped.

"Go on."

"When I want you, I'm not trying to *punish* you."

"I know, Em." She looked hurt. And extraordinarily attractive. But then, glancing around, she laughed when she saw what he had in mind. "You're kidding."

"Nope. If this ain't imagery rehearsal, I don't know what is." Standing back, he waited until a throng of Japanese tourists had filled the first seats in the Manhattan Express. The roller coaster train resembled four New York taxis jammed bumper-to-bumper in traffic. The taxicab seats were high backed, creating enough privacy from the other riders for Anna to eye Emmett apprehensively as he helped her into the last car. The restraining bar lowered across their laps, locking them in.

The train rolled outside and started ratcheting up a towering incline with no guardrails. The weight of the climb pressed them back into their seats, but Anna looked over at him. "You getting tired of me, Em?"

Of this endless wait for something he'd wanted to do since the first time he'd seen her? Yes. *God, yes.* With his right hand, he reached a few inches under her skirt and brushed the backs of his knuckles against the smooth skin of her thigh.

She braced slightly at his touch, but whispered, "Go on."

Before he could continue his exploration, they crested the top of the steep incline and began hurtling down toward Tropicana Avenue. He let go of Anna as they plummeted, and gripped the handles to the sides of his head. Now he knew what it was like to auger into the ground in a jet fighter. Las Vegas Boulevard, twinkling with white headlights and red brakelights, flashed past in a dizzying corkscrew.

He wanted off this mechanical aberration. He had no faith in something that didn't share his instinct for self-preservation. But his only escape was to close his eyes.

The Japanese screamed gleefully.

Anna shouted something he couldn't make out over the rush of the wind. Opening one eye, he glanced at her—she looked exhilarated. And, like some of the tourists, she was actually waving her arms over her head as the car completely inverted again.

An object slid across Emmett's chest. His BIA-issued encrypted cellular phone creeping out of his jacket pocket. It took all his willpower to let go of the handle with his right hand and grab the phone before it fell out. As the train slowed for its reentry inside the casino, he realized that the cellular was ringing.

"Let's go again," Anna said with a huskiness in her voice he'd never heard before. She further encouraged him with a fast, hard kiss.

But Emmett, rubber kneed, pulled her out of the car and answered his phone. It was from his supervisor in Phoenix, a Mescalero Apache of few words.

Twenty seconds later, Emmett disconnected and led Anna toward the escalator.

"What is it?" she asked.

"We've got an unwitnessed death in Oregon."

"Who?"

"Nobody can tell."

She grimaced, no doubt thinking of maggots and decomposition. She wore a certain perfume for homicide calls. Strong. "How recent was it?"

"Several thousand years ago—at least."

2

Anna drove down into John Day Canyon.

Landing in Portland at dawn, Emmett and she had borrowed a Ford Explorer from the FBI field office, then sped up the Columbia River to The Dalles. In that town, Emmett and she picked up Colonel Deborah Carter, the district chief engineer of the U.S. Army Corps of Engineers. Now, as the Clarno Reservoir came into view, Carter said from the backseat of the Explorer, "Take that road alongside the fish ladder down to the powerhouse, Turnipseed. I want to tell my people I'm in the neighborhood."

Anna didn't meet Carter's eyes in the rearview mirror. One didn't idly look at Deborah Carter. Stopping beside the concrete block of a powerhouse, she let the colonel out. In her early fifties, the uniformed woman was attractive but unremarkable from behind.

"Keep the goddamned peace," Emmett griped as soon as the colonel was out of earshot. His suit was rumpled from his trying to sleep in the cramped airplane seat. "Keeping the peace is a job for the county sheriff here."

"Not according to the Attorney General," Anna said. The dash clock read 1:30. Half the day was gone, and they had yet to inspect the site where the skeletal remains had been discovered. Not that it probably mattered. Emmett was right: There was no investigative work to be done. Still, two investigators had been sent to the Oregon boonies by the Attorney General in Washington on the recommendation of the U.S. Attorney in Portland. They were to stand by in the event federal laws had already been broken or might be broken in the coming weeks. And keep the peace, of course.

Fingernails tapped Anna's window glass, startling her.

She tried to show no reaction. But the second time did little to soften the shock. Deborah Carter's face was split diagonally by a scar that ran from her forehead across the bridge of her nose and down her right cheek. Apparently, the scar tissue had been smoothed out but not erased by repeated plastic surgeries. And, almost sadly, the original wound had spared enough of her features to show the beauty that had been ruined. That morning at Carter's headquarters in The Dalles, Anna had thought that she and Emmett hid their shock fairly well, until the colonel explained matter-of-factly, "Rocket attack in Vietnam, in case you're wondering. The administrative facility where I worked in Saigon was hit."

Anna lowered her window, letting in the whine of the power-house turbines. Carter's green eyes fixed on her. "Park near those other vehicles," the colonel said, pointing at them. "I'll join you two at the trailhead."

"We walk from here?" Anna asked.

"Yes." Carter briskly set off toward the opposite end of the lot.

Anna nosed in alongside a pewter-colored Lexus sport utility. Dark-skinned feet in sandals were dangling outside an open rear window, but the rest of the reclining figure wasn't visible. Also in the lot was a van with University of Oregon Department of Anthropology decals and a white Honda Accord with Confederated Tribes of Warm Springs stenciled on its driver's door. Anna locked up the FBI loaner, then Emmett and she joined Carter at the trailhead. It overlooked the dam sluice gates, from which foamy tan water gushed out and flattened into a river running low and scummy.

"Follow me to the festivities." Carter started down a footpath that wound through the thickets along the east side of the river. With the modern reservoir to her back, Anna found the landscape raw and primeval looking. The broad chasm belonged to an alien age, when volcanoes belched plumes of ash over an Africa-like savanna crawling with American camels, rhinoceroses and giant sloths. Modoc legend didn't dispute the existence of this scientific epoch. In fact, it told of such a time before the demigod Kumookumts plucked out his armpit hair to add human beings to a rich mix of other creatures.

Still, this country felt strange to Anna, even though she wasn't far from her tribe's ancestral territory along the California-Oregon border.

Walking directly behind Carter, Emmett asked, "Who arrested the fossil hunter, Colonel?"

"Nobody—*yet.*"

That was news to Anna. But Emmett and she hadn't wanted to phone the U.S. Attorney upon their arrival in Portland late last night, and this morning his secretary reported that he'd be in court all day.

"Then how'd you get the remains?" Emmett asked Carter.

"Let me start from the beginning. The last week of September, Gorka Bilbao—"

"What kind of name's that?" Emmett interrupted.

"Basque," Carter and Anna said simultaneously. There'd been a handful of Basco sheep ranchers in Modoc County, hardy transplants from the Pyrenees Mountains between France and Spain. The colonel went on, "Bilbao was spotted by my powerhouse people going to and from the canyon below the dam. This area's closed to fishing, so they were curious enough to call the law enforcement ranger for the Bureau of Land Management. The ranger, familiar with Bilbao's reputation as an illegal fossil hunter, questioned him."

"What makes Bilbao's hunting illegal?" Anna inquired.

"Basically, you can't collect the fossils of any creature that had a backbone. Naturally, Bilbao denied doing anything of the sort." Carter shooed a horsefly away from her face. "Next, Dr. Rankin phoned me."

"*The* forensic anthropologist?" Emmett asked, sounding slightly incredulous.

"The one and only Thaddeus Rankin," Carter said. "And right off, Dr. Rankin admitted to me that Bilbao had given him some human bones. That bowled me over. Rankin knows the game. This wasn't an authorized dig on Corps of Engineers lands. What surprised me is that he tried to palm the remains off on me after he only had a quick look at them. I thought he'd play cat and mouse with the Corps—you know, drag it out while he finished a complete evaluation in his own laboratory."

"*Tried* to palm them off on you?"

"That's right, Parker. I said no—the bones go to the Wheeler County coroner before I'll even touch them."

Emmett asked, "Who did the exam for the coroner?"

"A local pathologist. But after Rankin submitted a forty-page statement to the federal judge, detailing why he thought the skeleton was very ancient, the bones were transferred to my custody."

"And where are they now?" Anna asked.

"The safe in my headquarters. What a mess."

They rounded a bend in the trail, and in the distance Anna could see tiny figures on the sun-hardened mudflats.

"I'm not sure if Rankin violated the law in how he got the remains," Carter continued. "Bilbao broke the law but then turned the skeleton over to science, so I doubt the U.S. Attorney will file on him. But that's all beside the point. You both know the drill here. The Native American Graves Protection and Repatriation Act says the remains go back to the Indians with the closest link to them."

"The Confederated Warm Springs tribes?" Anna guessed, given the marked tribal Honda parked at the trailhead.

"Right," Carter said. "I was ready to comply with NAGPRA and hand over the bones to the tribes when Rankin used his connections to get a court order to block immediate reburial. That forced me to submit the remains to limited scientific analysis. He argued there's no racial or cultural tie between John Day Man—that's what he calls it— and any of the three Warm Springs tribes. That fired up the reservation, believe me." Then Carter repeated, "What a mess. If the skeleton had been found two hundred yards uphill from the river, the Bureau of Land Management would be handling all this. My mission is flood control, watershed management, river navigation—not sorting out the cultural patrimony for some old bones."

"Were any of them radiocarbon-dated, Colonel?" Emmett asked.

"Yeah, the court let a metacarpal be shipped down to the lab at the University of California at Riverside."

"Finger bone just above the knuckle," Emmett explained quietly to Anna.

"I know what a metacarpal is," she snapped.

"What was the result?" Emmett asked Carter.

"The bone's between 14,300 and 14,600 years old."

Emmett stopped dead in his tracks for a moment. "Christ, that'd make them the oldest human remains ever found in North America."

"All I do know is that the test results blew the lid off the pressure cooker," Carter said irritably.

Emmett looked stunned, a rarity for him. "What do you mean?"

Carter halted and turned. Again, Anna had to guard against an overt reaction—the colonel looked so normal from behind. "Don't you two know?"

"No," Anna answered for both of them.

"The pathologist reported to the Wheeler County coroner that the skeleton was male—and *Caucasian.*"

Anna's astonishment was so great she almost laughed out loud. "Come on, what was a white man doing tramping around Oregon more than 14,000 years ago?"

• • •

Anna's wasn't a new question, Emmett reflected as he trailed Colonel Carter down to the river. However, amazing as it seemed, this was not the first wrinkle in the favored theories—both white and native—of how human beings had appeared in the Americas. Skulls approximately 10,000 years old had been unearthed throughout the West, some with seemingly Caucasoid features—a long, narrow head, flat cheekbones and protuberant chin—and some with the rounded heads and pronounced cheekbones of modern northern Asians and Native Americans. Spirit Cave Man, discovered in a Nevada rock shelter in 1940, had been one of the puzzling Caucasoid finds. His mummy was radiocarbon-dated to be 9,400 years old. But Buhl Woman, a 10,700-year-old Idaho skeleton, clearly did resemble a contemporary Indian to a slight majority of her examiners, so her remains were repatriated to the Shoshone-Bannock tribes for reburial in 1992.

At last, Emmett understood why Anna and he had been sent here: John Day Man was too dangerous to long-held beliefs to go untended until the court decided what to do with him. And the U.S. Attorney in Portland was counting on two native cops to defuse Indian outrage over disturbing the remains while keeping the white scientists from exceeding NAGPRA's provisions. As usual, Anna and he were caught hopelessly in the middle. "We've got to get a copy of that court order ASAP," he said to her.

"Are you telling me to get it?"

"I said *we,* dammit."

Ignoring their bickering, Colonel Carter announced, "Welcome to the zoo, Turnipseed and Parker."

Emmett had never met Dr. Thaddeus Rankin before, but there was no mistaking the legendary anthropologist in the small crowd along the river. Rankin dominated the scene like an old lion, shaggy and scornful looking. Although semiretired from the University of Oregon, Professor Emeritus Rankin was still square-shouldered. Garbed in a campaign hat and khakis, he looked born to fieldwork. When not helping law enforcement distinguish between modern murder victims and Indian burials, Rankin spent most of his time stirring up controversies about the origins and habits of Native Americans. Emmett could trace the route of Rankin's journeys by the Indian enemies he'd left behind.

The dig was cordoned off with yellow tape. Rankin loomed at its center, using a cane to orchestrate the activities of a half dozen assistants. His students groveled around him with trowels, brushes and sifting screens. Recognizing Carter, Rankin offered a mock aside in a rolling baritone, "Be on your toes, boys and girls. It's the bloody army." Then he gave the colonel a jaunty salute. "Why, good afternoon, ma'am!"

Carter stopped with Emmett and Anna outside the tape. "Afternoon, Doctor."

"You've brought scouts, I see."

"Cops."

Rankin grinned slyly. "One of them appears to be the illustrious Emmett Parker of the BIA. A vaunted son of the Nuumu." Comanche, pronounced perfectly.

Emmett didn't respond at first. He never liked it when a stranger had advance warning of him.

"Who's your lovely assistant, Parker?"

"Not my assistant. My partner. Special Agent Turnipseed of the FBI."

"And what tribe are you, Ms. Turnipseed—Yahooskin Paiute?"

"Modoc." Anna smiled.

"Oh drat!" Rankin theatrically tossed his hat to the ground, and his white locks tumbled around his shoulders. He had abundant hair for a white man in his sixties. "I'm slipping. But Klamath or Modoc would've been my next guess."

"I'm also part Japanese," Anna confessed.

"Ahhh, there you have it. I was put off by the dilution of blood. Mingled blood confounds the holy shit out of identification." He stooped—a bit unsteadily, Emmett thought—to retrieve his hat. "Well, not only is the United States Army pitted against me, but now an FBI operative of the most ungovernable aboriginal tribe in North America has arrived to call the shots. Is that how it'll be, Investigator Parker?"

"That's how it'll be." Two Indian women stood on the hillside above, watching this exchange in silence. "Excuse us, Colonel," Emmett said, breaking away from Carter and leading Anna up the slope toward the pair, one old and one young. Impossible to tell which tribe they were from: A trio of them—the Sahaptin, the Wasco and some Northern Paiute—had been forced onto a large but reportedly worthless tract of land between here and the Cascade Mountains from 1855 to 1879. Whites hadn't valued hydroelectric potential in those days, so the combined tribes had prospered unexpectedly.

"I'll have to break this up," Emmett joked. "Too many Indians standing around in one place."

The old woman chuckled, but the pretty mixed-blood in her mid-twenties didn't. She had auburn hair down to her waist and a honey-brown complexion. She offered her hand to Emmett and shook firmly. "Elsa Dease, Warm Springs Tribal Cultural Resources. I'm an archaeologist by trade, so I got tapped to keep an eye on things here." The Native American Graves Protection and Repatriation Act on-site monitor. At least, Dease had a better-defined role than his and Anna's: to keep Rankin from desecrating the remains of ancient Americans, allegedly Caucasoid or otherwise.

Anna introduced herself, and Elsa's look became a little less officious. "You're part Japanese?"

"Yes," Anna replied. "There was an internment camp for Japanese Americans near our ranchería during the Second World War."

"My dad was white," Elsa said, "but my mom's full-blooded Warm Springs." Her mother was a Sahaptin, then, as the speakers of that Indian language had been first on the Warm Springs reservation.

"Mrs. Dease?" Emmett immediately offered his hand to the old woman, who accepted his in both of hers, warmly. She wore a kerchief around her head and a hearing aid.

"No, Minnie's not my mom." Elsa smiled at last. "This is Minnie Claw, one of our elders."

The introductions out of the way, Anna asked, "What makes Dr. Rankin think the remains aren't linked to the Warm Springs tribes?"

"We always been here," Minnie asserted. "First Man and First Woman sprung from this land before the Great Flood."

Anna showed deference to her by letting a contemplative silence hang in the air. "What's the archaeological record say, Elsa?"

"The ancestors of at least two of our tribes utilized the John Day area for at least eleven thousand years. This ended only with the reservation era."

"Utilized or occupied the area?" Anna asked. Good, Emmett thought, she's getting right to the point at the crux of cultural patrimony.

"Utilized." Elsa rearranged a strand of hair that had been shifted by the breeze across her face. An unconsciously sensual gesture, and Emmett pretended not to have noticed when Anna suddenly eyed him. "It's too hard a country around here to have supported even seasonal settlements, Ms. Turnipseed . . ." Elsa abruptly looked around, not as if she were trying to imagine those distant times, but as if searching for someone on the garishly colored cliffs above. Eroded palisades of red, yellow and an otherworldly turquoise. An inhospitable landscape that appealed to Emmett, to his Comanche affinity for desolate places.

"But there was always some nice patches of wild celery in the springtime," Minnie Claw added. "We come all the way from the big river to dig the roots."

"Yes, Minnie, that's right." Elsa stopped scanning the heights. "I see what you're getting at, Agent Turnipseed. Rankin and the other anthros wonder the same thing. How can we say these bones belong to our Ancient One if we used this country only part of the year? Well, maybe he came here to hunt antelope or watch over his wife as she dug wild celery. Do you have to build freeways and convenience stores to call a country your own? Do you have to have tombstones over your dead to prove that they're your ancestors?"

"No," Anna said. "But how do you account for the thirty-five-hundred-year gap between your known use of this area in the archaeological record and the age of these remains?"

"I don't. The record's just a white guess on how things might have been. It's not how they truly were. For that, you turn to your elders, who heard the stories from their elders. Oral history is really just one voice coming down through the centuries."

"You're Mowatak?" Minnie asked Anna. The Columbia Sahaptin word for Modoc, Emmett surmised.

"Yes, I am."

"Say somethin' to me in your di'lect. I want to hear how you folks talk down there in the tule lakes country."

Anna rattled off something. Modoc was derived from Sahaptin, the old woman's tongue, but the elder scrunched up her face. "No, it's too diff'rent for me to understand."

"I thought so, Grandmother. My uncle tells me our Modoc traders had to use Chinook jargon when they came up to the Columbia River to deal with you folks." Chinook jargon was a trading language of a few simple words. "But we're alike, I hear," Anna noted. "We both believe the dead live in the west . . ." As if disturbed by the thought, Anna didn't go on. Was she thinking of her father again? Emmett wondered if that man's shadow would always fall between them. It was uniquely frustrating to hate a dead man you'd never met.

"Mowatak are crafty," the old woman observed undiplomatically.

Emmett asked Elsa, "I thought most of the skeleton had been recovered."

"Most but not all. Rankin's been given permission to search for the missing bones. Especially the lower jaw."

"Any teeth affixed to the upper jaw?"

"None," Elsa responded. "All of them were blown out of the

maxilla." Meaning that the tooth sockets had been ruptured. Possibly by violence.

No doubt Rankin wanted the mandible so he could extract collagen, the protein structure of the bone, for DNA analysis. The most durable bone in the skeleton, the lower jaw—especially its molar cavities—offered the best chance of recovering intact collagen, or fibrous protein. DNA testing might establish the racial pedigree of the remains. Most Indians were the carriers of four identifiable DNA lineages. If the John Day specimen could be placed in another group, say modern Caucasians, give or take several thousand years of genetic diversification, Thaddeus Rankin would be celebrated as the most revolutionary anthropologist of the twenty-first century. The repercussions to American Indians could prove disastrous. A mysterious race of Caucasians had been here first. What would that do for the public's support of treaty rights if Indians went from original inhabitants to second-wave interlopers?

At that moment, Rankin's thundering voice drifted up from the riverbed. "The natives are conspiring, boys and girls."

"Not at all, Professor," Elsa called down to him. "We were simply discussing our origins."

"Which are, my dear?"

"First Man and First Woman, who were placed atop Mount Jefferson in a canoe by Coyote long before the Great Flood that nearly wiped out all life."

"How quaint. Indian Creationism, falling from the lips of one of my own former students. Were all my pearls of wisdom wasted on you?"

"Afraid so."

"I think I'll go home and shoot myself." Rankin's head sagged briefly in feigned despair. "Dear Elsa, didn't I teach you how to interpret figurative notions like the Great Flood? There was no such thing, neither Noah's version nor yours. Generations of retelling around campfires distorted the original reality—your forebears crossed the Bering land bridge exposed by the last ice age. Someday I'll unearth the skeleton of one of these east Asian pioneers, these missing links of the second wave, and the issue will be resolved. Now, dear child, it only seemed as if they were walking through the middle of a great flood.

And can we be sure that the word for sea and flood weren't the same in your earliest dialects?"

"We can't," Elsa said.

"And how can we be sure they weren't met by a seafaring Caucasoid people who'd beaten them here?"

"Again, we can't. But I like our version of the events better than your scientific racism."

"Even if it keeps you from understanding your true place in the grand scheme of things?"

"Who decides what's true? You?"

"Yes—I." Then Rankin exclaimed, "Coyote sent me to you, the bearer of great truths!"

"Blasphemy," Minnie spat. Then she asked Elsa, "What's that bridge talk suppose to be about?"

"The professor thinks we Indians walked to America over a land bridge from Asia."

"Oh no," the old woman said solemnly, "if that was so, my grandmother would've told me."

"Well, that proves it, ma'am!" Rankin laughed. Then his laugh turned into a growl as he ordered a student, who'd taken a water break, to get back to work. Elsa explained to Emmett and Anna that Rankin's team had only until sundown. Then the site would be closed to them forever.

Colonel Carter trudged up the hill to Emmett's side. The strong sunlight had pinked up her face, all but the scar tissue. "Listen, Parker, I'm going to check on my operations here, then catch a ride back to The Dalles with my powerhouse supervisor. If you need anything else, just give me a jingle."

"Thanks."

Carter faced Elsa Dease. For a second, Emmett thought the colonel was going to acknowledge the young woman. But then, without another word, she set off for the path back to the reservoir. Elsa watched her go until she vanished behind the bend in the trail.

Carter had claimed she'd made every effort to get along with the Warm Springs tribes by honoring NAGPRA. Anna, too, had been struck by the strained moment, for she asked Elsa, "You and the colonel aren't speaking?"

"No," the young woman said tonelessly, "we're speaking."

Below, Rankin again stooped, almost toppling over in the process. He plucked a piece of driftwood out of the dried silt and waved it over his head. "Elsa, look—a chunk of First Man and Woman's canoe!" He laughed uproariously, then once more sobered and told his people to hurry. "Ignorance is breathing down our necks, boys and girls!"

3

Anna overheard a man with a bad haircut ask the waiter in a German accent, "Vhat is your tribe?"

The waiter in the Juniper Dining Room had already mentioned to Anna and Emmett that he was Northern Paiute, but he now said, "Why, I'm a Holiday Inn-dian."

The tourist chewed his fry bread, apparently satisfied with the answer.

However, the Kah-Nee-Ta Resort was a cut above any Holiday Inn Anna had ever stayed in. Nestled in the Cascade foothills eleven miles north of the reservation capital, the tribally owned lodge boasted 170 luxury rooms in an arrowhead-shaped complex. It included a casino and a conference center. Below, an eighteen-hole golf course bracketed the Warm Springs River. Country club ambiance in the midst of sun-browned hills where wild mustangs still roamed.

Emmett's salmon dinner was untouched. Anna watched him flip through the court order that had just been faxed to them by the U.S. Attorney's office in Portland. Emmett had let her read it first, then seemed relieved to have something to do during dinner other than talk about themselves. She wondered if some crucial chance had been missed yesterday evening in Las Vegas. For a minute on the roller coaster, spiraling through the velveteen air, she'd felt as if she'd outdistanced memory. Would she ever recapture that physical sensation of absolute freedom?

"The judge settled nothing," Emmett interrupted her musings.

Anna agreed.

Citing the provision in the Native American Graves Protection and Repatriation Act that allowed a reasonable amount of scientific inquiry into newly discovered human remains, the judge had ruled against immediate reburial by the Warm Springs tribes. Dr. Thaddeus Rankin and a trained team—excluding any "amateur fossil procurers" like Gorka Bilbao—had been permitted to search for John Day Man's missing bones until 6:00 P.M. on October 18. Anna realized that it was now two hours past that deadline. Dr. Rankin and his field team had found nothing by 4:00 P.M., when Emmett and she had left the canyon. Even if Rankin had uncovered the mandible in those last two hours, the order didn't include permission for collagen to be extracted for DNA analysis. The judge had already sided with the tribes on this issue by "abhorring unduly invasive technologies that might violate the dignity of the remains." Still, the anthropologist had petitioned the court for further forensic testing.

Anna glanced up.

A filthy man in a military overcoat was descending the stairs from the casino level. He tapped the handrail all the way down with his earth-stained fingernails, slinking along as if at any turn he expected to be thrown out of the place. Earlier, she'd noticed him at one of the video poker machines overlooking the lobby, and his dark stare had made her uncomfortable. Now, he conferred in terse whispers with the hostess as he pointed directly at Anna and Emmett. The hostess seemed to be on the verge of calling security when Emmett took notice—and inexplicably waved the man over to their table.

"What're you doing?" Anna demanded as the shabby little figure with the crazed eyes drew closer. The other diners shrank slightly from his passing.

"It's our fossil hunter."

"What makes you so sure?"

"I doubt he's the concierge." Emmett folded up the court order and pocketed it. "And I've been waiting for Gorka Bilbao to plead his case to us."

The man stood over them, baring some very bad teeth in a tense grin. "You the feds they sent on account of me findin' the skeleton?"

"Gorka Bilbao?" Emmett asked.

"Yes, sir."

Thank God, he didn't offer his right hand to shake. Anna saw that Bilbao had cultivated a long index fingernail, probably as a nostril-scraping tool. Emmett gestured for him to sit in one of the empty chairs.

"Sorry to butt in on your dinner," Bilbao said. "I been waitin' for you two to finish . . ." He eyed Emmett's yet full plate to explain his intrusion. "But it's gettin' late, and I only got one headlight workin' on my pickup." Stone-faced, Emmett said nothing, and Bilbao's nervousness increased. "Mind if I get somethin' to drink?"

The reservation was dry with the exception of the lodge, where fine wines were served with lunch and dinner. At last, Emmett said, "Free country."

Bilbao raised his hand for the waiter, who was on the telephone at the hostess's desk. Frowning, the Paiute hung up as if he hadn't gotten through and came over. Bilbao ordered a glass of Gallo Hearty Burgundy, but the waiter drolly informed him that the Juniper Room didn't serve Gallo products, although they were available at the convenience store just outside the reservation on Highway 26. Obviously, he knew Gorka Bilbao and didn't care for him.

His civility spent, Bilbao snarled, "Anything red'll do."

The waiter withdrew, but Anna noticed that he went back to the telephone instead of making for the beverage service area.

"Bad news, bad news," Bilbao mumbled.

"What?" Anna asked.

"Those bones. Should never've found 'em. I wish to hell they was still buried in the riverbank."

"Why?"

Leaning closer to her, Bilbao dropped his voice. "I could feel the evil in 'em as soon as I uncovered 'em. On the drive home to my place in the Ochoco Mountains, I started gettin' cold. Terrible cold. Made no sense till I figured what was causin' it—*those bones*. Vapor was comin' off 'em like dry ice. They chilled the cab of my pickup just like air conditionin'—'cept I ain't got no air conditionin'!" He laughed in a shrill way that made it impossible to tell whether he was embarrassed by his admission of fear or believed none of what he was saying.

"Then that night the damn things heated up my cabin so bad I had to take 'em outside so I could sleep. God's my witness—they glowed like coals till I got 'em outside. Shit on milk, eh?"

Anna frowned.

"Pardon my French, ma'am," Bilbao prattled on, "but that's what my papa always said when somethin' was just too hard for a Basco to swallow. If you two wasn't Indian, I wouldn't even be tellin' you all this. But Indians know how weird this world can be."

Ignoring the backhanded compliment, Emmett asked, "Why didn't you leave the remains where they were and notify the sheriff?"

"Oh no. No way. Me and that sheriff go way back. His people was cattlemen, and mine ran sheep. Hell, that lyin' son of a bitch would've framed me for murder no matter how old the skeleton was."

Anna sat back, hoping to get farther from the stench of perspiration and wood smoke that wafted off Bilbao. "Then why didn't you go to the BLM ranger instead?"

"Worse yet, lady. Land Management wants to run me clean out of this country." He scratched his beard with the vigor of a dog going after a flea. "Didn't catch your names."

"I'm Investigator Parker from the Bureau of Indian Affairs and this is Special Agent Turnipseed of the FBI."

"You two from any of the local tribes?" Bilbao then tried to mask his paranoia with flattery. "You're as pretty as Miss Dease any day, ma'am."

"No," Anna said, "Mr. Parker is a Comanche from Oklahoma and I'm Modoc." She was tempted to add that Warm Springs scouts had helped the U.S. Army track down her renegade ancestors during the 1872-73 war. But she felt her impartiality was already clear.

The waiter deposited the glass of wine in front of Bilbao, who slowly dug from his coat pocket three crumpled dollars, some kitchen matches and a wad of foul-looking lint. He spread the bills flat on the tablecloth. He was a dollar fifty short, but Emmett told the waiter to put the wine on Anna's and his tab.

"Thanks, Mr. Parker, I'm a little low right now," Bilbao said, raising his glass. "*Ossagaria* to both of you. Good health." He took a gulp, then explained, "No, I took the bones right then and there on account I expected another flood most any time. I knew this skeleton was valuable to the college boys. Not to me, mind you. Law says I can't trade in vertebrates, and I'm all for the law protectin' vertebrates . . ." The Latin term wouldn't have sounded more surprising if it'd rolled off the tongue of a big mongrel. ". . . and I'm thankful too—what if all skeletons behave the way these done to me? I want no part of these old bones. They got terrible evil in 'em."

"What flood?" Anna asked.

Bilbao slugged down more wine. "Pardon, ma'am?"

"You said another flood was coming anytime."

"Oh, right. The flood for the fall salmon run uncovered the bones. The next dam release comes any day now. That'll be for the steelhead. Then the skeleton would be lost, washed down to the Columbia and lost forever to the college boys. I'm no educated man myself, but I respect what the college boys are doin' for science."

Anna had to bite her tongue.

"Were you working John Day Canyon for any particular scientist?" Emmett asked.

"Oh no," Bilbao replied. "Just freelancin' like usual. The canyon's a hot spot. Couple years ago, I come across a dandy pocket of jasperized viviparus where the Clarno dam is now. Pond snails to you," he clarified. "Each as pretty as a gem."

Anna asked, "What made you turn the skeleton over to Dr. Rankin?"

That gave the fossil hunter pause. "Well, ma'am, Doc Rankin's been good to me in the past."

"Meaning he paid you for fossils?" Emmett asked.

"Oh, nothin' like that," Bilbao quickly answered. "Sometimes I go to him, say I'm a little short, and he grubstakes me for a while. So when I saw this real old skeleton—and figured the flood would carry it away any minute—I made up my mind then and there to repay Doc Rankin for bein' so kind to me. I mean, a professor for a state school is just like a government guy, ain't he? I was turnin' the remains over to a branch of the government, just like I'm supposed to . . . right? Never had no notion I was violatin' anythin', otherwise I might've let the floodwaters sweep that old skeleton on down to the Columbia and out to sea." Bilbao's glass was empty, and he grinned hopefully at Emmett. "One more drink, and I'm on my way."

• • •

Emmett and Anna strolled back to their rooms along an exterior corridor. She walked in front of him, hips swaying voluptuously if only from the casual pace. He watched her from behind with a wistful sense of hopelessness. She was his Mount Everest, and in the last few weeks he'd begun to doubt that, at forty, he had the energy to take her on. Tonight, he was almost grateful for his fatigue; it was reducing his desire to a low throb. Like a carnal toothache.

She spun around, nearly catching his gaze on her shapely fanny. "Steelhead don't run until December."

"What?"

"I grew up in steelhead country. Seagoing trout."

"I know what the hell they are." Emmett knew this was payback for his having told her what a metacarpal was.

"Steelhead don't migrate upstream until December or even January. Bilbao would know that. But he said he took the skeleton because he was afraid another dam release would carry the bones away."

Emmett stopped in front of his door. "It's not going to take much to trip old Gorka up, if push comes to shove. And his pupils were dilated, so he probably uses more than wine to elevate his mood." Emmett yawned. "Just sharing the same table with that piece of vermin makes me want to take two showers." Then, a second later, the implication of "showers" hit him. He studied Anna for a reaction. Lately, he realized, they watched each other like the finalists at the World Series of Poker.

"Maybe I can join you for one of them," she said quietly.

He glanced down to remind himself that he wasn't wearing old Levi's. Slacks. *Good.* But then he began running through the mind-numbing calculus of their affair. Was he too tired to venture into unexplored territory tonight? Without benefit of imagery rehearsal and a safety net, would she freeze in the coming minutes? And what would Dr. Tischler say about the rash spontaneity of this? Despite these calculations, Emmett's blood was racing. "You sure?"

"Just open the door, Emmett."

Fumbling, he tried to insert the key in the lock, but she was running her hands over his shoulders. Her touch felt so good he turned and folded his arms around her. Pressing against him, she said, "I'm sorry for making you wait like this."

Did that mean his wait was over? *Christ Almighty—tonight might be the night.* He got light-headed.

He was about to kiss her when he saw a battered Datsun pickup with one headlight. The little truck started down the road from the parking area that was cut into the bluff behind the resort. Two seconds later, a diesel engine rumbled to life in the lot. Blinding high beams came on like twin suns, making Emmett squint. A Dodge crew cab pickup with dual rear wheels. Its windows were tinted, so he couldn't make out the driver.

Bilbao drove slowly, seemingly oblivious to the big Dodge that was swiftly closing on him.

"Give me the car keys," he said to Anna.

"What?"

"The keys to the car, quick. Follow me by way of the stairs."

"Why?"

"Just meet me on the road. I'll pick you up in a minute." Not waiting for her response, Emmett jumped over the parapet, thrashed through the waist-high bushes and up the embankment to the road. The Dodge was riding Bilbao's rear bumper as the two vehicles made their way down to the river. Emmett climbed a second embankment to the parking lot and unlocked the FBI Explorer.

Anna was waiting for him beside the road, putting back on a shoe that had slipped off during her own dash. "Your lights," she said, getting inside.

"How about that." Emmett sped down the road blacked-out, keeping to the low-drive gear rather than tapping the brakes.

Anna asked, "Did you notice our waiter go to the phone as soon as Bilbao walked over to our table?"

"No."

"You notice *everything*, Em."

"Do I?"

"Yes. What were you thinking about, the court order?"

"Not really," he said grudgingly.

"Then what?"

"Us. I was thinking about us."

"Honestly?" She sounded pleased.

He shrugged.

"Come to any conclusions?" she asked.

"Unrack the shotgun."

"Sounds ominous." But she reached up, removed the shotgun from its roof rack and slid the Remington into the space between their bucket seats.

The Dodge accelerated, and Bilbao could no longer ignore it. He had to take the road at speeds that made him weave back and forth across the center line.

"Hold on." Emmett bore down on the gas pedal. The two vehicles had disappeared around a curve, and he let down his window to listen. He could still hear the thunder of the diesel punctuated by the tinny rattle of the Datsun's four-cylinder engine. "See if there are any maps in this damned yuppie wagon."

Anna riffled through the glove box, came up with a topographical of the reservation and a flashlight. The vehicles had come into view again. The driver of the Dodge was strobing his high and low beams on Bilbao as if commanding the fossil hunter to stop. Bilbao refused to obey, and the Dodge and Datsun sped as one along the golf course. Scanning the map, Anna said, "One of three ways to go—"

"Never mind that. Bilbao's turning right."

"It'll be Whitehorse Rapids Road. Winds down to a town called Whiskey Dick."

At last, it was fully dark, and Emmett had to flip on his headlights. It had no effect on the driver of the diesel, who went on chasing the Datsun at freeway speeds. "License plate light is out on the Dodge. Can you tell what state the plate is?"

Anna strained forward against her seatbelt. "No."

"Raise tribal police to head this off."

She advised the dispatcher, who laconically notified all her units of the unusual pursuit. Anna hung up the microphone.

"Bilbao said he lived in the Ochocos," Emmett said. "Where's that?"

She hunched over the map again. "Mountain range about fifty miles to the southeast."

"Could be a long night." Emmett touched off the yelp siren to let the driver of the Dodge know a cop car was behind. This too had no effect on him. The narrow road became serpentine in its descent toward Whiskey Dick, and Emmett had only intermittent views of the two vehicles. Far below, pinpricks of headlights were twinkling up the mountainside. An oncoming car. When it met Bilbao, there would be a crash. Emmett was so sure of that, he sped up again. On a sharp curve. Brush slapped against the mirror on Anna's side, and she braced her hands against the dashboard. "Easy," she cautioned.

He held his tongue. The possibility of a shower together still loomed in the back of his mind.

Rounding the last of the hairpin curves, they plunged into a cloud of dust.

"Shit!" Blind, Emmett jammed on the brakes. Still, he nearly skidded into the same ditch that had claimed the Datsun.

Bilbao staggered out of the dust, shading his eyes against Emmett's high beams. He was bleeding from a cut on his nose, and his eyes looked hysterically large. He grabbed Emmett by the arm as soon as he got out of the Explorer. "Did you see it, Parker? Did you see!"

Shaking off Bilbao's grasp, Emmett peered through the clearing dust for the Dodge. Anna joined him at his side. There was no sign or sound of the diesel pickup, just the far-off headlights of the oncoming vehicle growing larger.

Bilbao had sunk to the weedy edge of the road and was babbling. "It was Tennyson. You can be damn sure it was Tennyson. I felt his power."

Anna asked, "Someone named Tennyson was driving the big pickup?"

Bilbao stared up at her as if she were out of her mind. "No."

"Then why are you sure it was Tennyson?"

"Nobody was drivin' that truck."

"What do you mean?"

"I saw when it went past after drivin' me off the road—*nobody* was behind the wheel!"

The headlights were close now. Emmett returned to the Explorer. There was no place to pull off, so he punched on the emergency flashers. The approaching vehicle slowed and stopped. It had a light bar, which came to life. A tribal cruiser. Emmett showed his credentials. A

police sergeant stepped cautiously out of the sedan. Emmett esti-
mated the man to be his own equal in height and weight, although—
judging from the lack of gray in his thick, black hair—ten years
younger. The sergeant didn't introduce himself, but his nameplate read
Gabriel Round Dance. He had quick, nervous eyes. He asked what
was going on, but Emmett had a hunch Round Dance had already
been alerted by the reservation grapevine to Bilbao's appearance at the
Kah-Nee-Ta.

Instead of explaining, Emmett asked, "A Dodge diesel pickup go
past you?"

His gaze slid past Emmett to Anna, but Round Dance said nothing.

"You hear me?" Emmett asked.

"Yeah, I heard you. No. No vehicles at all." The sergeant shined his
flashlight on the cowering Bilbao. His face screwed up with distaste for
the fossil hunter.

Emmett scanned the country to the north. "What hills are those?"

Round Dance looked. "Mutton Mountains."

"Any four-wheel-drive trails into them?"

"None I'd take my own rig up. You must be the BIA and Feeb
team."

"I'm Parker, and that's Agent Turnipseed."

The sergeant and Anna exchanged reserved nods. "Gabe Round
Dance."

Bilbao was still carrying on in the background. "It was Tennyson, all
right. He sent that truck to kill me. And he damn near done it too. He
can do that. Send things to do a soul harm."

"Is there such a person as Tennyson?" Emmett asked.

"Oh yeah. Tennyson Paulina. Lives down in the South End."

"Where exactly?"

"Seekseequa Canyon, the old Paiute colony."

"Does Paulina own a new Dodge diesel dually?"

"Never met an Indian rodeo cowboy who can hang on to his prize
money. Especially a Paiute cowboy. They do love to honky-tonk. No,
Paulina doesn't care about money or fancy trucks." Round Dance
flicked his chin toward Bilbao. "He drunk?"

"I doubt he'd graduate summa cum laude from the University of

Sobriety," Emmett said. "Combination drugs and alcohol, if you ask me. You might want to run him in for his own safety."

"No way, Parker. He's white, and under the influence is a cheap misdemeanor. I'll have to wait half the night for a deputy sheriff to take him off my hands. I've got better things to do." Then Round Dance asked somewhat disingenuously, "Where was he coming from?"

"The lodge," Emmett replied.

Round Dance glared at Bilbao. "You weren't anywhere near Elsa, were you, Gorka?"

"No, no, no."

Round Dance warned, "If you're lying to me, I'll find out."

"I ain't."

"What's that about?" Emmett asked.

"Bilbao's infatuated with a local woman. Been making a nuisance of himself. She got a tribal restraining order against him, but the magistrate said there wasn't enough to file a stalking charge."

"Is the woman Elsa Dease, the NAGPRA monitor?"

"That's her," Round Dance said. "Your pickup drivable, Gorka?"

Bilbao visibly contemplated this through his shock. Finally, he seemed to realize that he was being offered a choice between freedom and a night in county jail. Crawling over to the Datsun on his hands and knees, he examined the undercarriage. "I guess."

"Good. Then get off my reservation."

Bilbao rose and grabbed the door handle. He didn't seem to be going after something inside, but Round Dance's right hand tightened around the grips of his revolver. Bilbao meekly got inside his cab, and Round Dance relaxed slightly. Just slightly. He was working scared. Each cop had a tone to how he carried himself in the field. Working scared didn't necessarily mean cowardice, Emmett reflected. But it meant something.

Bilbao's pride demanded a parting shot at the Indian cop. "You don't fool me, Round Dance. You Wascos are just too chickenshit to tangle with Tennyson Paulina. That Paiute's got the power over you fish-eaters, and you know it too!"

"Move," Round Dance ordered Bilbao.

• • •

Anna had forgotten the false spring that came to this country in October—until the sun cleared the eastern horizon and Seekseequa Canyon became luminous with saffron-colored blossoms. This was the season the golden rabbitbrush bloomed, and the plumes seemed to burn yellow in the flat rays of the sun. Anna finished the last of a convenience store mocha coffee while Emmett left the paved road and started up a rutted lane. It was lined at quarter-mile intervals with mobile homes and simple frame houses. This was the heart of the South End, which in 1879 had been given over to a late-arriving band of Northern Paiutes who'd held out against the army with their charismatic leader, Panaina, or Paulina as he was known to whites.

Following Sergeant Round Dance's directions, Anna and Emmett were looking for a mom-and-pop grocery store that had been hauled from the town of Madras and converted into a home. Gorka Bilbao may have been right: The Wasco cop wasn't eager to tangle with Tennyson Paulina, otherwise he would have insisted on accompanying the federal cops on his home turf, standard operating procedure. And the Wascos, as a people, were known for their assertiveness.

Anna had enjoyed the silence with Emmett on the forty-minute trip down from the Kah-Nee-Ta. Early morning seemed to be a kind of truce between the sexes. There were fewer expectations than in the evening, she thought, less of that unavoidable tension between man and woman. Admittedly, this belief had exceptions, as her father's abuse had depended more on alcoholic whim than any set time of day. Late last night, Emmett had gone to his separate room without mentioning her earlier offer to shower together. Her weariness had made her vaguely grateful, yet she drifted off to sleep disappointed that they'd failed once again.

"That's it." Emmett now turned off toward an old storefront with sheets for window curtains.

The door was wide open.

He drove completely around the place. There was no Dodge diesel pickup on the premises. A 1970ish Cadillac El Dorado was parked to one side of the building, a can of Coors beer balanced precariously on the front fender. Close by, the remains of a campfire smoldered in front of a beehive-shaped hump of earth. Grabbing the mike, Anna ran the Cadillac's Oregon plate through the tribal police dispatcher. Registration came back to a Tennyson Hadley Paulina of P.O. Box 52, Seekseequa Junction.

"You still want to talk to him?" Anna asked.

"Might as well," Emmett said. "If only to cover our asses."

Technically, Bilbao was the victim of a vehicular assault. A felony. And he was Caucasian. All that gave jurisdiction to federal law enforcement instead of the tribal police, even though the offense had occurred on Indian lands. In the nineteenth century, white pioneers had refused to subject themselves to native justice, and so began the slow erosion of sovereignty promised by treaty.

The partners got out and spread apart to approach the front of the store. The end of a bed was visible through the open door. From it dangled two feet, one in a cowboy boot and the other unshod.

Emmett rapped on the doorjamb with his left hand. His right was poised near the .357 magnum holstered on his belt. Anna had taken to carrying her pistol in an ankle holster, which she found less obtrusive. Shifting her view, she saw that two people were in bed together, an Indian male in his forties and a white woman curled up against the dawn coolness. Both the man and the woman were entirely naked—except for the single boot he wore. At Emmett's second loud knock, the man's eyes slid open like a reptile's. But there was nothing lethargic about this; he seemed instantly on guard. "Cops?" he asked in a gravelly voice.

"BIA, FBI," Emmett replied. "Tennyson Paulina?"

"Yep. What're the charges?"

"None. We just want to talk to you."

"On that positive note, I'll get up." Paulina slapped the woman's bare buttock, and she gave an ill-tempered grunt. "Rise and shine, Trish. The feds are here."

Sitting up, she peered indifferently at Anna and Emmett, then slowly offered a smile that seemed more of a challenge than a greeting. She was striking looking but not pretty. The faint quilting of the skin on the backs of her hands said that she was in her forties.

Paulina rubbed his calves as if to knead some sensation into them, then reached for his Levi's on a bedpost. A silver belt buckle caught the sunlight streaming in through the door. He kicked off his solitary boot and stood, a gaunt figure with an insolent leer.

Anna busied her eyes with the interior of the former store. The grocery shelves were sparsely filled with saddles, ropes, tack and a few willow baskets, for which the female weavers of Seekseequa Canyon had once been famous. There was a telephone on the floor but no sign of foodstuffs, the lack of which was confirmed when Paulina lit a Lucky Strike and muttered to the woman, who was finally putting on a white blouse and a long, dark purple skirt, "Ain't shit in the pantry, Trish. Unless you can conjure up some donuts and coffee with one of your spells, how about takin' my Caddy into Warm Springs and gettin' us some?"

As she began to make a hasty exit, Emmett said to her, "Some I.D., please." Still smiling, she fished a California driver's license out of a tasseled leather handbag and held it up to the partners. Patricia Sward of Guerneville. A town along the Russian River deep in the redwoods.

"Satisfied?" she asked.

"Seldom, but you're free to go, Ms. Sward."

As the woman hurried out, Tennyson Paulina stopped in the midst of searching for something and stared at Anna. He was thin for a Paiute. Lumps under his drum-taut skin marked where calcium had built up over healed bone breaks. He went on staring at her through the smoke of his cigarette for a moment longer, then shuffled around and located a dirty towel on the floor, which he looped around his neck.

"You own a late-model Dodge diesel pickup?" Emmett demanded.

"No, sir." Shirtless and barefooted, Paulina hobbled out the door. He moved as if his broken bones had never knitted properly. He had yet to ask what the intrusion was all about, which Anna found telling: The guilty invariably waited for the police to explain themselves.

Emmett and she followed the man outside. It would be a hot autumn day, despite the night's chill.

"You have access to a late-model Dodge diesel?" Emmett continued.

"All I got access to is that ol' El Dorado, and Madras Used Cars is gettin' ready to repo it. Thought I'd do better up at the Tygh Valley Indian Rodeo this year, but I didn't. All I came home with was Trish, I'll be damned if I know what she wants from me. No doubt you know how it goes with white pussy, Parker. You wind up takin' even though you're never exactly sure what's bein' given." A forked stick was leaning against the side of the old store. Paulina grabbed it, and both Anna and Emmett stiffened. Chuckling at the partners' defensive instincts, he used the stick like a golf club to bat aside the Coors can that had apparently fallen off the fender when Patricia Sward drove away. Then he dug the forked end into the ashes of the dying fire and fished out a cantaloupe-sized rock.

Emmett asked, "You know Gorka Bilbao?"

"Yep." Paulina carried the rock toward the mound of earth.

"Ever had any run-ins with him?"

Paulina ducked through a low opening in the mound, which Anna then recognized to be a Paiute sweat lodge. He promptly appeared again, nursing a crick in his back with his free hand. "I don't have run-ins no more. Time was when I had a bad temper, but those days are over. All I got are pains and a box full of belt buckles for rodeos I can't half remember." Paulina got another rock from the fire pit and started back for the sweat lodge. "What's that loony son of a bitch sayin' about me now?"

Anna replied, "Mr. Bilbao accuses you of attacking him last night."

"How?"

"Sending a driverless Dodge truck to force him off the Whitehorse Rapids Road." She decided not to add that Emmett and she had witnessed the attack.

Paulina didn't laugh, and Anna wasn't sure if she had expected him to. Instead, he gave a sad shake of his head as he deposited yet another rock inside the lodge. Emerging halfway out the opening to toss the stick and his cigarette away, he said, "Jim Beam sour mash and Coors beer are my personal demons, and I got to sweat 'em out of me. Come inside or go away—choice is yours."

Emmett seemed reluctant to enter, but Anna trailed Paulina into the gloom. A sweat lodge was like a church; even the most depraved wouldn't violate its sanctity. She made herself not glance away when Paulina dropped his Levi's and sat nude on the hard-packed earthen floor. He draped the towel over his head like a hood.

The rocks pulsed with dry heat. Emmett crawled in behind her, and they sat with elbows touching to one side of the opening.

Paulina dipped a spray of sage boughs into a Tupperware bowl of water and flecked the droplets onto the rocks. There was a sound like bacon crackling in a skillet, and steam wrapped around Anna's face, opening her sinuses. "You two got names?" he asked.

They introduced themselves.

"Well, Investigator Parker, I don't know how things are with you Comanche . . ." There'd been no prior mention of Emmett's tribe, Anna realized. ". . . but it seems strange to me how somebody gets accused of havin' bad power in this neck of the woods. Agent Turnipseed's Modoc, I hear, so she's local enough to understand." Paulina reached back to let a deerskin flap down over the opening, and Anna tensed as the sultry darkness enveloped her. "It starts with your family—don't it, Turnipseed?"

Anna didn't answer. But he was right.

"If you come from a line of difficult folks," Paulina went on, "or just different folks, you can plan on being accused. It's said to be in your blood. Add in the fact you had nightmares or was sickly as a kid, and the rumormongers will say you resisted the power inside you. Now, I'll admit I been foolish. I gave these waggin' tongues ammunition to use against me. I'm competitive by nature and won me a lot of rodeo prizes, even though I gave away most the money to my kin and friends. The tongues said I used bad magic to get the bulls to let me ride 'em so long. And one time when I was drunk, I admit I picked a rattler up off the road and kissed the damn thing without gettin' bit. After that, everybody said I had Snake Power. They said I kilt a guy— a guy who happened to be white—clear up in Simnasho on the North End while I was down here in Seekseequa. Before he died, he told his wife he could feel a snake coilin' round his throat. The coroner said heart attack, but everybody in Simnasho swears evil ol' Tennyson kilt him with bad power." Paulina laughed bitterly. "Well, trust me, Parker and Turnipseed—I don't have no Snake Power. Kissin' that rattler was the same as fallin' down stairs drunk. Try it sober and you're bound to get hurt."

"What reason would Bilbao have to accuse you of sorcery?" Emmett asked. "He's white."

"Some white folks believe more in Indian ways than many

Indians." Paulina again sprinkled the rocks. "But that's just part of the situation we got here. Bilbao and his anthro boss, Dr. Rankin, offended my people by takin' our Ancient One out of his restin' place. A body's supposed to stay buried for all eternity. Bilbao has a guilty conscience—that's all you heard talkin' last night. Thaddeus Rankin has no conscience."

Anna felt sweat collecting in the small of her back. "Who do you consider your people, the confederated tribes?"

"No way. The Sahaptin and the Wasco never made us welcome here. My people are the Hunibui Eaters. That's my band of Paiute."

"Yesterday, a Sahaptin elder told us that the skeleton belonged to her tribe," Anna pointed out. "That her people dug wild celery in John Day Canyon for countless generations."

"Not true," Paulina rebutted. "We alone gathered in those badlands, and the other tribes were afraid to mess with us. Where do you think the best *hunibui*, or biscuit root, comes from? Along the upper John Day River, that's where. Us Paiutes welcome the support of the salmon-eaters in gettin' the remains back in the ground where they belong. But this John Day Man, as the press calls him, is Paiute."

"Dr. Rankin would say that the skeleton can't be linked to any of the three tribes," Emmett noted.

"I know," Paulina said crossly. "On account his skull don't resemble ours. Well, the old folks tell us the Biscuit Root Eaters didn't always look the way we do nowadays. Jesus Christ, Parker—don't you see where this is headed? Whitey already took most our lands. Yours too, Comanche and Modoc. Gone. Turned into farms and cities. What's he want now? To prove we don't have original title to this country? That means he aims to take what little we all got left. So we're not goin' to let Rankin and his lapdog, Bilbao, dig up our Ancient Ones no more. We'll do *anythin'* to stop 'em."

Suddenly, it sounded as if Paulina dumped the entire bowl of water on the stones. The cloud of steam made Anna cover her face with her hands, but still her eyes and nostrils felt as if they'd been scorched. "You all right?" Emmett asked.

"Yes." Although she was gasping for breath.

Emmett whipped back the deerskin cover, and light shafted inside.

Paulina was no longer sitting on the other side of the opening from them. His clothes were gone too. "Christ Almighty," Emmett said as he rushed outside.

Anna was right behind him. The morning air now felt icy on her skin. She and Emmett looked all around, but Paulina had vanished into the brush. There was no trace of him in the canyon, seemingly no more bare foot tracks on the soft ground around the sweat lodge than those he'd made to draw the hot rocks.

"He had this planned," Emmett said sourly. "That's why he had the woman drive out someplace to meet him."

"Want me to have tribal police stop and hold him?"

"For what? Suspicion of using bad power?" Shading his eyes against the dawn sun, Emmett scanned the bluffs above the canyon. "Paulina wouldn't even own up to being a medicine man."

Anna studied him a moment. The Comanche were inclined toward skepticism; they'd even discounted the Ghost Dance, which had promised the demise of the whites and the resurrection of the vanquished Indian world. She finally explained, "Out here, that's the first promise a sorcerer makes to the spirit who helps him learn his craft."

"What?"

"He promises always to deny that he has the power." Then she headed back to their vehicle.

4

Emmett took the handicapped space in the otherwise full parking lot of the Corps of Engineers headquarters in The Dalles. Bailing out, he noticed a CAT-scan unit trailer backed up to a side door in the complex. Anna had to half-jog to match his long-legged stride.

A graying blond man with a hawkish nose sprang up from the picnic table that employees probably used for lunch. Although dressed like an FBI agent, he shouted at Emmett and Anna, "I demand to be included!" No self-respecting cop demanded to be included in anything; involvement was always imposed from above. A handful of reporters and cameramen were poised to delay the partners' entry into the building, but the blond man's shout swiveled their microphones and cameras toward him for an explanation.

Emmett pushed his way through, Anna clasping his jacket sleeve to keep up.

Early this morning, while they'd been driving out of Seekseequa Canyon, the U.S. District Court for Oregon had handed down its second decision on John Day Man. The U.S. Attorney's secretary in Portland had left a message at the Kah-Nee-Ta Resort for them. When no response had come within the hour, the secretary had contacted Emmett's supervisor in Phoenix, who had raised Parker by cell phone and instructed him and Anna to get to The Dalles as soon as possible.

Colonel Carter's male assistant, a bland-looking civilian named Michael, was waiting for them in the foyer. "This way." Michael led them down a corridor, through a security door and into a room without windows. The first thing to catch Emmett's eye was a chunky

Mosler safe in a far corner. Drafting tables and computer stands had been shoved against the walls to make room for a conference table. Around it stood Dr. Rankin, Colonel Carter and Elsa Dease. The young NAGPRA monitor wore a wing dress, a native white buckskin garment reserved for high ceremony. A medicine bag dangled from her hip, and she held a silver bell by its handle. She offered an uneasy smile to Anna and Emmett.

Rankin had bound his long white hair into a ponytail. He made a point of looking at the wall clock—it was almost 11:00 A.M.—then barked at the partners, "The judge gave me only eight hours of examination time, and I'll be damned if your fucking tardiness is going to be counted against me!"

"Can it," Emmett said.

Rankin flared his eyes. "What'd you just say to me?"

"Special Agent Turnipseed and I aren't tardy. We got word to report here little more than an hour ago, and I believe we just set the land speed record from Warm Springs to The Dalles."

"Why the devil do you two have to be here at all? Carter just kicked out my assistant, an osteological technician, so we could make room for two gumshoes!"

"It had nothing to do with space, Doctor," the colonel said with patience that was clearly fraying—the scarred rift in her face had turned slightly purple. "I was only enforcing the court order. In deference to the remains, technical support staff is to be kept to a minimum. *You* were granted a look, not a mob of people in lab coats. There's already a CAT-scan technician in the trailer outside—at your request."

Emmett said, "We'll need a tape recorder, Colonel. Special Agent Turnipseed and I had no time to bring our own equipment." He and Anna would treat this exam as a law-enforcement–witnessed autopsy.

Carter jerked her head at Michael, and her assistant scurried out. Emmett strolled over to the safe. To his back, the colonel said, "We ordinarily keep sensitive plans and blueprints in there. This is the first time for a 14,600-year-old skeleton."

"And hopefully the last," Rankin said. "There's no temperature and humidity control in that damned iron crate of yours."

"We've done the best we could under the circumstances, Doctor."

"The federal government's best is seldom good enough. What do I have to do to convince you people you're not qualified to store human remains?" Rankin had come in his field khakis to remind everyone that he was the expert here. "Contaminate this specimen with mold, and I'll make sure the world never forgets you!"

Carter sighed. "Anyone care for something to drink?" She was looking directly at Elsa Dease as she asked this. Everyone declined, but only the Warm Springs woman ignored the offer. Elsa seemed withdrawn this morning—unlike her assertive, almost cheeky self of yesterday afternoon at the dig in John Day Canyon. Did her remoteness have something to do with Carter? If so, Emmett again wondered where the tribes and the Corps had gotten off on the wrong foot. Carter had every reason—land use, fishery and hydroelectric issues—to get along with the tribal bureaucracy. But that didn't appear to be the case.

Michael finally returned with the tape recorder. As he left, Carter ordered him to lock the door behind him.

Emmett handed Anna the recorder. Frowning at him, she extemporized into the tiny microphone about the purpose of the forensic examination, naming those who were present for it. Then she replayed this much to make sure the recorder was working.

"For Christ's sake," Rankin growled, "can I begin already?"

"Begin already," Anna said stridently. "The clock is running on your exam."

The anthropologist smiled, as if her show of backbone made her more interesting than she'd been just minutes ago.

Wheeling a cart before her, Carter joined Emmett at the safe. She shielded the lock with her body while dialing in the combination, then swung open the ponderous door. A gust of something akin to cold electricity hit Emmett. That was the only thing he could liken it to: a sudden and chilly snapping that poured out into the otherwise heavy atmosphere of room. Emmett had felt it before, not specifically with Indian remains but upon approaching murder victims in a darkened bedroom or a roadside ditch. As if the wronged dead were frenetically restless.

There were three white wooden boxes inside the safe. One by one, Carter stacked them on the cart. Each was about twenty inches square and ten inches deep. The air around the boxes seemed to crackle with outrage at the coming defilement by modern science—Emmett recalled Gorka Bilbao's claim that the bones had been incandescent.

Rankin spread a sheet of butcher paper over the table as Carter wheeled the cart over to him. Then he began removing the bones from the boxes and laying them out in anatomical order.

They weren't glowing, Emmett saw to his relief.

Elsa took a step back from the table.

"You all right?" Carter began to reassure the young woman with a touch on the shoulder, but then let her hand fall to her side again when Elsa brusquely nodded.

Emmett checked on Anna. Sweat from the steam in Tennyson Paulina's lodge had plastered her bangs to her forehead, making her look a bit wilted, but she watched entranced as the skeleton took shape on the table.

For the tape recorder, Rankin noted the absence of the fifth metacarpal, which had been sent to UC Riverside for radiocarbon dating and not returned as yet to the custody of the Corps of Engineers.

The remains gave off a strong earth smell. It suggested great age, century piled upon century in which this jumble of now articulated bones had lain forgotten in the volcanic silt of John Day Canyon. They had been ancient already when Christ reportedly spun fishes and loaves from thin air. Older still when Moses allegedly parted the Red Sea.

At last, Rankin brought out the partial skull. "That's it, all we'll ever have," he said. "About seventy percent of a complete skeleton." His expression had turned pensive. Was he too being affected by the remains? "Speak to me, old friend," Rankin addressed the skull, cradling it in his hands. Excited hands, Emmett noted. "Who were you?" The anthropologist tilted the cranium forward. "Well, first off, you were middle-aged, weren't you? Your skull sutures are fused." He nestled the skull in a donut-shaped beanbag and encouraged Emmett with a wave to have a closer look.

Emmett beheld the eye orbits, wondering if it was possible that the irises had been blue—contradicting everything he believed about the distant world those eyes had gazed out on. Somehow, had prehistoric Europeans crossed the Atlantic or skimmed the Arctic ice shelf and reached the Americas centuries before the arrival of Asiatic pioneers?

There was controversial evidence to support this hypothesis—an uncanny similarity between the stone-tool–making techniques of ancient peoples in Spain and the Paleo-Indians of North America. Or was John Day Man simply one of Emmett's own ancestors, physically differing from the Comanche and other tribes only because of 14,600 years of genetic diversification? Some DNA and evolution-of-language studies, also controversial, suggested that Indians had been in the Western Hemisphere for at least 40,000 years.

"I'd like a moment," Elsa Dease said quietly.

Rankin glowered at her for delaying him, but then something came over him—perhaps attraction for the young woman in native dress—and he backed off with a stagy bow.

Elsa rang her silver bell three times. The doorbell to eternity, Emmett thought, recalling how Buddhists clapped to awaken spirits. "Grandfather," she intoned, "we apologize for disturbing you like this. For ripping you out of Mother Earth and bringing you into the light of day again. It's not the doing of your descendants. You might very well be First Man, and if that is so, we sprang from you and First Woman. After the flood, you two stepped from the great canoe that still can be seen on top of Mount Jefferson—"

"Oh God," Rankin muttered.

"Grandfather—"

"Forgive me, Ms. Dease," the anthropologist interrupted, "but this isn't your grandfather. At least not your Indian grandfather, given your white blood." As Elsa smoldered, Rankin held up the partial skull like Hamlet contemplating Yorick. But something spoiled the melodramatic effect he probably wanted—his hands were now quaking so badly it appeared as if the cranium were trying to wiggle out of his clutches. "Note the narrow braincase and face. Classic Caucasoid characteristics. Let me refer to the living models of Mr. Parker and Ms. Turnipseed . . ." He regarded Emmett first. "Are you a full-blood, Investigator? With a name like Parker, I doubt it." Not waiting for Emmett to reply, he explained to the others, "Cynthia Parker was a white captive from mid-nineteenth-century Texas who spawned Quanah Parker, the last war chief of the Comanche. Looking at Parker, I'd guess that this touch of the whitewash brush has been diluted by several generations of pure Nuumu ancestry . . ." Once again, his pronunciation of the Comanches' word for themselves was infuriatingly perfect; he rolled out the vowels like a native speaker. "As you can see, Ms. Dease, Mr. Parker's braincase and face are moderately round. Now, Ms. Turnipseed provides us with a fascinating morphological specimen, as she has some Japanese blood in a predominately Modoc matrix. In fact, she represents both geographical ends of a relatively recent human migration that began in northeast Asia and ended in the Americas. Her head and face tend to be more oval than elongated, in marked contrast to my own northern European example, which is extremely elongated, and Grandfather's here, which is moderately elongated."

Elsa finally appealed to Carter. "I'd like a moment alone with the remains—after Dr. Rankin leaves."

"Granted."

"Get on with it, Doctor," Elsa said. "I tired of your lectures years ago."

Just when Rankin looked like he was going to erupt again, he cooed sarcastically, "Then you were in the minority, my dear. A pity Affirmative Action let you jump the waiting list for my classes and deny your seat to a more interested party." Rankin pointed out John Day Man's slightly projecting upper jaw. "Look—see how it sticks out like mine, and Ms. Dease's to some extent . . . but not Parker's or Turnipseed's?"

Emmett had had enough too. "According to the American Anthropological Association, race cannot be determined scientifically."

"Hogwash," Rankin retorted. "Swill dumped into the trough of political correctness by professional mediocrities."

"Then are you actually claiming that this skeleton is Caucasian?"

"Oh, I won't open that can of worms, Mr. Parker. The term *Caucasoid* doesn't make the full leap to *Caucasian*. *Caucasoid* simply refers to a set of physical features that, in contemporary racial subgroups, are possessed by some Aryan-Asians as well as Europeans. The Ainu, the indigenous folk of Ms. Turnipseed's Japan—"

"I'm Modoc," Anna said firmly.

"Of course, my dear." Rankin flashed her a cold, mercurial smile. "We are what we believe we are. As I was saying, the Ainu and the Laplanders of northern Scandinavia are definite Caucasoid types. Do I rule out a European migration to the Americas before those of your Indian ancestors? Of course not. Time will confirm it, but my own few remaining years will run out before it's conclusively proved, particularly if the tribes continue to use NAGPRA to stymie science." Rankin looked too robust to be talking about his own death. But there was that trembling of his hands—and the cane he'd hung by its crook on the back of a chair. The anthropologist rested John Day Man's cranium on the table again. "I too finally know who I am, Ms. Turnipseed. Just a human being who comes from a long, convoluted line of other human beings, none of whom crawled out of a magical canoe on Mount Jefferson to inhabit the earth or, as you Modoc presume, came into existence when your curiously asexual god plucked the hairs from his body." He turned on Elsa. "And when I lie in Mother Earth, as you so charmingly anthropomorphize this spinning ball of rock, no bell can awaken me to the disappointments of this life."

With that, Rankin fell silent and examined the skeleton.

Two hours later, he straightened after inspecting a femur through an illuminated magnifier. "V-shaped cut marks," he announced, "on both ends of the bone."

"You sure?" Emmett asked.

Rankin offered him a look.

Leaning into the magnifier, Emmett scrutinized the earth-stained thigh bone. And there they were: minute marks from a stone knife. The cuts were exquisitely fine because the blade had probably been fashioned from obsidian, volcanic glass so sharp it was being tested at present for use in surgery. Emmett itched to find evidence that Rankin was grossly mistaken. But no, he'd seen such marks before on antelope and deer bones. The V-shape indicated repeated hard strokes with an implement.

"What's this mean?" Colonel Carter asked with rising concern.

"John Day Man was butchered and eaten," Rankin said flat out.

"By whom?"

"Ah, that's the question, Colonel. The one that can turn the universe upside down."

"Cannibalism's not the only explanation for marks like these," Emmett argued. "In some cultures, the dead were stripped of their flesh before they were buried. No part was eaten. And the bodies of witches were often cut up, defleshed and crushed to erase their power."

Rankin hoisted an eyebrow. "And where'd you receive your training, Mr. Parker?"

"Oklahoma State."

"Master's in anthropology?"

"Bachelor's in criminology, minor in anthropology."

"Ah, Oklahoma State. Good football program."

"Yeah," Emmett fired back at him, "which gives me just enough knowledge to lateral the ball to five court-recognized experts who'll disagree with your cannibalism theory."

"Disagree with it or *disprove* it?"

Glancing across the table, Emmett saw that the color had dropped from Elsa's face. And she was tottering. "Grab Dease!" he told Deborah Carter, who was standing beside her. The colonel took hold of the young woman just as she began to sink to the floor. Elsa let go of the silver bell. It chimed against the linoleum. Carter went down in a heap with Elsa but managed to keep the young woman from striking her head. The colonel touched two fingers to Elsa's wrist, then said, "Her pulse is wild."

"Hysterical reaction." Rankin blithely went on with his examination. "It's what happens when you take myth too literally."

"Or lock your knees and cut off your circulation," Anna said.

Elsa's eyes had never completely closed, but all at once they were alert again. "Let me up." Carter tried to hold her still, but the young woman insisted, "I want to stand."

Carter looked to Emmett. Elsa's color had improved, and Anna was filling a paper cup with water from a sink. "Let her, if she wants," he said.

With the colonel's help, Elsa came to her feet, shook off Anna's offer of water, then shuffled on her own around the table to Rankin. "Show me what you're talking about."

"Be my guest." The anthropologist stood back from the magnifier.

As Elsa studied the femur, Rankin whispered in her ear, "Have you seen the big obsidian knives at your museum in Warm Springs? The legend in the display case says those gorgeous black blades were for ceremonial use. But it fails to say what kind of ceremony. I can tell you. They were used to sever the tendons so the muscles could be pried off the bones and roasted over an open fire. Imagine a world in which cannibalism was not linked to insanity—"

"Control yourself, Doctor," Carter demanded.

Elsa adjusted the position of the bone under the lens. "What's this?" she asked Rankin.

"What's what?"

She pointed at a small round puncture in the femur.

"Who knows?" Rankin replied. "Minor scavenging damage from a rodent, maybe."

Elsa indicated another spot. "And this?"

Emmett came around the table so he could see it: a quarter-inch-wide ellipse of black matter imbedded in the bone. Clearly not bone itself. Rankin examined the inclusion, then said to Colonel Carter, "I'll need a CAT scan on this."

A half hour later, Carter returned the femur and a computer-enhanced image to Rankin, who definitively answered Elsa, "It's the broken-off tip of an obsidian atlatl point. That confirms the violence inferred by the blown-out tooth sockets in the maxilla."

Looking over the anthropologist's shoulder at the image, Emmett had no difficulty recognizing the remnant of the lithic projectile. The complete point had been attached to an arrowlike dart that was hurled by a throwing stick. The atlatl predated the bow and arrow, which never matched the killing velocity of its more primitive antecedent, although the throwing spear went out of use with the extinction of the mammoth and other huge prey.

Anna squeezed in around Emmett to view the image. "Did the bone fuse around the point?" she asked Rankin. Good question. If bone tissue had healed around the bit of stone, John Day Man had survived this particular wound.

"No, the injury was perimortem," Rankin answered. At the time of death. "The projectile is situated close to the track of the femoral artery." Hand quivering, he used his pen to point. "I see intimations of a leaf shape and side notching. What style would that suggest, Ms. Dease?" He waited for her answer.

"Cascade, maybe. But it seems to be too crudely made to be true Cascade."

"How about Proto-Cascade, if I might coin a term?"

"Perhaps," Elsa said as if it pained her to say so.

Carter picked up on this right away. "What's so bad about that?"

In silence, Rankin returned the femur to the rest of the skeleton.

Emmett told Carter, "The doctor thinks he has evidence John Day Man was killed by Paleo-Indians in this region."

"Well, don't I?" Rankin scoffed.

"I'm not getting it," the colonel said in dismay. "Caucasoids, as you call them, and Native Americans living in the Columbia basin at the same time 14,600 years ago?"

Rankin just shrugged.

Elsa Dease looked sickened. "So what're you going to say to the press, Doctor?"

"What would you say, Elsa, if you were me?"

"I'm not you."

"You've just answered your own question." Rankin checked the wall clock, making Emmett do the same. Incredibly, it was 6:46 P.M.—exposure to John Day Man somehow made time evaporate. "It's my opinion this skeleton can't be associated with any existing American Indian group. However, I believe this middle-aged male was a victim of Paleo-Indian violence." Then, surprisingly, Rankin's tone toward Elsa turned consoling. "But look at it this way, my dear—all three of the Warm Springs tribes are relatively new to this region. The archaeological record's clear on that. Your ancestors pushed out people who were already here, and they no doubt pushed out the group who fashioned the atlatl point that felled our specimen. By no means am I saying your tribes are responsible for this poor fellow's death. His remains just wound up on your turf."

Elsa Dease said with an icy determination, "I'm going to ask for further analysis."

"By whom?" Rankin asked.

"Maybe one of the court experts Mr. Parker mentioned." Tears of anger welled in her eyes as she faced the anthropologist. "You're not going to have the final word on this. Believe me."

Rankin looked flabbergasted. "Even if it means Grandfather is subjected to *unduly invasive technologies?*"

Elsa clenched her teeth together, visibly trying to control her temper before she further contradicted herself. Rankin had bullied her into sounding pro-analysis. Carter handed her the cup of water Anna had drawn at the sink, and the young woman finally drank.

• • •

After Dr. Rankin's press conference in front of the Corps of Engineers headquarters, Anna didn't feel like eating. But she did want a cup of coffee before tackling the drive back to the Kah-Nee-Ta, so she persuaded Emmett to go around the corner with her to the local Starbucks. However, Rankin and Elsa Dease could be seen through the windows of the coffeehouse, arguing heatedly at a table—the other patrons were staring at them. Elsa had taken off her wing dress and was in a sweater and slacks.

There was a neighborhood bar directly across the street from Starbucks, but Anna wasn't sure how Emmett would feel about going inside. His drinking years were behind him.

"It'll do," he said, as if reading her thoughts.

They took the booth in the front of the dreary tavern and ordered coffees. The patrons, all white, were hunched over the long bar. Emmett was unusually quiet. Ordinarily, Anna would let a silence between them mellow out, but this one made her uncomfortable. Any more silence felt like defeat. Despite her weariness, she decided to get the two of them back on Dr. Tischler's therapeutic bicycle—tonight. "How're you doing, Em?" she asked.

He gazed through the tinted window, which made the night seem even darker than it was. Rankin and Dease were still going at each other in Starbucks. "Pacific Northwest depresses me."

As if waiting for this cue, veils of drizzle started falling through the streetlights.

"Me too," she confessed. Even though she'd been born on the edge of it. The Dalles had been the site of an aboriginal slave market, where the Modoc had brought Shasta, Pit River and Paiute captives to trade for goods. Perhaps the lingering presence of all those displaced souls was getting Emmett and her down. Or maybe it was how Rankin was trying to repaint with gore and blood a native past that had seemed reasonably humane in her mind.

Staring across the wet pavement at the anthropologist, Anna asked, "What's his agenda? I've never read his works."

"There are two major prongs to his latest hypothesis—Caucasoids were first to people the New World, but their small numbers were wiped out by more numerous invaders from northeast Asia."

"Our supposed ancestors?"

"Yeah. And forget *Hiawatha* and *Dances with Wolves*. We Indians were a barbarous bunch, murdering and eating the Caucasoids at the drop of a hat."

"What's Rankin's proof like?"

"Sketchy. He claims he had everything he needed in a New Mexico dig—including human remains in coprolite, dried fecal matter. But, in the first big test of NAGPRA, the Zuni tribe shut him down and had all the specimens reburied on site. It damn near destroyed Rankin, according to the BIA archaeology investigators with our Albuquerque office. Years of work down the drain." Emmett's brow wrinkled. "But he wasn't always obsessed with trying to prove Indians were cannibals. A couple decades ago, he joined the American Indian Movement in occupying BIA headquarters in Washington, then later bankrolled the Wounded Knee standoff. He called the United States' treatment of native people its original sin."

"What turned him around?"

"I don't know," Emmett said. "Maybe he felt time and fame slipping away. His father was an even more renowned anthropologist." Anna reached across the table and took his hand. He returned her caress but asked uneasily, "We're not going to talk about showering, are we?"

"No, I think we've beaten that horse to death." Anna paused. "Is there anything else you have in mind?"

He stopped blinking. "Like what?"

"It's a long, dark drive back to the Kah-Nee-Ta." She rose. "You get going on the imagery rehearsal while I visit the restroom." She headed for the rear of the building.

A hand tapped her shoulder from behind. "Excuse me . . . Ms. Turnipseed?"

Anna turned on a thin white man in his fifties with an aquiline nose. He wore a conservative charcoal-gray suit. She'd noticed him before at the bar, where he seemed to be keeping watch on the street.

"Yes?"

"Pardon me. I'm—"

Emmett swiftly came from the booth and spun the man around. "Who are you?"

The stranger didn't seem to be intimidated by Emmett, although he said, "Forgive me for interrupting, Mr. Parker."

"Who're you?" Emmett repeated.

"I'm Nels Sward. You've heard of me?"

"Nope." But then it seemed to hit Emmett the same instant Anna realized: The white woman with Tennyson Paulina this morning had been named Sward too. Patricia Sward. *Too old to be this man's daughter*—Emmett must have been thinking the same thing, for he said, "Do you have any I.D.?"

"Of course, sir." Prying a California driver's license out of his billfold, Sward said matter-of-factly, "I'm the high priest of the Norse Folk Congress. Do you mind if we all sit? I promise to state my business promptly and then go back to the bar." He handed the license to Emmett, who underscored Sward's hometown with his thumbnail for Anna—*Guerneville*.

"All right, Mr. Sward," Emmett finally said. "If you keep it brief."

"Join you in a minute." Anna continued on to the grimy restroom. She was sure Sward had said "high priest of the Norse Folk Congress," but on a day that had included a vanishing Paiute sorcerer and 14,600-year-old Caucasoid bones, she no longer completely trusted her take on reality. Might Patricia be Nels Sward's sister? Intuition told Anna no.

When she returned to the booth, Emmett was asking Sward, "Norse Folk *what*?"

"Congress. We're Old Norse pagans." Sward showed amusement at Emmett's surprise, then stood politely with him as Anna slid past her partner. "I understand your reaction. I'm used to it. Especially from Native Americans, who somehow think Europeans were always Christian. Well, we weren't." Sward and Emmett sat. "The Jesus Road, I'm afraid, was a Middle Eastern import. Before that, we looked at the world much as traditional Indians still do. We honored Mother Earth and Father Sky. The four cardinal directions were sacred to us. We planned our lives by the sun, the moon and the stars. Animals were our brothers and sisters, our protectors and advisors, and plants our doctors. We lost all that, and our lives have been empty ever since. A few of us are looking back to recover some of the old ways . . . before the world is destroyed by the dominant culture."

"Pagans," Emmett muttered, still disbelieving.

"Indeed, sir."

"Honest to God pagans."

"I swear on Odin's head."

Sward's accent was unrecognizable to Anna, maybe Scandinavian but with another influence as well. "Where are you originally from, Mr. Sward?"

"Sweden, Ms. Turnipseed, but in my early twenties I went to the Navajo Nation. I spent nineteen years there."

"What'd the Dine think of your pagan beliefs?" Emmett asked, using the Navajos' own word for their tribe.

"I wasn't a pagan then, Mr. Parker. At least not until the very end. I was a Lutheran missionary." When neither partner said anything, Sward added, "A woman. I'd begun to question the value of my missionary work. At the same time, a beautiful Dine woman came into my life and acquainted me with the possibilities of paganism. Naturally, Navajo beliefs didn't work for me. I'm not Navajo."

Anna asked as if she hadn't met Patricia, "This woman became Mrs. Sward?"

"No, I'm afraid not," Sward said with a trace of sadness. "But I'm grateful to her for putting me on my present path."

Emmett asked, "What's this have to do with us?"

"I and some members of my kindred have—"

"What's a kindred?"

"My local group in northern California, Mr. Parker. We've been in the area since shortly after the discovery of John Day Man was announced. I've arranged with the Forest Service to set up a camp. Tomorrow, we'll move out of our motel and pitch our tents just north of the reservation along the White River."

Emmett yawned. "I still don't understand why you're here."

"To reclaim our Nordic ancestor and properly bury him so his spirit will be at rest. We consider it a sacred obligation."

"Hate to disappoint you, but I don't think it's been proven John Day Man is a Viking."

"Agreed, Mr. Parker. And your sarcasm is quite understandable." One of Sward's large, bony hands checked that his tie was still knotted snugly against his Adam's apple. "I listened to Dr. Rankin this evening with much interest. But I was disappointed his craniometric analysis fell short of the truth."

"The truth about what?" Anna asked.

"The origins of the skeleton. John Day Man is more than a Caucasoid. He's Caucasian. Additional work needs to be done. Now, if . . ." Sward keenly watched Deborah Carter come through the front door. "Colonel, we have to talk before you leave."

Emmett recognized the craving in her eyes, the intense irritation that the work world was once again delaying its gratification at the bar. All of this was familiar. "Tomorrow, Sward," she said tersely.

"I must formally protest my exclusion from today's exam."

"Make an appointment with my assistant. I've had enough of this crap for one day."

As soon as Carter was out of earshot, the pagan priest said to the partners, "What I've heard of her, I thought the colonel would be more sympathetic to our point of view." He returned to the matter at hand. "Anyway, additional forensic work must be done on the remains."

"So . . . ?" Emmett asked.

Anna could tell that he was at the end of his patience, so she interjected, "This sounds like something for your group to pursue with the scientific community, Mr. Sward."

"Few of that community have taken us seriously. As the federal investigators on the scene, you two have authority."

"Neither of us is an anthropologist," Anna pointed out, "so forensic work is outside our expertise. We're just here to keep the peace, Mr. Sward."

"Then why don't you start by keeping the peace with the Norse Folk Congress?" The bartender appeared. Sward asked for a Manhattan, then turned back to the partners with a tepid smile he kept putting on like a mask. He couldn't hide the fact that he was intensely angry, and his anger unsettled Anna a little. "You can order any forensic work you require, correct?"

Anna wasn't sure, and Emmett kept silent. She'd just observed Deborah Carter knock down a double shot of amber-colored liquor, then turn from the bar and slip out the back door.

Sward went on, "My kindred is willing to gamble that there's one process that will settle the matter of John Day Man's racial patrimony once and for all. We believe that a forensic sculptor can reconstruct the partial skull—and show us most of his face as it was in life."

"No crime's been committed that warrants a request for a sculpture," Emmett said. "And there are budgetary considerations."

"Always." Sward reached inside his suit pocket and produced a check, which he laid on the table between the partners. It was made out to the Oregon State Police Laboratory in the amount of $10,000. "This should cover the costs of the reconstruction."

Anna asked, "How do you already know how much it'll be?"

"My attorney phoned the lab manager. If the NAGPRA monitor or the federal investigators authorize the work, his sculptor could do it for that amount. But he stressed the need for authorization. Ms. Dease has snubbed us."

Emmett nudged the check back toward him. "Special Agent Turnipseed and I have no grounds to order a sculpture. Have your attorney petition the court. I wouldn't be surprised if Dr. Rankin helped your cause. If the tribes consent, you might have a shot."

Sward was returning the check to his pocket when his hand froze. His attention was riveted across the street. Anna looked. The silent commotion behind Starbucks' windows was breaking up. Elsa had stormed outside. Rankin was still inside at the cash register as she unlocked her Honda and got behind the wheel. He limped out with the aid of his cane, but she'd already sped up the rain-slick street by the time he reached the curb.

Seconds later, the silver Lexus four-by-four she'd last seen in John Day Canyon pulled up for him. The street lighting was too dim for Anna to see much about the driver, although the profile of his features and his hair suggested that he was black.

Rankin gazed after Elsa's Honda one last time, then got inside the Lexus.

"Please don't take this personally," Sward said as he stuffed the check back in his pocket, "but I intend to complain to your superiors. You are proving to be as intractable as Colonel Carter."

Emmett stood and stretched. "My boss is the Secretary of the Interior. Ms. Turnipseed's is the Attorney General. The area code for Washington, D.C., is 202. Skoal."

5

Once Wapinitia Road climbed out of the reservation border town of the same name, there were no houses until the village of Simnasho, where Elsa Dease lived with her mother. Twisty and scarcely wide enough for two cars, it was no road for a drifting mind. Yet, Elsa kept replaying the day's events in an effort to loosen their grip on her. Thaddeus Rankin had finally gotten under her skin. He'd never lived on a rez, nor did he really understand Indians, otherwise he would've known that believing human beings were adrift in an amoral universe was dangerous. If you didn't know where you came from, you didn't know who you were. And if you didn't know who you were on a reservation, you might behave destructively.

I failed my people today.

The tribes had counted on her to get the Ancient One repatriated as soon as possible. But Rankin had tricked her into losing her temper. She'd had no intention of asking for further testing; that was the last thing her people wanted. Then he'd trumped her at the news conference by sounding so reasonable and conciliatory. But Rankin had a temper of his own, and maybe that was why she'd agreed to have coffee with him. To find the chinks in his armor. However, despite his bursts of ill humor, he'd been in control at Starbucks too, and at the end of the half hour she'd blown it again and threatened to ask the court for another forensic authority to study the skeleton. In defense of his cannibalism theory, Rankin had regurgitated the same hollow spin that other tribes—not the Sahaptin, Wasco or Paiute—had inhabited this country on that day 14,600 years ago when John Day

Man took an atlatl point to the thigh. That gave no solace to peoples who believed that they and this land were linked from the beginning of time. Land, time and the people were conceptually inseparable.

She took a hairpin curve too fast, and her outer tires flirted with the shoulder, spraying gravel against a paddle marker.

Slow down—don't let Rankin get inside you. Keep your mind on the road.

But it wouldn't stay there, not after a bruising day like today.

Again, her people were being told that they were superstitious children who couldn't interpret their own past. Every time that message had been shoved down a tribe's throat, either by missionaries or government bureaucrats, there'd been more withdrawal into alcohol, more promiscuity, more wife and child abuse. Even well-meaning whites just didn't get it: The ethical bedrock for a native society was its origin story. People behaved well because the Forces of Creation had punished previous beings for misbehaving. The human world was built on the ruins of other worlds that had been out of sync with natural goodness. Geologic features like mountains weren't just humps of stone— they were primal beings petrified by the gods for immorality.

Elsa slowed for the big turn below Neva Spring. Her headlights swept over some sumac bushes. Autumn red, they looked like dollops of blood against the golden grass. She almost gagged as she recalled the horrific vision that had made her faint while viewing the Ancient One: an illusion of a corpse, freshly flayed and still bloody, yet crawling with maggots. The elder, Minnie Claw, had cautioned Elsa to respect powerful visions. What did this one mean?

She cracked her window for air.

Rankin's voice was back inside her head, booming like thunder: *What do I think of NAGPRA? It's the most mindless assault on science since the Catholic Inquisition's prosecution of Galileo for heresy!*

The Native American Graves Protection and Repatriation Act was not mindless. It was a reaction to two centuries of shameless grave robbing. Entire native burial grounds had been rooted up, skeletons and mummies shipped off in the hundreds of thousands to rank charnel houses dignified with the name of museum or university. On the frontier, army surgeons had routinely shipped the severed heads of deceased native men, women and children to physical anthropologists in the East. These early anthros had subjected the skulls to craniology and phrenology, pseudosciences that held brain size and cranium characteristics to be proof of white superiority over other races.

The asphalt glistened under Elsa's headlights.

She'd driven through occasional drizzle since leaving The Dalles, but now it began to rain. She switched on her wipers. Only one set of headlights showed in her rearview mirror, also coming south on Wapinitia Road, but miles and miles behind.

She shivered. So violently she wondered if she'd left the car's air conditioning on this morning.

No, it was off. She turned on the heater.

Minutes later, she held her hand up to a vent. The engine temperature gauge registered warm, but the air whispering through the plastic grille was positively arctic. She felt as if she were sitting on a block of ice, and the metal cage of the Honda itself seemed to suck the warmth out of her body.

Elsa glanced into the back for her parka.

She hadn't brought it along. The morning had been balmy, so she'd taken only a sweater. Her wing dress was carefully laid out across the seat, and the bell she'd borrowed from her mother's church was on the floor mat. It chimed softly on the curves. The Honda labored up the last stretch of grade before the divide. Fog crept from the creek below and covered the road in patches. Headlights flickered behind, closer than before, sparkling crazily like diamonds. They were savagely pretty. As were the quicksilver droplets of rain slanting through her high beams. But menacing too. Over the last several minutes, the world had changed in a fundamental way she couldn't put her finger on.

And now, abruptly, she was hot.

Had the heater finally kicked in?

No, the fan was shut off. When had she done that? She touched a hand to her forehead. Her palm felt icy, but her head was burning up. Feverish. And she was slightly nauseous. Coming down with a flu bug explained everything.

Except the loud rattle that came from the other side of the car at that instant.

Sitting up, she gripped the steering wheel tighter. Had she hit something in the road? She looked back, but at that instant another band of fog wrapped around the car. She braked, and the mist glowed like an explosion of blood behind her.

Had her bell somehow made the noise? But the sound had been nothing like the chiming of a bell. She really couldn't pinpoint where it'd come from.

Hunching forward, she peered into the fog. The whole divide was cloaked in it. She lowered her beams so the swirling pall wouldn't reflect the light back into her eyes.

Just then, another sharp rattle made her jump.

This time it had come from the passenger side of the dashboard. She was certain of it. Was something coming loose in the engine compartment and banging against the firewall? She wasn't far from Simnasho, three miles at most, and any vehicle following was probably a Warm Springs family returning to the reservation after a day's shopping in The Dalles. Still, Elsa dreaded breaking down in the bleak hills of the North End. There were creatures here that could steal your sanity. Elders like Minnie Claw insisted these awful, ghostly things existed as surely as the wild horses that sheltered in the ravines and lava caves.

Listening intently to her engine, she tried to diagnose the trouble. She told herself that the engine was the source of the sounds. In the perverse ways of machines, it was playing games with her. She and her mother missed her late father's mechanical skill. He'd been supervisor of the tribal motor pool.

Unexpectedly, she saw his face. Amazingly clear and lifelike. Just when she'd feared that she was beginning to forget it. But this flicker of joy died when she saw rattlesnakes coiling around his head, more and more serpents constricting around him until his likeness was obscured by a slithering, crawly ball of snakes.

She nearly retched before she gulped down enough air to quiet her stomach again.

Another rattle made her startle.

She coasted to listen for the next one.

Exasperatingly, it didn't come, even after several minutes, and she accelerated again.

Then it sounded as if somebody had hit the dashboard with a sledgehammer. "My God!" she cried, pulling over.

She grabbed the flashlight under the seat, but the bulb filament barely lit up. She popped the hood release and got out, stretching her sweater over the top of her head against the rain. The drops sizzled against the engine. She aimed the faint beam this way and that. Nothing seemed out of order to her. No stink of oil smoke. No anti-freeze hemorrhaging out of a hose.

Elsa hurried back inside the car and drove on.

She felt so very young. There were times, especially during meetings for which she'd prepared herself, when she felt adult and competent. But this day hadn't left her feeling that way. She'd done better when she'd had a mentor, a confidante, somebody with whom to talk over these attacks of insecurity. Someone who knew how hard it was to force your way through a hostile world. But, sadly, she no longer had that mentor, so she wanted to rush home and toss the bedcovers over her feverish head. The morning light would help restore her spirits. It always did.

Hot, so hot. Her stomach was churning again.

She rolled down her window all the way, and needles of rain blustered in with the cool wind. There was a whoofing-flapping noise, like a turkey vulture taking off, and then arms wrapped around her throat. Gasping, Elsa let go of the wheel to get the thing off her. As the Honda careened toward an oak tree, she realized that the arms were flat and lifeless cloth. Her wing dress had been blown off the backseat. She jinked the wheel, avoiding the tree by inches, then laid the dress on the passenger seat beside her. *Calm down . . . calm down . . . this day has chewed up your nerves.* She wished she could be little again and doze off in her mother's arms. Her mother had been good at comforting back then. But Vernita Dease didn't know how to talk to a grown daughter. She could read minds, often see things before they took shape, and that made talk almost an annoyance to the woman.

Then another deafening thump made Elsa brace.

And another, coupled to the previous one by a low chattering of metal against metal.

In the greenish shine of the instrument lights, she watched the glove compartment lid vibrate. As if something wanted out. Elsa wasn't ready to let go of reason, to declare that all of this was a fantastic nightmare, so she ignored her trip-hammering heart and asked herself what she might have left inside the glove box that could create such a pounding.

She stopped in the middle of the road but set the parking brake and shifted into neutral to keep the engine running.

Reaching up, she turned on the dome light.

Then she waited.

Oddly, she thought of what she'd seen while turning off the main street in The Dalles: Deborah Carter standing on the darkened corner, arms stiffly down at her sides, her eyes not letting go of Elsa until the night separated them.

A birdcall, poignantly shrill out in the hills, snapped Elsa back to the present. She'd never heard such a call after sundown.

A minute passed, and nothing more happened.

Two minutes.

The only sound was the tapping of the rain on the roof. Pecking the sheet metal like beaks. She knew she couldn't drive on until she opened the glove compartment and looked inside.

Slowly, she reached for the latch. Her fingers were within inches of it when a skeletal foot slammed through the lid. An entire lower leg began slinking into the cab. Not clean white bones or even earth-stained ones. They were splashed with red, partly defleshed and still bleeding.

Elsa screamed.

•   •   •

It was Anna's turn to drive and Emmett's to navigate. They no longer had an excuse to switch on the Explorer's emergency flasher and break the speed limits, as they had up U.S. 197 on the drive to the Corps of Engineers headquarters. So Emmett suggested the shortest route back to the Kah-Nee-Ta from The Dalles, the serpentine Wapinitia Road. It was marked on the map as a vague gray line, and he suspected that Anna had already had this route in mind when she mentioned a long, dark drive back to the lodge. *Jesus, is she honestly ready to go all the way tonight? Or is she just testing herself again?* So many times before, her unmistakable signals of arousal had gradually given way to an air of forced experimentation. Then backsliding.

"Em?" she asked, eyes on the road.

"Yeah."

"What's it mean—Nels Sward's wife with Tennyson Paulina?"

"Nothing, if Nels doesn't know about it. Patricia's just sneaking into a tepee for some extracurricular sport." Immediately, Emmett regretted his choice of words—did Anna think what he wanted with her was merely sport?

Fortunately, she seemed too engrossed in her own train of thought to take note. "But what if Nels does know?"

"I'm not sure." He had no experience with white pagans, and the Swards' motivations for doing anything were beyond him.

As they left the few scattered lights of the town of Wapinitia behind, he decided to hold Anna to her promise. He reached across the space between their bucket seats and rested his hand on her knee. No nylons. The silken feel of her skin made the hair on the back of his neck snap. *I'm back to adolescent shit. I'm getting a rush from her goddamned knee.* Ever so gradually, he started up her thigh, but she suddenly laughed. "Tickles."

"You think *that* tickles . . ."

"Wait until I pass this car."

But distance on a stormy night was illusory, and almost ten miles went by before Emmett could even tell that it was a foreign compact. By then, the rain and fog made further dalliance with Anna too risky. She concentrated on the road, and Emmett sat back in frustration.

Out of a glum silence, Anna said half teasingly and half placatingly, "We'll be around this car in a minute. Just no parking until we get to the lodge, okay?" Then she added breathlessly, "That's the only condition I'm putting on this, Em. Whatever happens has to be finished by the time we reach the Kah-Nee-Ta."

"Then I'm glad we won't be alive for the accident investigation."

"What accident investigation?"

"The one ordered by the Department of Justice when two half-naked federal officers are found dead in a single-car rollover."

"Anybody else you'd rather be found dead with?"

He was about to say something smart when, finally, after all these months, after all of Dr. Tischler's tedious coaching, after all the dry runs at intimacy, Anna began running her hand along his inner thigh.

She was actually exploring *his* body. A groan broke from his lips, which he quickly tried to cover by clearing his throat.

"Does it feel good?" Almost as if she had no idea that such tender contact could feel exquisitely good.

"Slow down," he said.

"Don't you like it?"

"There's a car parked in the middle of the road—stop!"

She stomped on the brake pedal, and the Explorer sideslipped on the rainy pavement. Emmett cringed for the collision. But, wisely, Anna gave up braking and instead punched the accelerator to swerve around the white Honda. The Explorer came to a sliding stop in front of the other car. The Accord's headlights blazed directly into Emmett's eyes, but he could tell that the driver's-side door was wide open and the dome light was on.

"It's Elsa Dease's."

"Are you sure?"

Emmett let down his window. "Turn off your engine."

"What?"

"Cut the engine—fast!"

Anna did so, and then he heard only the pattering of the rain on the two cars and the murmur of the Honda's idling engine. He strained for the sound of a Dodge diesel pickup retreating down the grade toward Simnasho. He'd seen no lights other than the Honda's on the road, but finding the Accord in the middle of the road had made him think of Gorka Bilbao's encounter with the Dodge the night before.

Emmett got out with the flashlight in hand.

Squinting through the rain, he looked for a figure behind the wheel. Even a slumped-over one. In Anna's gut-wrenching pass around the Honda, he believed he'd spotted no one inside the Honda. But his mind had been on a crash.

Anna joined him. "Did Elsa hit something?"

"No front-end damage. No blood from a road kill."

Together, they circled around the Accord and approached it from behind. Right hand on his revolver grips, Emmett scanned the hillside above. Something had made Elsa Dease stop with no thought for where she was—a blind curve. That *something* might still be watching the road from the wooded heights.

He tried to take in the whole of the night with his senses. The rain made the air smell like bleach. A creek burbled on the downslope side of the road, although it was hidden by the fog.

He turned to the car.

The first thing he noticed through the open door was the floor mat on the driver's side. It was bunched up under the pedals. As if, in panic, Elsa had jammed it there. No bullet holes in any of the windows. No apparent blood. And he doubted that the tribal police had ever taken a report on a carjacking. That was an urban crime. Kneeling, he ran the flashlight back along the pavement. Elsa had probably hydroplaned—actually floated on a thin film of water— when she first hit the brakes. But hit the brakes she certainly had: The rubber had finally grabbed the road while the Honda was going sideways, leaving fresh, helixlike patterns on the asphalt.

Anna leaned over him to look inside the car. "What do you want me to do?"

He had the feeling her asking was a concession to his wounded male vanity of late. During one of their interminable hand-holding sessions, he'd explained the importance the Comanche place on face, the maintenance of personal dignity. "Get the hazard lights going on the Explorer before somebody slams into us."

"Then what?"

He tossed her the flashlight. "Look over the drop-off for Elsa."

Just when he was about to remind her, she said over her shoulder, "Don't step on any tracks in the dirt, Turnipseed."

The wing dress.

It was lying in human outline on the passenger seat. As if Elsa had been dissolved right out of it. But then Emmett recalled that the young woman hadn't been wearing the dress at the press conference or in Starbucks while she argued with Rankin. He had liked that: Some native things weren't to be shared with the world at large. She'd worn the dress solely to honor her ancestor, and with that purpose completed she'd taken off the garment.

Had she been abducted?

Careful not to touch the outer handle, he closed and reopened the door. The hinges screaked. They'd been sprung by force. Had someone wrenched the door open from the outside, or had Elsa thrown it back from inside?

The glove box lid was down.

The high angle of the dome light kept it from illuminating the interior. And Anna had the flashlight. There was one on the passenger floor mat. He thumbed it, but the batteries were dead. Emmett reached inside the glove box, felt around. A few maps, Kleenexes, little else.

Had Elsa opened the glove box to take out the flashlight, only to be disappointed that it didn't work? What had she meant to use the light on?

"Not a thing," Anna said from behind.

"Okay." Emmett stood and faced her. Her hair and shoulders were already soaked. "Radio the tribal P.D., ask them to roll here from both directions, if possible. Stop all vehicles leaving the area. Then you call out Elsa's name on the P.A. every minute or so. There's a chance she was injured somehow and wandered off, dazed." He relieved Anna of the flashlight. "Maybe she has a medical condition we don't know about."

"The fainting spell at the headquarters?"

He nodded. "I'll have a quick look around."

"Be careful."

"You too." Then he felt the need to add, "I really liked it."

"What?"

"You know."

Anna smiled briefly, beautifully, then jogged for the Explorer.

Emmett hiked back along the road, searching for a second set of tire tracks. If someone had been pursuing Dease—conceivably blacked-out, for Emmett was positive he'd seen only one pair of taillights ahead of Anna and him—the driver of that second vehicle would've been forced to lay on his brakes when Elsa did.

But there was no sign of that having happened.

The rain refused to let up, even though thick fog kept scudding over the crest. *Goddamned Pacific Northwest.* Emmett about-faced and worked along the upslope shoulder of the road with the flashlight.

He reminded himself that young people are new to life's troubles.

Shouldering archaeological and cultural protection for three tribes was no easy task, particularly with glib adversaries like Thaddeus Rankin to ridicule you at every turn. And Elsa had looked pained during the press conference; her words had come with difficulty in the glare of the camera lights. Native sentiments weren't easily translated into sound bites. Maybe it had all overwhelmed her on the drive home, and she'd gone off into the trees for a cry.

Emmett hoped so.

But didn't really believe that this was about a crying spell.

"Elsa Dease," Anna's voice came over the Explorer's public address speaker, *"this is Anna Turnipseed of the FBI. If you can hear me, please respond. . . ."*

Nothing but the sounds of the rain in the vegetation, the creek below.

Then Emmett saw where small foot tracks had cut the berm above the road. They continued at a running pace up the slope, then stopped where the ebony basalt of this country began. Impossible to hold any sign of a person's passing when wet.

Still, Emmett hiked up the hillside.

There was both hope and cause for alarm in the discovery of this short section of tracks. Hope because there were no accompanying foot impressions to indicate that Elsa had been dragged along against her will. But she'd been running. From what? Or, if not that, toward what? That was possible too: She'd been retreating toward the privacy in which to be alone.

But in this weather? And she'd already been alone, unless she'd picked up somebody after roaring away from Starbucks.

On a hunch, Emmett followed a ravine. The ridges on both sides were too precipitous to climb, but thanks to a wildfire the gully was fairly easy going. Until he came to a burnt copse of scrub oak. The wildfire had seared away all the foliage, leaving only the skeletal remains of the stand: limbs rearing up from crotches, many-fingered branches splayed against the sky. The night seemed to swallow his flashlight beam, so he had to push half-blind through the spindly maze. Wood crunched underfoot like dry bones being snapped.

Anna's amplified voice rolled up from below: *"Elsa Dease, if you can hear me, please respond. . . ."*

The ravine narrowed. There was little wind in its confines, and Emmett paused to listen. He could sense frenetic energy in front of him in the same way long ago he'd felt the onset of a supercharged Midwestern thunderstorm: The fillings in his teeth were buzzing.

An admittedly strange thought made him turn off the flashlight. What if the small, almost bony foot impressions he'd seen angling up the berm had not been Elsa's?

He moved on, groping his way through the gradually thinning burnt oaks with his hands. Something globular bobbed in his path. He touched the skull-shaped object, only to jerk his palms away—he'd been pricked. The cone of a downed yellow pine. It was still attached to its denuded branch, which was waving in the slight breeze.

Water sheeted down the rocky bed of the ravine, lapping into his oxfords.

A snort sounded in front of him. Indignant.

Emmett reached for his revolver. Before him, the higher reaches of the ravine were pitch black.

Something horny and bonelike could be heard beating the flooded ground. A clear warning—*stay away*. Then, the presence out there seemed to swell with fury.

Emmett held the flashlight away from his body, so as not to illuminate himself, and switched it on.

At least ten pairs of big, inhuman eyes shone back at him, freezing him for a split second. He barely had time to flatten himself against one wall of the gully before the stallion charged past, snorting a fetid breath in his face. The lead wild horse was obediently trailed by his mares and colts. One whipped her tail at Emmett's eyes, making him flinch. The thuds and splashes of the hooves faded down the defile, then broke across the hillside and became inaudible.

Another minute of silence was ended by Anna's voice: *"Elsa Dease . . . ?"*

• • •

The bells, the hypnotic songs sung by Indian women in white dresses and their men in white T-shirts, the all-white interior of the Shaker church made Anna feel disembodied. Ethereal. And yet, she could feel Emmett's hand touching the back of hers in the privacy of the pew. As if they had made love last night in such innocence that neither misplaced guilt nor flashbacks could haunt her this morning. She wished it'd been so, but they hadn't made love last night.

They hadn't even slept.

No cars had been found leaving the area where Elsa Dease had vanished, so Sergeant Round Dance had organized a search and rescue party of tribal police and Wasco County deputies to comb the hills above Simnasho. An almost impossible terrain to thoroughly cover, the basalt heights were pitted with caverns and craters like Swiss cheese. S&R worked throughout the night despite the rain and fog. Anna and Emmett assisted by manning the field command post, passing along messages, making sure coffee and sandwiches were available. At dawn, the state police provided a helicopter that whined up and down the ravines. All of this effort produced nothing, so at noon Anna and Emmett took control of the missing person investigation, as it involved a native woman who had been on federal business. Elsa's car was towed to the tribal police compound in Warm Springs. There, the senior FBI evidence technician from Portland went over it. He confirmed at least one thing: no traces of blood.

The search was scaled back, and the chopper buzzed off toward its home base.

As Anna and Emmett finished closing down the command post, Gabriel Round Dance took them aside and said with an air of certainty, "Elsa's mother will know where she is." Then the sergeant led the partners to the Shaker church in Simnasho, where the three of them slipped into a service that was already under way.

A handsome, middle-aged Warm Springs woman was seated in a chair set before a prayer table. She was dressed entirely in white. After staring owlishly at Anna and Emmett, she shut her eyes and appeared to meditate. The male members of the congregation took handbells from the table and began ringing them to the beat of a song that gradually grew louder. The tune itself sounded like a curious blend of Indian chant and Christian sacred music. Both men and women stamped the floor around the seated woman.

"Which one is she?" Emmett whispered to Sergeant Round Dance.

"That's Vernita Dease in the chair."

Shakers from Warm Springs had come to Anna's ranchería when she was a child. She still remembered the mesmerizing effect of the songs, the bells and the tramping feet. The white clothes of the faithful made her ask her mother if they were angels. Indian Shakers weren't to be confused with the nearly extinct white sect now more famous for its furniture than its beliefs. Indian Shakerism was born in the 1880s in Washington around Puget Sound when John Slocum, a Skokomish Indian and hell-raising timber worker, had a near-death experience—or actually died, according to believers. From heaven, he saw how his fellow Indians of the Northwest were being destroyed by vice: gambling, alcohol and tobacco, plus the traditional practice of sorcery, which caused so much strife through scapegoatism on the dispirited reservations. Slocum didn't accept the Bible as the word of God, preferring personal revelation instead. But he and his followers adopted many of the trappings of Roman Catholicism, such as candles, bell-ringing and genuflecting. Added to this culture-bridging mix was his wife Mary's hand-trembling, a widespread native diagnostic and healing technique. Thus, the name Shakers was given to the faithful.

A pause. Anna ran a fingertip over the bridge of Emmett's knuckles. He smiled faintly.

Then the song was repeated. Louder. Until the old frame church was shaking to its foundations. The white cross was bouncing on the chains that attached it to the rafters. Some of the congregants were gazing heavenward as they tramped around; others warmed their palms over the candles blazing on the prayer table. A wizened old woman gasped toothlessly at something invisible hovering in the air near her. She reached out and trapped it. Her clasped hands vibrated wildly as the thing—a spirit perhaps—tried to escape. Gingerly, the old woman carried it to Elsa's mother, rubbed it into her hair and onto her face. Vernita Dease's eyelids began to twitch. Others touched her with their candle-chafed palms. Others yet caressed a second, smaller cross on the prayer table and brought its power to Mrs. Dease, massaged it into her arms and shoulders. More and more hands were laid upon her as the singing, bell-ringing and tramping went on.

Brought up Catholic, Emmett looked slightly bewildered by the Shaker ceremony. Portions were familiar to any altar boy, others probably seemed like a burlesque of the mass.

Mrs. Dease's right hand began to quake. It seemed to do so of its own accord; the rest of her body remained motionless. The shaking spread into her arm. Soon her whole being convulsed with all the forms of energy, both native and Christian, that had been used to anoint her.

Emmett leaned forward in concern.

Just when it appeared that the power would tear her apart, Mrs. Dease gave a moan and slumped exhausted in her chair. The singing and the tramping ceased. The chime of the last bell faded to silence.

Mrs. Dease cracked open an eye. Anna thought that it was fixed on her.

"My Elsa is somewhere under the ground," the woman said disconsolately. A wail went up from some of the women, but, sitting up, Mrs. Dease cut it short with a gesture. "I didn't see if Elsa's alive or dead. Maybe she's only dead as Brother Slocum was, and soon she'll return to us with a message. . . ." This optimistic interpretation of her trance-induced vision was greeted with approving murmurs. "That's all I have to say right now, brothers and sisters. Thank you for your help. I thank the Father, the Son and the Holy Ghost for Their guidance."

Round Dance approached Mrs. Dease. He waited several feet short of her until she crooked a finger for him to step up to her chair. There was a whispered exchange during which both the police sergeant and the Shaker woman looked at Anna and Emmett, then Round Dance returned to the pew. "She'll talk to you outside."

The storm had moved on before dawn, and the early afternoon was warm and hazy. The snow-dusted summits of Mount Jefferson and Mount Hood rose out of the green-black forests. The rain-washed air smelled good after the thick, waxy-smelling atmosphere of the church. Anna recalled that tribal police throughout the Northwest used extrasensory Shakers like Mrs. Dease to give them leads on lost people and objects. She had the impression that Round Dance had asked for her services before, although never for something as emotionally wrenching as the possible loss of the woman's own daughter.

Mrs. Dease emerged into the daylight on the arms of two male Shakers, who promptly withdrew. She looked as spent and sleepless as Anna felt. But very much in control of herself. As soon as Round

Dance had made the introductions, Mrs. Dease asked, "Did you hear what I said about my daughter?"

"Yes," Emmett replied, "but I don't understand."

"Neither do I. Not yet." She smiled wanly at Anna. "Are you the Modoc FBI girl they've been telling me about?"

"Yes."

"There were some fine Modoc and Klamath Shakers in the old days. Did you know any of them?"

"Not really. I remember a service, but it was put on by Warm Springs people."

"I was probably there." The pleasant memory dimmed in Mrs. Dease's eyes. "There are beings who'd like to steal my Elsa away. To re-make her in their own mold. Lately, I've had to use all my power to protect her. But I guess my power isn't enough. Maybe I let pride get in the way. Maybe I should've just left it up to God. I don't know. Life can be very confusing, yes?"

"Yes." Anna resisted glancing at Emmett. Somehow, she sensed that Mrs. Dease knew about their troubled relationship. Even sympathized.

Emmett asked, "What do you mean by 'beings'—human beings?"

The woman seemed to take his measure. "When people are consumed by bad desires, I don't know how human they still are, Mr. Parker. To forgive, I try to believe that they are possessed by spirits, and once those evil spirits are removed . . . humanity returns."

Emmett pressed, "Did someone threaten to abduct Elsa?"

Mrs. Dease said nothing.

"We're trying to find your daughter."

"I know, Mr. Parker. It's just that I think maybe this is all God's plan. A few years ago, Elsa got away from her faith. Became caught up in Indian magic. And I don't like all this bother about some old bones—it sounds like sorcery to me. Maybe this disappearance is the way for Elsa to return to her church."

"Was it God's plan for your daughter to be possibly kidnapped?"

"Maybe, Mr. Parker. And if it is, who am I to question His means?"

"Mrs. Dease," Anna said, "are there things we can look into without making God think you're doubting Him?"

Another benign smile. "You are very pretty, Ms. Turnipseed. Like my Elsa. And that can attract certain spirits."

"From another world?"

"No, this one."

"Where, if I might ask?"

Mrs. Dease hesitated, then said, "Mount Hood. Timberline."

"When can they be seen?"

"The third sabbath's eve of the month."

The Shaker sabbath was Sunday, so the spirits that coveted Elsa gathered on the third Saturday evening of the month atop Mount Hood. Tonight, Anna realized, made slightly uncomfortable by this coincidence. She'd begun to distrust coincidences in Indian Country.

The audience was over, for Mrs. Dease began to turn back for the church. But the rattletrap janglings of an approaching pickup truck delayed her. An old GMC pulled up to the churchyard. Its front seat and bed were crammed with Warm Springs men, mostly young. Some wore mirrored sunglasses, others red bandannas as headbands. All had their game faces on, all except the gaunt man sitting snugly against the passenger door. Grinning, Tennyson Paulina got out of the cab and, alone, strode up to Mrs. Dease. He paid Anna and Emmett no mind, as if his disappearing act yesterday morning had had no purpose other than to show the federal cops that he could slither out of their hands anytime he chose.

Paulina touched two fingers to the brim of his dusty brown Stetson. "Vernita."

"Tennyson," Mrs. Dease said guardedly. The Shaker men began drifting out of the church and forming a line behind her. No one greeted the Paiute cowboy, even though he went on grinning amicably all around. Round Dance had strolled off a short distance to light a cigarette.

"We heard," Paulina said to Vernita.

"What'd you hear?"

"That they got Elsa."

"Who?"

"Why, Rankin and Bilbao. Who else?"

"I'm not asking you to make trouble in my daughter's name."

Paulina hooked his thumbs behind his silver belt buckle. "Look,

Vernita, I'm here to bury the hatchet. This is the time for the three tribes to stand together. Me and my friends want to help any way you see fit."

"Generous of you," Mrs. Dease said, although she didn't sound appreciative.

Paulina shook his head at her indifference. "Wearin' down your hate is like wearin' down granite with a toothbrush. But I'll keep tryin' because I see no purpose in dividin' up the rez worse than it already is." He faced Emmett and Anna for the first time, tipped his hat to her. "Officers."

"You sure beat a hasty retreat yesterday," Emmett said.

"Had business."

"Legal, I hope?"

"I'm off parole and as clean as a whistle. But I'm sure you already checked on that."

Emmett frowned. He and Anna had, by radio through the tribal police communications center. Paulina had served six months for an aggravated battery in Spokane, Washington. A few drunk-driving arrests.

"Besides," Paulina drawled, "ain't *my* criminal history you should be runnin'."

"What do you mean?" Anna asked.

"Take a gander at Gorka Bilbao's rap sheet, Ms. Turnipseed. Makes fascinatin' readin'." Then he nodded goodbye. "Vernita, folks." He sauntered back to the pickup, and it splashed off through the rainwater pooled on the muddy road.

Anna asked Vernita, "What reason would Paulina have to bury the hatchet with you?"

"Tennyson Paulina's a snake."

Anna shook her head that she didn't understand.

"Tennyson looks like a man, but he's just a snake walking around. His spirit has been possessed by Snake. Some say he killed my husband with Snake Power."

6

Twilight, the timberline on eleven-thousand-foot Mount Hood.

This tundralike zone between the last wind-stunted pines and Palmer Glacier seemed very much like an abode of malevolent spirits capable of seizing Elsa Dease and carrying her off into the night. Maybe it was the colors of the overripe sunset, Emmett thought. The sky was the garish blue of a lizard's belly. Except where it limned the white pyramid of Mount Hood. There it was an intestinal pink. And the single band of cloud in the west was the same maroon as two-hour-old blood at a homicide scene.

"We can go if you want," Anna said morosely from the passenger bucket seat in the Explorer.

"Go where?"

"I don't know, just go."

She'd trusted that Vernita Dease wouldn't send them on a wild-goose chase—that something up here on Oregon's highest peak was keyed to Elsa's disappearance. Emmett had his doubts. Sending cops on wild-goose chases was a popular sport on most reservations. And Anna instinctively gravitated toward charismatic mother types, like the Shaker woman or Dr. Tischler. In Emmett's eyes, Vernita's credibility had plummeted when she'd claimed Tennyson Paulina possessed Snake Power, this right after complaining that her daughter had lapsed into Indian magic. Yet, he hadn't argued with Anna about coming here on Vernita's counsel. So the Shaker woman believed and didn't believe in native spirituality. Self-contradiction was the rule in human nature, not the exception. And Anna and he had pulled out all the stops to locate Elsa, including calling in bloodhounds. They'd even asked Crook County to send a deputy up into the Ochoco Mountains to learn where Gorka Bilbao had been last night: apparently at home, his Datsun pickup broken down, having barely made it back after his encounter with the Dodge diesel on Whitehorse Rapids Road.

So, twenty hours after finding Elsa's tribal Honda abandoned in the middle of Wapinitia Road, Anna and he had no leads, and grasping at straws was probably in order.

"Mount Hood . . ." Emmett repeated the particulars of Vernita Dease's grudging revelation. "The timberline. The third Sabbath's eve of the month. Which happens to be tonight. Now ain't that a dandy coincidence?"

"I *said* we can go."

"Settle down. I'm trying to work through this." Emmett yawned. "I asked Vernita if these spirits were of another world, and she was firm—*no, this one.* So I'd say we're looking for a spirit still very much in the flesh. . . ." He gazed around the scenic overlook for people, but the October chill had driven the last hikers indoors. *Timberline,* Emmett repeated to himself. He sat up. *The Timberline.* "Shit," he said, starting the engine.

"What's wrong?"

Emmett pointed down at the rustic hotel below them. "That's the Timberline Lodge."

It hit her too. "What were we thinking?"

"We weren't. We're tired."

He parked in the lodge's lot and grabbed several flyers off the back seat. The tribal police had produced a missing person bulletin with Elsa's photograph and vital statistics. The photo had been taken at an All-Indian Pageant a few years before. As Miss Warm Springs, she'd been first runner-up.

Anna threaded her arm through his as they walked across the lot, skirting the patches of black ice. "Slow down a little."

He thought he'd already cut his long-legged stride in half. "Any slower and I'll be moon-walking."

The fireplace in the lobby was crackling. Its warmth invited lingering, but Emmett led Anna to the front desk. Holding up his credentials and the flyer, he asked the white female clerk if she'd ever seen

Elsa at the lodge before. No. The woman was new here. "That makes two of us, honey," he grumbled. "Mind posting this on your employees' notice board?"

"Not at all."

Emmett asked Anna when they'd last eaten. She couldn't recall either. Fall was the off-season on the mountain, and the clerk said reservations wouldn't be needed this evening at the Cascade Dining Room. Passing by the open double doors to a small conference hall, Emmett peeked inside. Propped up against walls were blown-up black-and-white photographs of nude women standing artfully under waterfalls or stretching out on tree limbs. The dozen or so diners inside were all female, and a woman with bifocals and a boot camp haircut glared up at him from her place next to the podium.

Anna and he continued on to the main dining room, which was virtually deserted.

They weren't even finished with their salads before the day's work was tugging at Emmett. Vernita Dease wouldn't have couched her disclosure in a riddle unless she feared the consequences of informing on somebody. That was understandable, given the eye-for-an-eye character of reservation sorcery. So if a lead developed out of this, the Shaker woman wanted to make it appear that Anna and he had discovered it on their own. "Is Vernita afraid of getting witched?" he asked.

"Maybe. She said Paulina's been possessed by Snake."

"Then hedged that *some say* Tennyson killed her husband. Aren't Shakers supposed to give up belief in sorcery?"

"Ideally," Anna replied. "But who measures up to the ideal?"

Is she referring to me? Ignoring the possible slight, Emmett glanced into the adjoining cocktail lounge. Sedate and tasteful, Chopin tinkling through the sound system. "Don't suppose Tennyson comes up here on Saturday nights, do you?"

Anna shook her head.

Emmett didn't think so either. Right now, no doubt Paulina could be found in some honky-tonk just off the dry reservation. Emmett felt too antsy to eat and regretted having ordered a big cut of prime rib. These, the first twenty-four hours of a disappearance, were critical. After, progress would come in bits and pieces. If at all. And he'd let

Anna talk him into straying from Simnasho, the locus of the search. "All right . . ."

"All right what?" She picked at her salad again. No hungrier than he was, probably.

"Round Dance told us Bill Dease turned down Paulina for a job at the tribal motor pool years ago." The Wasco sergeant had given this as the explanation for the brittle reception the Paiute got from Vernita in front of the Shaker church. "That's where the bad blood began. Still, in my book, not much of a reason to kill somebody."

"If that's what you think."

His fork stopped halfway to his mouth, and a cherry tomato plopped back down onto its nest of greens. "What's that supposed to mean?"

"You didn't grow up in a reservation environment."

"How dang thoughtless of my parents."

"Stop it, I'm just saying that tribal employment stirs up a lot of bitterness. Especially on a shared reservation where the most powerful tribe controls the pork barrel. This isn't an insult. You Comanches lost your rez when the Allotment Act broke it up into private holdings."

"Seems I've spent a good part of my working life on rezes."

"Not the same as *living* on one. Like mine. Modoc, Klamath and Paiute pressed together, competing for too few jobs. So I can see how Paulina might've wanted to get back at Elsa's father for refusing him a job."

"Never met a rodeo cowboy yet who'd work out of the saddle. I wouldn't be surprised if Paulina asked Bill Dease for a job just to keep qualifying for his state unemployment."

"Fine," Anna said curtly, "then that's how it was."

Their dinners arrived. They ate without further conversation, although their silence was soon interrupted by a strident female voice coming over speakers from the conference hall: "The photographs of Claudia Burgoyne transport us into the hidden places of the Cascades, timeless glades and mountain pools where women can be women without apology. While subliminal in effect, they still evoke the bedrock unity of women in concert with nature. Their dappled, almost mystical light recalls a time when goddesses reigned supreme, an age before fanatical God worship and other male inventions eclipsed the pristine beauty of the world. . . ."

Emmett rolled his eyes.

• • •

Anna listened to Emmett say to the desk clerk, "Two rooms."

It was her turn to take the wheel. By spending the night here at the Timberline and not forcing her to drive eighty miles of mountain roads back to the Kah-Nee-Ta, was he resisting the tide of irritation that had made them quarrel at dinner? The possibility touched her, and she quickly responded to the overture: "Make that one room with two beds." When both he and the clerk stared quizzically at her, Anna added to Emmett, "Let's save the government a few dollars. We've already got rooms at the Kah-Nee-Ta."

"I'm putting this on my *personal* credit card," he said.

"Then you don't want our government rate, sir?" the clerk asked.

"No, this isn't government business."

Behind the privacy of the chest-high counter, Anna furtively took his hand, and he squeezed back.

"Do you belong to AAA or some other travel group, sir?"

Disengaging himself from Anna, Emmett went through his wallet. "Uh, no."

"What's that card there?"

"National Native American Law Enforcement Association."

"Good enough for the discount. We're almost vacant." Along with a solitary room key, the clerk gave them each a toilet kit—toothbrush, small bottle of mouthwash and disposable razor.

Their tryst exposed by this offering, Anna blushed, then noticed that Emmett's color had deepened too. Yet, reaching their wood-paneled room, he collapsed fully clothed across the double bed closest to the door. She thought he was out for the night, but he pawed for the telephone on the nightstand and dialed a number. "Watch commander, please," he requested. Warm Springs Police Department, undoubtedly. He had an infallible memory; once dialed, a number was locked almost eternally in his mental Rolodex—the result of having learned to read late and letting his aural memory develop first, he claimed. "Yeah, Lieutenant, this is Emmett Parker. Agent Turnipseed and I are tied up at the Timberline Lodge. We'll return to Warm Springs first thing in the morning. Any messages?" Emmett frowned. "*Nothing* back from Portland P.D. Investigations?" Another pause. "Well, I gave them my cell phone number, but by chance if they contact you, please tell them where I am tonight. And don't hesitate to call with any news about Elsa. . . . Thanks." He hung up, and Anna put the telephone back on the stand for him. "You can take the first shower," he said, his voice too flat to read any suggestibility into it.

She unlaced his shoes, shucked them off. Then she stripped away his socks and began rubbing his bare feet.

"Nice," he murmured. "But go ahead and shower."

Instead, she kissed his toes.

His eyes popped open.

She tried to smile, but couldn't. Having failed to put any conditions on this, she was frightened, and the temptation was to plunge blindly ahead and simply get it over with. That might put this vexing obstacle behind them once and for all. But simply getting it over with had been one of the mechanisms she'd used to cope with the sexual horrors of her youth. She wished she could be back on the roller coaster with Emmett, corkscrewing side by side through the Las Vegas twilight, her skin tingling as if she were shedding all memory of the past on the long plunges.

Sitting up, he asked, "Want me to turn out the light?"

She'd stung him with hesitation before, so she rushed to say, "Yes." She hoped he took her fear for excitement. She could feel herself deserting her body, retreating into numbness. *What made me suggest taking a single room?* He stretched across the bed and switched off the lamp. In the darkness, she listened to the rustle of his clothing as he removed it.

The phone rang.

"Ignore it," she urged. Hypocritically, for she knew that they couldn't, not with Elsa Dease still missing.

The phone went on ringing. Was Emmett testing her? Why did everything between them have to feel like a test? Anna grabbed the handset as Emmett rested his head in her lap. "Turnipseed."

"*Special Agent* Turnipseed?" Male, middle-aged.

"Speaking." She tried to sound more like an FBI agent. The caller identified himself as a Portland Police captain in Investigations. "Oh yes," she said, "thanks for getting back to us."

"How can I help you?"

"My partner and I understand you worked a sexual assault case on Gorka Bilbao in the mid-1980s."

"Yeah, back in my rookie days. It was more than sexual assault. Kidnapping, rape and battery."

"Who was the victim?"

"A nineteen-year-old Yakima woman. Streetwalker."

"Full blood?" Anna asked.

"No, half white. Why do you ask?"

"Elsa Dease, our missing person, is half white too. . . ." Through her slacks, Anna felt Emmett caressing her thigh. "How'd it go down?"

"Brutally," the captain replied. "Bilbao stalked the victim for a week, then forced her into his vehicle at knifepoint. . . ." Anna found that odd. Persuading a streetwalker to enter a vehicle was no great feat. Obviously, Bilbao had wanted the thrill of abduction. Had he somehow reenacted the same scenario with Elsa last night? "And then he took her to an abandoned cabin on Tanner Creek."

"Where's that?"

"Up the Columbia about thirty miles from Portland," the detective said. Anna rested her hand on Emmett's shoulder. It was bare. Her fingertips slid down to his hips. He was still in his briefs, which reassured her that he wasn't prepared to go all the way until she consented. "Bilbao bound and gagged her," the captain went on emotionlessly. "Bit both breasts so savagely she needed a total of sixty stitches. . . ." Anna froze, no longer hearing the cop's voice. She was back in that shanty on her ranchería, squirming against the unimaginable being performed with hideous tenderness on her adolescent breasts. She shoved at the shadow, trying to get it off her. And then, without transition, without a crisp demarcation between past and present, she found herself in the room at the Timberline again.

Emmett's silhouette had risen from the bed, and he was putting his clothes on.

"May I phone you right back?" she asked the captain.

"Sure. Is everything okay?"

"Yes, just give me a minute." Anna hung up just as Emmett flipped on a light to locate his shoes and socks.

"Emmett—"

"Don't say a thing." He grabbed a pillow and then a spare blanket off the shelf in the closet. Before going out.

• • •

The chill beyond the lodge's rear entrance nearly turned Emmett around and sent him to the front desk to get a separate room. But the thought of admitting defeat to the clerk made him plunge ahead. He marched around the building to the front lot. The night was starry in the way only sharp cold can make it. He unlocked the Explorer, crawled into the back seat, plumped the pillow under his head and covered himself with the blanket. He had to bend his legs to fit on the five-foot-wide seat.

You, Emmett Parker, are a fucking nitwit.

This crippling relationship was more than stupid. It was potentially dangerous. He'd never been this distracted on an assignment, even in the throes of his divorces. But then again, his wives had not gone to work with him. Now, he was involved with a female partner, and there was no getting away from Anna Turnipseed.

Shit.

And there was something unexpectedly frightening in being the partner to an abuse survivor—the looking glass it held up to the darkness in your own heart.

Never get involved with a female partner.

This had always been such a powerful prohibition, he suddenly realized that it would reassert itself in the coming days. How? He wasn't sure. But sound judgment would be restored.

Gazing up, he began tracking the arc of the Big Dipper through the fogged-up window over his head, hoping the monotony of this task would make him drowsy.

Some time later, feminine laughter awakened him out of a light doze. He reared up on his elbows. Two women strolled in front of the

Explorer. The lot was steeped in darkness, but Emmett recognized one of them as the bespectacled female with the cropped hair he'd seen in the conference hall. She opened the passenger front door of a Volvo sedan for the other figure, and Emmett was lowering himself onto his uncomfortable bed again when the women embraced. They kissed. At first he was unable to look away, despite a tug of shame over this accidental voyeurism. But after a moment, he made himself drop down again.

A door thudded shut, then another, and the Volvo's engine was gunned before its sound receded down the road.

By no means did Emmett consider himself homophobic, but the kiss and the mirrorlike image of joined femininity had struck him as being unnatural. He neither approved nor disapproved, just disliked the ambiguous feelings the sight had given him. An unpleasant voice broke from some dark corner of his mind and asked if this was Anna's problem. Instantly, he dismissed the notion. Mean-spirited. And untrue.

Or is it?

Were Anna and Dr. Tischler making him jump through therapeutic hoops that had nothing to do with the underlying problem? Did Anna's experience with her father make all men revolting to her?

The Big Dipper was now blocked from view by Mount Hood. No guiding stars in any of this. And the interior of the SUV was even more frigid than before. He draped the pillow over his face and bundled himself in the blanket again.

After a minute, he sprang up. Snatches of scenes from the past few days, fragmentary and meaningless of themselves, had just been fused by his subconscious. "Christ Almighty," he said, throwing off the blanket. He got out and headed for the front desk.

•   •   •

Anna said nothing as Emmett parked along Cherry Heights Road and shut off the Explorer's engine. She was too sleepy to argue with what he was doing. The neighborhood was on a bluff overlooking The Dalles, and the lights of the city shone steadily through the cold, still air. The dash clock read 4:11. Too early for dawn, but Anna looked east anyway. Nothing but a gray darkness cut in two by the black flow of the Columbia. Sirens wailed and a fire truck horn blatted in the distance.

At two o'clock, Emmett had burst back into their room at the Timberline. Startled awake, Anna had expected some momentous decision from him concerning them, their relationship, even a possible breakthrough that would usher in the natural intimacy that had eluded them so far. But Emmett dropped a different kind of bombshell: Over the past year, two connecting rooms had been taken on the same third Saturday nights of the month by Deborah Carter and Elsa Dease. And the Athena Society, the women's self-awareness group on which they'd eavesdropped during dinner, had convened the same evenings.

Then Emmett had announced that he was off to The Dalles. Anna could come along if she wanted.

So they were now parked outside a modest brick house with a river view. Colonel Carter's. Emmett had gotten the address by having Warm Springs tribal police run her name through Oregon DMV.

Anna ended the silence that had lasted the entire drive from Mount Hood. "Aren't we pushing it by talking to Carter at this hour?"

"I want to catch her with her guard down. Carter and Dease last met at the Timberline in August. Nothing since, according to the front desk computer. Three days ago in John Day Canyon, they snubbed each other, though Dease told us she and Carter were still speaking."

"So?"

"Speaking maybe, but somebody called something off, and I'll bet one of them took it hard. They walked on eggshells around each other at the exam in Carter's headquarters on Friday. And the colonel left the tavern minutes before Dease ran out of Starbucks. What if Carter flagged Elsa down and rode with her up to that curve on Wapinitia Road?"

Anna objected, "But does their past relationship—whatever it was—justify an interrogation in the middle of the night?"

"It's morning," Emmett dryly noted.

"Okay, it's morning. But are Carter's proclivities—"

"Christ, woman, you've got a vocabulary. Is that what a Berkeley education does to a poor soul?"

"Are Carter's proclivities solid enough probable cause to roust her at this hour?"

"We didn't think twice about rousting Gorka Bilbao with a deputy because of his proclivities."

"That's because his were criminal. Carter's aren't."

"As far as you know." Emmett reached for his door latch. "Listen, you can always come up with a reason to stand back and do nothing. Some cops make a habit of it, and they invariably make rank. Stay in the car if you think I'm out of bounds. Consider it a good career move."

Sighing, Anna followed. The cold jolted her fully awake.

As they strode up the colonel's unlit driveway, a sudden whine broke the quiet. Carter's automatic garage door opened, and a sedan with federal plates rolled outside. Emmett rapped his knuckles on the car roof, making the woman brake so forcefully her tires chirped against the cement. She powered down her window. Her low beams reflected off her reclosed door, making her scar look especially sinister. "What is it?" she asked, her eyes shifting from partner to partner.

"We need to talk to you."

"No time, Parker."

"What?"

"I have no time!" With that, Carter backed onto the road. She cut a turn that made the sedan sway and accelerated east along the bluff.

For a second, Emmett stood motionless in apparent disbelief. Then he ran for the Explorer. Anna fell in beside him. "Are we in pursuit?" she asked.

"Hell if I know." He jumped in behind the wheel. Anna grabbed the microphone as soon as she got inside. It was almost to her lips when Emmett said, "Don't advise the local PD."

"Why not?"

"Let's see what she does. If she crosses the river into Washington, she tips her hand and violates federal law."

7

Deborah Carter didn't commit interstate flight.

Instead, she sped into the parking lot of her headquarters, bolted from her sedan and through the building entrance. The lot was already crowded with emergency vehicles, and a fire hose kept the front door ajar. Emmett saw no evidence of smoke, but as soon as he stepped out of the Explorer he caught a whiff of something acrid in the air. The bones. This involved the bones in a way that defied rationality. What had Gorka Bilbao said the other night? *The damn things heated up my cabin so bad I had to take 'em outside so I could sleep. God's my witness— they glowed like live coals till I got 'em outside.* Fantastic. Improbable. But now there were fire engines in front of the Corps of Engineers headquarters.

"Wait for me, Parker," Anna said from behind.

He slowed, but only because a patrolman blocked his entry. "BIA and FBI," he said, showing his I.D. The cop motioned them past.

The fire hose led them to the windowless room in which Dr. Rankin had examined John Day Man's remains. The door had been blown out into the corridor. The hose proved to be a precaution; there was no fire. But the fluorescent fixtures had been shattered, and the only illumination came from the flashlights of the firemen.

Emmett and Anna entered the room, their shoes crackling over debris. He could taste the plaster dust still hanging in the atmosphere. The conference table was on its side, and the rest of the furniture lay in a jumble against one wall. The clock on that wall had stopped at 4:01.

Ignoring the partners, Carter talked in low tones to the fire battalion chief.

Emmett drew Anna's attention to the safe, and together they approached it. The escutcheon plate behind the combination dial was warped and scorched. The dial itself was missing, although Emmett could retrace its trajectory to a round hole that had been punched in the opposite wall. "This blaster was no pro," he said quietly, relieved that he now had a rational explanation for the violent force that had ripped through this room.

"What do you mean?" Anna asked.

Emmett pulled on the handle to the safe's door with the shaft of his ballpoint pen, even though he had no expectation of finding latent fingerprints. The door didn't give. "The right way to do the job is to drill a hole and pour in some nitroglycerin to take out the locking mechanism. This blaster just blew off the dial, which accomplished nothing."

"He didn't get inside?"

Emmett shook his head. "Now the only question is, what kind of shape is the skeleton in?"

Carter had overheard him, for she said, "We're to touch nothing, Parker. The police department already phoned ATF, and they're on the way from Portland."

Usually, the Bureau of Alcohol, Tobacco and Firearms was prompt. "What's their ETA now?"

Carter joined them at the safe. "About forty minutes." She looked directly at the partners for the first time since tearing out of her driveway. "City police called me," she explained with no hint of apology. "That's why I couldn't dally up at my place."

Emmett let that slide for the moment. "Is this room wired?"

"No, just the outer openings of the building."

"How'd the PD learn of the blast?"

"The alarm went off," Carter said. "It automatically phones them."

That probably meant the rumble of the explosion had triggered the sensors on the exterior doors and windows. Most likely, one of those sensors had been bypassed or deactivated by the blaster to get inside the headquarters.

Forty minutes passed, and still no ATF.

The firemen set up portable lights in the room. The bored-looking patrolman drifted in from the entrance and rubber-necked around a splintered doorjamb. "Officer," Anna asked, "did your arriving units see any vehicles leaving the area?"

"None," he replied, "streets were empty. No peds either."

Emmett realized that Carter was looking at him. He had the impression that she'd been doing it for some seconds. "Any word on Ms. Dease?" she asked.

He let her wait—just to watch her. She didn't take a breath until he said, "Nothing yet."

Instantly, the colonel shifted gears and became all business again. "Well, it's obvious I've got to get these bones out of here."

"Where can they go?"

"Devil if I know, Parker. I'm just sick of the responsibility." Carter paused. Then inspiration lit her eyes. "The Department of Energy's Hanford nuclear reservation—that's where. It's the most secure facility in the Northwest."

Emmett didn't object to that idea. "How far?"

"About a hundred miles over the river into Washington, but I'll insist that armed federal rangers escort the remains all the way."

Anna had been strolling around the room. Emmett waited until she returned to his side before he asked Carter, "Where were you Friday evening, Colonel, after you left the tavern?"

Carter's eyes fixed intently on Emmett again. "I don't see where that concerns you."

Emmett felt Anna rest a hand on his forearm. Her tag-team signal that she'd spell him before he lost his temper. "Colonel," she said evenly, "it concerns us in that you might know about Elsa's habits, things to help the investigation."

"Why would I know about her habits?" Again, no sign of being flustered. It seemed as if some sort of preset mental conditioning had dropped into place like a cog.

"Mr. Parker and I have indications you two were close friends."

"Such as?"

Anna checked behind: The cop and the firemen were out of earshot in the corridor. "Adjoining rooms at the Timberline Lodge."

Emmett thought Carter was on the verge of smiling, but then the colonel shrugged her shoulders like a prizefighter trying to keep loose. Her words came with the heavy cadence of hammer blows: "What are you two pulling? You think you can just waltz into my headquarters and insinuate any fucking thing you want!"

"Would you care to continue this conversation in private?" Anna calmly asked.

"I don't care to continue this at all!"

Emmett jumped back in. "How would you characterize your relationship with Elsa Dease?"

"None of your goddamned business!" Carter's shout was still reverberating around the room when she grinned at the partners. The grin was angrily defiant, but her eyes had clouded. And she finally lowered her voice to a fierce, tremulous whisper. "Is it so hard for you to understand that when your own looks are taken . . ." She gestured with clawed hands at her scarred ruin of a face. ". . . you appreciate physical beauty all the more in others? Do your pathetic little imaginations have no better take on my feelings than this? Damn you and your vulgar thoughts! Damn you both!"

Anna could tell by Carter's sudden composure that somebody had entered the room. She and Emmett turned.

Thaddeus Rankin stood in the door frame, a trench coat draped over his shoulders. His eyes were rheumy, as if he were feverish, and he spoke in a throaty growl. "What's the game here, Carter?"

She said nothing.

Rankin limped into the room, the rubber tip of his cane tapping against the floor. "Will you kindly tell me what's going on?"

Carter had crouched slightly under questioning, a normal reaction, but now she straightened to her full height. "An attempt was made to get inside my safe."

"Jesus H. Christ!"

"Parker here doesn't believe the lock was compromised," Carter went on while the anthropologist fumed. "So spare me your theatrics, Thaddeus. The bones are probably okay."

"Not as long as they're in this building!"

"Agreed." The colonel seemed to enjoy how this knocked the wind out of Rankin's sails. "That's why I'm going to have them transferred to the Hanford reservation by federal rangers as soon as the ATF does its work."

"I warned you, Carter!"

The colonel righted a chair, dusted the seat off with her palm and sat haggardly as if she had no intention of saying anything more. It puzzled Emmett how swiftly her anger had played itself out, as if she had weightier things on her mind than anything Anna and he could throw at her.

Rankin motioned for Anna and Emmett to follow him out into the corridor. The patrolman, standing just outside the room, touched two fingers to the bill of his cap. "Doc."

"Morning, Bob. How's the missus?"

"Fine, sir. Just fine."

Only when they had reached the privacy of the foyer did Rankin say, "Explain the crime to me."

Emmett's eyes narrowed. "First tell us how you found out about it."

"I heard the sirens from my estate across the river. I've been on pins and needles ever since my specimen was brought here. I had my assistant phone The Dalles Police Department, then came over as soon as I was told about the break-in. These mindless army bureaucrats will screw it up yet." Sighing, he clasped his ponytail, which had wound around his neck, and squeezed it until his fist shook. "Doesn't anybody understand how precious this skeleton is? Some of the biggest questions about human prehistory in the Americas could be solved by John Day Man. Am I the only person on the face of the planet who doesn't want to see him reburied or destroyed?"

Anna asked, "Do you object to the remains going to Hanford?"

His expression softened as he looked at her. "I have mixed feelings about that, my dear. The deeper John Day Man goes into the bureaucracy, the less chance for science to ever see him again." He inhaled exploratively. "Bomb?"

"Explosives of some kind," Emmett said. "Apparently not enough to blow open the safe."

"Why not?"

"We're not sure yet."

"An amateur?"

"Possibly. ATF will tell us more about the blaster. Here they are now. . . ." Through the glass door, Emmett tracked the progress of a van as it parted onlookers who, over the past forty-five minutes, had materialized out of the neighborhood. Three agents in ATF jackets filed from the van. Two began working the small crowd, one with a videocam and the other with a bomb-sniffing German shepherd. Like arsonists, some blasters got a sexual charge out of hanging around the scenes of their handiwork. The third agent came inside. Rankin vehemently declared, "If that bomb damaged the most valuable skeleton of this century, I'll own the federal government!"

"I thought you already did, Doctor," the supervising agent quipped. Then he ambled down the corridor toward the crime scene.

"Brief him," Emmett told Anna.

"Where are you going?"

He didn't have time to explain. He'd just spotted Nels Sward. In the few seconds it had taken Emmett to speak to Anna, the pagan leader had melted into the darkness. Trotting outside, Emmett waved his credentials at the ATF dog handler and said, "Got somebody I want you to shake hands with."

The agent understood at once. "Lead the way."

They caught up with Sward midway down the street. The man was dressed in an overcoat and fedora. A thin red stripe of dawn showed behind him. "Morning, Mr. Sward," Emmett said.

Sward halted, pivoted and smiled, although the dog seemed to unsettle him a little. The agent directed his flashlight on the pavement, using the muted edge of the beam to illuminate the man's face. Sward's hawkish nose threw a shadow across his cheek. "Good morning, Mr. Parker."

"Tomorrow's the big day."

"I beg your pardon?"

"You and your people are going to set up camp along the White River, aren't you?"

"Oh yes. Quite. It'll be nice to get outdoors."

All the while Emmett palavered with Sward, the dog sniffed the man, paying special attention to the bulges of his hands in his coat pockets. The shepherd was trained to sit if he detected traces of explosive. He began to lower his haunches onto the pavement at one point, but then raised up again and circled frenetically at the limit of his leash. While not prepared to signal that he'd caught an incriminating scent, the dog still found something troubling about the man.

"Oh," Emmett said to the ATF agent as if he'd just remembered his manners, "this is Nels Sward of the Norse Folk Congress."

The agent gave his name, and Sward took his right hand from his coat pockets. Good, no glove. The two men shook perfunctorily.

"What's all the commotion about?" Sward asked. "I heard it from my motel."

"We're not sure," Emmett replied.

"Is the skeleton in jeopardy?"

"I don't believe so."

"I see. Well, if you don't mind, I'd like to get out of the cold."

Emmett didn't mind. Sward was eager to go, and he let him.

"Are you contaminated by the crime scene, Parker?" the agent asked as they rushed up the street toward the lot. The dog kept peering nervously back at Sward's retreating figure.

"Yes."

"Then I'll ask you to stay outside the van."

The agent ducked inside with his canine, but left the door ajar so Emmett could witness the procedure. Immediately, the man ran a cotton swab over his right palm. Then he plunged the swab into a vial of clear liquid, a reagent, or reactive agent, that would change color if the ATF man had taken away even the tiniest trace of explosive from the handshake with Sward. He held up the vial so Emmett could see.

The liquid remained crystal clear.

"Well," the agent said in disappointment, "I wouldn't rule Mr. Sward out just because of this. He could've worn plastic gloves, then changed clothes and showered. He was creepy enough to be a blaster. He sure spooked my poor dog."

Emmett nodded. He resisted adding that the Navajo, among whom Nels Sward had lived for nineteen years as a Lutheran missionary, believe that dogs can detect witches.

• • •

Anna stood in the background as Dr. Rankin used his considerable charm to convince the supervising ATF agent to open the safe without further delay. She understood his sense of urgency. Earlier, when no one had been looking, she'd held her hands as close as she could to the steel without making contact. The safe had seemed to vibrate, as if something charged with an electric rage was trying to get out. She felt as if she were separated by a few inches of metal and fireproofing material from seeing the world in an entirely new and frightening way. On second thought, maybe it wasn't new. Maybe it was the worldview of her Modoc ancestors, who had respected the invisible forces surrounding the dead. Maybe she and all moderns had grown dangerously callous toward the powers of the dead.

A high-pitched whine made her jump as the ATF supervisor pressed the trigger on a power drill. He bored a hole in the back of the safe, then used that hole as a starting point in which to insert the blade of a metal saw. Sparks flew and bounced on the floor as he cut. Within minutes, he had a square opening.

Rankin pushed forward to look inside the safe.

"Only the FBI is to handle the remains," Deborah Carter ordered from her chair. "That's the way it'll be until the rangers get here."

Anna went to the safe. Rankin and the ATF supervisor stepped aside, the anthropologist with an impatient gesture for her to hurry. The musty odor of the bones was strong, despite the competing smell of the overheated saw. The ATF man aimed his flashlight through the opening. She could see the white wooden boxes inside. The uppermost one was tottering over. She reached in and was righting it when her hand recoiled. It'd been a split second of sensory confusion over whether the box was very hot or very cold, for both fire and ice burn.

"The mind can make the body feel *anything*," Rankin said with an amused look.

His words made her feel foolish, and she resolutely took the boxes out and carefully laid them on the linoleum. They were room temperature— no more, no less. She opened each for Rankin's inspection.

He finally said with relief, "John Day Man survives."

• • •

Emmett got his first coffee of the day in the squad room of the Warm Springs tribal police station. Anna declined Gabriel Round Dance's offer of a cup, perhaps hoping that as soon as this business was wrapped up she might catch a nap in her room at the Kah-Nee-Ta. Emmett had no such expectation. The sergeant had urgently summoned them from The Dalles, and his tone of voice hadn't augured sleep anytime soon.

The details of the investigation inside the Corps of Engineers headquarters were still floating around Emmett's brain like confetti, although one fact had risen above the confusion. The ATF supervisor, who knew explosive residues the way a confectioner knows candy, was almost positive that the blaster had used military dynamite. Lab testing would confirm or deny his suspicion in a day or two.

Round Dance's voice brought Emmett back to the present. "This morning around four o'clock, our Seekseequa patrolman arrested Tennyson Paulina for public intoxication. Paulina was raising Cain out on the road in front of his house. We also detained him on a charge for you feds."

"Why us?"

"He thumped a white woman, Parker."

Here it was again. The baffling conundrum of racial justice. American society didn't entirely trust an Indian department to look after the interests of a white victim on tribal lands, although Emmett suspected that Round Dance was freely surrendering jurisdiction in this case. "Patricia Sward?"

"Yeah. You two met her when you were down there?"

"In the flesh." Emmett caught Anna's frown from the corner of his eye.

She took a swig of Emmett's coffee. "Where's Ms. Sward now?"

"In my lieutenant's office," Round Dance replied. "Already treated at our hospital for a few facial bruises. Nothing life-theatening, but it was still a righteous thumping."

Rising from her chair, Anna said to Emmett, "I'll talk to her while you see Paulina."

Emmett gave her his revolver for safekeeping in her purse, then heaved himself to his feet and followed Round Dance into the weapons-restricted detention wing of the complex. Tennyson Paulina was visible through the chicken-wired glass of the drunk tank, sprawled out on a bench in an orange jumpsuit. His eyes opened and fastened on Emmett even before Round Dance turned the key in the lock. Emmett entered the concrete cubicle, and Paulina sat up stiffly, his joints cracking and popping. The whites of the Paiute cowboy's eyes were inflamed by drunkenness, and he stank of a hard night. But he sounded reasonably coherent as he drawled, "I'm dyin' for a smoke, Parker. Got one?"

"Nope." Emmett sat on the bench across from Paulina's.

Withdrawing, Round Dance said, "No smoking in here, Tennyson. I'll get you a pack if and when you're moved to one of the blocks."

"Obliged, Gabe." Paulina winked at Emmett. "He ain't goin' to have me for long. I got nineteen hundred dollars, cash money, for bail. Poker game Friday night."

The evening Elsa had abandoned her car on Wapinitia Road. "Where was the game?"

"Little club down in Redmond. And I got witnesses who put me there from sundown to two A.M., in case you're wonderin'. You got to learn to relax, Parker. I bet you got a bad gut."

"Stow it." Emmett had been put off by how Round Dance had treated the inebriate. Civility to an inmate was one thing, deference was another. Was he afraid of the alleged sorcerer, as Bilbao had suggested? "Are we going to be able to finish this chat, Tennyson, or are you going to vanish in a cloud of steam again?"

The Paiute chuckled thickly. "Sorry about that. It was really on account of Trish, her bein' caught in a compromisin' situation. She's a married woman, you know."

"I know. Met her husband in The Dalles."

Paulina got serious again. "What's he like?"

"Different. Real different. Makes me look at white people in a whole new light." Emmett leaned his back against the wall. It ached from the hours of driving. "What are Patricia's damages?"

"Oh come on, I'm not goin' to tattle on myself." Paulina rubbed one bare foot atop the other.

"Well," Emmett went on, "it's hard for me to imagine that she'd go into anything without her eyes wide open. Frankly, my biggest concern right now is finding Elsa Dease as soon as possible."

"Mine too," Paulina said earnestly. "That's the only reason I'm talkin' to you without my lawyer present."

"Then let's postpone this till we can all sit down together."

Paulina loudly exhaled. "You really want to know what went down between me and Trish last night?"

Emmett inclined his head as if it might be of casual interest. He was on the brink of achieving his objective—getting a voluntary statement out of Paulina in spite of a virtual Miranda warning.

"She was goin' through that hippie handbag of hers," the Paiute offered, "and out falls a condom."

"How disappointing. You figured she was a cherry?"

"It was one of mine, Parker. *Used.*"

"How do you know it was yours?"

"I fancy the colored sort. Pink. I'd just blown my wad into it, okay? Tossed it in the trash. She'd gone and fished it out."

Emmett tried not to smirk.

"You don't get it, do you, Parker?"

Emmett glanced at his wristwatch—8:30 P.M., and he was lusting for sleep. "Probably not."

"The white bitch took it so she could make a charm against me. She's workin' that white pagan medicine against me, man!" Paulina seemed genuinely alarmed by the prospect. "By all rights, I can kill her for tryin' to witch me. That's the law of my people, and you and the whole government can't say otherwise."

"You think her husband knew she was spending time with you?"

"Shit yes, now I do!" Paulina shouted so loudly a jailer checked to make sure everything was okay. "I damn well guarantee it!"

Emmett flashed four fingers at the jailer through the window. Code Four—all's well. The prisoner was just venting.

"It was a setup from the get-go," Paulina went on, controlling himself again, probably so as not to jeopardize Round Dance's gift of cigarettes. "I should've known better up there at the Tygh Valley Indian Rodeo. When white pussy comes lookin' for you, it only means trouble. And Trish picked me out of a whole mess of cowboys like I had horns. Christ, she let me half undress her before we was out of the parkin' area. I'd already had her by the time we reached that beer joint in Maupin." He rubbed his gnarled hands over his head as if trying to erase a now troubling memory. "Let it go, Tenn, let it go. My own damn fault." He looked up at Emmett. "You tappin' my phone?"

"No. It involves more paperwork than you're worth."

Paulina visibly considered the answer, then seemed to accept it. "Okay, okay. You workin' on Bilbao like I suggested at the Shaker church?"

"Some."

"Was I right about his rap sheet?"

"He bears watching," Emmett said.

"That's all? Anybody check where he was the night Elsa disappeared?"

"Yes. Apparently, he was up at his cabin in the Ochocos."

"Apparently?" Paulina sneered.

"Don't push it. My partner and I were almost on Elsa's bumper when it went down. There were no other vehicles in the area."

"Parker, them ol' Basco shepherds can walk to hell and back—with two rams slung over their backs. Bilbao could've parked his dinky pickup in Simnasho and hotfooted it up to the top of the grade in no time. I wouldn't be surprised if Rankin sent him to get Elsa out of the picture so he could have the bones back." Paulina slapped his knees in summation. "Well, that's that. As usual, the feds won't do jackshit. It's up to the people to get to the bottom of this."

"Watch your mouth," Emmett warned. "Some impressionable kid's apt to get carried away by your pearls of wisdom, and then I'm coming after you for conspiracy."

"Do what you got to, Parker."

"You and Bill Dease . . ." Emmett let the rest of his question dangle.

Paulina bit. "What about us?"

"Why the bad blood?"

"You don't want to know."

"Try me."

Paulina closely watched Emmett as he said, "Elsa was in love with me. . . ." Emmett's doubt that a devout Shaker family would let their daughter cavort with a rodeo bum must have shown, for the man tacked on, "You don't have to believe it if you don't want to."

"Make me believe. When was this?"

"Nine years ago."

"Elsa was—what, sixteen, seventeen then?"

"Sixteen."

"How'd you two get any time together?"

"You know well as me that Indian beauty pageants and rodeos go hand in hand. We started eyein' each other, then talkin' between events, and one thing led to another. I was headed to Canada for the Calgary Stampede and maybe a job with a cattle outfit up there. She wanted to go with me, but I said absolutely no. Wasn't goin' to take jailbait across a state line and an international border. Elsa followed me anyways, caught up with me in Spokane. So'd Bill Dease. Fit to be tied. He acted like it was all my idea from the start, and I couldn't make him see the truth. Or maybe I just didn't have the patience. I was drinkin', sure, but I wasn't mean drunk. Before I knew what happened, Bill was out cold on a barroom floor, Elsa was cryin', and the cops were puttin' the chrome bracelets on me."

It sounded plausible to Emmett. More plausible than Paulina despising Elsa's father because the man had denied him a job.

• • •

Inside the lieutenant's office, Patricia Sward smiled vacuously at Anna's intrusion.

"Ms. Sward, I'm Special Agent Turnipseed from the FBI."

"I remember you." She submerged the smile in a yawn. Her pale skin was almost translucent, so the bruises looked worse than they probably were. "Have I been waiting all this time for you?"

"Yes." Anna sat behind the desk. "This offense may fall under federal jurisdiction. I'd like to discuss it with you."

"But I already gave a statement to the policeman."

"A tribal officer. I know it's all repetitive, but I have to interview you again."

Patricia Sward shook her head in quiet exasperation. Her eyes had a damp gleam to them, probably more from the travails of the night than any emotion she was presently feeling. She looked used up.

"You must be tired," Anna commiserated.

"Utterly. As if I'm dead and dreaming."

The answer sounded so ethereal in the golden morning light spilling through the venetian blinds, Anna asked, "Are you a member of the Norse Folk Congress too?"

"*Too,* Ms. Turnipseed?"

"My partner and I met Nels the other night."

"Oh." The woman looked through the window at the juniper- and grass-covered hills that ringed the tribal capital as if she'd been dropped at the ends of the earth. "Yes, I'm a member too." As Anna watched, her thin defenses collapsed, and when she faced Turnipseed again there were tears in her eyes. "You know what the toughest thing in the world is?"

"What?" Anna asked softly.

"To have faith. To have true faith when the world prefers that you believe nothing at all." Then she laughed miserably through her tears. "You think we're all crazy, don't you?"

"Pagans, you mean."

"Yes, crazy pagans."

"Well, you're a new experience for me. I had it pretty well set in my mind that European Americans are Christians."

"I don't know what I am anymore." Patricia Sward hid her eyes with a hand. The skin was like ice, and the traceries of veins showed through it. She was so transparent, yet difficult to read. She'd just mentioned dreaming. When she dreamed, was it of Scandinavian woods and fjords? Why were she and her husband dipping into racial memory for emotional sustenance, and what did any of this have to do with Tennyson Paulina, a Paiute of the Hunibui Eaters band?

Anna waited a moment, then asked, "Did the tribal patrolman see Paulina hitting you?"

"No," she snuffled into a Kleenex. "Why would that matter?"

It had implications for the prosecution in the event Patricia Sward didn't want to talk, although Anna doubted that the U.S. Attorney would go ahead without her full cooperation. There were too many other cases already on his plate. "I'd advise you to seek a complaint against Paulina . . . even in the tribal court."

"Why, Ms. Turnipseed? Aren't you loyal to your own kind?"

It was odd to hear of a member of the Northern Paiute, periodic foes of the Modoc in the old days, as her own kind. But she responded, "Yes, but I draw the line when it comes to abusive behavior. You're probably not the first woman Paulina's beaten. If we do nothing, you won't be the last."

Yet Patricia Sward said, "I'm not going to press charges. I just want out of here."

Anna could no longer hold in her dismay. "Why were you with Tennyson?"

The woman's unhappy blue gaze flickered around the office as if explaining was useless.

"I'm trying to understand, Ms. Sward. Not accuse."

"I know," Patricia Sward said, "but you have to be part of the kindred to understand. Understanding's in the blood, not the mind." Then she seemed to fasten hopefully on an idea. "We all make sacrifices for what we believe, don't we?"

"Like what?"

"I prefer to keep that my secret. But I'll say this—our faith is just being reborn. We need to protect it, nurture it, whatever the cost to us as individuals."

"Protect against what?"

"You know about Paulina. Surely you know what kind of creature he is." Patricia Sward took her compact from her purse and examined her face in its little mirror. She winced at the sight of the bruises and quickly snapped the case shut. "I've tried so many things, Ms. Turnipseed. And all of them left me empty. Except Norse paganism. I feel connected now. To Nature, the whole Cosmos. And there must be something to it if so many of my race practiced it for thousands of years. As an Indian woman, you understand that kind of continuity . . . don't you?"

8

Gorka Bilbao lit his propane lantern and hung it from a branch of the pine tree that stood in the front of his cabin. It'd been another warm autumn day; the evening was just as pleasant. He filled his tin washtub at the hand pump to his well, then dragged the basin over to the tree and poured in a pail load of fossils he'd collected some weeks ago. Taking a bottle of Thunderbird wine from his rear trouser pocket, he eased onto a camp stool and began scrubbing the claystone off his specimens. Silt soon clouded the water.

Slow down on the wine.

He had only two and a half bottles left out of an entire gift box of twelve. How could he get down the hill to Prineville, the nearest town, for more? His Datsun's right front wheel tie-rod was bent from his encounter with the Dodge diesel on Whitehorse Rapids Road. The tire had shimmied and pulled all the way back to the Ochoco Mountains, then blown within sight of his cabin. His spare, he discovered, was flat too.

However, except for his dwindling supply of Thunderbird, he was in no rush to leave the mountains. Danger was brewing outside them. That'd become clear yesterday afternoon with the arrival of a Crook County deputy sheriff. Bilbao surmised that he was under suspicion, although the cop refused to say why. *Where were you around nine last night?* In answer, Bilbao showed him his disabled Datsun just down the dirt road. He even proved that the pickup was undrivable, but cops never offer absolution.

Let it go. They've got nothing on you.

"I'll drink to that." Bilbao was sweeping the bottle up to his lips when a flicker of movement in the tub caught his eye. Pink tentacles shrinking back into a shell. He put down the Thunderbird, slowly reached into the muddy water and grabbed an object that was floating just under the surface.

Then he stared, flabbergasted, paralyzed, into his hand.

He was holding an ammonite, a large snail-like marine creature long extinct. There were no sea fossils in this part of Oregon, and he'd never found an ammonite. He'd only seen them in his fossil book. Yet, the big whorl of shell was undeniably an ammonite.

And it was alive.

Bilbao looked up into the sky. He took big, slow breaths, trying to empty his head so reality would seep back in. *The wine, too much wine.* It'd left him feeling both hot and cold at the same time. *Wine will be the death of me.*

Finally, hesitantly, he peered down—and chortled out loud to himself. "Shit on milk!"

It wasn't an ammonite. He was clutching a mammoth's tooth. Almost as common to this country as jackrabbit bones.

He plunked it back into the water and had his drink.

But then he froze while wiping his mouth on his sleeve. He'd heard a thunderous noise in the distance, half masked by the hissing of the propane lantern and the shrill cry of a bird he'd never heard before.

Coming to his feet, Bilbao shambled away from the noisy lantern and out into the deepening twilight. He halted, braced his hands on his wobbly knees. He could hear only his own wheezing, and it took a minute for him to gather enough air to hold his breath and listen.

It was definitely the rumble of a truck engine.

Like a diesel.

He started shivering, recalling the headlights of the big truck burning on the back of his neck the other night. His stomach cramped with fright.

The Dodge. The driverless pickup was coming after him again.

What to do?

His gun.

Bilbao ran toward his cabin. He was nearly there when he remembered that, as soon as the deputy left, he'd hidden his .45 revolver in the rocks above his homesite. A convicted felon, he wasn't allowed to keep a weapon, and if the law came back with a warrant for his arrest he didn't want a gun charge tacked on.

Bilbao rounded the cabin and staggered up the slope. After only a few yards of climbing, his legs ached too badly for him to go on. He waited again until his breath quieted, then listened.

Nothing. Just the familiar sound of his propane lantern.

And there were no headlights on the road up from Prineville.

That made him feel better. "Fuck you, Tennyson Paulina!" he bellowed. "And stop tryin' to witch me! Have the balls to come after me yourself, you red son of a bitch!" His echoes mingled in the canyon below.

Darkness had fallen.

The circle of light cast by his lantern seemed small against this overwhelming gloom, but he was drawn back to it.

He returned to his camp stool, planning to get his gun later.

A ghostly mist lingered over the water in the tub. He broke it up with a wave of his hand. "Stop tryin' to witch me," he repeated, but this time he whined instead of shouted. And his teeth were chattering. He was wearing down under the relentless pressure of Paulina's magic. This morning, or maybe yesterday morning, he'd been walking along the dry creek below his cabin when a skeletal hand thrust up out of the sand and snatched at his trouser cuff. Screaming, he ran. It was ten minutes before he could force himself to return to the spot, and by then Paulina had cleverly transformed the bony hand into a forked manzanita branch that resembled human fingers.

And this afternoon, or maybe yesterday afternoon, he'd spied a gray-blond devil standing on a far ridge. He'd known it was a devil because, even at that distance, he could tell that it had a horn in the middle of its face instead of a nose. Paulina was now manufacturing devils that appeared to be white. To deceive Bilbao into trusting them.

He glanced down.

Two primitive-looking eyes jutted above the surface of the water on antennae-like spindles. Gawking at him. They taunted him, mocked his fear, and Bilbao lashed out in sudden anger, "You goggle-eyed son of a bitch!" He plunged his arm into the basin and rooted around for the offending creature. But he found only clumps of stony fossils. He withdrew his hand from the water—and moaned. A glistening mass of slime was clinging to his forearm. It had snakelike tentacles, and they bit into his wrist, gnawed on his flesh.

Reeling backward, he knocked over the stool as he tried to shake off the prehistoric jellyfish. This creature too had previously inhabited his fossil book, but now it was horribly alive, attacking him. The more violently he shook, the more tenaciously the thing tightened its grip on his arm. Finally, he slammed it against the trunk of the tree. There was an explosion of jelly, splattering his face. The stuff stung his eyes like acid.

Blinded, Bilbao groped for the tub.

Kneeling beside it, he splashed his face again and again. At last, the pain subsided, and he could see once more.

The lantern was swinging on the limb. There was no breeze, and he couldn't recall knocking against it.

No more wine. Ever again.

He'd bitten his tongue in his terror, and the salty taste of blood filled his mouth. Panting, he cupped his hand for a rinse. And caught his reflection on the surface. Something was stuck to his cheek. He ripped the thing off and examined it in his trembling hand. A trilobite. The crablike anthropod had been extinct for more than 350 million years, yet this one was rolling up into a ball before Bilbao's eyes, protecting its underbelly and scores of wriggling legs.

Repulsed by the thorny feel of its shell, he rose and hurled the trilobite against the side of his cabin, smashing it into a crusty goo that slid down the wall.

He bent over to dump the water out of this Pandora's box of a washtub. But things were scuttling up his trouser legs. More trilobites, thousands upon thousands of them. They spilled over the lip of the tub and fanned out in all directions, clicking as they moved to recolonize the world. The relentless clicking made Bilbao plug his ears with his fingers. He stamped his feet, but his frantic effort was futile. Those trilobites flung off his legs were instantly replaced by countless others.

Dropping his hands from his ears, he kicked over the tub. The water slopped out, and he was sure that this would end it. "There . . . there!"

But then the tub, rolling around on its side, became a pipe from which surged a boiling torrent of primordial life. Trilobites mixed with marine scorpions and urchins as big as footballs. Monstrous sea slugs slithered out and wallowed around Bilbao's boots like grotesque seal pups. Lizards with cruel snouts and razor-sharp teeth squirmed from the teeming chaos, reared on their hind legs and streaked into the night.

Bilbao righted the tub again, praying that that would cut off the hideous parade of long-dead life.

He waited breathlessly. "Please . . . please . . ."

A fountain of brown water burst from the basin and shot twenty feet into the air, littering his yard with more and more impossible beasts that thudded sickeningly against the sopping ground. Bilbao backed away from the writhing deluge that went on and on and on.

Still backing up, he bumped into something large.

As large as himself.

Turning and facing the thing was beyond his courage. So he shut his eyes and whimpered as long, bony fingers wrapped around his neck.

• • •

Anna took one ravine, Emmett the other. Hot. Too summery for a fall day. She stripped off her FBI windbreaker and tied it around her waist. There were no tracks in the gully, as if even the animals of these hills avoided it because they knew something tragic had happened here.

Except one.

A hummingbird flitted out of the red sumac bushes and hovered directly before Anna. She tried to take a step forward, but the bird darted aggressively toward her face.

"What are you doing?" she asked.

Its tiny black eyes were fastened on her in such a way that the bird almost seemed capable of speech.

Anna continued up the ravine while the blur of wings buzzed around her. She shooed with her hands, but the hummingbird refused to go away.

Then she found a woman's shoe. Stooping, she pried it out of the dried silt. A seven. Elsa's size.

The hummingbird grew even more insistent as Anna tried to push on.

"I've got to look," she said.

The bird circled her one last time, the rasp of its wings loud in the confines of the ravine, then vanished in an iridescent flash. The dark opening of a cave beckoned Anna on. She clambered over a boulder toward the cave. On the other side of the big rock, a cloud of flies spiraled up from something that was partly entombed in the silt. The exposed skin of the withered body looked leathery, but the auburn hair shone as lustrously as if Elsa had just run a brush through it. This jarring mixture of the grisly and the lovely rang inside Anna's head like an alarm going off.

Again.

And again.

Her head jerked up off the pillow.

By the glow of the digital clock, she could make out the telephone on the nightstand. "Turnipseed," she answered.

"This is Vernita Dease. I'm sorry to bother you."

Quickly, Anna's mind caught up with the present. It was only 8:30 P.M. After leaving the tribal police station this morning, she and Emmett had recombed the hills above Wapinitia Road where Elsa had left her Honda. They'd found nothing, other than a partial shoe print that may or may not have been Elsa's. Dead tired, they'd then both turned in early to their rooms at the Kah-Nee-Ta. "That's okay, Mrs. Dease. What can I do for you?"

"Something bad's going to happen tonight."

Anna flicked on the bedside lamp, squinted against the glare. Her purse was safely in reach. In it were her semiautomatic and a mummified hummingbird, a Modoc talisman given to her by an uncle to ensure her safety. To make her as nimble as a hummingbird in the face of danger. "What's going to happen?"

"I heard this from a relative, so I don't want you to use my name."

"All right." Anna realized that she might be promising too much too soon, but she also sensed that the woman would clam up if not given this guarantee.

"Tennyson Paulina and a bunch of his hotheads are going up to the Ochocos to get Gorka Bilbao to talk."

"And if he doesn't talk?"

"I think they'll kill him. I don't want that, and my Elsa wouldn't want it either."

Anna carried the phone to the table, where earlier she'd spread out a map of north central Oregon. Her eyes had finally adjusted to the light. The Ochoco Mountains were less than fifty air-miles southeast of Warm Springs, but they were crisscrossed by thin red filaments of Forest Service roads. For an instant, she thought that Paulina was in the tribal detention facility, but then recalled that Patricia Sward hadn't pressed charges. The Paiute had then been free to walk out of the jail as soon as he was sober. "When did Paulina and the others leave?"

"I'm not sure. Maybe a half hour ago."

"What're they driving?"

"I don't know. Please hurry."

"We will." Hanging up, Anna went to the wall separating her room from Emmett's and pounded on it three times with her fist.

• • •

Anna studied the map while Emmett drove at breakneck speed up Barber Creek Road. It was one of two unpaved routes entering the Ochoco Mountains out of the north. Over the radio, the agencies involved had agreed that Anna and Emmett would approach Bilbao's cabin by Barber Creek. An Oregon state trooper would use Trout Creek Road, the other byway out of the north, while units from the Crook County sheriff's office raced up from Prineville on the improved route Paulina and his friends would most likely use.

Anna's call sign came over the Motorola, interrupting her map deliberations. "Go ahead with your traffic, Crook County."

"Be advised, our responding units have requested heavy equipment to remove fallen rocks on the Allen Creek Road."

Anna turned to Emmett. "Meaning?"

He took the mike from her. "Crook County, are you advising that your units can't presently respond to the site?"

"That's affirmative. They'll try an alternate route, but that gives them an ETA of at least an hour."

"Copy." Emmett hooked the microphone back on the dashboard. "Shit. Looks like Paulina knew which way the cavalry would come."

Anna removed the shotgun from the roof rack. All of a sudden, she and Emmett were the most likely respondents to face Paulina and his followers. Parker topped a crest at sixty miles an hour and the Explorer landed on its skid plate with a teeth-gnashing crunch.

Anna checked the map again. "Turn right."

Emmett fishtailed through the remote intersection.

An unnatural light was breaking from the canyon below. As Emmett continued to barrel down the road, a small cabin came into view, as did the source of the illumination, a lantern hung in a tree. Something unrecognizable was crouched at the base of the tree, maybe a chained dog.

Without warning, Emmett stomped on the brakes and shut off the headlights.

Anna asked, "What're you doing?"

Emmett bailed out with the only flashlight, stooped and ran the beam along the surface of the road. Three seconds later, he was back behind the wheel, punching up his headlights again. He peeled off onto a barren pumice flat that gently descended to the cabin. "Don't want to cover up the bald light-truck tire tracks leading out of here," he explained. "Somebody's tied to the tree."

He was right. As they drew nearer, Anna saw that a stocky, bearded man was tethered by a rope to the trunk.

Emmett parked with the high beams shining directly on Gorka Bilbao.

"Oh God," Anna murmured before she could stop herself.

"Cover me with the scattergun," Emmett said. "Keep it trained on the cabin door." Then he got out, again crouching and holding his light flush to the muddy ground as he looked for the path that would least damage the numerous tracks in the yard.

Emmett went forward, revolver drawn.

Anna stepped out into the stench of roasted meat. She almost retched. Recovering with a gulp of air, she angled her vehicle door back to give her some measure of protection against any oncoming bullets. She stared briefly at Bilbao, then quickly focused on the unlit cabin. The ghastly image of the man remained imprinted on her mind's eye, almost obliterating everything else. The fossil hunter had been gagged with his shirt, for he was barechested. Worse than that, he'd been slit from his belt to his sternum, the skin stretched back and held open with wooden skewers to reveal his sagging entrails.

She checked on Emmett.

He was examining the rope on which Bilbao had been dangled over a fire. There were no flames, just coals, but the heat continued to roast his viscera, accounting for the nauseating stench. Emmett shifted his revolver to his left hand and touched two fingers to Bilbao's neck. The carotid artery there was apparently lifeless, for Emmett shook his head at Anna and pantomimed punching the talk button on a microphone.

"Crook County," she transmitted, clasping the mike to the receiver of the shotgun, "ready to copy emergency traffic from FBI at the scene?"

"Go ahead, FBI."

"We have a homicide here. All responding units—use extreme caution." She retraced the webwork of roads in her mind. "No vehicle description, but bald light-truck tire impressions lead away to the north."

"Copy, are you Code Four?"

Anna scanned all around for the brutal danger that still might be here. But the fresh tire tracks had strongly suggested flight, and that knowledge made her say, "Affirmative."

Emmett returned to the Explorer, using his outbound tracks on the way back. He was shaken too. Nothing extraordinary betrayed that, but his eyes were bright and glassy. "The bastards took no chances. They hamstrung Bilbao with a knife, cut the tendons right through his boots. Then did a helluva job of tying him up with a stick for a back brace and leaning him over the fire."

Anna had taken a small bottle of perfume from her windbreaker pocket. Desert floral scents collected by a Moapa Paiute woman who lived near Las Vegas; her homemade blend suggested sunny and breeze-swept places beyond death. Anna splashed some into her palm and dabbed her throat—barbecues, she feared, would never quite be the same for her. "It's how they kite salmon up here."

"What do you mean?"

"Kiting salmon. Skewering the fish open with sticks and leaning it over an alder fire." Something came to her. "Where's Bilbao's pickup?"

"We'll clear the cabin first, then hunt for the Datsun. Put out a BOLO if it's gone." Be-On-Look-Out. "They might've taken it. Hope they did—that nails it down for the county D.A."

Anna didn't have to ask who "they" were, even though it was hard for her to imagine that Northern Paiutes had done something this vicious. She'd grown up among the Yahooskin, a band of this tribe, and torture-murder didn't fit the character of those people. Emmett, she suspected, would disagree.

She switched the radio on to the public address speaker so they could continue to monitor traffic, then joined Emmett to go through the cabin. Nothing but years of filth, fossils crammed in every nook and cranny. With only one flashlight between them, they stuck together as they began a wide circle around the homestead. Within the first quarter of that orbit, they found Bilbao's truck parked on the shoulder of the road to Prineville, the right front tire completely off the rim. ·

"I'll start the sketch and evidence inventory," Anna said, knowing that she had to test herself by returning to the heart of the horror. Avoidance was addictive at a homicide scene. "You keep the flashlight."

Emmett raised the nimbus of the beam just enough to examine her eyes. He seemed reassured by the look in them. "Okay."

She started back toward the lantern. Although the sibilant hiss obviously came from the lantern, Anna could easily imagine it issuing from Gorka Bilbao's slitted belly. He'd bled so copiously it was a wonder he hadn't put out the fire with his own blood. Emmett had kicked some dirt onto the coals to stop the grisly roasting.

She reracked the shotgun in the Explorer, grabbed a notebook, then walked toward the corpse. Her shadow stretched out in the headlights to overlap it. She stepped aside and, from a distance of about ten feet, saw that Bilbao had nearly chewed through his gag. It must have taken him several minutes to die, an eternity of indescribable suffering. She despised what he'd done to that Yakima girl, but no rap sheet in the world justified a death like this.

Then she tried to visualize a beginning to the attack.

A camp stool lay on its side next to a tin washtub, the kind that had served as a bathtub in her shanty before federal housing brought modern plumbing to her ranchería. It was filled with muddy water. Had Bilbao been washing when he was assaulted? No soap scum on the surface. Clamping the notebook under her arm, she unbuttoned her blouse sleeve and reached into the distasteful-looking water.

She felt along the bottom.

Something bumped against the back of her hand, then evaded her grasp. She groped all around before finally seizing it—only to be pricked under her fingernails by spines. No—not spines, bristles. It was a scrub brush. She explored some more and brought out a fossil. Some kind of mollusk. Pouring off the water, she revealed more fossils.

So Bilbao had been caught unaware at one of his most common chores. He hadn't been forewarned by the sound of an approaching vehicle; otherwise, she suspected, someone as guarded as he would've put out his lantern. Paulina owned a Cadillac, an unsuitable vehicle for these rutted mountain roads. But that afternoon at the Shaker church, he'd shown up with his friends in an old pickup.

A radio transmission came over the P.A., the male voice garbled and unreadable but undeniably tense. The Crook County dispatcher quickly relayed, "Units and stations, state police unit Paul Fourteen reports a stop on an older model GMC half-ton pickup along Trout Creek Road one mile south of Amity Creek. Numerous Indian male subjects. He requests an urgent back. Any unit in position?"

"Emmett!" Anna called out into the darkness.

His voice drifted across the canyon to her. "Tell them we're rolling!"

• • •

Emmett felt no hesitation in abandoning a homicide scene that had just been secured. A frightened cop was asking for help. That plea superseded any other obligation. And having seen what had been done to Bilbao, Emmett believed that the trooper had every reason to be scared. As Anna and he dropped over the crest and started down the north slope of the Ochocos, the man came in loud and clear. "Where's that back?" he pled over the radio.

Anna broadcast, "Paul Fourteen, we're about two minutes from you. Copy . . . ?"

Then there was no further response.

Anna tossed the rumpled map into the backseat and fed a round into the chamber of the shotgun. Emmett could smell her perfume. He thought he could pick desert lavender and honey mesquite out of the mix. Pleasant, although the fragrance now evoked carnage to him. If and when they ever made love, he'd insist that she not wear it.

Ahead, a film of bluish light was fanning over a hill. Emmett put down his window to listen for shots.

"Crook County," Anna radioed, "FBI and BIA are on the scene. Will advise."

A new voice carped over the airwaves, "Advise Jefferson S.O., FBI. You're now in our county."

All they needed—a jurisdictional scrap.

The clash of headlights told Emmett what had happened. The trooper had blindly met the GMC pickup on the curve around the hill, giving him no chance to let the truck pass by. That way, he might have fallen in behind it before making his felony traffic stop. As it was, the two vehicles were almost butting grilles. Emmett let up on the brake, shifted into four-wheel drive and pressed the accelerator. *Don't get caught in a crossfire with the trooper.* He left the road and bounced over sand mounds of sage and bitterbrush. Anna yowled as her seatbelt kicked in too late to save her head from crashing against the ceiling.

"You okay?" he asked.

"Go, go!" she hollered.

Emmett spun the Explorer around so the headlights converged with the trooper's on the aged pickup. But both the state cruiser and the GMC vanished as dust sifted down over the windshield. "Get out on my side," he told Anna. Then he tumbled out his door and flopped down in the soft tire-churned sand. Coughing, he peered over the sights of his revolver.

The pall of dust soon floated back down to earth.

He didn't know what he'd expected to see. Certainly not Tennyson Paulina standing stark naked on top of the pickup's cab. His scrawny body was motionless, as if he'd turned to stone.

"Tennyson!" Emmett shouted.

No reaction. Had Paulina been hit? No sign of blood, but some wounds didn't bleed.

Anna crawled across the driver's seat with the shotgun and exited the Explorer on Emmett's side. She played out the microphone cord behind her. "Paul Fourteen," she asked by radio, "are you all right?"

Nothing for a count of three, then a shaken voice broke the static: "I guess so."

"What happened?"

"All the war-whoops bailed out and crawled under the truck. Next thing I know, this joker's tearing off his clothes and jumping up on top of the cab. You see a weapon?"

Anna began to say something, but another transmission overrode hers, creating an ear-splitting squeal.

Emmett asked for the flashlight. She tossed it to him, then radioed, "Units and stations, FBI—be advised Paul Fourteen is uninjured. But continue to roll all available backs."

Both Crook and Jefferson counties acknowledged.

Emmett couldn't see any of Paulina's buddies. Rather than raise his head, he crept forward to the next sandy mound. It was thickly crowned with sage, and through the foliage he could count four or five figures huddled together under the bed of the pickup.

"You on top of the truck!" the trooper instructed over his P.A., his voice jittery, "Climb down *now* or I'll open fire!"

Paulina didn't climb down, and the trooper didn't open fire.

The Paiute began serenely turning to the cardinal directions, supplicating with cupped hands toward each as if making an offering of sacred smoke.

"Tennyson, this is Emmett Parker. Come on down before somebody gets hurt."

"That's entirely up to you people," the man responded woodenly. Was he stoned?

"Do you or your people have any weapons?" Emmett demanded.

No answer.

Paulina's clothes were strewn around his feet. Without warning, he reached down into them and came up with his left hand fisted. He was no sooner standing erect again than there was the sharp crack of a pistol. Paulina pitched off the cab roof and into the darkness on the far side of the truck.

Emmett rose. "Christ Almighty."

Five Indian males, the oldest no more than his early twenties, inched up into view. They looked shell-shocked. The trooper's voice boomed over the P.A. again: "You want me to take them down, FBI?"

"No," Emmett yelled, "stay where you are." One shooting was enough for tonight. He waved for Anna to come forward with him to provide cover with the shotgun.

"Put your hands behind your necks and lace up your fingers," Emmett ordered the young men. They obeyed. "Now turn around and drop to your knees." When their backs were to Anna, Emmett checked on Paulina.

The Paiute was sprawled nude across the sand, eyes open. A bloody graze was visible along the right side of his rib cage. In his open left hand was a pack of cigarettes, badly crushed. The silver foil at its top glinted in the flashlight beam.

Emmett kept his revolver aimed on the man. "Can you hear me?"

"I want you and your Modoc partner to transport me, Parker. Don't want no white cop sayin' I got killed tryin' to escape."

• • •

Paulina got his wish. Anna pointed out to the assembled deputies that summoning an ambulance would double the gunshot man's arrival time at the nearest hospital in the town of Redmond. They agreed. Emmett put down the backseat in the Explorer, creating a makeshift bed for Paulina, and Anna covered him up to the waist with a blanket. His clothing had been seized and bagged as evidence. No weapons had been found, although those could've have been easily ditched between here and Bilbao's cabin. Emmett reclined beside the prisoner, wearing surgical gloves and holding a compress to the wound. Anna had done this while Paulina still lay on the ground. She'd felt his splintered ribs through the wad of cotton, but the stoical Paulina was breathing without difficulty, so the bullet probably hadn't penetrated his lung.

Anna drove.

"You see a gun in my hand?" Paulina asked when they were miles down the dusty road.

"I don't know what the trooper saw," Emmett answered. He'd already told Anna that the cigarette pack foil had sparkled like gunmetal when he'd shone the flashlight on it. Her own view of Paulina's left hand had been blocked by the man's legs. She felt sorry for the trooper: He now faced an administrative inquisition to explain what—in his own fear-juiced mind over the space of a microsecond—had seemed entirely justifiable. She'd been there.

"How about you, Turnipseed?" Paulina asked. "You see me with a gun?"

Anna kept silent.

"Okey-doke," the Paiute sighed. "I've run into this before. Even with Indian cops. Hell, 'specially with Indian cops. You always got to prove you're part of the congregation." As Anna turned off the last dirt road onto U.S. 26, Paulina added, "But I'll give you both this much—it's all in the eye of the beholder. And there's been some mighty strange beholdin' lately."

"What do you mean?" Emmett asked.

"You mind takin' off these cuffs?"

"Yes, I do. What strange beholding?"

"I heard on the radio that a lady across the Columbia in Wishram Heights looked out her kitchen window and saw a turkey vulture roostin' on her sill. Swore that the buzzard had a human ear in its beak. What d'you make of that, Parker?"

Anna forgot to dim her high beams, and a logging trucker flashed his own lights at her.

"Sounds like a tall tale to me, Tennyson," Emmett said. "What other tall tale do you have—like how you spent your evening?"

"Mirandize him," Anna interrupted before Paulina could reply.

"Tenn and I are just jawing."

"I *said* give him his rights," Anna said adamantly, "or wait for the county investigators to question him. This isn't our case."

"Anna—"

"Just do it." It was the first time she'd called Emmett on his habitual fast-and-loose play with rules, and she waited for him to blow up, realizing that their frayed relationship might not withstand one more rift. But she refused to back down. He was wrong.

Finally, Emmett exhaled, then began reciting Paulina's rights to him in a monotone.

But the Paiute cut Emmett off before he got to the end. "I don't need my rights to tell the truth." A remarkable statement from a prisoner accused of a capital offense. Even if Paulina had a genius for lying, he could be demolishing his own defense. But she could now honestly testify that the man had waived his rights. "All five of my compadres will tell this same story, as much as five different humans can ever tell the same story. . . ." Paulina paused on a seething breath. "Hold that bandage a little easier on me, Parker. Sure," the man went on, "we came to the Ochocos tonight to rough up Bilbao. Get him to say what he done to Elsa. And if he touched one hair on that girl's head, I would've had no problem killin' the son of the bitch. But he was already dead when we got there."

"Bullshit," Emmett said.

"Then hook me up to the lie box. Scrape under my nails and check my clothes for Bilbao's blood. You can't do what was done to old Gorka without gettin' blood all over yourself, right?"

"Why'd you get on top of the truck?" Anna asked.

"Guess, Modoc."

Paulina's sarcasm was understandable: It was no great mystery. Among the tribes of the region, there were traditional forms of power to ward off specific dangers. One of these magical ways had been an overly optimistic solution to the slaughter being inflicted on native peoples by repeating rifles. "Bullet Power?"

"There you go, sister." Paulina made a clucking noise with his tongue. "I had to calm down my boys. God knows how many of us that trooper would've wasted if I hadn't shown him that his bullets was nothin' to me."

"I thought you didn't have powers."

"Hell, I don't, Parker. I got a hole in my side to prove it, don't I? But I saw some power tonight that scared the holy shit out of me."

"What are you talking about?" Emmett asked.

"The Ancient One's on the loose now," Paulina said quietly. "And I got no idea how we'll ever get him back in the ground again. He's pissed off, bad, and he don't care who he hurts. So hold on to your hats. Buzzards with ears in their beaks and gutted Bascos won't seem like anythin' out of the ordinary before long. Believe me."

9

"Too bad the weather has turned," Dr. Rankin's driver said as he opened the passenger front door of the Lexus for Anna. "I don't care much for the cold." A placid black man in his mid-thirties, he had an accent Emmett couldn't place. The dry spell since Elsa Dease's disappearance four days ago had given way to rain again. Five hundred feet below the bluff, the gray waters of the Columbia glinted briefly under a weak sun, then all was swallowed up by the downpour once more.

Emmett got in the backseat, and Rankin's driver started down the long driveway to the mansion. This white Normanesque castle stood on the Washington side of the river within sight of The Dalles. The anthropologist had tersely explained over the phone that he permitted no outside vehicles on his estate, so somebody named Kawatu would meet the partners at the gate, where there was ample parking.

Rankin's driver was apparently Kawatu. He wore a lab coat and tweed trousers. Taking the lane at a leisurely glide, he obviously savored the feel of the luxury sport utility.

"How long have you been Dr. Rankin's driver?" Silences didn't bother Anna, so she must have been genuinely curious about the man.

"I'm an osteological technician, actually, not a driver." Kawatu grinned good-naturedly at her mild chagrin. "The doctor calls me his number one bone picker."

"Sorry."

"No matter, Ms. Turnipseed. Lately, his health has gone downhill, so I've stepped in to help get him around. I'm afraid he's a very bad passenger. How do you call it . . . a seat-of-his-pants driver?"

"Backseat driver," Emmett said, yawning.

"Yes, that's it, Mr. Parker. Thank you."

"Too bad about his health." Emmett paused, hoping Kawatu would fill in the ailment that was affecting Rankin's nervous system. His best guess was Parkinson's disease. Or early Alzheimer's.

But the man only smiled and said, "I'm sure he'll appreciate your sentiment."

Rankin didn't want to hear Emmett's true sentiment. Over the past thirty-six hours, while Anna and he had been assisting the Crook County detective with his grisly homicide investigation, the anthropologist had been pulling political strings. The result was this visit. On the day Anna and he had hoped to rest and collect their thoughts, the U.S. Attorney in Portland had ordered them to brief Rankin on developments. The man had complained that the partners had purposely cut him out of the information loop. False. It was just that events had rippled far beyond any concerns about the John Day skeleton, and there were things Rankin had no right knowing, even though his forensic expertise made him a valued friend of regional law enforcement.

Kawatu parked under the porte cochere, and the overhanging projection from the house sheltered the Lexus from the rain. Getting out, Emmett saw that there were wrought iron bars over the basement windows. "This way, please," Kawatu said, unlocking the massive front door for the partners.

Inside the dim foyer, Emmett was struck by the musty smell of catalogued death. The house felt more like a museum than a mansion. He hoped that the rooms beyond would grow brighter, but each mahogany-paneled chamber grew successively darker until Kawatu opened a door on an absolutely dismal library. On the walls were funereal artifacts from all over the world, some Southwest Pacific but most Native American. Rankin might as well have decorated with tombstones and casket lids. If he realized the effect this display might have on two Indians, he didn't show it as he swiveled his recliner chair away from the fireplace and toward the partners. He was wearing a cream-colored Irish knit sweater, loose-fitting slacks and carpet slippers. His ponytail was undone, and his long white hair cascaded over his brawny shoulders.

"Your guests, Doctor," Kawatu heralded.

Rankin didn't rise for Anna, although he bowed his head toward her. "Delighted, delighted. Sit by the fire, both of you. Winter's arrived early." His palsied hand indicated a love seat. "Something to drink?"

"Coffee," Emmett said. At only 1:00 P.M. his energy was already flagging. Which made this day-wasting trip all the more galling.

"Coffee sounds good," Anna said, although her gaze was on the cocktail table set before them. Under its glass was an array of trade beads, some showing slight melting from the same fires that had cremated their owners.

"Two coffees, Kawatu. And bring a scotch and soda for me. One for yourself too, if you like."

"It's not five o'clock, Doctor," Kawatu said with affectionate reproach.

"Yes, but weather like this makes it feel very, very late to me." Rankin said this with such melancholy the man looked thoughtfully at his boss before going out. As soon as Kawatu was gone, Rankin explained, "New Guinean. A magnificent specimen of the Fore tribe, although God knows I found him far from the highlands his people call home."

"*Found* him?" Emmett asked, too far gone to hide his growing ill humor.

"Yes, Mr. Parker, I believe that's the correct term. I was headed back to Port Moresby, and a Fore friend asked me to look up his sister in that sprawling slum of a city. He hadn't heard from her in some time. Unfortunately, she'd slid into prostitution and was dying of syphilis. You die of things like that in Papua New Guinea. She had an eleven-year-old son, and he'd become quite an adept thief. Not entirely adept, for the police were holding Kawatu in a squalid prison camp. The poor woman begged me to take him. . . ." The anthropologist stirred the fireplace coals with a brass poker.

"So you took him," Anna finished the story for him.

"And I took him." Rankin smiled at her, his head twitching slightly. "Sent him to university. Made a competent osteologist out of him. Almost a Pygmalion tale, except I was careful not to change Kawatu's essence. And for that I'm completely to blame. But I've always valued naturalness over convention."

"And what's Kawatu's essence?" Emmett asked.

Rankin put the poker back in its rack. "He's living proof the primal mind is grossly materialistic. He covets all I own and asks for a raise at least once a week. You see, the Fore invented their gods not to moderate their own behavior, as you Native Americans did, but rather to serve their greed."

"What were you doing in New Guinea, Doctor?"

"Studying cannibalism, Ms. Turnipseed," Rankin said, and Anna looked as if she was sorry she'd asked. "That was twenty-five years ago, my dear, and the highlands of New Guinea were the last bastion of the taboo to beat all taboos. Really a pair of taboos, because there are two varieties of man-eating. Exocannibalism, in which one's enemies are the fare, and endocannibalism, the former practice of Kawatu's tribe. It's said the bellies of the Fore are their cemeteries . . . isn't that so, my boy?"

Emmett saw that the New Guinean had come silently back into the room, burdened with a service tray. "Isn't what so, sir?"

"That you Fore eat your deceased relatives."

"So I've been told." Kawatu gracefully lowered the tray so that Anna could take a china cup of coffee. "Before my time."

"Nonsense, my dear boy, you were just too young to remember."

"Thanks," Emmett said to Kawatu, accepting a steaming cup. So that was it. Rankin had used New Guinea as his living laboratory on cannibalism, then returned home to superimpose his passion for this ghoulish subject on prehistoric North American cultures, ignoring the protest of the descendants of those cultures that he was misinterpreting the evidence, even sensationalizing science for his own self-aggrandizement. And, in the last decade, he'd slipped in an additional premise that Paleo-Indians had killed off an earlier arriving race of Caucasoids and cannibalized them.

Kawatu carefully handed a mixed drink to Rankin. "I really must get back to work, sir."

"As you wish," Rankin said indifferently as the man went out again. The anthropologist was staring at Anna with intense interest. After a moment, he became aware of Emmett's eyes on him. "Busy week—what, Mr. Parker?"

"Yeah." Here it came. Emmett could almost feel the love seat heating up under him.

Rankin took a sip. "I just don't know what to think."

Emmett was tempted to volunteer that he didn't either, but had a hunch the anthropologist would offer his own opinion soon enough.

"Gorka Bilbao was a disgusting little fellow," Rankin went on, "but he served his purpose. The academics like to rail against the Bilbaos of this world, rooting up bones and fossils out in the great pristine wilds, slashing through the stratigraphic layers of prehistory like warthogs. The sad truth is, millions of tons of precious specimens weather out and crumble to dust each year simply because there aren't enough Bilbaos to salvage them. I could care less that he collected them only to supply himself with cheap wine." Rankin lifted his glass in salute. "To Gorka, may you rest in the peace you have allegedly denied John Day Man." He drank, slopping a dribble of scotch and soda down his chin. Wiping, he asked, "Who's doing Bilbao's postmortem?"

Anna named the pathologist out of Bend, the biggest town in central Oregon. The autopsy had been scheduled to begin at 10:00 A.M.

"Pathologist my ass," Rankin growled. "He's a country butcher. If this job's botched, the whole parade could march down the wrong street for months."

"And what's the right street?" Emmett asked.

"Certainly not that two-bit medicine man, Paulina, and his hooligans. The luminol test should've put that idiotic hypothesis to rest."

As silence hung over the library, Rankin's eyes roved uneasily from partner to partner. "What?"

The results of the test were a closely guarded investigative secret. The Crook County I.D. technician had sprayed luminol reagent on Paulina's clothes and those of the other five suspects. Under blacklight in a darkened room, only one spot of blood had shown up. On Paulina's Levi's, which had been at his feet when the trooper's bullet grazed his side. Another test had suggested but not confirmed that it was the Paiute's own type, not Bilbao's—unfortunately luminol destroys many blood factors used in forensic characterization.

Emmett stood. "Why are you bitching to the U.S. Attorney for us to keep you in the loop, when you obviously have your own sources on everything related to this fiasco?" He was more than ready to leave, but Anna tugged surreptitiously on his sleeve.

"It's a fair question, Doctor," she observed.

The anthropologist made a deflated little gesture for Emmett to sit again. Parker did so, reluctantly, after a second tug from Anna. "Forgive my ill humor—I have good days and bad days," Rankin continued, "and this is a bad one. You two are the only competent investigators on the ground here, and you alone can keep things on track. Don't you see the undercurrent here? Someone is conspiring to make sure science never gets its paws on John Day Man again."

Before Emmett could say anything more, Anna asked Rankin, "What's 'on track' in your definition?"

"Bilbao was tortured. That's a physiological fact. But why would someone do that? We can safely say it was on the assumption Bilbao abducted Elsa Dease. If Paulina and the Warm Springs crowd were responsible, I believe at least one of them would've broken by now, claimed minor involvement as an accessory and glossed over the affair by claiming Bilbao confessed to the abduction before dying." Emmett had to resist nodding in agreement: Last night, Paulina had again demanded a lie detector test, although the state police polygraph examiner wanted to wait until the Paiute was off painkillers. And as Paulina had forecast, all the Indians had told essentially the same story of finding Bilbao already murdered. "Knowing the practicality of the primal mind," Rankin said, "I also believe the Warm Springs boys would've tortured Bilbao only enough to learn Elsa's whereabouts, dead or alive, and then made him show them where she was. *That* is where they would have slain him, if at all."

"So you think the killer wanted to punish Bilbao," Anna said.

"Not entirely, my dear. But passion took over, especially after this person most likely learned from Bilbao that Elsa had been raped and murdered. We both know Gorka's past."

"And who is that person?" Emmett asked.

Rankin took a deep breath as if forcing patience on himself. "The other morning at the Corps of Engineers headquarters, I couldn't help overhear Deborah Carter's outburst about her feelings for Elsa.

Disturbing, terribly disturbing. Not morally, for I believe genetics is behind that sexual inclination. But materially. It clarifies so very much. After reflecting on the matter, I now wonder if it was Carter who tried to open the safe and make it look like a burglary."

"For what purpose?" Anna asked.

"Why, to make a gift of John Day Man to Elsa. That way, the Warm Springs tribes could've reburied him in secret while you two wasted time and effort looking for an imaginary safecracker." Rankin sat forward. "Carter's the only person at the emotional epicenter of all these unfortunate crimes."

Not true if Tennyson Paulina had once loved Elsa Dease as much as Carter possibly did, Emmett thought. Most of the Warm Springs reservation believed that Bilbao was responsible for Elsa's disappearance and wanted him dead, particularly Paulina, and it was a stretch to imagine that the slender colonel had restrained a bruin of a man like Bilbao, hamstrung and hog-tied him before slicing open his belly to the flames. Emmett told Rankin so.

"Unlikely on the surface, Mr. Parker. I agree. But can you eliminate the possibility at this point?"

Emmett didn't answer.

ATF's test on the explosive residue was finished, and military dynamite was confirmed to have been the type used on the safe in Carter's headquarters. The ATF investigators were following up on an anonymous lead, possibly from a Corps of Engineers employee, that some dynamite was missing from the Corps' magazine on the army's Boardman Bombing Range upriver of The Dalles. Identifying threads put by the manufacturer in the explosive could eventually corroborate this source down to the lot and batch numbers. Also, the blast had occurred at 0401 hours, the time of the shift change for the federal rangers who patrolled government facilities and installations in the Mid-Columbia area—something that smacked of insider knowledge.

"This is why I invited you two here," Rankin explained. "To beg you to make absolutely sure that that possibility is eliminated. Eliminate it, and no one will be more satisfied than I, believing that Colonel Carter has suffered enough in this lifetime. But she's not an obvious adversary, and that makes her insidious."

Anna looked sideways at Emmett, then asked, "Adversary of whom, Doctor?"

"I see the handprints of the same old clique," he said, evading her question. "The Milquetoast academics, the Christian fundamentalists and Indian fakirs who pushed the Native American Graves Protection and Repatriation Act through fucking Congress." He spat out the full title of NAGPRA with caustic precision. "What price political correctness? I'm being worn down by these idiots. The evidence in the archaeological record is overwhelming. Cannibalism was here right into the nineteenth century. When the Caucasoids were depleted, the Indians fell upon one another. Right until the last century." He turned on Emmett. "What'd Herman Lehmann have to say about this? He and his band of fellow Nuumu found some enemy Tonkawas eating the leg of a Comanche warrior . . . !" While Rankin ranted on, Emmett was struck by how, despite his paranoia, the anthropologist could draw up an obscure historical account like this out of a prodigious well of facts. A white captive, Lehmann had risen to warrior status among the Comanche and left the best surviving description of that nomadic life. "And this is nothing compared to the evidence revealed by my own work at Arroyo del Huesos in New Mexico, which these ignorant bastards are doing all they can to erase! A pocket of thirty Caucasoids—men, women and children—of nine thousand years ago had been undeniably killed, butchered and cooked. Undeniably!"

"Excuse me," Emmett interrupted, "but I'm confused by how John Day Man fits into this pattern of cannibalism."

Rankin calmed himself. "In what way?"

"Well, I read somewhere that you yourself believe several factors must be present to add up to a cannibalistic signature."

"Yes, yes, that's right," Rankin said impatiently.

"What were they? Bone breakage by hammering against a stone anvil. Cracking of long bones to get at the marrow. Burning after butchering. I forget the rest, but my point is, John Day Man's skeleton shows none of these. Just V-shaped cuts possibly made by an obsidian knife."

"Yes, Mr. Parker, we're dealing with something new here. The first discovery in a possible series. Picture this: A lone Caucasoid is caught alone on the colder Oregon steppe of 14,500 years ago by half-starved Paleo-Indians on a hunting or gathering foray. This target of opportunity is killed and eaten—hastily, mind you, before his own band can come to his rescue. Only the choicest cuts, the biggest muscle masses, are devoured. Then our Paleo-Indians dump his remains in a ravine along the John Day River and move on, hoping for another windfall of the same kind." Rankin grinned in frustration. "John Day Man expands the hypothesis by demonstrating another variation on the same theme. He doesn't disprove cannibalism. Don't you see what's going on here? I'm being coerced to pretend that the North American holocaust never existed. Well, I will not be coerced! I will not!"

"Doctor, please." Kawatu was standing in the doorway with a worried expression.

Rankin held up a hand for him to be silent. "With you in a minute, my boy. Well, my friends, I'll continue to amass my proofs until I have an avalanche of them to pour down the throats of these gutless morons. The facts are waiting in the dirt out there, and I encourage all interested parties to start searching!" He pointed south, toward Oregon, so vigorously that something spilled out from under his sweater. "And neither homicide nor superstitious claptrap are going to keep me from bringing them to light! The bones will speak!"

Rankin finally realized that the partners were staring at the object that had fallen from the waistband of his slacks, a snub-nosed revolver. Emmett didn't feel threatened by the unexpected appearance of the weapon. The opposite was true. He felt pity for Thaddeus Rankin, a sick and aging man, ridiculed by his peers and frightened for his life. Bilbao's murder had shaken him, and he was holed up in his musty fortress with a handgun and a New Guinean tribesman, waiting for the killer to make his next move, wildly accusing anyone and everyone of being that killer.

Kawatu helped Rankin to his feet. The anthropologist looked confused, but in his distraction he remembered his guests. Enough awareness survived in that troubled mind for him to seem slightly embarrassed. "Again, it's been a bad day. Good days and bad days. Thank you for coming. Kawatu will take you back to your car."

10

Through the rain-streaked glass of her window, Anna watched the dark shape of a head break the surface of the swimming pool. It was Emmett's. Returning from Dr. Rankin's estate to the Kah-Nee-Ta late this afternoon, they'd planned to have dinner together. Yet, after a brief parting to freshen up, Emmett showed up at her door in a pair of swimming trunks and announced he was going to skip dinner. That was it. No invitation to join him in the pool. He then went down the stairwell, his rubber thongs slapping the wet cement.

At first, Anna passed it off as his exhaustion. And, on the drive back, he'd said he expected the dining room, like the rest of the reservation, to be in an ugly mood after the wounding of Tennyson Paulina by a white state trooper. But then, as she sat alone in her room, Emmett's skipping dinner with her took on such dire overtones she broke her vow never to disturb Dr. Tischler at home. She left a message with the psychiatrist's answering service, trying not to sound hysterical to the operator but making it clear that she needed help this evening.

Then Anna sat beside the window to wait.

Maintenance had turned off the pool lights, probably because there were few bathers this time of year, and only the casino sign made Emmett visible. He backstroked across the pool, leaving a phosphorescent wake. Was he thinking of a graceful way to back out of Anna Turnipseed's life? Would her circle of intimate relations be reduced again to a mother with Alzheimer's who no longer recognized her? Loneliness was obscene to a Modoc, and she knew that a solitary, work-oriented existence would only intensify the sense that she'd done something terribly wrong to wind up alone.

At last, her phone rang.

"Special Agent Turnipseed," she said, in case the call was job-related.

"Anna, how are we doing tonight?"

The quiet calm in Dr. Tischler's voice somehow promised that everything could be worked out, given patience and effort. But this burst of dependent euphoria swiftly faded and Anna had to admit, "Not so well, Myra."

"Going through a particularly tough memory right now?"

"No."

"Then what?"

"I really hate to bother you like this."

"Tell me."

"Since leaving Las Vegas, Emmett and I have been drifting apart."

"And how's that make you feel?"

"Pissed off, powerless. The same old demons."

"I know—I can hear them in your voice." Then Dr. Tischler asked, "Where's the 541 area code?"

"Oregon, we're up here on a case together. I'm sure part of it is that we're both so tired. We've been run ragged ever since we arrived almost a week ago, and there's been no time for us, the exercises you gave us. Still, I don't want to read too much into his mood."

"Might be wise," Dr. Tischler interjected.

"But it's more than that."

"How can you be sure?"

"I just am, and now I'm afraid we won't ever get back together again." Anna didn't realize how distressed she was until her voice suddenly cracked. Talking to Myra always seemed like a one-on-one with God, an all-seeing female deity who could make pretense crumble with a simple *How does that make you feel?* "And . . ." She couldn't make herself complete the thought.

"And what, Anna?"

There was an evil here that was drawing more and more victims into its vortex. Over the last few days, she had begun to wonder if, before that faceless evil had run its course, she'd be counted among those victims. Too paranoid an intuition to be shared with a psychiatrist. "I guess that's it, Myra."

On the other end of the line, there was the rattle of ice in a glass. "I really don't understand why anybody would want to go into law enforcement." Strong words from a woman who measured everything that came out of her mouth. Did she have that many screwed-up cops for patients? "Where's Emmett now?"

"Out in the swimming pool," Anna replied.

"Did you swim together before you called?"

"No. He made it pretty obvious he wasn't in the mood for company."

"So he went down to the pool fully clothed?"

"No, in a suit. What're you saying, Myra?"

Then, without precedent, the psychiatrist sounded exasperated with her. "Did he stand in front of you dressed only in a swimsuit and say 'Don't bother me, Anna'?"

"Kind of."

"Part of healthy sexuality is the ability to look at your partner's unclothed body and not numb out or lapse into dissociative fantasies, right?"

Anna tried not to sound too hopeful. "You think that's what Emmett was asking me to do?"

"I can't answer for him. But healthy sexuality is playful. Go play with Emmett, Anna."

With that, Dr. Tischler hung up.

Stung, Anna stared at the receiver in her grasp. *Well, screw you too, Myra.* She swore to herself that she wouldn't go down to the pool if it were the last option on earth. She felt as if she'd just been unfairly spanked. But then fear rushed in, fear that the gulf between Emmett and her would only widen if left untended. She always packed her swimsuit, thinking to soak in the hotel's Jacuzzi if the day's work left her too wired for sleep. She'd never used a hot tub on the road, but the suit always found its way into her carry-on bag.

She decided not to give herself time to invent an excuse.

So, five minutes later, she crept out into the exterior corridor, clasping her semiautomatic and room key in a bath towel. The rain seemed within a degree or two of turning to snow, and as she padded from the building the drops felt like ice on her bare skin. Emmett's face was turned away from her. He didn't react to the sound of her scooting a lawn chair over to poolside. She wrapped the towel around her 9mm several times, then set it on the chair. All gooseflesh, she felt ridiculously vulnerable. And prudish in her modest bathing suit that was the same blue as her FBI-issue windbreaker.

She dived in.

She'd braced for cool water, but it was very, very warm. Her plunge felt like gliding into another world, an entirely new dimension with a caressing atmosphere in which all sound was softly muted behind a rush of bubbles. She was a river otter, sleek and buoyant. Movement was not only effortless, it reminded her that she had a body, and that awareness was exhilarating. She waited for the sensation to fade, or to sour into guilt. But it didn't. There were no terrible memories involving water.

Feeling liberated, she flutter-kicked to the surface and splashed Emmett in the face.

• • •

Emmett liked the patter of the rain on the pool. Floating on his back, he peered up into the dark murk, his eyelids twitching from the cold strikes of the raindrops. The past five days had been crammed with too much dulling detail, and now—suspended on a liquid membrane between sky and earth—he waited for an overview to take shape in his weary mind. Years ago, he had levitated much like this on a cushion of excruciating pain. That had been during the Gaze at the Sun Suspended finale of the Sun Dance, when he'd hung on tethers attached to his pectoral muscles. In a godlike flash, he had seen how alcohol and divorce had fractured his life. Left unresolved, these issues would consume him. Since that day eleven years ago, he had mastered booze, but the relationship with a woman that would free him to explore the neglected corners of his life—that remained doggedly elusive.

What is Nels Sward up to?

The question shot up out of his subconscious. All human beings have an agenda, however outwardly irrational those purposes might seem to the uninitiated.

But what the devil had Nels Sward tried to do by sending his wife to capture some of Tennyson Paulina's semen?

Sward had spent much of his adult life among the Navajo, who carefully guarded their cut hair, their fingernail clippings, even their feces from falling into the hands of others. The reason was simple, once you understood the Navajo. These by-products of the body could be used by a skinwalker, or male witch, to cast spells to sicken and even kill a careless person. Had Nels Sward fused this concept with something in white paganism?

If so, why would he want to destroy Tennyson Paulina?

Emmett couldn't project himself inside Sward's head. Although he could see how ancient Norse religion resembled traditional Indian spirituality in some ways, he just couldn't believe that modern whites would put stock in spells and charms. Maybe he was out of step with the New Age. What had that feminist speaker up at the Timberline Saturday night said about goddesses? *A time when goddesses reigned supreme?*

He was trying to fit this insight into the conundrum of Elsa Dease's disappearance and Gorka Bilbao's murder, when something plunged into the water beside him. Instantly, he thought of his revolver, still in his room, until Anna's laugh made him lower his upraised hands. He started to yell at her for scaring the crap out of him. That left his mouth open for a splash full in the face. He swam toward her, puzzled by her mood. She laughed again, teasingly. Was she setting him up for another disappointment?

She darted out of reach and somersaulted under the surface.

He circled around, looking for her in the depths. He'd heard something new in her laughter, a natural abandon, nothing forced or uneasy about it. Had she been drinking? It seemed inconceivable to Emmett, given her bitterness toward her father's alcoholism, but this notion seemed no more inconceivable than her frolicking around him like a porpoise.

There was a yank on the fanny of his trunks, and he tried to catch her hand. Missed. And she was gone again.

Submerging beneath the surface, he glimpsed her spiraling off toward the far end of the pool. He gave chase, a slow and plodding farm-pond swimmer. She, on the other hand, seemed born to the water. Reaching the shallow end, he stood, wiped his eyes and searched for her. He'd just shuffled halfway around when something wet slapped into his face and clung to it. He pried it off—her suit.

Heart quickening, he thrashed out into the middle of the pool, wondering if she'd ever let herself be caught now. He was tempted to beg her not to do this. Given one more letdown, he didn't know what he'd do.

The water got quiet around him. There was no sound but that of the rain. "If you don't want to be found," he called out huskily, "tell me, for godsake."

From somewhere across the pool, she said, "Polo."

He stroked for the last position of her voice, expecting her to be gone. But she was there, defined by a shadow and the turbulence of her churning legs.

"Marco," he whispered.

"Polo," she repeated.

"You lost this." He handed her the suit, and she heaved it over her shoulder. It landed with a plop on the deck. Then he said, "I didn't know you liked the water so much."

"Neither did I."

He reached out and took hold of her thin waist. The smooth feel of her skin made him hungrily draw her into him, but at that moment she let out her air and slowly sank. He followed her down until his toes touched the bottom. Her face approached his. Her underwater kiss tickled his lips with a frenzy of tiny bubbles.

Then they both had to rise.

He gulped in the rainy night air and chuckled. Her fingers were busy at the cord that held up his trunks. He'd accidentally knotted it, but felt that helping her would somehow be wrong. Her head bobbed as she struggled to loosen his suit and tread water at the same time.

Behind her, a fountain of wicked-looking orange whooshed up into the sky. The fireball illuminated the parking lot above the lodge, and the blastlike concussion tripped off car alarms. Anna looked and groaned, "No, no, no."

"Stay here," Emmett said, hopping up onto the deck, "while I get my revolver."

"Take my nine-mil. It's in the towel."

Climbing out, he tossed her suit to her, took his room key from the small pocket in his trunks and laid it on the deck chair. "Get my revolver and join me in the lot." Grabbing her pistol, he ran for the fire, which was getting bigger.

At its flaming core he could make out the boxy shape of a Ford Explorer. He was already halfway up the landscaped slope when he realized that he'd left his thongs at the pool. The cold asphalt of the road burned the soles of his feet, reawakened the twinges of old frostbite damage to his toes. Quickly, he decided not to come into the lot by the only lane that entered and left it. That approach might deliver him directly into the high beams of a fleeing Dodge diesel. Instead, he angled up the barren extension of the slope above the road. It was in shadow, but the steep surface was a slick gumbo of mud and pebbles. He had to dig his fingers of his left hand into the ooze as he laboriously ascended.

Reaching the lot, he knelt behind a car and studied the scene. All doubt was erased: The engulfed vehicle was the Explorer Anna and he had checked out of the FBI motor pool in Portland. The hottest part of the fire was located under the chassis of the sport utility, which meant that the tank had been punctured to let the gasoline pool beneath the vehicle. The tank had been less than a quarter full—Emmett had intended to fill up tomorrow morning in Warm Springs—and the blaze was already starting to subside.

Arsonists are often drawn like moths to their own handiwork. Advancing on the Explorer with the pistol down at his side, Emmett checked the hillside above the lot and the parked cars. The only onlookers were gathering outside the entrance to the lobby. The auto alarms had quit.

Anna's voice echoed up from the road. "Em?"

"I'm okay."

"Is it ours?"

"Yeah." He decided that if the gas tank hadn't blown by now, it wouldn't. Thankfully, the lot was unpaved, so there'd been no asphalt to catch fire. The last orange flickerings were dying on the ground, but there was a glow of combustion inside the Explorer, no doubt from the arsonist having splashed gas around the interior—the driver's door lock button was up. The paint was still bubbling on the facing surfaces of the cars to either side of the FBI vehicle, and the rain sizzled against the hot metal.

Anna joined him in front of the grille, the coolest place to stand, and draped a blanket around his shoulders.

She had his revolver, and they traded weapons.

Then she froze. "There's something inside."

The windows were sooted over, proof that the interior fire was extinguishing itself for lack of oxygen. "What?"

"I don't know—something's behind the wheel."

Peering through a clear patch on the windshield just above the defroster vents, Emmett believed that he could make out a headlike shape bending forward from the neck-rest. His stomach knotted up. Would the victims now be delivered to Anna and him? It would be a convenience he didn't want, for it meant that the two of them were being watched.

Once again, he scanned all around. No one.

A jingling of keys and the bob of a flashlight marked the arrival of hotel security. The two guns made the guard uneasy until Anna showed her credentials. "What's the ETA for the fire department?" she asked.

"Three or four minutes."

"Excuse me," Emmett said, borrowing the flashlight from the man. Using the blanket as a heat shield, he stepped up to the driver's-side door and aimed the beam through the black-coated window. Impenetrable. He would wait for the firemen; opening the door might only reignite the oxygen-starved fire. Withdrawing, he stepped to the front of the Explorer once more, trying to recall any vehicles that had left the lot while he was in the pool. But Anna had had all his attention. She took his hand. Was she frightened, simply trying to reassure him, or both? Her eyes were inscrutable, and she was fully dressed again.

They tracked the progress of emergency lights up the hill. The sirens died, and the engines lumbered into the lot. Emmett and Anna let go of each other and backed off while a tribal fireman doused the

Explorer with foam. As soon as the retardant stopped boiling off the vehicle, Emmett waded through the knee-deep suds to the driver's door again. The scum left by the foam only made the glass more opaque. He motioned a fireman over. The man wore protective gloves. "Open it for me, will you?"

Anna came to Emmett's side.

The fireman wrenched back the door, and all three of them gasped as a gush of noxious-smelling air flowed out of the interior.

Choking, Emmett pushed forward and directed the flashlight on the front seat. A fully articulated skeleton sat there, hands braced on the steering wheel as if the phantom were driving. It seemed animated, alive for a split second. To Emmett's back, Anna said, "Oh God." This seemed to trigger the collapse of the charred bones. The skull pitched off the shoulders and bounced to the floor. Vertebrae and limb bones tumbled helter-skelter around Emmett's bare feet.

Stooping, he picked up a femur and examined it. Small. Indicative of a woman.

Anna must have recognized the same fact, for she asked under her breath, "Do you think it's Elsa?"

• • •

At nightfall, Minnie Claw was returning to her home village of Simnasho along the Wapinitia Road when her headlights blinked twice, then went out for good. Darkness immediately enveloped her old Chevy Biscayne, but she saw that the windshield wipers had stopped in mid-stroke. She'd turned her hearing aid down because road noise bothered her, so she wasn't aware that the engine had died too until she pressed the accelerator and the car continued to slow. She began to veer off the pavement, but the darkness to the right suggested a plunging cliff. She held the heavy steering wheel straight as she braked to a stop in the right lane.

The Sahaptin elder sat back.

She had spent the day in The Dalles, selling her beaded cloth bags on consignment to the trading post stores. She would've made it home before nightfall, but a strange sight along the White River had made her pull over. White people queerly dressed in cloaks and animal skins.

Holding torches, they were scattered along the banks of the river as if searching for something. It had given Minnie an uncomfortable feeling to see white people behaving even more strangely than usual, so she drove on without asking them what they were doing.

Turning the key now, she tried to restart the motor.

But it was no good, so she sat back again.

The rain came down hard, like fingers drumming the Chevy's roof. As the minutes passed, the interior of the car got chilly. With her hearing-aid volume at its next to lowest setting, Minnie could barely hear the downpour. But suddenly a sound broke through this soft roar, a bird trilling sweetly. Its song was startlingly clear. "Oh no," the old woman said out loud. No bird sang in the darkness until shortly before dawn. There was only one thing to do. She fumbled inside her purse for a book of matches. This was no bird calling. It was a stick Indian, a bonelike spirit that dwelt in forlorn places. By mimicking enchanting birdsong, a stick Indian could beguile a person out into the wilds, then deprive that poor soul of reason. Eternal madness and wandering ensued.

Minnie Claw knew how to handle a stick Indian.

She ripped the paper matches from the book, then climbed out of the car. It was very dark, and the rain quickly soaked through her kerchief. But, feeling her way around the Chevy, she dropped the matches in a protective circle. Stick Indians were fond of matches, as they dwelt in darkness, so the offering was bound to send this one away, satisfied.

But then a troubling thought occurred to Minnie.

Elsa Dease had vanished not far from here. The girl's mother didn't like to hear such things, but Minnie resolved to tell Vernita that a stick Indian was to blame. The moment she'd heard of Elsa's disappearance, Minnie had suspected that the Ancient One's disrupted burial along the John Day River was the cause. Now she knew how. Outrage had transformed the Ancient One into a stick Indian.

Lights broke around a bend in the road.

Minnie faced them, shading her eyes with a hand. Brakes locked and tires skidded. The vehicle, a police car, came sideways at the old woman, and she cradled her head in her hands. But it stopped a few feet short of her. The tribal policeman put on his blinking blue lights and got out. It was Gabriel Round Dance.

"Minnie," he loudly exclaimed, "what're you doing stopped in the middle of the road!"

Gabriel was respectful of the old ways, so she told him, "A stick Indian was tryin' to snatch me."

He gave her a long, thoughtful look, then indicated her Chevy with his flashlight. He said words in a normal voice, but she didn't catch them.

Minnie boosted her hearing-aid volume. "What, Gabe?"

"Something wrong with your car?"

She'd forgotten. "Oh yes. The stick Indian made it stop workin' so he could get me. Nothin' works on it. Lights, wipers, nothin'."

Gabriel took off his jacket and covered her, then tried to start her car.

"See," she said with satisfaction. After telling Gabriel about the stick Indian's mischief, she'd been afraid the motor might fire right up.

Gabriel popped the hood and studied the engine. "Battery," he declared after jiggling something. "The connection for your negative battery cable is all corroded." He got in behind the wheel, and her engine coughed to life, her lights came on. "This will get you home, Minnie. But get that cable fixed at Warm Springs Chevron tomorrow."

"Okay."

Gabriel got out and stretched a kink in his back. Minnie returned his police jacket to him, and he paused while putting it on to listen to a voice on his radio. There was talk of a car fire at the Kah-Nee-Ta Resort. Arson, the woman's voice said.

"Thank you, Gabe," Minnie said.

"No problem."

She expected him to head south toward the Kah-Nee-Ta, but Round Dance continued north toward Wapinitia. Soon his lights were lost in the rain. Minnie had to wipe the mist off the inside of her windshield before going on. Gabriel was a nice Wasco boy, but she would not go to the Chevron station tomorrow. A battery cable had not been the cause of the energy being drained out of her Chevy. That, clearly, had been the work of a stick Indian. It was horribly dangerous to have one loose in the countryside. This hadn't happened in many years. She must warn all the people to be on their guard until this spirit could be coaxed back into the ground.

Nearing the crest, Minnie suddenly let up on the gas pedal.

There was movement across the road.

She expected to see a wild horse, a deer or even a rare mountain lion, but—as she coasted nearer—what she saw made her gasp. Everything became clear with a heart-wrenching shock.

"Poor child," the old woman whispered mournfully as she sped up again. "Poor, poor child."

11

"Appreciate you doing this on such short notice, Doctor," Anna said. Thaddeus Rankin was leaning on Kawatu's arm in the lobby of the Mid-Columbia Medical Center in The Dalles. "And sorry for the hour." One-thirty in the morning.

Rankin waved off her apology. He still looked sickly, but his head and limbs were slightly less palsied than they'd been this afternoon. "Where are the remains?" he asked.

"Emmett's bringing them from the unit." They'd borrowed a tribal police cruiser for the seventy-mile dash from the Kah-Nee-Ta.

At that moment, Emmett burst through the emergency entrance, wheeling a gurney before him. On it were several boxes.

Rankin and Kawatu led the partners to the elevator. Once inside the car, the anthropologist glanced at the boxes and asked incredulously, "The bones were actually articulated in a sitting position behind the wheel of your vehicle?"

"That's a fact," Emmett replied. "Then they collapsed around my feet."

"Curious," Rankin murmured.

Emmett exchanged reserved nods with Kawatu, who so far had said nothing. This made Anna suspect that the New Guinean might be put off by this unreasonable demand on his ailing mentor.

But it didn't feel unreasonable to Anna.

She and Emmett had to know if this was Elsa Dease. Tonight. If so, her killer had come to the Kah-Nee-Ta six hours ago, and the trail would never be hotter. Apparently, Rankin had grasped the urgency as well, for he'd immediately agreed to meet the partners in The Dalles, even though Anna had given him the chance to beg off because of his health. She'd pumped a fist in the air when he didn't, for God only knew how long it would take to hunt up a certified osteopathic pathologist in the boondocks of Oregon.

They got off the elevator in the basement. Rankin's halting gait slowed them all to a crawl, and he winked self-consciously at Anna and Emmett. "Thankfully, I was already awake when you called. Waiting."

"Waiting for what?" Anna asked.

"Kawatu to return from the Okanogan Sheriff's Office along the Canadian border with some specimens. They wanted me to look at a few bones, possibly human. Wasted trip—turned out to be mule deer."

"No matter, sir," Kawatu said, "I feel fine."

Anna was still running on adrenaline, but she offered, "Can I get you two some coffee?"

Rankin shook his head as Kawatu opened a wide door for him and switched on the lights inside the autopsy suite. At its center were three human-sized stainless steel trays. Emmett pushed the gurney up to the first of them, then looked at Rankin.

"Begin," the anthropologist told Kawatu.

The Warm Springs firemen had offered a body bag in which to transport the skeleton, but the fire-blackened bones were as brittle as chalk. Anna and Emmett had had the tribal cops ransack their station for all the packing material they could find.

Kawatu unraveled a wad of bubble wrap. In it was the toothless lower jaw, and he pivoted in obvious surprise to Rankin.

"What is it, Doctor?" Anna asked.

"As you'll recall with John Day Man, the mandible was the major bone we never found. Interesting. Any teeth still affixed to this specimen's upper jaw?"

"No," Emmett said.

"And what do you make of that, Mr. Parker?"

"Could be an attempt to delay identification. But most of the bones were too charred for me to tell if the teeth had been yanked after death."

Anna could no longer hold back the question that'd been gnawing at her since her shock wore off in the lodge's parking lot. "Do the remains look ancient to you, Doctor?"

"Patience, Ms. Turnipseed."

The man was right. So far, Kawatu had unpacked only a half dozen bones. Unsteadily, Rankin rested the mandible near the head of the table, then asked her, "Do you have Ms. Dease's dental records?"

"With no teeth in these jaws, are they needed?"

"X rays might show unusual mandible and maxilla characteristics."

Anna made a mental note to contact Vernita Dease for the name of Elsa's dentist. She didn't look forward to telling the Shaker woman that her daughter's remains might have been found. The tribal police had debated contacting Vernita earlier tonight, but in the end decided to ask Round Dance first. Numerous radio attempts to reach the sergeant, who was on duty, had gone unanswered.

"Elsa's height?" Rankin asked, inspecting a femur.

"Five four," Anna replied.

"Is that *confirmed*?"

"Yes." By the records of a tribally hosted beauty pageant.

"Sliding caliper," Rankin said to Kawatu, and the assistant smartly slapped the instrument into his palm. Steadying his hands with a visible act of will, the anthropologist measured the head of the thighbone—and frowned. "Forty-two millimeters."

Anna had to ask. "Meaning?"

"Probably female," Emmett answered quietly for Rankin. "In fact, right in the middle of the range for a modern female."

Rankin gave Emmett a grudging smile. "Bravo, Oklahoma State."

Kawatu had finally laid enough bones out on the table for the skeleton to take on dimensions. Short. It was clearly short enough to be Elsa Dease's. Emmett had doubly wrapped the skull, so a minute passed in prickly silence before the New Guinean nestled the cranium in a donut ring.

"Is that all?" Rankin tipped the last box to glance inside.

"Yes," Emmett answered. With all remains now exposed, the atmosphere in the suite stank of char.

"Grand. We're missing the pelvic bone." Rankin rotated the blackened skull so that he could peer into the face. It was narrow to moderately round, Anna thought, trying to recall Rankin's lecture last week on the racial differences between braincases and faces. Her imagination superimposed Elsa's arresting brown eyes over the hollow sockets. "Definite Caucasoid characteristics," Rankin proclaimed.

Anna's heart sank. Elsa, of course, was half white.

"Magnifier, Kawatu."

As soon as the assistant brought an illuminated magnifier from a cabinet across the room, Rankin motioned for Emmett to have a look through the big lens. "All right, Mr. Anthropology Minor from Oklahoma State, age this specimen."

Accepting the challenge, Emmett shifted the cranium. The contact left soot on his fingertips. "Surface texture's been badly scored by the fire."

"I didn't ask you for reasons why you can't age it, Mr. Parker." While Emmett ignored him and studied the skull from various angles, Rankin said to Anna, "The distinct plates of a baby's skull gradually fuse together over a lifetime. The cracks in those plates are called sutures—"

"There's some obliteration of the interpalatine suture," Emmett interrupted, "and moderate obliteration of the incisive." He stood erect and waited for the anthropologist's reaction.

Rankin scowled.

Anna asked, "Wrong?"

"No," Rankin said with a belated smirk, "he's right. This individual was between eighteen and fifty years old."

Again, Anna had to fight her disappointment. Elsa was twenty-six. Only a year younger than herself.

Kawatu was taking out a vertebra when something fell out of the bubble wrap and floated delicately down to the surface of the autopsy tray. "What's that?" Rankin asked.

Emmett, who was closest to it, said, "Looks too fragile to pick up with my fingers."

"Tweezers, Kawatu."

Given them, Emmett gingerly transferred the fist-sized piece of mesh to the magnifier. "It appears to be a Mid-Columbian fishnet," Rankin said, his right eye made big and blurry by the lens, "probably woven from nettle fiber, as it's still fairly pliable. Size of the mesh—say,

two inches—indicates use for catching salmon. Preserve it, Kawatu."
While the New Guinean put the artifact in a plastic bag, the anthropologist further explained, "Might be the answer to the collapse of
your skeleton. The bones were wrapped in a fishnet, which was weakened by the flash-fire inside your vehicle. The net disintegrated as soon
as you opened the door and let oxygen into this virtual vacuum."
Rankin moved on to some vertebrae. "Also, there could've been enough
desiccated tendons and ligaments remaining on the bones to keep portions of the skeleton articulated. Note this, Kawatu—arthritic lipping
on five of the lower discs. From repetitive activity of some sort, possibly horseback riding."

Kawatu wrote down the observation.

Again, bad news. On her beauty pageant application, Elsa had listed
horseback riding as one of her hobbies.

Rankin picked up the mandible again, scanned it under the magnifier. He pointed out a pit that was twice as large as the hole left by the
roots of a molar. "Have you ever seen a truly bad abscess before, Ms.
Turnipseed?"

She was in no mood for guessing games. "No, why?"

"One like this would have been excruciating. The most penniless
street person would seek and receive treatment for inflammation
this advanced." Rankin held her eyes with a tenderness she found
disarming—it disconcerted her that he could be appealing as well as
tempestuous and arrogant. Before the onset of his illness, he must
have been enormously attractive, although in a way that brought out
any self-destructive tendencies in his admirers. "I doubt antibiotics existed when this white male was at the height of his suffering."

Male? She began paying complete attention again. "You mean, we
have another fourteen-thousand-year-old skeleton?"

"No, my dear. These remains are probably nineteenth century,
which accounts for the individual's diminutive stature. Five four or
five was average height for a man in those days. He might've lost his
teeth while still alive due to lack of care and nutrition. No evidence of
trauma to any of the bones, but there are enough unfused sutures in
the cranium for me to suggest he died well before the age of fifty. We'll
run some further tests, but only to satisfy our curiosity. In terms of a

homicide case, it's safe to say this is beyond the province of modern law enforcement." Then he turned on Emmett with a smile. At first, Anna thought it was relieved, but then Rankin's sarcasm was unmistakable. "Any idea, Mr. Parker, who would leave such a macabre calling card on your doorstep?"

Emmett wiped the soot off his fingers into his handkerchief. "No, not yet."

Rankin continued, "Then you're a better man than I."

"Why's that?"

"I can't imagine myself taking this sort of intimidation lying down."

"Lying down?" Emmett repeated hotly.

Kawatu stepped between the two men, and Anna realized that Emmett's frustration was about to boil over. Parker had an inch in height over the New Guinean, but both were heavily muscled. As she tried to think of some way to defuse the moment, Rankin nudged his assistant back out of the way with his cane. "Everything's quite all right, my dear boy," he said unconvincingly. "I understand your defensiveness tonight, Mr. Parker."

"Who's being defensive?"

"Then forgive my choice of words. You and your partner have been targeted, and that has to be upsetting."

"Do I look upset?"

Anna decided to intervene before she wound up alone on this detail. "Why do you think we're being targeted, Doctor?" she asked.

"You're the principal investigators."

"But we're not," Anna argued. "We're heading up the missing person investigation on Elsa, but Bilbao's murder is Crook County's case. In the end, we'll do little more than testify as witnesses to the crime scene."

"I mean, you two are perceived as being the principal investigators," Rankin said ambiguously.

"By the local Indians? Paulina's still in the Redmond hospital under guard, but you mean some of his followers?"

Rankin had to ponder that for a few seconds. "Possibly, but I'd take a hard look at any aboriginal touches to these crimes. They could be intentionally misleading."

Emmett asked acidly, "Then who left a Sahaptin salmon net and a skeleton in our cruiser this evening? Deborah Carter? As what, a warning for us to back off?"

"To the best of my recollection, you got in the colonel's face over something at her headquarters." Rankin looked tired and sick again. "I don't pretend to know all the nuances involved here, Mr. Parker. My concerns are purely evidentiary. Do what your instincts tell you to do. Kawatu, I believe we've used up all the gratitude we earned by coming here in the middle of the night." The anthropologist went out on his assistant's arm, his shoes skimming the tile floor.

Once alone with Emmett, Anna spun on him. "What'd you do that for?"

He shrugged.

"Don't repercussions mean anything to you?"

"Fuck the repercussions. When you're given a difficult and thankless job, be difficult and thankless." Emmett began repacking the bones. "Rankin wants to personally ramrod the investigation. He figures two native cops aren't smart enough to do it. That's all this little head-butt was about. Control. Let's get the skeleton to the Wasco County coroner for safekeeping, then try to get some sleep."

"Two o'clock, Sunday morning . . ." She paused to get a grip on her temper.

"What about Sunday morning?"

"You insisted we come here to The Dalles to jack up Carter about Elsa's disappearance. What's changed your mind about her?"

"Finding Bilbao the way we did." He finally looked at Anna. "I don't give a damn what makes Deborah Carter tick, I don't care about her proclivities—they don't teach you in engineering school how to do the kinds of things that were done to Gorka Bilbao."

• • •

The repercussions began at 6:17 the next morning with a phone call from the U.S. Attorney in Portland. Not from one of his aides, the man himself. Despite her fuzzy-headedness, Anna quickly surmised that Thaddeus Rankin had called in some favors, and the federal prosecutor was doing the anthropologist's bidding, however much he tried to make this sound like a few words of friendly advice. "By chance, is Parker KMA?" he asked, obviously familiar with FBI acronyms. *KMA* stood for *kiss my ass* and was used to describe agents eligible for retirement.

Sitting up in bed, Anna resorted to some CYPA—*cover your partner's ass.* "No, sir. Rankin was throwing his weight around, trying to call our shots for us, and if Parker hadn't put him in his place, I would have."

"Well, Thad Rankin's been a tremendous ally of law enforcement in the Northwest for a long time, so I think we can put up with a little of his eccentric bluster. I can't begin to name all the cases he's closed for us. Usually pro bono." Free of charge. "The crime labs in the region are swamped all the time, and you can't imagine the load he takes off them. Do I make myself clear?"

"Yes, sir." Through the open door to the adjoining room, she heard bedsprings clack. As a precaution, Emmett and she had taken new rooms at the Kah-Nee-Ta last night, and he'd suggested that they not shut the connecting door.

The U.S. Attorney sighed. "You guys getting *any* fix on what's going on out there?"

She decided a confession of ignorance wouldn't be well received. "Political heat could be coming from the tribes."

"Oh?" Instant worry. "What're you hearing?"

"The Warm Springs council, especially the Paiute councilpersons, feel Crook County is holding Tennyson Paulina and his followers without cause."

"That true?"

"Their shoe prints were all over the scene at the cabin. But Parker and I had a voicemail message from the state police polygraph examiner waiting for us when we got back to the lodge last night. . . ."

"And?"

"Paulina passed the box." The Paiute had refused to take his pain pills until he was given the test. Anna didn't mention the examiner's question to her—*Are there any meditative aspects to Indian spiritual practices that might be used to defeat the exam?* He had also reported that the sheriff doubted the veracity of the test. "And," she went on to the U.S. Attorney, "Paulina's followers are sticking to the story he told Parker and me—Bilbao was dead when they got to his cabin. There's no blood evidence to link them to the fossil hunter's body, and a killing like that had to be bloody."

"You and Parker witnessed the trooper shooting Paulina?"

"Yes, sir."

"Either of you see a weapon in the Indian's possession?"

"I didn't," Anna replied, "but from my angle his right hand wasn't visible. Seconds after the trooper fired, Parker saw a cigarette pack in Paulina's hand. The foil glinted in his flashlight beam like gunmetal."

"Lord. What's the Crook County sheriff up to?"

"Not sure. Maybe he and the local state police commander are afraid to release Paulina. He'll stir up trouble over the shooting."

"You sure? That's no reason to hold, what—six people?"

"Yes, sir. Six." Though tempted, she didn't add that, in much of the rural West, Indians were invariably the usual suspects.

"Doesn't the sheriff trust the polygraph?"

She finally admitted, "I hear there's talk in the department that Paulina witched the box."

"*Witched the box?*" the prosecutor echoed skeptically.

"Used Indian magic to mask deceitful responses."

"Is this sheriff Native American?"

"No."

"Then what's with him? Why would he believe in Indian voodoo?"

"Surprising the number of whites in Indian Country who believe in our voodoo." Something even Gorka Bilbao had known.

The prosecutor didn't catch her mild protest. "What's the polygraph examiner make of all this?"

"He says Paulina's probably clean."

The U.S. Attorney sighed again. "You think I should get the Bend FBI office ready for a civil rights investigation over this shooting?"

Anna hesitated. That would end any cooperation from all the local sheriffs' offices; the detectives would speak to Emmett and her only through their association attorneys, weighing every word as if they might accidentally incriminate themselves. "Let's see what happens in the next few days, sir. If none of the Paiutes crack, they might get kicked loose with no pressure from us. And in fairness to the sheriff, he might be waiting for just that—one of Paulina's people to break ranks and talk."

"Okay, keep me informed." Cupping his palm over the handset, he still could be heard speaking to someone in his office. "Listen, Turnipseed, I'm going to fax you guys some material on Deborah Carter. It's sensitive, so stand by in the hotel office for its arrival. . . ." He then proceeded to lay out the need for follow-up on the colonel, just as Rankin had mentioned, but made it sound as if Emmett and she were to go through the motions only so some investigative legwork could be reported back to the anthropologist. "Use the leverage of the missing person case. Can you do that for me to help keep Thad Rankin on our team?"

Anna agreed, knowing that there was no choice in the matter.

Hanging up, she saw Emmett standing sleepily in the doorway. He was shirtless but had remembered to put on his trousers. "What's up?"

He'd caused all of this with his burst of ill temper at the hospital last night. "Not much, Em. You can fuck the repercussions and stay here. I'm going to kiss ass and start working Carter by reinterviewing Vernita Dease."

Emmett muttered something surly under his breath and padded back into his room, but when she returned from the office twenty minutes later with the bulky fax, he was dressed to go. Grabbing two cups of coffee from the breakfast buffet, they trooped wordlessly down to the maintenance garage, where their loaner vehicle from the tribal PD was secured. Another Explorer was on the way from the FBI motor pool in Portland. On his hands and knees, Emmett scanned the undercarriage of the patrol car for explosive devices.

It was only thirteen miles to Simnasho, but Emmett refused to drive, even though it was his turn. Stretched out in the passenger seat, he thumbed lethargically through Deborah Carter's service record. The clouds were low on the hills, and the road wound up into the drizzle. Wild horses stood on a ridge, their coats slick from the rain that had fallen on and off all night.

Anna hadn't had a chance to read the fax, and she didn't want this brooding silence to last the rest of the day. "Anything interesting?"

"Yeah," Emmett said, "Carter's in the army." But several minutes later, he threw Anna a tidbit: "And she's fluent in Russian."

"Then this might have international implications?"

"It better. Otherwise the Crook County sheriff is going to be damned ticked about us horning in on his homicide."

It was a hint of humor, which encouraged Anna that he was coming around. Yet, when she pulled up in front of Vernita Dease's trim little house near the Shaker church, he declined her offer to go inside and went on reading Carter's file. Getting out, she slammed the car door.

The tempo of the rain had picked up again.

From the way Vernita answered the bell, it was clear that she already had company. And was expecting bad news. Invited inside the living room, Anna quickly explained, "I have nothing to report, Mrs. Dease. I just needed to talk to you again." After an aching pause, she added, "The tribal police told me where you live. Do you mind giving me a minute?"

The Shaker woman exhibited no relief, just the weight of her vigil falling around her shoulders again. "It probably doesn't matter," she said, puzzling Anna.

There was no opportunity to ask Vernita what she meant, for an elder was sitting hunched on the sofa. Anna had last seen the old woman with Elsa at the dig along the John Day River—the kerchief and hearing aid jogged her memory.

"Ms. Turnipseed," Vernita said, "this is Mrs. Minnie Claw, a long-time member of our community." Not how one introduced even the remotest relative.

Minnie's eyes showed recognition. "Ah, the Modoc girl who talks funny Sahaptin."

"That's right." Sitting in an armchair, Anna knew that any questioning would have to wait until Minnie excused herself. The woman gave no indication that she intended to leave anytime soon, and it'd be a breach of etiquette to ask for a moment of privacy with Vernita. The interior of the Deases' living room was as ethereally white as that of the Shaker church itself, and an ersatz ivory cross hung on the wall behind the elder.

Vernita said, "Minnie, you may as well tell Ms. Turnipseed about the sighting."

"You Modocs got stick Indians down your way?" Minnie asked outright.

Anna searched her exhausted mind. "I don't believe so."

"Maybe you call them *skep-ma*?" Vernita prompted.

Anna was familiar with the term *skep*, which was pronounced *scape*. The spirit of a deceased person, often glimpsed as a skeleton, that had such a genius for evil that no human could remain sane in its mind-warping presence. "Yes, I know what you mean. Did you see a *skep*, Minnie?"

"Last night," the old woman said confidentially, "a stick Indian made my car quit up on the grade. Motor, lights, everythin' went out."

"The grade on Wapinitia Road?" Anna tried to clarify, already not liking the sound of this.

"Yes, that's the place."

"Did you actually see the stick Indian, Minnie?"

"Oh no, girl, they're sneaky. But I heard its birdcall. And then I put matches all 'round my car, so the stick Indian would take the matches and not come close to me. That worked fine."

Anna asked, "And your car started up again?"

"Gabe wouldn't say so," Minnie equivocated, "but I'm sure the matches did the trick."

"Gabe?"

"Gabriel Round Dance," Vernita answered for Minnie, "the policeman who introduced us."

Anna looked back to the old woman. "Sergeant Round Dance helped you with your car?"

"Yes. He said it was a cable gone bad, but I don't think so."

"What time yesterday night was this?"

"Two hours after sundown. Maybe a little longer."

Roughly thirty minutes following the torching of the Explorer at the Kah-Nee-Ta, Anna realized. "Which way was Sergeant Round Dance headed?"

"North."

Away from the lodge. The reservation, like most, was checkered with dead spots for radio transmissions, which might explain his lack of response to repeated attempts to raise him. "Go on, Minnie. I'm sorry for interrupting." Vernita had brought Anna a cup of coffee on a tray with cream and sugar. A touchingly traditional gesture: Grief was no excuse for a lack of hospitality. "Thank you," Anna mouthed, and Vernita patted her hand.

"So I went my way, and Gabe went his," Minnie continued. "I was farther on when I seen it. . . ." Pausing, she deferred to Vernita, who dipped her head as if to say that she could stand another telling of what was coming next. The old woman caught Anna's eye again. "I seen Elsa. All confused in my lights, standin' on the edge of the road. Her skin was like ashes, her hair was a mess and her clothes tore up. She run across the road like a scared deer and was gone before I could think. Otherwise, I would've give her some matches so she could get the stick Indian off her trail." Tears had welled in Vernita's eyes as she listened. "I knew right then what this was all about. It all made sense." Minnie sat back as if that concluded her story.

"What made sense?" Anna pressed.

The old woman dropped her voice as if she feared it carrying beyond this small room. "The Ancient One the Basco dug up along the John Day—it's turned into a stick Indian. Now it won't let go of us till it's back under the earth. As long as we put off doin' the right thing, folks will disappear and die." Another uneasy glance at Mrs. Dease. "I know you don't like me talkin' this way, Vernita, but that's how it is. This stick Indian will go on hurtin' folks till we use good medicine to stop it."

Vernita glossed over this previous disagreement with a preoccupied smile. "Thanks for sharing this with us, Minnie. I hope you weren't too frightened."

"Me? No. It was Elsa who was scared. Scared out of her mind. We got to find a holy person to help us get her back. There's suppose to be an ol' Yakima over in . . ." Minnie's voice trailed off.

Vernita had come to her feet, an unexpected signal of dismissal to the old woman, for she looked slightly miffed as she rose and the Shaker woman helped her into her cheap plastic raincoat. As soon as Minnie was out the door, Vernita said piteously, "Poor superstitious soul."

"Do you think Minnie just imagined the sighting?"

"Oh no, Ms. Turnipseed," Vernita said, sitting again. "Minnie saw something. But it wasn't Elsa being chased by a stick Indian. She saw Elsa's ghost. My daughter's gone. Before I had a vision of her under the ground—alive or dead, I wasn't sure. But now I see her wandering the night as if she can't find the gate to heaven." Vernita buried her face in her hands. Anna detected no racking of sobs, so she remained quietly seated. Finally, the woman pulled her hands away and, in a remarkable recovery of composure, asked, "Did you and Mr. Parker go to the Timberline last sabbath's eve?"

"Yes."

"And?"

"That's why I'm here. To follow up on what we learned about Elsa and Deborah Carter."

A glimmer of respect broke through Vernita's pained expression. "I see. So you two learned of this on your own?"

"That's right," Anna replied, keeping up the pretense that Vernita hadn't guided them to the discovery about the colonel's relationship with Elsa. Nor would she ever reveal that the Shaker woman had informed on Paulina and his followers the night they went to Bilbao's shack.

"I don't believe it was a carnal thing. Please don't think that of my daughter."

"I don't."

Vernita fixed her gaze just above the level of Anna's head, as if something were unfolding there, something unpleasant. "You know what it's like to be young and unhappy, don't you?"

"Yes." Anna surprised herself with how emphatically she admitted this. Was it a measure of how helpless she was beginning to feel in regard to Emmett?

"And sometimes there's so little a mother can do or say." With that, Vernita abruptly got up and left the room. Anna thought she might have gone to release the crying fit she'd just suppressed, but in a moment the woman returned dry-eyed with an envelope. "Go ahead and read this." Addressed to Elsa at this house, but with no return address. A postmark of July 10, this year, at The Dalles.

Anna's palms tingled as she began reading the tight scrawl:

My dear Elsa—
Please don't take this as an idle threat,
but any continued persistence to avoid me
will only drive me to desperation. If
desperation is my only means to convince

you of my respect and admiration for you,
then so be it. I have no fear of death.
In fact, it's a desired release, particularly
if you continue to hurt me with your silence.
Have you forgotten what Watson did for both
of us . . . ?

It was signed *Debbie*. Anna read the entire letter twice, then tried to hide how badly she wanted this powerful piece of evidence. "I'll need to take this, of course."

"No," Vernita said adamantly.

"I beg your pardon?"

"When you find my daughter's body, you can have the letter. Not a minute before."

"Mrs. Dease, I assure you that we're doing everything we can to find Elsa."

"I know." Her stubborn look softened slightly. "I just want to make sure Elsa is never hurt by this. Can you understand that?"

Returning to the car minutes later, Anna tried excitedly to tell Emmett about the letter. But he had his own urgency to share, for he thrust a page from the fax under her nose. "Prior to being assigned to the Corps of Engineers," he said, "Carter was an instructor at the army's Survival, Evasion, Resistance and Escape School in North Carolina."

"So?" Anna asked, then started the engine and ran the defroster—his breath had fogged up the windows.

"You've never heard of it?"

"No. Let me guess what they teach—escape and evasion?"

"Plus how to stand up to torture. The instructors are specialists in torture techniques."

• • •

Gabriel Round Dance knelt naked in his Warm Springs house. The bungalow was on a back street of the tribal capital, distant enough from neighbors for him to use his sweat lodge in the traditional way some on the reservation might find immodest. He'd just dashed without a stitch on through the rainy darkness, and, despite a quick rinse of cold water in his shower, his skin still steamed from the hot interior of the lodge.

Purified, he prepared himself, trying to concentrate.

But his father's eyes were on him. Roland Round Dance, also a tribal police sergeant, stared down from his framed picture on the wall. The same old question burned in his gaze: *How can a man turn bad power back on his enemies?*

Roland Round Dance had never learned the answer, and died as a consequence. There were no spiritual road maps left. All the medicine men among the Wasco were long dead, the fearless sojourners to the dream world who could ferret out those who carry out their abominations in shadow.

Round Dance knelt before his coffee table. The only light in the living room flickered atop it, a small fish-oil lamp. The flame bent with each of his breaths, as if his thoughts could travel through the air and impact the physical world. A dangerous place, this world, with perils that could scarcely be fathomed, let alone countered.

"Help me," he prayed.

From a Baggie, he sprinkled dried sage leaves into a stone incense burner, then touched the flame to them. The acrid smoke rose into his face. He cupped his hands to capture it, rubbed it over his bare arms and shoulders, caressed it into his hair. Then he took his .357 revolver from the holster on his Sam Browne belt and wafted smoke over his service weapon.

Strange, nothing was more common than sage on the Columbia Plateau, yet nothing was quite as cleansing and power-infusing. He'd gathered this sage in the Ochoco Mountains, where it grew tall and robust. Sliding his Buck knife from its holder on his belt, he held the blade to the stream of incense and watched the steel glint in the dancing light of the flame.

"Make me strong," he implored.

12

Anna asked out of the blue, "Are we now part of a witch-hunt?"

Emmett had her hold her question—Deborah Carter was speeding up the westbound on-ramp of Interstate 84. Seven minutes ago, the colonel had left the Corps of Engineers headquarters and climbed into her sedan. Digging his cell phone out of his pocket, Emmett punched in the number to Carter's office from memory. Her assistant, Michael, answered. "Yeah, this is Emmett Parker from the BIA. May I speak to the colonel, please?"

"I'm sorry, Mr. Parker," the aide said, "she's on her way to Portland for a meeting. May I take a message?"

"No, that's all right. Will she be in Monday?"

"Yes, sir."

"I'll catch her then." Disconnecting, Emmett fell in behind a Greyhound bus so that Carter, several vehicles ahead, wouldn't catch sight of Anna's and his new loaner from the FBI motor pool. It was another Ford Explorer, which had made him uneasy tailing the colonel these past thirty-six hours—she would already associate the partners with the Explorer that had been torched. Emmett switched on the windshield wipers to clear the spray tossed by the bus wheels. Ahead, the Columbia Gorge was obscured by the morning drizzle. "What's this about a witch-hunt?"

Anna was nursing a double mocha coffee she'd picked up at an espresso drive-through in The Dalles. "I was wondering how much the establishment wants to get rid of an outspoken officer who won't declare her sexual orientation."

Emmett grimaced—his back ached from having slept fitfully in the vehicle last night. "What establishment?"

"The military, for sure. Maybe government officials in the Northwest. I'm not sure. All I know is, I don't like the U.S. Attorney faxing us her complete service record. How'd he get it? What are we doing here, Em?"

He understood Anna's growing disillusion after shadowing Carter since Wednesday afternoon. He checked the dash clock. It was now 9:00 A.M. on Friday. They had nothing to show after a day and a half of following the colonel to Corps-managed sites, watching her run off-duty errands around The Dalles for what seemed a lock-step, insulated life. Nothing to remotely suggest that she'd murdered a man and set fire to an FBI vehicle within the week. Last night, Carter had even lingered for an hour at the New Age shelf in a bookstore.

However, minutes ago, she'd walked out of her headquarters with urgency in her step. Perhaps explained by running late to the meeting in Portland, which was eighty miles away. Perhaps not.

Carter was doing ten miles an hour over the posted limit, forcing Emmett to jockey through traffic to keep up.

The rain began beating the windshield.

Boosting the wiper speed, he found himself missing Phoenix's clear autumn skies. The divide between the arid Columbia Plateau and the lush west slope of the Cascade Mountains had been crossed. Dashes of autumn-red maples failed to brighten the somber woods. This was dreary country to a Comanche, who often visualized sunlit plains to drift off to sleep. Undulating seas of grass. This morning, his head felt as thick as Oregon's skies.

Anna finished her mocha coffee, crushed the cup and tossed it onto her floor mat.

Something had been missed Tuesday evening in the pool at the lodge, an opportunity that he sensed might not come again. Neither of them had mentioned this latest near miss at intimacy. Too busy, he supposed. Or beginning to drift apart with the tectonic slowness that had characterized the beginning of the end of all his other relationships. And she was looking at him differently now—as if wondering what she'd ever seen in him.

"She's getting off," Anna cautioned.

Deborah Carter exited at Bonneville, the town on the south anchorage of the huge dam of the same name. Emmett calculated that they were midway between The Dalles and Portland. Gas stop?

No, Carter barreled past two stations and continued east on the frontage highway. Then she turned up a logging road.

Emmett shifted into four-wheel drive for the mud-slick track. He followed the colonel at a distance through the shadowy tunnel formed by the overarching trees. "Where are we?"

"Hang on." Anna was flipping through maps she'd taken from the glove compartment. After unfolding one and studying it, she said, sounding stunned, "Tanner Creek."

"What about it?"

"Don't you remember what I told you?"

Then it came back to him. "Right, Tanner Creek." Where, according to the Portland PD Investigations captain, Gorka Bilbao had taken the nineteen-year-old Yakima prostitute he'd abducted at knifepoint. To an abandoned cabin. A minute later, Anna pointed at one set back off the road, its roof sagging as if from the weight of the moss heaped on top of it. Carter's tire tracks went past the shanty with no sign that she'd gotten out. Instead, the impressions showed that she was weaving from excessive speed on the slimy road.

Emmett could make out the snow line on the hill looming ahead. That would stop Carter, who had only two-wheel drive.

Anna and he were finally onto something. Yet he also sensed that there was a fly in the ointment. Bilbao had been murdered five days ago. If Carter had tortured the fossil hunter to learn where he'd dumped Elsa's body, why had she waited all this time to act on the information?

Emmett braked.

"What're you doing?" Anna seemed eager to keep pursuing Carter.

He pointed out two spots on the road where mud had been flung back from spinning wheels. "She stopped here. I'll bet to listen for somebody following." A former instructor at the U.S. Army's Survival, Evasion, Resistance and Escape School wouldn't blithely ignore the possibility she was being tailed. Several times over the past thirty-six hours, Emmett had suspected the colonel knew she was being watched.

He shifted into reverse, looking for an opening. A hundred yards down the road, he found one: a skid trail cut by the lumberjacks through the dense young firs to drag logs. He backed up until the boughs were pressing against the side windows. "We'll hoof it from here." Both Anna and he had to push their doors against the foliage to get out, but he was satisfied the Explorer was well hidden.

Big wet snowflakes whirled down among the raindrops. Anna snapped her parka hood over her head and asked, "What if Carter drives on for miles?"

"She can't without chaining up. I doubt she'll do that."

They took off through the sopping growth, traversing the hillside above the road. Emmett mentally tried to tighten down the probable sequence of events. Bilbao had kidnapped and murdered Elsa Dease. He'd let his previous victim, the Yakima streetwalker, live to testify against him, so he'd learned from that. Using almost indescribable torture, Carter had pried Elsa's burial place out of Bilbao, then killed the fossil hunter. Now she was confirming her own guilt of murdering Bilbao by making a beeline to Elsa's grave.

A sound penetrated the rustle of the rain.

He pulled Anna down beside him behind a fallen log.

She shrugged questioningly at him.

He pantomimed digging. He'd heard the unmistakable crunch of a shovel blade biting into the earth. Anna turned her head to listen, then nodded that she heard it too.

Motioning for her to follow, he slipped quietly through the trees. The sodden debris and moss on the forest floor helped deaden their footfalls. They walked for five minutes before halting and concealing themselves again.

It wasn't hard to spot Deborah Carter.

She'd hiked up into the snow on a slope denuded of timber, and her drab-green uniform stood out against the whiteness. As did the mound of freshly turned earth beside her. She worked maniacally, at a pace impossible to sustain, then leaned over the hole, chest heaving, and examined its bottom before digging with a wild fury again. She did this again and again until finally, throwing down her shovel and gripping herself in her arms, she sank to her knees on the slushy ground.

Her sobs carried clearly to the partners.

• • •

Nels Sward glanced across the cab of their Volkswagen van at his wife. He'd met Patricia twelve years ago at a gathering of neo-pagans in a Marin County meadow overlooking the Pacific. He particularly remembered the bonfire, whipped a riotous orange by the wind off the ocean. At first, her free spirit had put him off, intimidated him even, and he'd kept his distance from her during the rites and feasting afterward. Yet, somehow, she'd seen through his remoteness and glimpsed the sexual attraction underlying it. They made love in the grass where the firelight blended into the night. Her casual approach to intimacy amazed him. With time, she emancipated him from much of his inbred Swedish reserve, even though grappling with her desires felt like trying to snatch fireflies out of the night before they winked off again. Patricia could turn icy on the heels of a fiery passion, melancholy after great joy. Their courtship was tempestuous, but they'd wed as soon as her divorce from a Sausalito psychic was final. A psychic who'd foretold that she would betray him. It was Sward's first marriage, her fourth. It hadn't been easy. Yet he believed Patricia and he were bound in a spiritual way that transcended the occasional infidelities committed by both partners. Norse paganism seemed to best define the truce that was their relationship, the tumultuous union of the male and female elements of the universe.

It was their only common ground.

He felt uneasy that, all morning, he'd been going through the history of their love in search of something. Something, perhaps to put his mind at rest.

"Nels?" Patricia awakened him from his reverie.

Sward realized that they'd come to the T in the Forest Service byway. He had stopped without thinking. He didn't need to check the map to confirm that this was where Barber Creek Road intersected

Allen Creek Road along the crest of the Ochoco Mountains. He'd driven this way before.

"This is it," he told Trish, backing up to park on the shoulder.

They got out of the Volkswagen, and he studied her for a moment. Her facial bruises had turned a faint green. The sight of them made Sward sick. Perhaps his Lutheran upbringing was to blame, but he couldn't come to grips with the fact that he had dispatched his wife to another man's bed.

"Let's see what we can find," he said.

Side by side, they hiked down the road and into the canyon. Snow flurries came and went on blasts of wind, and Trish buttoned her coat around her throat with an elegant play of fingers that captivated him. She could be as graceful as a goddess. And as ruthless as one.

Paulina.

Sward was familiar with Indian witches from having lived among the Navajo. He admired how they could bend reality to their own purposes. Their notion of power had become a template for him. Big-city alienation and rampant materialism had reduced the white concept of power to subordinating others to one's own will. Ball-busting. Indians knew better. Power came from subordinating one's self to supernatural forces that were neither good nor evil, in the Judeo-Christian vein, but nevertheless could be diverted to satisfy human desires—if properly entreated.

Did it work?

Without a doubt. Nothing confirmed fact like experience. As a Lutheran missionary, Sward had been the object of a Navajo sorcerer's wrath, suffering a prolonged ailment that resisted diagnosis by modern medicine. At the same time, membership at his mission fell off, his ministry was incessantly criticized by the tribal newspaper, and his car and house became the favored targets of a relentless youth gang.

From that, he'd learned that when absolutely nothing goes your way, it's not an accident.

So, arriving in Oregon and immediately sensing strong spiritual opposition for possession of John Day Man, he'd known what he faced in his quest to claim the skeleton. He initiated a discreet investigation that soon netted the name of the man who might be wielding that formidable energy. His name was Tennyson Paulina. A dangerous sorcerer, according to Sward's Warm Springs informant, a member of the tribal police. Sward and his kindred cast counterspells on the Paiute, but these failed. Paulina grew stronger, and he even got the government to send two Indian cops as watchdogs over the situation. Wolves in sheep's clothing.

Patricia and he slowed. The shack had come into view. No police vehicles were parked around it, no cars at all. The light snowfall had cleared momentarily on a Wagnerian sky—billowing ramparts of cloud and shafted sun.

They resumed their brisk pace.

Paulina, Paulina.

At his wit's end, Sward had turned to the oldest member of his kindred, an Englishwoman and lifelong pagan who'd suckled Druidic wisdom from her mother's teat. She explained, *Nothing is more potent than blood and semen. Life and new life, the hot vigor of the eternal circle. But of the two, semen is the greater, for it has within it the formula for blood.* She recommended a desperate measure: A female from their group should steal the Paiute witch's essence, which could then be used in an amulet to weaken his powers. As wife of the high priest, Patricia felt it only right that she did this. Reluctantly, Sward let her go. But the sorcerer had uncovered her theft of his semen. In the bitter aftertaste of failure, ugly mental pictures of Paulina and Patricia had begun to torment Sward.

They'd come to the shack.

It was ringed by fluttering yellow tape strung from whatever was available—bushes, trees, fence posts. Sward looked all around for police, saw none, then ducked beneath the tape and held it up for Trish to pass under.

She was highly sensitive to the Unseen World. He asked, "Do you feel anything special about this place that might help us?"

She scanned the homesite. "No." He found her terse, pouty-lipped *no* enormously sensual—Paulina was back inside his head with Patricia, coupling with her. The image both repulsed and aroused Sward. He was used to complicated sexual feelings, but this mood was different. It was tinged with violence. His lust was mingling with an urge to do her harm. It was insane. She'd only gone to Paulina for the good of the kindred, to make sure John Day Man was returned to the care of his descendants. Something dreadful was getting inside his head. Paulina's power. Sward had to guard against it.

He loved his wife, deeply.

There were chalk marks around a pile of ashes in front of a pine tree. The wet snow was already erasing them.

"Here." Trish had stopped dead in her tracks. She extended her arm toward the dissolving chalk. "Pain, fire, death," she said in a distressed hush. It wasn't necessary for her to feel this; they knew how the man had died. Swiftly, Sward took her by the arm and led her away from the pine tree. The door to the cabin was unlocked. In fact, there was no lock. Sward pushed it all the way open for light. He'd never seen such squalor—even in the most unkempt hogan on the Navajo reservation. Spoiled food offended his nostrils, but it was impossible to locate the source in the police-ransacked mess.

Trish wrinkled her nose, but then ran her fingers along a shelf overloaded with fossils and bones. More specimens were heaped in the corners. Evolution's junk shop. None of the bones looked human to Sward.

"Bilbao wasn't a man," he said.

Trish turned bright-eyed toward him. "What's that?"

"Judging from the way he lived, I think Bilbao was a troll."

She smiled prettily. "Don't trolls hide treasures?"

They went on searching.

In addition to fossils and bones, Bilbao had been an avid collector of pornography. The police had obviously gone through the magazines, for some were still folded open on the gritty floor to flagrant examples of bondage and sadomasochism. Sward disliked this take on sexuality. While he respected physical desire, he also saw sex as an expression of worship, a link to divinity, communion with the goddesses.

Trish must have picked up on his musings, for she suddenly sat at the table and stared up at him.

He too eased down into a rickety chair, avoiding the tabletop with his elbows—the police had dusted it for fingerprints with black powder. "What're you thinking?"

"It's all so easy for you, isn't it, Nels?"

Her acrimonious tone didn't surprise him. This had been building for days. "The path we've chosen, you mean?"

She nodded, lips pressed together.

"I'm sorry if I've given you that impression. I'm a searcher too, Patricia. A wayward searcher, hunting for the wisdom of his ancestors. Sometimes I feel very lost. And it seems as if ridicule awaits me behind every corner. It's so difficult to find our way back to the heart of the circle. After all the persecution, the Burning Times. But no, I'm not in total control. I'm not in control at all. And all I really want is an easy mind, a feeling of grace. As you do, my love."

She looked away from him. "I'm sorry for the pain these past days have given you, Nels." Without warning, she drew his hand up and kissed it.

Disarmed and moved, he couldn't speak for a moment. She had a gift for the unexpected. "We shouldn't dawdle," he finally said. "The police might come back."

"All right." She stood.

Sward had hoped to find maps, but there were none anywhere he looked.

"What's this mean?" Patricia asked, handing him an entire newspaper page torn from *The Madras Pioneer* of September 2, this year. One side was an advertisement for the Sears catalogue store, touting a clearance sale of washers and dryers. But on the flip side was a notice by the Army Corps of Engineers of scheduled water releases from dams throughout north central Oregon, signed by Colonel Deborah Carter. *The Judas,* Sward thought to himself, a duplicitous and repulsive woman. Clarno Reservoir—along the John Day River—had had a release on September 27. The very next day, Sward recalled, Bilbao had found the specimen. There were numerous other releases, but most of them were outside the fossil- and bone-rich region the man had worked.

All but one.

Yesterday, October 25, a man-made flood had issued from Willow Creek Reservoir. Less than forty miles east of the John Day River on the edge of the army's Boardman Bombing Range.

"Where'd you find this?" Sward asked Trish.

"In a jar with some loose change and dollar bills in it."

"You may have just found the troll's treasure map." He pulled his coat sleeve back from his wristwatch. "I see no option other than to run this past Dr. Rankin."

"Are you sure, Nels?"

"Yes. We can't always pick and choose our allies."

•   •   •

Four in the afternoon.

An hour ago, Anna had been relieved when the rain let up, but a freeze had sifted in from the northeast behind it, bejeweling the evergreens with ice droplets. An all-terrain vehicle was putt-putting back and forth across the slope in which Deborah Carter had dug three shallow holes. Mounted on the ATV was a ground-penetrating radar that could actually peer into the subsurface soil.

At 11:35 this morning, Carter had given up trying to find Elsa Dease's body. Anna and Emmett had trailed the colonel back to the interstate, where she turned east toward The Dalles, not bothering to shore up her cover story by going into Portland. As soon as the partners were convinced that Carter was headed home, they broke off surveillance and asked the FBI resident agent out of Yakima, Washington, to head south and continue shadowing the colonel. Then they had the Forest Service district office barricade the logging road behind a *Flooded* sign. In short order, the Portland FBI office flew in a consulting team from Seattle that specialized in detecting ground disturbance—and buried bodies, as a by-product of that highly technical process.

The ATV operator crisscrossed the slope in a grid pattern, searching for electrical properties in the ground varying from those of virgin soil. Earlier, Emmett had wondered out loud to Anna if Carter had done any digging prior to the storm and if those mounds might be hidden by the snow.

Three hours later, they still had no answer.

It was rare for wide-ranging federal cops to meet crime victims prior to their being victimized, Anna realized. Particularly homicide victims.

There was a blessing in that, for it was awful to imagine a young woman she'd known and liked now entombed somewhere in this half-frozen muck, her beauty already eaten away. The ATV operator had mentioned that, in a moist climate, most bodies were soon scavenged by insects and burrowing rodents. *Stop picturing that.* What was the next step? By no means was she prepared to arrest Deborah Carter. She might have, had this been the day after Bilbao's murder. But an impulsive act like that followed by days of superhuman restraint? It made no sense, and that no doubt is why Emmett had wondered if Carter had come here before this morning to dig.

Emmett ambled over, hands in his pockets, but stood off from her several feet. "How you doing, lady?"

"Okay." Although she wanted to be busy. Only that made the waiting at a scene bearable.

The ATV operator parked beside the team leader. They conferred briefly over a printout of radar readings, then the leader strode for the partners. "Finished." The man's nose was red from the cold. "No disturbance other than the three holes you two saw being dug. We covered a full acre around the big snag . . ." Anna figured that Carter had used the standing dead tree as a landmark to find the grave site. Is that what Bilbao had told her under torture? "You have any other areas for us?"

"Yeah," Emmett said, "all of northern Oregon and southern Washington."

"Know how you feel," the man said sympathetically.

"Thanks for your help," Anna said. "We'll be in touch."

The team leader walked off to begin shutting down the search, and the partners were left alone with their quandary. Emmett puffed air in his cheeks and slowly let it out. She could almost read his mind. Had Bilbao, in the midst of his death throes, actually lied to Carter? Or, worse yet, had he been blameless in Elsa's disappearance?

She had a sudden, peculiar sense that the distance between Emmett and her was measured in miles, not feet. But he narrowed his eyes at her, and that emotional distance seemed to close a little, although his tone then seemed sullen: "I want to have another go at Carter."

"When?"

"Soon."

"We tried that just last Sunday," Anna pointed out. "What good did it do? And by now the colonel has circled her legal wagons, so she's ready for anything we have to ask."

"Agreed. That's why I'll make damn sure all our ducks are in a row before we interrogate her again."

"How will you do that?" Anna asked.

Emmett's gaze slid off into the woods. "Everybody has a closet with skeletons in it. In Carter's case, we just have to turn back the clock far enough to find that closet."

13

Emmett's heart squeezed up into his throat as the U.S. Army Blackhawk helicopter swooped down on a landing zone in the piney woods of North Carolina. He was reminded of Anna's and his roller coaster ride in Las Vegas as he leaned his upper body outside the open side door. Just beyond the LZ was a compound straight out of a Chuck Norris movie: weather-stained concrete huts and a rickety-looking guard tower, all surrounded by a ten-foot-high razor wire fence.

The bespectacled major sitting next to Emmett in the chopper cabin raised his voice over the engine noise. "I ask that you don't talk to any of my little lambs, Mr. Parker. This exercise has value only as long as the students suspend disbelief. Your presence could bring them back to the real world, making our job tougher."

Emmett said, "Agreed."

The major wore no nameplate and had simply been introduced as "Doc." He was a psychiatrist assigned to the Survival, Evasion, Resistance and Escape School run by Military Intelligence at Camp Mackall in the Fort Bragg complex. He reminded Emmett of a young Catholic priest, the same self-conscious effort to appear tranquilly empathetic.

The pilot touched down, and Doc jumped out. Emmett followed, ducking his head as the rotor above him whispered like a guillotine blade. The chopper promptly lifted off again, and the psychiatrist led the way to the compound's gate. Guarding it was a banana republic guerrilla dressed in the same grunge Emmett had seen college students wearing late last night at Portland International Airport. "Papers," he growled with a foreign accent.

Doc showed his I.D., and they were let through. "The course is three weeks long," he explained as they crossed a quadrangle scuffed barren by boots. "In the first half, we teach the students survival and hiding skills. After that, they're on the move through Occupied Pineland, a mythical country just conquered by Opfourland, America's enemy in the region. They have to link up with the Pineland resistance for help, not an easy chore when you're exhausted, drinking muddy water, and subsisting on bugs and swamp grass. Inevitably, they're captured and brought here."

"Are they taught the use of explosives?" Emmett asked, recalling the safe in the Corps of Engineers headquarters.

"Not at this school." Doc unlocked the back door to the largest structure. Inside was a console of TV monitors. An enlisted man sat before it in the semidarkness, making notes. The scene resembled the security viewing room in a casino. The soldier smiled up at the intrusion. "Howdy, Doc."

"Hi, Stevens. How are my little lambs doing this afternoon?"

"Number Fifteen has been puking on and off for the last hour. One of his buddies fessed up to Ivana that he ate raw acorns out in the bush. He's refusing his bowl of water."

"Poor ignorant lamb. You've got to leach the tannic acid out of acorns." Doc leaned over the console for a closer look at one particular screen. All of them showed solitary American soldiers crammed into three-foot-square cement cells. These cubicles were illuminated by bare lightbulbs that Emmett suspected never went off. It was impossible for the captives to either stand up or lie down, so they huddled in fetal positions. The prisoner in question had the dry heaves. "If he won't drink by 1700 hours, medevac him."

"Yes, sir."

Doc said to Emmett, "This is what my job's all about. It's not the staff's aim to break a student either physically or emotionally, but he must understand from this experience that that's exactly what his real-life captors will try to do."

One cell was different from the others. It was round and filled with filthy-looking water. Protruding just above the surface was a man's face, just his nose really, for the low ceiling prevented him from raising his entire head above the swill. At that moment, Doc tapped this screen. "He's ready for Ivana, Stevens." The enlisted man made a phone call, and Doc ushered Emmett over to a small window set in an interior wall. He surmised that it was a mirror on the other side. Obviously an interrogation chamber. The walls were splattered with what appeared to be dried blood. A desk faced a small chair that was secured to the floor. Sitting behind the desk with a cool look of unconcern was a young woman in faded fatigues. She had short blonde hair, a style that made her blue eyes seem large. Emmett felt a twinge of desire. He'd had several since being dropped off by Anna at the airport, all dampened by worry over Anna returning alone to the Warm Springs reservation. He'd agreed to it only by making her promise that she'd lie low until he returned to Oregon.

"That's Staff Sergeant Kelly," Doc went on. "Better known to the students as Ivana the Terrible. She's one hell of a military interrogator. To be an instructor here, you must've gone through the SERE course yourself. Kelly was a student under Carter. Turnover is such that nobody else remembers the colonel."

Is it so hard for you to understand that when your own looks are taken, you appreciate physical beauty all the more in others?

Emmett studied his own dim reflection in the glass. He'd done the same in the mirror of the 737's lavatory last night—and been struck by what chronic stress, restaurant food, inadequate sleep and the years of alcohol had done to his looks. The episode with Anna in the swimming pool the other night was a puzzle to him, for over the past few days he'd come to the conclusion that, her trauma-induced chastity aside, she just wasn't physically attracted to him.

Movement brought him back to the interrogation chamber.

A figure was shoved blindly into the room by a gigantic guerrilla. The captive had a sandbag over his head. Emmett could tell that he was the same student who'd been immersed in the tank; his pajama-like prison garb was still dripping. He was slammed down into the chair by the big man. "That guard is known as The Intimidator," Doc said needlessly. The hood was whipped off, and the student tried to make sense of the delusion of a sexy young woman facing him. He sniffed the air, tentatively. "Kelly wears a perfume that drives you nuts," Doc murmured.

Over a speaker in the wall, she and the guard could be heard exchanging a few words. In Russian, Emmett believed.

Doc was one step ahead of him. "Nearly all staff in the compound are military language specialists." That explained Deborah Carter's fluency in Russian.

The captive waited with an apprehensive expression for Kelly to say something. His eyes were red rimmed. All the visible skin below his head was wrinkled and pallid. He was shivering despite a fist-clenching effort to control the shaking. Emmett pitied him. Arriving at the airport in Fayetteville this morning, he'd found the weather surprisingly balmy. Now, seven hours later, a cold front had drifted in, and North Carolina felt as frigid as Oregon had been.

"What is your name and rank?" Kelly asked with a Russian accent.

The captive had to clear his throat after his hours of isolation. Still, his voice was no more than a rasp. "Captain James T. Kirk, commanding officer, Starship *Enterprise*." If he thought his answer was funny, he didn't show it.

Kelly nodded, and The Intimidator seized the student by the shoulders, picked him up like a rag doll and held him over the desk. Kelly roundly slapped the captive, and the guard plunked him back in the chair. It had happened so swiftly, the student looked stupefied.

"In the debriefing at the end of the course," Doc observed, "most students describe that slap as one of the most intensely sexual experiences of their lives."

"I'll pass," Emmett said, although he'd noticed that the fatigues failed to conceal Kelly's shapely hips and legs.

"What is your name!" she shouted. No wonder Carter had kept her balance when confronted about her relationship with Elsa Dease. She'd had more interrogation experience than Emmett did after fourteen years as a cop.

The captive also decided to pass on another slap. "Taylor, John B."

Kelly stood, strolled around the desk and got right in his face. "What?" she asked with a seductive smile.

Her smile made him uneasy. "Taylor, John B. Lieutenant, United States Army."

"No!" She punched him in the stomach and he doubled over so that his face rested between his knees. "You are Prisoner Thirty-two! You are a prisoner of the Opfourland Liberation Forces!"

The student sat up again. "Yes, ma'am," he said with a hangdog lack of eye contact.

"Now, Prisoner Thirty-two," she asked menacingly, "what were you doing in my country . . . ?"

• • •

The dancing around the bonfire reminded Anna of the countless Indian powwows she'd attended since childhood. Except that these dancers were Caucasian. She parked a short distance from the other vehicles beside the White River. She'd spent the day resting at the Kah-Nee-Ta, leaving the surveillance on Deborah Carter to the resident FBI agent from Yakima. At three this afternoon, he'd phoned her to report that the colonel was spending her Saturday closeted inside her house. He had yet to learn her whereabouts on the evening Bilbao was killed, but Anna didn't want him to interview the colonel's work associates until Emmett got back from North Carolina. She decided to free the agent to go home. Congress was wrangling over the budget, and FBI headquarters had ordered overtime to be held to a minimum.

Minutes later, her phone had rung again. She'd expected a call from Emmett but was surprised to hear Thaddeus Rankin asking her to join him at something called a Vetrnaetr Blot at the pagan encampment north of the reservation.

"What's a Blot?" she asked.

"You'll see. It begins at six-thirty." When she hesitated, Rankin added urgently, "You absolutely must meet me there. Something's happened that requires your immediate action. I wouldn't bother you otherwise, believe me."

She had agreed to go, although it'd struck her as odd that the anthropologist had invited just her. As if he knew Emmett was gone. Then she realized: Rankin was being kept abreast of developments by a law enforcement insider, probably the U.S. Attorney. Did that mean Rankin wanted only to help the investigation? Were Emmett and she resisting that help simply because they found his scientific theories distasteful?

Stepping out of the Explorer, Anna zipped up her parka. The snow-capped cones of Mount Hood and Mount Jefferson shone through the frigid darkness. Walking past Rankin's Lexus, she heard muted music from inside. Kawatu got out, the harpsichord concerto of the Brandenburg Concerti gushing richly around his muscular body. "Good evening, Ms. Turnipseed," he said, his eyes fixed alertly on her.

"Kawatu. I'm here to meet the doctor."

"I know. You'll find him at the fire."

Applause came from that direction. It followed what had sounded like a toast. "You don't care to take part in the celebration?" she asked.

"Oh, it's a white man's thing," he replied without rancor.

Anna wondered where that left her.

"If you'll excuse me." Kawatu got back inside the Lexus, shutting in the strains of the concerto with him.

Anna moved on.

Nels Sward was standing with his back to her. The pagan leader seemed animated as he chatted with a follower—in sharp contrast to his subdued demeanor in the tavern a week and a half ago. In his hand was a ram's horn, and a honey-colored liquid spilled over the lip as he turned around at Anna's greeting. "Hello, Mr. Sward."

He looked nonplussed, but he quickly hid his displeasure behind a polite smile. "Why, welcome, Ms. Turnipseed. How nice to see you again. May I get you a horn of mead?"

"I don't drink."

"Understood. But the purpose isn't intoxication. You'll find no drunks here, just men and women with tongues loosened by the nectar of the gods. That way, we can count on one another to speak the truth."

"I see." Anna tried not to stare at his costume—a hooded cloak belted at the waist over baggy trousers. His followers were similarly attired, although the women wore white homespun dresses under their cloaks and their long hair was plaited. Both sexes were laden with gaudy jewelry. Obviously, Sward didn't know why she was present. "I'm looking for Dr. Rankin," she said. "He asked me to meet him here."

The pagan leader bowed. "Allow me to take you to him."

As they wound through the dancing, babbling throng, she inquired, "What's a Blot?"

"The word itself refers to blood. It harkens back to the era of blood sacrifices to the gods, but nowadays we make do by anointing the altar with mead. Blots are our major ceremonies. This is the Vetrnaetr, or Winter Night, rite, when we honor our male ancestors . . . like John Day Man."

They passed by a very old white woman. Her lower lids sagged off the eyeballs, making her leer at Anna seem wraithlike. "Caution's in order, Nels," she said with an English accent, "caution."

Sward cupped a hand to her wrinkled cheek, but kept moving.

Rankin rose from a camp chair at Anna's approach. There was strong color in his face tonight, which could have been explained by the horn of honey liquor in his grasp. The grasp itself seemed steadier than at past meetings. "You're looking well, Doctor."

Rankin shrugged off her compliment. "It'll pass. Please, sit." He gave her his chair and settled onto the end of a log that served as a bench. "Quite a show, Nels," he commented.

"And what a pleasant surprise to have the FBI present."

"Ms. Turnipseed's here at my request to receive a forensic report." Facing her, Rankin briefly rested a hand on her knee. "The toxicological results have come in on the skeleton the arsonist left in your vehicle. . . ." He paused, and Anna noted to herself that the toxicology return had come in record time. Two weeks was the norm. "Extremely high levels of mercury were found."

Sward looked interested, despite himself. "Which means what, Doctor?"

"Of itself, little. Miners in this country were exposed to hazardous levels of mercury. But I recalled the pitting on the specimen's forehead—barely noticed for all the fire damage." He shifted toward Anna again. "That worm-eaten effect was from either advanced syphilis or some other treponemal infection. I'd say syphilis because mercury was the most common treatment for the social disease in those days."

Sward asked, "So what does that tell you about the identity of this—" Without warning, a woman grabbed him by the cloak and pulled his head down to hers for a bawdy kiss. When she laughingly disengaged herself to the raucous cheers of the other celebrants, Anna saw that it was Sward's wife, Patricia. Still clinging to her husband, she offered Anna an amused smile, betraying none of the remorse and uncertainty she'd shown last Sunday morning in the Warm Springs police station. The bruises Paulina had given her were still visible.

"Bravo, Trish," Rankin chuckled. "The ancient Greeks believed the brain and not the gonads to be the source of semen. I congratulate you, dear girl, for going right to the source."

The woman gave Rankin an odd look. As if he'd said something inappropriate. But then she pecked him on the cheek and danced away, her copper arm rings glinting in the firelight.

Sward asked, "Do you know who this nineteenth-century fellow was, Doctor?"

"No. But he had a lifestyle that included regular visits to prostitutes, I'm sure—miner, cowboy, soldier perhaps."

"Fascinating." Sward flipped back the edge of his cloak to check his watch. "But you must excuse me, I have duties." He withdrew.

Anna knew that Rankin had not summoned her here to report high traces of mercury in some bones. That could have been done by phone or fax. He was looking at her, examining her face as if for bone structure—it made her feel oddly transparent, fleshless even, yet not violated. Something in his look seemed to deaden the incessant tension within her. Like venom numbing muscles and nerves. "The Modoc and Japanese blood mixed well in you, Ms. Turnipseed."

Ignoring the comment, she asked, "Isn't this strange company for a man of science?"

"Not for an anthropologist, my dear. I'm here observing the rebirth of an extinct religion. The traditionalists among your own people are making the same quixotic attempt, going back to the trash pile of history to piece together a belief system. A hit-and-miss proposition at best, but I can't blame them for trying." Rankin took a quaff from his horn. "There must be some special stress, some inner lack at the outset of the twenty-first century that's making otherwise rational people do this."

"Indians," Anna said tartly, "wouldn't have to go back to history if they hadn't been barred from practicing their religion."

"Agreed, my dear. But the same's true of pagans. They were burned at the stake for their practices, something I'm sure the Bible Belt fundamentalists and native Creationists would love to do to me. So I'm in sympathy with these exuberant neo-heathens."

"How long have you known the Swards?"

Rankin made a dismissive gesture. "Not long. They've rather made pests of themselves."

Nels Sward stood on a flat, altarlike rock. "Brothers and sisters," he began, his voice echoing dramatically in the river valley, "we, as a true Northern people, have many gods and goddesses. Of our gods, there's Thor, whose chariot's wheels rumble through the clouds, giving us thunder and rain. Odin, the Allfather, traded one of his eyes for wisdom, and we thank him for instilling a thirst for knowledge in us, otherwise we'd be powerless against the magical arts of our enemies. Of the goddesses, there is Freya, giver of love and beauty. Frigg, Odin's wife, also one-eyed, is so honored by her husband she alone of all the other gods is allowed to share his throne with him. But tonight, as we welcome in the snows of winter, I'd like to pay special homage to Sigyn. . . ." His gaze fell on Patricia. She waited for him to go on with an uncertain smile. "Sigyn, as you know, is wife of Loki, the most mischievous of our deities. She sits faithfully beside her troublesome husband, vigilant against those who would spit venom in his eyes." Sward paused again, staring at Patricia with a twist to his face. Was he drunk? He had to be, Anna suspected, given the size of his drinking horn. "Sigyn, the faithful, the goddess of forgiveness. And so I would have us begin the dark season with the spirit of forgiveness toward all those who have transgressed against us recently. . . ."

Rankin whispered to Anna, "I suggest you get a warrant."

She wasn't sure she'd heard him right. "What'd you say?"

"Please keep your voice down. Get a search warrant."

"Why?"

The anthropologist leaned closer. "In the large tent, you will find skeletal remains. I'd estimate them to be at least thirteen thousand years old."

Automatically, Anna thought of the burglary attempt last Sunday at the Corps of Engineers headquarters. "Are you telling me John Day Man has been stolen from the Hanford facility?"

"No. Sward and his wife found these bones along Willow Creek just this morning. I don't know how the devil they did it. Beginner's luck, I suppose, although he's had his people scouring the countryside for bones for weeks."

Anna caught the old white woman glaring at her again. "Why do they want them so badly?"

"A bona fide Caucasoid skeleton?" Rankin asked rhetorically. "It'd be their Holy Grail, their Ark of the Covenant. All religions long for tangible proofs. Science has made them touchy about their credibility. A Norse ancestor would unite these misfits, show other Nordic Americans that their roots go back to these very rocks and forests, that they're not gate-crashers on this continent. *They* were the original pioneers. But all this is beside the point—Sward invited me here earlier to examine the remains. Their antiquity, sex and Caucasoid characteristics are unequivocal. And there are butchering marks on some of the larger bones."

"Wait—these people have found *another* cannibalized specimen?"

"Need I draw you a picture, Ms. Turnipseed?"

"What sex is this skeleton?"

"Female, so I'll refer to her as Willow Creek Woman. I don't think you realize how important she is. She puts John Day Man in context. He was unique, an anomaly, until this second discovery." Rankin's whisper grew high pitched from an effort to hold down his excitement. "Now he's the first find in a series!"

Anna was mystified that he wasn't keeping this to himself. Apparently, the pagans were giving him unlimited access to the remains in order to authenticate them. Because of NAGPRA, the federal government wouldn't be so generous. "Why're you telling me this?"

"Extralegal means to study these skeletons won't do me a damned bit of good. How can I announce my discoveries to the scientific community if it's against the law for me to even handle the bones? Now, we both know the legal tide is running against me on John Day Man, and you can help me by reporting to the court that I helped you confiscate Willow Creek Woman. I'd appreciate it if you listed me as an unnamed reliable informant in the search warrant affidavit. Later, if the need arises, I'll come forward to assist the U.S. Attorney with any prosecution. But I want anonymity in the short term." He swept his eyes over the surrounding pagans. "God only knows how they'll react to my informing on them."

Anna's head was swimming. "Which tent?"

Rankin pointed, his hand doddering again. The tent glowed from within. And the flaps at its front were guarded by a fat, red-bearded man in a tunic. "I'd imagine you're resourceful enough to get a peek past that hulking Neanderthal."

Anna thought a moment. "Do you have a pocketknife?"

Rankin smiled as he reached into his trouser pocket. "You're a worthy daughter of your tribe, Ms. Turnipseed. . . ." His palsy increased, making it difficult for him to remove the knife while seated. He hoisted himself up on his cane. A look of astonishment came over his face, and he began stamping his feet in place as if he'd been possessed by some delirious martial spirit. His knees buckled from the fierce pounding. Then he pitched forward and landed face-first against the ground.

The pocketknife slid out of his open palm.

• • •

"What I wouldn't give for a face like yours," Staff Sergeant Christine Kelly said in her appealing Georgia drawl. "You've got the ultimate face for an interrogator."

Emmett put on a frown. "Well, I've been called ugly before, but never quite like that."

"Oh, you're not ugly, Parker, and damn if you don't know it too," she said.

That afternoon, when he'd asked her for an interview, Christine Kelly said flat out, "Dinner in Aberdeen." When he started to balk, mostly from the effects of jet lag, she confidently explained, "I'm not coming on to you, Parker. Dinner's all the time I've got free. Then it's home to bed and up at zero-dark-thirty for another day in the psychological paradise of Occupied Pineland." So he'd met her at 8:00 P.M. at a roadhouse between Camp Mackall and Fort Bragg. The hostess delivered them to an adequate table, but Christine insisted on another, one in front of the fireplace. Emmett hadn't minded. The East had a dank cold that took getting used to again.

He asked, "The military teach you Russian?"

She shook her head. "Master's in Russian lit from Emory. Though I was required to take the army's crash course."

"A master's degree? Then why aren't you an officer?"

"My daddy was a career NCO with the marine corps. He taught me to work for a living, mister."

Emmett smiled. The transformation from Ivana the Terrible to this frank and engaging woman was so abrupt he found himself smiling too much. All through the late afternoon, as she grilled student after student, he studied her demeanor as a military interrogator. Before he'd left Oregon, Bilbao's autopsy report had come in—the fossil hunter's abdominal artery had been clipped so precisely the man could have lingered at death's edge for as much as ten minutes while his entrails were slowly roasted. Did anything about Christine's—and Deborah Carter's—training evoke that kind of savage meticulousness? Kelly was certainly meticulous but not savage. And she'd been nothing but genial to Emmett from the moment Doc introduced them.

Her glass was empty, and he poured her more red wine from the bottle. "You don't drink?" she asked.

"No."

"Because you're Indian?"

"Because I'm me."

"Okay, enough of that. Say something in Cherokee."

"Comanche."

"Don't quibble, Parker."

Shaking his head, he sat back and looked into her appreciative eyes. Appreciative of his maleness, he was convinced. The situation was beginning to spin out of control, and he realized that he was letting it. Without a fight. He told her in Comanche that she was a breath of fresh air.

"Pretty. What's it mean?"

"I just made up a Comanche name for you."

"What gives you the right to do that?"

"Tribal custom. Everybody starts out with a childhood name. That's shed when a personal trait becomes apparent."

"So what's my grown-up name?"

"She Who Breaks Balls."

Christine hammered the table with her fists and laughed, drawing stares from the other tables, mostly military people. She dug into her purse for paper and pen, shoved them in front of Emmett. "I love it! Write it down phonetically!"

Emmett wrote down the rough equivalent of Breath of Fresh Air, trusting that it would be months or even years before she finally learned the true translation. Beaming, she examined the words, then folded the paper and put it away. For the first time since this afternoon, her expression got serious. "Let's get Deborah Carter out of our hair."

"All right. What do you have to say about her?"

"First, let me ask—is she in trouble?"

"Potentially. It's a homicide case, although no arrests have been made yet."

"Is she a suspect?"

"As much as some others."

Apparently satisfied with his honesty, she said, "Carter was the consummate pro in the compound. Some said it was her face that made her so effective, that with a face like hers you could scare Freddy Krueger. But it was more than that. She knew just where to twist the mental knife to make the student understand his vulnerability. At the time I went through the course under her, I believed Major Carter was singling me out for special maltreatment—"

She was interrupted by the arrival of their dinners. As soon as they were alone again, Emmett asked, "*Was* Carter singling you out?"

"Yes." She bit into her steak and chewed reflectively. "But that's standard operating procedure at SERE. A captured platoon is delivered to the compound and, as an interrogator, you begin chipping away at the weakest link. Not to sound sexist"—she smirked at her own irony—"but that's usually the female among the thirty-odd students. The physical challenges in the evasion phase are geared against the natural superiority of the female anatomy, so the gentler sex show up as the walking dead. At least I did. The interrogator goes after the woman or the youngest male in the party. Once somebody throws in the towel and starts cooperating with staff, it messes up the morale of the rest. Even the mentally toughest."

"So Carter was especially rough on you?"

"She broke my clavicle." Christine grabbed Emmett's hand and had him feel the slight dent in her collarbone visible over the top of her low-cut blouse.

He reluctantly took back his hand. Her skin was warm and satiny. "Was Carter disciplined for this?"

"Nope. Nor should she have been. I was tossing a punch at her at the time." Christine grinned. Great teeth.

"Did you believe Carter was gay?"

"Is she? Half the folks at Camp Mackall probably think I'm gay."

"What's the other half think?" Emmett asked.

"Wouldn't you love to know? Listen—that accusation goes with the territory. You're a trained interrogator, so you know that it's an acting job. You assume a role in order to persuade somebody to confide something he or she doesn't want to confide. I can't help it if narrow-minded people confuse you, the real person, with that role."

Emmett put down his fork. "Then what got her taken off the SERE staff before her normal rotation was up?" He'd finally figured this out, although the fact was carefully buried in her service record.

"Certainly nothing she did at the school."

"Then what?"

"You can do better than that," she said coyly. "Sum me up, Parker—how are you more likely to get this out of me? Rough stuff or making me trust you?"

•　•　•

Once again, Anna found herself on Wapinitia Road in darkness. She was really too tired to drive after the past five hours of whirlwind chores. Arriving at the Norse camp, the ambulance EMT had insisted on transporting Rankin to the nearest emergency medical facility, the Indian Health Service hospital in Warm Springs. Although he regained consciousness after collapsing, the anthropologist couldn't speak. Still, as Anna tried to comfort him, he adamantly clicked his eyes toward the big tent. In all the confusion, the red-bearded pagan remained at his post, so Anna made use of Rankin's pocketknife on the back wall of the tent, cutting a small slit in the canvas and then parting it with her fingers. The first thing to catch her eye was a ring of candles. At least fifty candles. These only accentuated the diabolical display: A scarlet cloak had been spread over the floor, and on it reposed an earth-stained skeleton.

Immediately, Anna had turned for her Explorer.

She'd driven the sixty miles to The Dalles, where the local federal magistrate resided. Using an office in the PD, she made a call to the U.S. Attorney at his home, explaining about the discovery of another skeleton illegally collected off Corps of Engineers–managed lands. He encouraged her to seek a warrant, promising that U.S. Marshals would do the dirty work of the actual confiscation later that night—she and Emmett were still the federal peacekeepers on the scene. He agreed with her that Willow Creek Woman should be taken directly to the Hanford nuclear facility to join John Day Man in the vault, by-passing Deborah Carter. This done, Anna typed out an affidavit and an hour later presented it to the sleepy-eyed magistrate, who issued the warrant.

Now, as she climbed the last grade before Simnasho, she made up her mind to check on Rankin. She'd not mentioned to the magistrate that her reliable informant had been transported to the Warm Springs hospital earlier this evening. Without Rankin's testimony in the future, the entire prosecution might implode over the probable cause for the search. The EMT hadn't said that the anthropologist's condition was life-threatening, but neither had he wasted any time getting him to the nearest medical facility.

Anna was suddenly chilled. As if she'd driven into a pocket of cold so unnaturally intense the heater seemed powerless against it. She glanced in her rearview mirror, thinking that she'd absently passed through a patch of ice fog.

"Jesus!" she cried, hitting the brakes.

A specter stood frozen in the red shine of her taillights, an unkempt female apparition in the middle of the road, arms extended like bony wings. Anna spun the Ford around and accelerated.

The road before her was empty.

Heart thumping, she jerked the steering wheel back and forth so her high beams fanned across the brush. Nothing. She stopped where she believed the thing had loomed, its magenta eyes fixed on her.

Reaching for the flashlight in the glove compartment, she startled when the lid fell open with a rattle. Of its own accord. The rectangle of black seemed more like the entrance to a void, an opening on unimaginable depths, than a mere storage bin. Cold seeped from it as if from an open freezer door.

Finally, she made herself reach inside and feel around. She found the flashlight, then took her semiautomatic from her ankle holster and bailed out.

She lit the darkened hillside above her.

Fright had opened her sinuses, and the cold stung her nostrils. Her legs felt weak beneath her. It was all she could do to approach the berm on the upslope side of the road. She examined it for tracks.

The ground, saturated by the rains, was now frozen so hard even an elephant wouldn't have left an impression in it.

She listened to the night—nothing but the sound of a creek flowing somewhere below the road. Backing up, she kept a keen watch all around. The conviction that she was not alone was overpowering.

She'd just reached the Explorer and was shutting her door when a bird whistled from the heights. The piercing song made her want to look for the creature that could sing so exquisitely.

• • •

Christine Kelly sublet her apartment from an Intelligence officer who'd spent a tour in Japan. The crisis in the Balkans had unexpectedly sent him to Kosovo, so Christine, who'd been in desperate need of housing in the Fort Bragg area, wound up with three sparse rooms and black-lacquered furniture, which she admitted ran counter to her plush Catherine the Great tastes. Lounging around a low table with her in the guttering light of a candle, Emmett tried to piece together how he had wound up here. It was late, very late, and twice today the military interrogator had given him contradictory signals. The first had come after asserting that she had only time for dinner with Emmett. Dinner had ended three hours ago. Then Christine had invited him over to her place for a nightcap—after it had been clearly established that Emmett didn't drink.

The meaning of nightcap had yet to be defined.

Following her to her place in his rental car, he'd made a little joke to himself that nobody said no to Ivana the Terrible. But that was an eva-sion. Ivana had been left back in the compound like a uniform hung in a locker, and this was entirely Christine, a funny and spontaneous young woman with no discernible hang-ups.

You can't guard against desire, so you guard against opportunity.

Still, here he sprawled on a tatami mat, swilling club soda and dis-cussing job satisfaction with Christine. "It really came together for me," she was saying, "when one of my students was actually captured."

"During Kosovo?"

"Sorry, that's classified." Her breath sounded like soft surf as she drank from her brandy snifter. "The kid came through it fine, and he credited his training. Man, what a high for me! I used to dwell on the misery of our little lambs, as Doc calls them. Tonight, if it were two years ago, I'd be thinking, 'Here it is Saturday night, I've got a full belly, a nice buzz on and stimulating company. And they're all squat-ting alone in those concrete boxes. Hungry, scared, afraid of looking weak when I show up in the morning.' But it finally hit me when that kid credited his training—I'm just inoculating them against future suffering." Her snifter floated up to her lips like a big bubble as she sipped again. "Enough about my satisfactions. What's it like being a cop?"

"We work Sundays too."

"Come on, you can do better than that."

After a moment, he offered, "Well, the shrinks say there are pre-dictable stages in a law enforcement career. First, the honeymoon, a kind of infatuation with the uniform, the action, the attention. Then after about six years, disillusionment sets in. You're fed up wearing the monkey suit, even the excitement is old hat, and you can't remember the last time anybody showed you any respect."

"And if you get past the disillusion?" Christine asked. "What then?"

"I suppose momentum takes over. I don't know."

She frowned. "You're thinking about Deborah Carter, aren't you?"

"Yes," Emmett lied. Actually, he was thinking about Anna. The heady sense of escape he'd experienced in the air last night was being replaced by a straitjacket of marital guilt. A marriage of the mind that included no conjugal rights. He fought down a rising resentment. He didn't belong here, but it was night back in Oregon too, and he wasn't welcome in Anna's bed.

Quit feeling sorry for yourself.

Christine volunteered, "Let's put Carter to rest once and for all."

"Does that mean you finally trust me?"

"For about three hours now. Fire away, Investigator Parker."

"If her conduct at the school didn't get her canned, what did?"

"All right," Christine said. "This is rumor, secondhand. . . ." At last, she sounded a little tipsy. "What's the legal term?"

"Hearsay."

"So I can't testify that it's a fact, right?"

"Most likely."

"I heard that Carter got careless. Something happened between her and a female captain in EOD at Fort Rucker in Alabama."

Emmett sat up. Explosive Ordnance Disposal. His mind sprang back to the safe in Carter's headquarters.

"Anyway," Christine continued, "I've got a hunch they pushed the don't-ask-don't-tell policy to the limit. Still, the beef might not have involved any sexual issues, okay? But the brass in Military Intelligence started taking a second look at Carter's treatment of female students here at SERE. I don't think she was ever truly out of line, and that's what I told the Criminal Investigation Division guys. But the brass must've figured where there's smoke there's fire, for the next thing we knew Carter was gone, reassigned to the Engineers."

"What was the name of the other officer?"

"Oh, you would ask me." Christine flexed her fingers against her forehead. "Evans. Or something like that. I never met her, know nothing about her." She gave Emmett a hopeful glance. "Enough?"

"Enough."

She swigged down the last of her brandy. "God, am I going to pay for this tomorrow."

Recognizing his cue, Emmett rose on legs that were half asleep and took numb steps around the table to Christine.

She tousled her hair with her fingers and squinted up at him. "It wasn't the booze I was talking about. Where the hell are you going?"

"It's late, and we're both bushed." He offered a hand to help her to her feet, but she seized his tie and yanked him down to her. Her mouth found his, and he tasted the liquor—more forbidden fruit.

"I will tell you when you are bushed," she whispered in his ear with her Russian accent, exotic and seductive-sounding now instead of ominous. He kissed her back, fiercely, and she laughed triumphantly. "You're a pushover, Parker." *No shit.* The frustration of nearly a year with Anna Turnipseed had turned his self-restraint into tissue paper. *No going back, no going back.* A rapidly fading voice asked where this could possibly lead. There were no BIA law enforcement postings in North Carolina, and he knew full well that Christine had no expectations beyond tonight.

But he couldn't stop kissing her, running his palms up and down her back.

Then, without warning, he had his first out-of-body experience since the Sun Dance more than a decade before. One self was still lying entangled with Christine on the tatami mat, but the other was looming dispassionately over the couple. This disembodied self went out the front door, down the stairs and stood confused and grossly embarrassed in the parking lot.

Above, Christine stood in her open door, clearly hurt.

He owed her an explanation.

Emmett drummed back up the stairs and took hold of her by the shoulders. "Look, I'm seeing somebody."

"Good," she said, "so am I." Then she pulled him by the wrists back inside.

14

Anna told Thaddeus Rankin, "U.S. Marshals are seizing the skeleton in Sward's camp right now."

"Good." The oxygen being fed by tube into the anthropologist's nose must have dried out his throat, for he reached for a glass of water on the stand next to his bed. Earlier, she'd guessed stroke, but he'd recovered his power of speech. The on-duty doctor at the Indian Health Service hospital in Warm Springs didn't seem to be sure what was wrong with Rankin, although he raised his eyebrows when Anna mentioned the curious foot-stamping that had preceded the anthropologist's collapse. "Not Parkinson's disease?" Anna asked, but the doctor had refused to confide in a non–family member.

Still shaken by what she'd seen along Wapinitia Road, Anna had resisted turning off to Vernita Dease's house. There'd been no use tormenting Elsa's mother with word of another sighting of her daughter's restless spirit. Hopefully, in the clear, hard light of morning, the incident would seem less real than it did right now.

Rankin set the glass back on the stand, then fixed his puffy eyes on the window in the door to his room. Kawatu stood on the other side of the glass, expressionless but obviously concerned, for he'd been waiting there upon Anna's arrival twenty minutes ago and hadn't budged since.

"He must be very loyal to you," Anna said.

Rankin chuckled sarcastically. "Sorry, my dear, you're reading too much into it. Kawatu's just waiting for the carcass to stop twitching." He gave a voluminous sigh. "When I was young, I saw nothing but virtue in the Fore tribe. Quintessential human beings, unpolluted by civilization—all that pious bullshit. I suppose I wanted to become one of them, so much so I went waltzing into their dark world with little thought that one day I'd have to pay the piper in this one. The fact is, the Fore are crass schemers."

"Schemers for what?"

"Material goods. Cargo. Just like we moth-eaten academics scheme for an immortal reputation. That's our mythology, you know, the touch of yearning that almost makes us human. We actually believe a spirit can live on in the intellectual esteem of others." He waved a tired hand toward the door window. "Please close the curtain around my bed. This is like coming face-to-face with the illusions of my youth." As Anna did so, he asked, "So you saw Willow Creek Woman in the tent?"

"Yes."

"Notice anything peculiar?"

Anna sat again beside him. "Like what?"

"The mandible—missing, just as with John Day Man."

She hadn't noticed; the face of the skull had been turned away from her. "You think the jaw's still out there along Willow Creek?"

Rankin shut his eyes. "Perhaps. Perhaps not. I'll rest tomorrow—doctor's orders—but Monday morning bright will find me out there. The truth can become a ravenous obsession, Anna. Don't make it your obsession . . . all right?"

He said nothing more, so after a few seconds she quietly got up and left the room.

• • •

Fog had closed in around the Holiday Inn in downtown Fayetteville. Swallowing down waves of saliva, Emmett stared through his window into this woolly dawn. The phone rang. He let it ring four times, then answered. "Hello."

"Okay, Parker . . . I think I got what you want." It was the BIA's liaison with the army's Criminal Investigation Division.

"Can you hang on just a minute?"

"Oh, did I wake you?" the CID man asked caustically.

"Just hang on a sec." Emmett put down the telephone and trooped into the bathroom, shut the door and threw up into the toilet bowl. This morning's emotional hangover was so violent it was difficult for him to believe that he hadn't fallen off the sobriety wagon last night. For the first time in his life, he realized how potent an ingredient the conscience was in the nauseating scramble of reactions called a hangover. The only thing missing was a sense of personal weakness. Pathetically, what he'd done last night had not come of weakness. It'd been too premeditated for that. Every step of the way he'd known how the night would end, and he'd plunged ahead. Why? He could come up with only one possible answer: to demolish his relationship with Anna Turnipseed with such finality there would be no going back, no matter how much he might want to patch things up in the coming weeks. Now, his conscience would never permit him to touch her. It all made cold, logical sense, but he'd been puking ever since he'd come back to the hotel at 3:30 A.M.

He rinsed out his mouth and went back to the telephone. "Sorry, nature called."

"Better than Emmett Parker calling at four in the morning," the CID man griped.

"So I owe you."

"Amen." There was a rattle of papers at the other end of the line in Silver Spring, Maryland. "Her name is Evanson. Not Evans, like you told me. Captain Margaret Evanson."

"Does she have a middle or hyphenated name of Watson?"

"Uh, no. Who's Watson?"

According to Anna, the name Deborah Carter had mentioned in her letter to Elsa. "Never mind. Go on."

"Evanson's middle name is Roberta."

"Where's she posted now?" Emmett asked.

"Resigned her commission, July 1992. Whereabouts unknown. Ineligible for retirement, so we can't trace her that way."

"Great." Emmett had feared a dead end like this. "Any idea why Carter got reassigned from SERE to the Corps of Engineers? Her service record says squat about it."

"That's to prevent some nosy PFC file clerk from getting the lowdown on his boss. But you're in luck."

"How?"

"The former commanding officer at Redstone Arsenal is a friend.

Know what's worse than you calling me at four? Me calling him at four-thirty. He'll talk to you. But not over the phone and strictly off the record. You agree to that?"

"Yeah," Emmett said glumly. Ultimately, he might have to find an informant who would testify.

"Got a pen?"

"Yes," Emmett fibbed. Easier than explaining that he could remember things without writing them down. The CID man gave him an address in Boca Raton, Florida. "Thanks, I'll be in touch."

"Normal business hours, Parker. I'm taking in the welcome mat after this."

"Yeah, yeah." Emmett hung up. He had to vomit again. This proved to be the last purging; his stomach was empty. His soul too. Freedom always felt like emptiness at first. Three divorces had taught him that. But something was different this time. He'd never cheated on any of his three wives. Other women had entered his life only after the legal separations. What was he doing? Or did it even matter in a world where everything was up for grabs, including the place his ancestral Nuumu had occupied in it? Was that it—had John Day Man left him in moral confusion?

That's just a dodge. You knew what you were doing.

He dressed, then spread a Southeast U.S. road map over the bed he hadn't slept in. Boca Raton was at least five hundred miles from Fayetteville. Too far to drive. He reached for the yellow pages.

Simply dialing the number got things in motion for him. What he'd told Christine was profoundly true. After disillusionment, you were left with momentum. Just momentum. He asked the United Express reservation clerk, "What do you have departing this morning for south Florida, say Fort Lauderdale?"

• • •

Lying in bed, Anna searched her memory for a face to the apparition that she'd glimpsed Saturday night along Wapinitia Road. She was no longer sure it had been Elsa Dease. Or had been anything more than a product of her own imagination.

A door latch disengaged with a click.

She didn't pay the sound immediate attention, for it hadn't come from the entry door to her own room at the Kah-Nee-Ta. Her mind waded back into the mist along Wapinitia Road.

Then it hit her with a crackling sensation at the back of the neck—the silence-cutting click had been from the adjoining room. Emmett's. He was still gone. He hadn't phoned even once over the two days he'd been gone to North Carolina.

Kicking off her blankets, she rose and took her pistol from her purse. She thought of phoning security but quickly decided that the sound of her voice would only alert the intruder to her presence. She and Emmett had left the connecting door unlocked, so now—without pausing to listen—she threw it open.

Two tall silhouettes loomed in the semidarkness. She shifted her muzzle back and forth between them until she comprehended that one was a reflection on the mirror that covered an entire wall.

"Don't move," she said, protecting as much of her body as she could behind the doorjamb.

"It's me, Anna." Emmett turned on a lamp. His airline carry-on bag lay on the bed.

She lowered her pistol. "What're you doing back?"

"Finished up everything I had to do."

"Why didn't you phone?"

Averting her eyes, he began unpacking. "Got to Portland so late, I didn't want to wake you. Renting a car was easier than having you drive two hundred miles round-trip."

"I mean, why didn't you call me before you left North Carolina?"

"I wasn't in North Carolina. Flew back out of Miami."

"What's that have to do with what I just asked?" But then his stung look made her regret her sharpness with him. "I'm sorry—glad you're back." She started to move toward him, intending to give him a hug and a kiss, but he ducked around the corner into the bathroom with his shaving kit.

"You run across a Margaret Evanson among the Norse pagans?" his voice came out to her.

"No. But listen, another skeleton has been discovered east of here. By Nels and Trish Sward, of all people. Tomorrow Rankin's going out there with a team to look for the mandible."

Emmett emerged from the bathroom. "*Another* skeleton with a missing lower jaw?" he asked skeptically.

"Yes. And the teeth blown out of the upper. What's that mean?"

He shook his head.

Anna went on, "A replacement NAGPRA monitor flew in today, and I'm to back him up at Willow Creek. The local tribes are going to send protesters, so I can use your help."

"Fine, it's Willow Creek first thing in the morning." He seemed submerged in thought. Distant.

"Who's Margaret Evanson?"

"I'll explain in the morning." Without giving her a peck on the cheek, he herded her back into her own room with a few light touches on her back. Then he shut the connecting door.

Anna was back in bed when a faint click cut through the hum of Emmett's shower running. He'd turned the lock on his side of the door.

• • •

As soon as Emmett saw the throng of vehicles parked alongside Willow Creek, he was thankful that Anna had asked the Morrow County sheriff's office for crowd control. He eased the Explorer through the milling crowd. Early this morning, the sheriff had forewarned Anna that the Warm Springs activists would be joined by Umatilla tribal protesters, whose own ancestral lands bordered on the creek. Several media interviews of Indian leaders were under way, and placards bobbed in the air. The most notable read:

FREE PAULINA

AND

OUR ULTIMATE ANCESTORS!

No white pagans were present, although the Swards had been persuaded by the federal marshals to show where they'd found the bones last Friday. Nor was Deborah Carter on the scene; she'd left Corps representation to an engineer type in a down-filled vest who stayed close to his government-plated Suburban. By having the marshals directly take Willow Creek Woman to the Hanford facility in Washington State, bypassing the Corps of Engineers, had Anna tipped off Carter that she was under suspicion? After seeing how intimately familiar SERE staff were with the art of interrogation, Emmett wanted to hit the colonel like a speeding dump truck.

A University of Oregon van and Dr. Rankin's Lexus were set off from the protesters' cars and guarded by a deputy sheriff with a grain-sack belly. Emmett showed the cop his credentials, then pulled alongside the Lexus.

"What'd the doctor at the Warm Springs Hospital say was wrong with Rankin?" Emmett asked Anna as he unhooked his safety belt.

"He wouldn't. I brought up Parkinson's disease, but he wouldn't discuss it." She glanced questioningly back at Emmett.

He knew that her look had nothing to do with Rankin's ailment. As they quickly broke off eye contact, she gestured at the Lexus. "Rankin's sitting in his car."

So he was, drooping in the passenger front seat with the engine running. Emmett got out of the Explorer and strolled around to the man's window. Anna followed him, her hands thrust in her parka pockets.

Rankin powered down the glass, and hot air steamed from the opening. He looked exhausted. "Did you have a fruitful trip back east, Mr. Parker?"

"It was all right," Emmett answered noncommittally. "You're not going down to the dig site?"

"No, I'll have to leave the work to Kawatu and my grad students. They'll keep me informed."

Emmett peered around to get his bearings. Willow Creek Reservoir lay thirty miles upstream, out of sight. According to the map he'd studied, the army's Boardman Bombing Range lay just east of this site. "So, Doctor, another flood and another specimen. This one also without a mandible and the teeth ruptured from the maxilla?"

"Unfortunately, yes."

"Doesn't that seem strange to you?"

"Not really," Rankin replied. "As much as I'd like to find both jaws intact, it's unlikely I will—thanks to the nature of prehistoric cannibalism. My discoveries in New Mexico confirmed that the jaws of victims were pounded and shattered to free the teeth, which were then strung on a necklace. So, realistically, I'm only hoping to find fragments of the mandible here. Is there some problem?"

"Nope," Emmett said, even though this new rendition was at odds with Rankin's previous one that the bushwhacking cannibals had hastily taken only the choicest cuts from John Day Man before pitching his remains into a ravine. So much for infallible expertise. "Think we'll mosey down to the dig."

"Keep a sharp eye out for bone fragments," the anthropologist urged. "The more searchers, the better." Then Rankin's window glided back up.

A camera team was moving toward them, so Emmett led Anna down a path too steep for the newsmen's city shoes. It merged with a cow trail that was marked every fifty yards with a strip of yellow tape hung from a bush.

On the drive here, she'd filled him in about everything that had happened to her in his absence, including her ghostly encounter on Wapinitia Road. Hearing that had made him wonder if their unraveling relationship was stressing her out as well. But he'd not been in the mood to discuss his trip with her. He still wasn't. However, it was time.

He halted.

She stopped too, looking up at him with a trusting expression that lanced him.

"I didn't learn much at the SERE school itself," he began. "The instructors are kept on a tight leash by Army Intelligence, so it's no place for a mental case. And explosive techniques aren't part of the curriculum."

Anna asked plaintively, "Then what *did* you learn that's got you so down, Em?"

His voice almost caught in his throat. *I learned that I've got limits when it comes to you.* "Carter had a close friend, a female captain with Explosive Ordnance Disposal assigned to Redstone Arsenal in Alabama."

"Margaret Evanson," Anna surmised.

"Correct."

"Why'd you ask me last night if I knew somebody with that name among the pagans?"

"My CID liaison turned me on to the former commanding officer at Redstone. A Bible-thumping fundamentalist lay preacher."

"So?"

Emmett checked around to make certain they were still alone. "There was an unusual problem on his base in 1991. Seems he had some practicing pagans among his troops."

"Norse?"

"No, something called Wicca, another brand of paganism. Not racially oriented like Sward's group, as best as I can tell. The general was ready to burn these witches at the stake—until the Judge Advocate advised him that Wiccans, in or out of uniform, are guaranteed freedom of worship by the Constitution. The general went ballistic, rallying conservative politicians in the area to help him drive 'the satan worshippers' out of the army. He was finally muzzled, but that just further convinced him that his cause was righteous."

"What's this have to do with Carter?"

"She was I.D.ed by the MPs at one of these rites. There, according to the general, at the invitation of Captain Evanson. He said 'they were queer for each other'—his words, but he was short on proof about that."

"So this general got Carter transferred from SERE?"

"Indirectly. The army doesn't want any spotlights on the school staff—rightfully so, they teach classified techniques to evade and resist the enemy behind the lines. Nor do they want the students to think their interrogators are into satanic torture, even though Wicca has nothing to do with devil worship. And I'm not even convinced Carter is a Wiccan."

"Still, she got reassigned."

"Yeah."

"And Evanson?"

"I don't know. She resigned her commission in 1992 and dropped out of sight."

"So she might be in Sward's camp," Anna said, "and could've been in The Dalles the morning the safe was dynamited."

"Possible. It'd be nice to get a look at the Norse Folk Congress's roster. What leverage do we have? Are the Swards still under threat of arrest?"

"No more than Bilbao was," Anna replied.

"But old Gorka turned John Day Man over to a respected anthropologist. You told me Rankin had to blow the whistle on the Swards to get these new remains into government hands."

"Right. But the U.S. Attorney seems satisfied now that both skeletons are safely locked up at Hanford. I doubt he'll file on the Swards. Especially after they showed the marshals where they found the bones."

Emmett glanced up: An attack helicopter, laden with missiles, whined overhead toward the bombing range. The chopper reminded him of North Carolina, and Saturday night came rushing back with a vaguely sickening bouquet of brandy and hot candle wax. Anna tracked the helo for a moment, then took the lead down the cow path.

He followed in silence. At least one thing made sense after his trip east. Nels Sward's caustic comment about Carter in the tavern at The Dalles: *What I've heard of her, I thought the colonel would be more sympathetic to our point of view.* Increasingly, the pagan priest seemed to have a wealth of privileged information.

Emmett kept his eyes on the trail, avoiding glimpses of her figure that might spark arousal. Arousal would torture him in a different way from now on. It would sting with loss instead of smolder with frustration.

"Where'd you stay Saturday night?" she asked over her shoulder.

He paused before answering, and instantly realized that the pause was fraught with guilt. "Holiday Inn in Fayetteville."

"Not on the post?"

"Why would I stay at Camp Mackall?"

"I don't know. I got caught late on an interrogation at an air force base once, and they put me up in an apartment. Bachelor Officer Quarters, I think they called it."

He no longer had to explain his actions to her. That was over. But crazily, he wanted her forgiveness. If not that, reassurance that she wouldn't hate him.

The archaeological dig came into view. Kawatu squatted on a sandbar in the creek shallows, placidly watching a bevy of graduate students laboring with shovels and sifting screens. He gave the partners a wave. Emmett nodded back at him, unsure how a man born on the trailing edge of the Stone Age saw all this. Apparently, the bustling activity amused Kawatu, for he was smiling to himself.

A mixed-blood man in an Eastern-style overcoat spotted Anna and Emmett. "Hello!" He churned up a dirt ramp the students had cut into the wall-like bank. He had enough white ancestry for male pattern baldness and a walrus mustache. He was grasping a video camera. "Special Agent Turnipseed and Investigator Parker, I presume?" A tenor voice and crisp diction.

Emmett let Anna tell the man his presumption was right.

"Mel Brantford, Mohawk tribal archaeologist here for NAGPRA." He felt moved to add, "I'm an enrolled Mohawk."

Maybe a quarter enrolled Mohawk, Emmett thought as he shook the man's pulpy hand.

Anna asked, "How's it going so far?"

"Fine," Brantford said with a twinkle in his eye. "Dr. Rankin's crew haven't found a thing. And an Umatilla holy man just finished a ceremony to beseech the forgiveness of the ancestor. I've got it all on tape." He said this as if one day it might prove to be crucial evidence.

To cover his ass, Emmett mused. He asked, "Who's going to do the preliminary exam on the female remains?"

"That's been done, hasn't it?" Brantford looked apprehensively from partner to partner. "The U.S. Attorney faxed me your search warrant affidavit before I left New York. Didn't you say your informant was expert enough to attest to the age of the skeleton?"

"Yes," Anna said, "but my informant's quick look at the remains in a nonlab setting shouldn't be taken as a forensic exam."

"But he compared Willow Creek Woman to John Day Man . . . right, Agent Turnipseed?"

"Well—"

"So," Brantford interrupted her, "it's obvious we're dealing with pre-Columbian age and a clear-cut need for repatriation here. Thankfully, I got the Warm Springs and Umatilla tribes to agree not to fight over cultural patrimony, so Willow Creek Woman can be jointly interred."

"You're not listening to my partner," Emmett said. "We're all for re-patriation. But there are reasons not to get carried away with it."

Brantford nervously stroked his mustache. "Such as?"

"Less than a week ago, somebody planted some nineteenth-century bones in Turnipseed's and my vehicle before torching it. Bones are cropping up all over the place, and no skeleton's going to get reburied before we can pin down its age. The county coroner has a stake in this too, and as cops we've got to back him—despite our sympathies for how the tribes feel. At the very least, John Day Man was examined by a pathologist and a bone was shipped off for radiocarbon dating. When can we expect the same for Willow Creek Woman?"

"You can't," the NAGPRA monitor said stubbornly. "The court already ruled against any invasive technologies being performed on the remains."

"We're not communicating here, Mr. Brantford. The court ruled that only after both procedures had already been carried out on John Day Man. Doesn't this mean those two procedures *aren't* invasive? Christ Almighty, the order let Rankin have a full eight hours with the skeleton."

"I believe the court will be receptive to my recommendation that nothing more be done to Willow Creek Woman, Mr. Parker."

"How the fuck do you know that?" Emmett felt Anna's fist bump against the small of his back.

"You don't have to curse, sir." Brantford took a step back before pulling himself up to his five-foot-eight height. "The potential for social unrest has increased markedly in the last week. More analysis will only inflame the situation."

"You've been here less than twenty-four hours," Emmett pointed out. "I don't think you've got a handle on the situation."

"Neither do you, according to the U.S. Attorney in Portland," the monitor said acidly. "And he's led me to believe that the court will concur with my assessment."

That was it then. The judge was going to let Brantford call the shots until Rankin's lawsuit for complete examination of the remains was adjudicated, which might take years. What had been deemed reasonable scientific inquiry into the age and tribal affiliation of John Day

Man was now held to be unjustified in regard to Willow Creek Woman. A politically motivated decision that flew in the face of judicial consistency. Emmett could care less if Rankin ever again got his paws on either skeleton, but the judge's backpedaling infuriated him. How could Turnipseed and he keep the lid on this pressure cooker if the law flip-flopped at every turn? Indian unrest would now be followed by white pagan unrest. Sward wouldn't take this lying down; he was a man of strong beliefs, however bizarre those beliefs might seem to Emmett. What could he say to pacify Sward? That the court was more sensitive to Indian spirituality than white?

Anna was glaring at him, so he controlled his voice as he asked Brantford, "Then you mean to tell me that no part of this skeleton will be sent off for carbon-dating?"

"That process entails the needless destruction of bone material. We both know that, Mr. Parker. I don't mean to be contentious, but you two seem to be parroting Dr. Rankin's side in an argument I had with him less than an hour ago."

"Fine." Starting back up the trail, Emmett took out his cellular phone.

"Where are you going?" Anna asked, alarmed.

"Find some high ground so I can get through to the U.S. Attorney."

"Why?"

"So he can drag his fat ass out here to keep the peace."

• • •

The pogonip seemed to have a life of its own. That was because this ice fog didn't exist as a compact bank. It was a many-tentacled creature, feeling out with its swirling white arms for the low places in the desert valleys, strangling all sound. *Pogonip* was derived from the Shoshonean word for cloud, but the phenomenon was more like an octopus. The law enforcement ranger for the U.S. Bureau of Land Management kept passing in and out of its blinding grip as he drove along the John Day River. His was a vast beat, as large as some states. And with fewer people than lived in a single New York apartment building. He prowled the night alone, looking for fossil and relic hunters, game poachers, campers who'd stayed on public lands long enough to qualify as squatters. Now and again, he busted methamphetamine manufacturers foolish enough to set up their crude laboratories on the assumption that no cops patrolled this wasteland of grass, sage and basalt.

The ranger was the law here, and few secrets escaped him.

Emerging from another band of fog, he sped up.

Wherever the pogonip passed, it left behind a fairyland of ice crystals. The flocked brush resembled decorative shrubbery in a department store window at Christmas. A sign loomed out of the darkness. The words had been frosted over, but the ranger knew them by heart:

CAMP WATSON HISTORICAL SITE
U.S. CAVALRY OUTPOST 1863–1866
LEAVE ONLY FOOTPRINTS, TAKE ONLY PICTURES

Not that there was much to take.

Time and the elements had erased nearly all vestiges of Camp Watson, which even in its heyday had been little more than a scattering of ramshackle huts around a dusty parade ground, nothing resembling the imposing stockaded fortresses of Western films. Outposts like Watson had been miserable places for their troopers. Suicidal loneliness assuaged only by rotgut whiskey and native prostitutes.

Some of those soldiers were still here.

The ranger flicked on his spotlight and swept the beam over the post cemetery. The wooden head markers had disintegrated or been carried off by souvenir hunters long ago. The graveyard was perched on a bluff above the river, and in moonlight the spot afforded a panorama of glimmering waters on three sides. It felt like an island cut off from the rest of the world, and that's probably what made it a passion pit for rural lovers. The ranger had requested a sign to warn parkers not to drive over the nearly invisible graves, but he was still waiting for it.

As he ran his spotlight over the cemetery, a wisp of fog rose eerily out of the ground. The pogonip had already moved from here on its nocturnal wanderings, so the wisp puzzled him.

Seizing his flashlight, he got out.

The icy ground squeaked under his boots as he strode into the cemetery. He slowed his pace as a strong feeling took hold of him. Someone—or something—was waiting for him out among the graves. His armpits went cold with sweat. He unsnapped the safety strap on his holster as he approached the spot where he believed the spurt of fog had flowed out of the ground. Frosted dirt lay on either side of a five-foot-deep hole. His first wild thought was that one of the desiccated bodies had shucked off its mantle of earth and bolted into the night. Is that what he'd seen as fog moments ago—the thing taking flight?

He made himself settle down. It was easy to spook yourself, alone on a night patrol in the middle of a fogbound desert.

An object glinted dully in the bottom of the open grave.

Climbing down into the pit, he examined the object. A tarnished brass button with an American eagle on it. Army issue. Stooping, he raked the ice off the dirt base, revealing tatters of a gray woolen blanket and dark blue uniform cloth—the snatches of material still held their colors after more than 130 years underground. He picked up something, believing it to be a shaving brush, then hurriedly dropped it in revulsion. A hank of light brown hair, as fresh-looking as if it'd been snipped off a living head only last week.

After that, it was all he could do to search the violated grave for its occupant.

But, after twenty chilling minutes, he found only one bone, so small he couldn't recognize it. He stood upright, thinking. Often, frontier graves caved in on themselves when the coffin lids rotted through. But no doubt this soldier had been buried in his blanket in the 1860s and then dug up sometime between the ranger's check of Camp Watson last week and the onset of tonight's fog.

Getting back inside his four-wheel drive and starting the engine, the ranger ran the heater full blast. He believed he now knew what it was like to lie in a grave.

Cold. Cold that made you sink through time like a hailstone.

15

"A syphilitic cavalry trooper dug up at old Camp Watson," Dr. Sinclair said, summarizing the verbal report Anna had just given him. The semiretired pathologist, who'd examined John Day Man for the Wheeler County coroner, lived just downriver from The Dalles on the Washington shore. He shifted in his worn easy chair as if trying to get comfortable with this information. "Well, that jibes with the finding of mercury in the bones and *Rankin's* observation that the forehead looked worm-eaten from a dose of Venus's curse. . . ." Anna caught the vinegary inflection the elderly man used on the anthropologist's name—and the lack of *Doctor* prefacing it. "So now all you two have to do is figure out who dug up this horse soldier and stuffed him in your car."

Emmett nodded agreeably enough, but Anna could tell that he was disappointed by Dr. Sinclair's condition. The pathologist had undergone cataract surgery two days ago, and a protective cup was taped over his right eye. One lens replaced and one more to go, he'd cheerfully explained. He was the expert who'd declared John Day Man to be Caucasian and modern, and since the failure yesterday of Rankin's team to find Willow Creek Woman's lower jaw, Emmett had been seeking support for expanded analyses of both sets of remains. For law enforcement, not anthropological purposes.

He'd counted on Dr. Sinclair to be his chief supporter.

Then the pathologist's front door had swung open, and the aged man goggled at the partners through his clouded left eye as if he could barely make them out. The interior of his Victorian house was gloomy, and it smelled musty from pervasive mold. The high, dim ceilings made her feel small. Compounding her low spirits was the realization that, since returning from the East, Emmett looked at her only when she spoke. And then briefly.

"Doctor, let me get something straight," Emmett said as politely as his foul mood of the past day probably allowed—thank God he hadn't phoned the U.S. Attorney as threatened yesterday morning along Willow Creek. "You had all the time you needed to examine the skeleton, right?"

"You bet. This was before the NAGPRA bureaucracy horned in."

"How long did your exam take?"

"About an hour. Maybe a little less."

Emmett frowned. "And it was your opinion that the remains were those of a modern white man?"

"Yes, sir."

Anna could see Emmett struggling with the credibility issue—a visually impaired rural pathologist who'd come up with a conclusion diametrically opposed to Rankin's. Thaddeus Rankin, the preeminent authority on questionable osseous remains.

And by now, Dr. Sinclair had caught on too. "What's eating at you, Mr. Parker? You *want* to believe Rankin that those bones are fourteen times older than Methuselah?"

"Frankly, no. But I'm looking for concrete evidence one way or the other."

"No such thing," Dr. Sinclair said. "*Concrete* is a building term, not a forensic one. As an investigator, you should know that. And how evidence fits into a theory is *always* in the eye of the beholder." He smiled at his own allusion, his cheek crinkling under the protective cup. "Here's the question that's chafing at you, Mr. Parker—how blind was this old sawbones a month ago when the Wheeler County coroner came running to him with a slew of dirty bones? Pretty damned blind, I'll admit."

"Did Dr. Rankin recommend you for the initial exam?" Emmett asked. A new line of inquiry he hadn't discussed with Anna. She looked to Sinclair, who straightened his shoulders.

"Hell no," the pathologist groused. "You think that arrogant bastard thinks anybody but him knows a scapula from a spatula? There's a rotation list of court-recognized experts, and invariably Rankin's name is at the top of it. But he screwed himself out of the job in this case because he accepted the remains from that Basco bone collector."

"So you were the next name on the list?"

"Yes, miss."

"We're in no position to question your credibility," Anna continued, "but you came up with such a different finding from Dr. Rankin's. And there's UC Riverside's carbon dating of the fifth metacarpal at over fourteen thousand years." She saw no other way to put it: "Have you had second thoughts about your report since you gave it to the Wheeler County coroner?"

"No," Dr. Sinclair said tenaciously.

"Did you observe evidence of possible cannibalism?"

"I saw a few cut marks. God only knows what they mean."

"Is it possible your vision was a factor in your evaluation?"

"Yes, Miss Turnipseed, an immaterial factor."

"I don't understand."

Dr. Sinclair raised his hands and showed them to the partners. "These were all I needed to evaluate those bones."

"I still don't understand," Anna said.

"I've *felt* fourteen-thousand-year-old remains with these hands, miss. Specimens from China. Ancient bones feel brittle like honeycomb candy. I tell you—the bones Rankin turned over to the Corps of Engineers felt *green*."

• • •

A large chamber opened off of Thaddeus Rankin's library. The original owner of the mansion had used it as a morning room, a sunny place for the women of the household to gather, to chat and sew. Rankin had installed wooden blinds over the windows and turned the room into a secret shrine to his late father. Here, he housed the man's artifacts. The most curious was a collection of penile sheaths. No self-respecting Fore tribesman would've gone out in public without one of these two-foot-long tubes covering his member, even though he was otherwise nude. The ornaments had appealed to the old man's dry sense of whimsy.

Herbert Rankin had been born to a Colorado mining fortune, and his early adulthood was devoted to a sinecure in banking punctuated by aimless world travel. But while in New Guinea during the 1920s, he came upon a Fore funeral feast in which the women of an extended family placidly ate the deceased, who'd been cut up into bite-sized chunks and lightly steamed in banana leaves. Thus began his fascination with one of the darkest threads in the tapestry of human behavior. Returning home to earn a master's degree in anthropology, Herbert Rankin had been astonished to learn that academia questioned the very existence of cannibalism, viewing it as a myth invented by Westerners to advertise their own moral superiority. It had not been a myth among the Fore, a protein-starved people who saw nothing immoral about ingesting their dead relatives. It fact, they thought this grisly last supper to be an act of piety. So, in 1936, Herbert Rankin published *Endocannibalism Among the Fore Tribe of the New Guinea Highlands,* the seminal work that vaulted the former polo-playing dilettante to a controversial preeminence in anthropology.

Thaddeus Rankin had labored all his life in his father's shadow, but only in the last few years had he realized that he'd never emerge from it. The same mindless forces that had questioned cannibalism in New Guinea were covering up its evidence in ancient North America, its devastating impact on a small number of Caucasoid pioneers, and Rankin was running out of time to make his case.

He now toasted his father's portrait with his third scotch and soda of the afternoon. "You win, Papa. The playing field was never level. But you taught me to enjoy a good irony, and that's what I intend to do."

Lately, the old man came to him in his dreams, a figure robed in patriarchal white. This was a disquieting experience for an avowed agnostic, although Rankin didn't believe that his father's spirit was trying to contact him. Rather, his own diseased and dying brain was crying out against its imminent doom, fabricating a personal myth to take the sting out of mortality.

Rankin's cordless phone rang. "Hello."

"There is a situation, sir," Kawatu said. "Colonel Carter is at the gate, demanding entry."

"What does she want?"

"To see you at once."

Rankin rose on his cane and shuffled across the room. He opened a panel of wooden slats for a view of the heights above his spacious lawn. Carter's Corps of Engineers sedan was parked squarely in front of the gate, and the colonel herself was standing at the intercom speaker set in one of the gateposts. Impossible to tell at this distance how agitated she was, but her unannounced appearance made Rankin suspect she'd finally learned that he had accused her of the safe job and Bilbao's murder. Had Turnipseed and Parker let the cat out of the bag?

"What shall I do, sir?" Kawatu asked.

Chances were that Carter would vent her spleen, threaten legal action, then depart in a huff. "Bring her down to the house, my boy. Remain on the line."

A few moments later, Rankin watched the Lexus speed up the hill toward the gate. Yesterday morning at Willow Creek, Emmett Parker had kept mum about his trip to North Carolina. When a veteran investigator clammed up, it usually meant that he'd hit pay dirt.

So the colonel might be growing desperate.

Carter got back behind the wheel of her sedan.

Kawatu stopped at least a car's length below the gate and stepped out. Rankin was about to warn him over the phone that he'd left too much space between the Lexus and the entrance, when the colonel accelerated around him and barreled down the slope, unescorted.

"Damn." Rankin turned and, as quickly as he could, made for his library. God only knew what this woman was capable of. He took the five-shot revolver from the top right drawer of his desk and cracked the cylinder to make sure it was loaded. Yes. He slipped the handgun into the pocket of his cardigan sweater.

"What do I do?" Kawatu's voice came from the cordless phone. He sounded unflappable, as always, but the Lexus's engine could be heard at high revolutions in the background.

"Is the front door unlocked?"

"Yes, sir."

"Let her come inside."

"Do I accompany the colonel?"

"No, my boy. Hang back and see what develops. This could all add up to nothing." Rankin sat behind his desk. The top of his head was on fire, a symptom that always came before another deterioration in his condition. How much worse could things get before his nervous system utterly failed? Medicine had no answer. Almost perversely, his illness ravaged his nerves without debilitating the muscles, so his old physical strength remained latent in his twitching body.

"Rankin!" Deborah Carter's shout came through the house from the foyer.

"This way, Colonel," he called out to her, putting down the phone but keeping the connection open with Kawatu.

The front door slammed shut.

Carter burst through the library doorway in a disheveled uniform. Her unscarred facial skin was ruddy, and Rankin thought he could smell whiskey on her. Her hands were tight around her purse. Odd she'd thought to bring it from the car. "Rankin," she said hatefully.

"Good afternoon, Colonel. Has the Corps of Engineers finally come to broker a deal with me over the specimens?"

Her mouth was bent by a cruel smile. "Yeah, that's it."

"Well, spell it out, dear woman."

"Do exactly what I say and you might live."

"I beg your pardon?"

Carter drew a pistol from her purse and leveled it on him. "You heard me, you son of a bitch." Rankin's first inclination was to go for the revolver in his sweater pocket, but he swiftly realized the futility in that. So he hoisted his tremulous hands and listened for Kawatu in the house to Carter's back. He remained calm. *You're already a dead man. A dead man can take anything. A dead man still on his feet is unstoppable.*

The colonel seemed to be distracted by his shaking. "What the hell is wrong with you?" she asked in obvious disgust.

"I'm dying, Deborah," he said simply.

If his words had any effect on Carter, her eyes didn't show it. "Get up. We're going for a drive."

"Where?"

"To find Elsa."

"I have no idea where she is," he answered, but this reply only incensed her.

"Get up and show me before I shoot you between the eyes right now, you crazy son of a bitch!"

Rankin coolly smiled at her. "You have a lovely anger, Deborah. We should let our angers out to play with each other sometime."

Carter rushed around the desk and slapped him. Before the shock had worn off his face, she'd seized him by the left forearm and jerked him to his feet with a painful wristlock. Hovering on his tiptoes, Rankin was astonished that his body could still move so quickly. At close quarters, Carter stank strongly of booze. She kept up the pressure on his bent wrist as she shoved him toward the hallway. He heard a creak of hardwood flooring somewhere out in the house—Kawatu, he realized, and he stifled a slight grin.

She must have taken Rankin's clumsy gait for resistance, for she began tapping the back of his neck with her pistol muzzle. "Move!"

The front door was wide open to the afternoon. Just minutes after Carter had slammed it shut. Pushing Rankin outside, Carter peered all around—for Kawatu, the anthropologist was positive, who was conspicuously nowhere near the Lexus.

"You drive." She manhandled Rankin past the rear of her sedan.

"I can't," he protested, knowing that his chances for survival improved with each additional thing to preoccupy her. "I'm in no condition."

Carter's lips thinned over her teeth, but then she opened the passenger-side front door of her car and thrust him into the bucket seat. She kept her pistol aimed on him the entire time she rounded the grille and got in her own side of the sedan. Her keys were in the ignition, and she started the engine with her pistol still trained on Rankin. "Right now—tell me which way to go . . ." She held the gas pedal to the floor. ". . . or I'll dump your corpse out on your own lawn!"

"Go where, Deborah?"

"To find Elsa!" The cords stood out in her neck.

Rankin shrugged helplessly. "I wish I could help you."

Midway up the driveway, she braked. So hard, Rankin was tossed against the dashboard. He recovered himself and sat back, nursing what he believed would be a badly bruised elbow tomorrow. If there were a tomorrow for him. Incredibly, the thought of imminent death made him want to giggle. Another symptom of his ailment, the uncontrollable laughter, but the impulse itself seemed to perfectly describe his contempt for the world.

Carter had pulled a large manila envelope out from under her seat and was offering it to him. When he didn't accept it, she barked, "Look inside before you lie to me!"

He undid the fastener and slid out two eight-by-ten photographs. The first was of a barren landscape. Local plateau country most likely. Shot from miles up. The colors were false: Vegetation was red and water yellow. He realized that, for readability, these hues had been superimposed on the gray tones of a satellite photo. Rankin recognized Lake Umatilla, a bladderlike swelling in the Columbia River, and the rest of the quilted topography fell into place for him. He traced Willow Creek up to its reservoir. "A satellite photograph, Deborah. So what?"

"Shot on Monday morning, October twenty-second."

Two days after Elsa Dease vanished along Wapinitia Road, Rankin recalled. "How's this involve me?"

"Accidentally," she spat at him. "The army was testing an air-to-air missile for the new attack helicopter, so a Department of Defense satellite turned its telescope camera on the west side of the Boardman Bombing Range."

"And?"

"Look at the next photo, you bastard. The resolution is amazing."

Not quite as amazing as Rankin had been led to believe military satellites were—but he could still pick out the Dodge diesel pickup parked within walking distance of Willow Creek. Thankfully, the license plate wasn't readable, perhaps more from the high angle of the camera than any deficiency in its ground resolution. But Rankin saw himself pointing with his cane toward the creek. For Kawatu's benefit. A man, obviously a black man, was setting out from the pickup with a canvas bag. All this was clear enough to be compelling evidence in court.

He faced Carter's pitiless eyes. Drunken green eyes. "Well," he muttered with a soft laugh, "there you have it."

"The Dodge is registered to a Kawatu *Rankin* of Klickitat Valley, Washington."

"I recently adopted the dear boy," Rankin said, "but he still insists on having a place of his own. I suppose I'm a bit too much to take twenty-four hours a day." Again, he thought of the revolver in his sweater pocket, but Carter's attention with her own weapon was unrelenting. "How'd you find out Kawatu is the registered owner? The license plate isn't visible in your photo."

"Ran your name for owned vehicles through the Washington State Police. No Dodges showed up, but the computer abstract showed a near miss—Kawatu's pickup."

"By chance, have you shared these photos with Turnipseed and Parker?"

"Screw them. They've been too busy investigating me. Screw all the cops, you've got them in your pocket. That's why I'm handling this myself." Without warning, she reached over and began frisking him. His hand darted for his pocket, but he was too late—Carter was already grasping his revolver. The discovery seemed to have no impact on her. She just let down her window and flung the piece out onto the lawn. The glass whined up, and she confronted him again with a look that said she could kill him with an utter lack of remorse. "What've you done with Elsa?"

"Nothing. That much is the truth, Deborah."

"Where is her body?"

"I really don't know."

She cuffed him on the side of the head with the butt of her pistol. His vision grayed out, and a little blood trickled around his ear. Carter's voice cut through his momentary confusion. "I'm going to the top of the driveway now. There are only two directions to go from there, right or left. Tell me which turn to make to go to Elsa, or I'll blow your brains out." She said this so apathetically it didn't seem like a threat—until she jabbed the muzzle of her pistol against his temple.

Rankin smiled at her.

"Stop smiling, you sick bastard!" she cried. They had come to the open gate. Her forefinger began compressing the trigger. It didn't take much pull to set off a pistol.

"Let's not make a scene in front of my own house, Deborah," he said, raising his voice for the first time.

"Which way!"

Rankin went on smiling. "Right, my dear. Turn right and follow Highway 14 until I tell you."

• • •

Emmett hurried up the stairs of the Oregon State Police crime lab in Portland. A hatbox was cradled in his arms. He'd tired of waiting for the elevator, but now had to pause on the second-floor landing for Anna to catch up. She was burdened with her own hatbox. "You didn't leave the copy of the court order in the supervisor's office, did you?" she needled.

"No." Not after spending most of last night fighting to get the order, he wasn't about to forget it.

But the victory had been limited.

Mel Brantford, the new NAGPRA monitor, had won on the radiocarbon-dating issue. Emmett had asked the judge for a tiny bone from Willow Creek Woman and a new bone from John Day Man to be sent to the UC Riverside lab. Refused. Choking down his frustration, Emmett had then petitioned for the atlatl point tip lodged in John Day Man's thigh bone to be obsidian-hydration tested. Once cracked open, volcanic glass absorbs water at a constant rate, a reliable means of determining the age of a lithic artifact. That too had been denied because the extraction would damage bone matter. But finally, claiming to see *"some merit for law enforcement questions about the discoveries"* in Emmett's brief, the judge allowed resin casts to be made of the incomplete skulls and delivered to the nearest forensic lab for reconstruction. While this left Emmett less than jubilant, the order could open the door to further testing—particularly if the partial faces didn't resemble the sculptures that had already been made of other ancient Caucasoid finds. Early this morning, the same CAT-scan trailer used by Rankin at the Corps of Engineers exam had been trucked to the Hanford facility. Three-dimensional images had been made of the two skulls, then cast in resin.

Emmett knew that he'd almost struck out with the court. It had come down to an argument of time and distance. The other alleged Caucasoid specimens, Spirit Cave Man and Buhl Woman, had been found forty-nine years and hundreds of miles apart. John Day Man and Willow Creek Woman had been discovered twenty-eight days and less than fifty miles apart. Also, these latter remains had been strewn along water courses, not in strata of earth that could have pinpointed the archaeological epoch in which these people had lived and died.

Once more, Emmett waited on the landing for Anna to catch up. Her hair was speckled with fine drops from the drizzle that had just blown in from the Pacific, and her eyes were glazed over as if something had just dawned on her. Something troubling.

"What's wrong?" he asked, impatient to get the casts into the sculptor's hands.

His brusque tone must have kept her from speaking, for she just shook her head as they started up the last flight together.

Naturally, the forensic sculpture laboratory was at the far end of the corridor. "Let's try to get hold of the carbon-dating folks at UC Riverside again before quitting time. . . ." He checked his wristwatch: It was already a quarter to five. At two this afternoon, he'd phoned to ask if John Day Man's metacarpal had ever been shipped back to the Corps of Engineers. The secretary hadn't known, and the rest of the staff was tied up on a test. "And I want to find out how that particular finger bone was chosen," Emmett went on to Anna, who continued to look stunned. "Did Rankin physically make the choice? Or did somebody from the Corps do it on his recommendation?"

Ignoring his questions, Anna said quietly, "You want off the hook, don't you?"

He stopped in the middle of the corridor. "What're you talking about?"

She halted too, her eyes moist. "You came to a decision about us on your trip back East. And now you want to call it quits."

Was his head translucent, like the resin cast of John Day Man's he was holding? "I don't know what you're talking about," he said hollowly.

"Yes you do, Em. Maybe you don't realize how different you've been since you came back. But you know what I'm talking about."

He had no idea what to say next. Asking her to postpone this talk for another time would only confirm to her what she'd already intuited. But he wasn't about to deliver the speech he'd prepared, not in the sterile, echoing hallway of a crime lab. Her eyes slowly filled as he racked his brains for something to say that might get him past this moment.

Then his cellular phone rang. Like a prayer answered. He set the hatbox on the floor.

He half expected somebody from the UC Riverside lab, but it was his army Criminal Investigation Division contact in Washington, D.C. A crackly connection. "Okay, Parker, I finally tracked down Evanson for you. Did it through some former EOD pals of hers." Emmett was so rattled by Anna's on-target observation, a second passed before he could recall—Captain Margaret Evanson, Carter's pagan friend with Explosive Ordnance Disposal. "She's dead," the CID man went on.

"Say again?"

"Evanson is *deceased*. In fact, she's been dead since 1992."

Emmett pivoted slightly so he wasn't facing Anna. "How?"

"After resigning her commission, she went to work for a private ordnance disposal firm. They got a contract from the Kuwaiti government to help with the cleanup after the Gulf War. Evanson was killed while clearing a minefield."

"What happened?"

"Who knows? Her mind must've been on something else," the CID man said wryly. "You want me to find out?"

Emmett considered it. Then he felt this entire lead totter and collapse in on itself. However promising the pagan link between Carter and Evanson had seemed on the flight back from the East Coast, someone other than Margaret Evanson had tried to blow open the Corps of Engineers safe. Someone else had tortured Gorka Bilbao to death. Somebody still at large. He would've never encountered Christine Kelly if he'd known all this a week ago. Last Saturday night would never have happened. Yet it all seemed inevitable. And every complex investigation had within it at least one utterly convincing but misleading coincidence. Like a false rhyme. "No," he told the CID agent, "don't bother following up on how Evanson died. I've already wasted enough of your time."

"Oh, thanks for making me feel this was worthwhile."

"It was—the lead had to be eliminated," Emmett said, "and I appreciate your help. Got to go." Pocketing the phone and swooping up the hatbox on the run, he said to Anna, "Well, Margaret Evanson isn't traipsing around Oregon behind our backs—she died in an explosives accident in Kuwait."

Anna made no comment, and Emmett pushed open the lab door.

The sculptor shyly introduced herself: Angela Bream, a graying woman of early middle age in a shapeless cotton shift. She was also wearing sandals, despite the onset of rain. It was soon apparent from her reticent manner that she preferred communing with the heads of the dead to dealing with talking ones. She read the note from her supervisor authorizing overtime, then the court order and finally the transcript of Rankin's examination of John Day Man. Thankfully, Anna had remembered to bring a copy along, having recalled from an FBI academy class that a forensic sculptor made fundamental deductions on age, sex and race based in part on the rest of the skeleton.

Emmett took stock of the laboratory. Numerous heads were in the process of being reconstructed. Some were girdled with straps of clay as if locked in medieval torture devices. A big tub labeled *Cornish Pot Clay* was the apparent source of an earth smell that filled the entire room. He reminded himself to find a motel here in Portland for the night. The long drive back to Warm Springs would be the perfect opportunity for the talk with Anna, but he no longer felt up to it. Tomorrow.

Bream went through the papers again as if something was missing, then asked, "Where's the report on the female specimen?"

"There isn't one," Anna replied. To Emmett's relief, she sounded all-business again. "Dr. Rankin had a brief look at the remains, but not under lab conditions. He told me he believes the skeleton to be at least thirteen thousand years old and Caucasoid. I'm sure he'll be glad to help you if any further questions arise."

Bream sighed. "How soon do you need the reconstructions?"

"As quick as possible," Emmett said.

"Two days, if I work late. That's time-and-a-half after five o'clock."

"No problem with your supervisor. Uncle Sam will foot the bill."

"I'd still like more time."

"Not possible," Emmett said. He was sick and tired of being behind the curve on this case. Forensic sculptors were artists, and in his experience even the most conscientious artists were wasteful of time. "And we'd like the female's done first." He hadn't discussed this with Anna, and the implication visibly hit her. Elsa.

Bream lifted John Day Man's resin cast out of the first hatbox and shed its protective bubble wrap. Emmett was reminded of Mesoamerican masks of polished alabaster he'd seen in a museum: This cast gave off the same inner glow of consciousness. Bream seemed to let the piece communicate to her, then rested it on the table. "The newspaper said the mandibles haven't been found. Still true?"

"Yes," Anna said. "Can you fill in the lower portions of the faces from what you have of the two skulls?"

Emmett had the same hope, but Bream answered, "No. The best I can do is smooth some clay over the top of the temporomandibular joint to infer some continuity down to the cutoff point on the rest of the reconstruction." She unpacked Willow Creek Woman and studied her until Emmett could bear the silence no more.

"What are you thinking, Ms. Bream?"

"Both specimens have recessive cheekbones and narrow nasal apertures. Those would be the Caucasoid characteristics Dr. Rankin cited in his report on the John Day specimen. But I'm also struck by their somewhat flat foreheads and circular eye sockets."

"Like Mongoloids," Emmett finished for her.

"Yes." The sculptor lifted Willow Creek Woman's head to the level of her own. "Nice symmetry, wide-set eyes. Pretty. She was very pretty."

• • •

Night fell as Deborah Carter drove Rankin northwest along State Route 241 through the Rattlesnake Hills of Washington. Twenty minutes ago, the sun had set behind the smoke-gray cloud bank of an approaching storm, and Rankin had smiled as the colonel boosted the brightness of the dashboard lights—to keep a sharper eye on him, he supposed. She was supporting her increasingly heavy pistol in the crook of her right arm, although she never failed to keep it pointed at him. And she still seemed worried about the police falling in behind her or setting up a roadblock ahead.

A sign alerted her to the intersection with Route 24 a mile away. "Which way?" she demanded.

"I'll tell you when we get there, Deborah."

She looked bitterly at him. "It was Kawatu who phoned me, wasn't it?"

"I beg your pardon?"

"Your man phoned me last Thursday night, telling me I could find Elsa's body seven miles up the Tanner Creek road near the big dead fir tree. Admit it, you son of a bitch!"

"Let's keep this civil, Deborah."

"Tell me!" Her whiskey buzz had probably worn off, and she was growing more and more frazzled by the minute.

"I can tell you that Elsa is nowhere near Tanner Creek."

Strangely, that settled Carter down somewhat. She'd been gripping the steering wheel too hard, and her right hand cramped. She shook it several times, and the pilotless car wavered back and forth over the center line. No other vehicle lights were visible. The colonel took hold of the wheel again as they came to the intersection with Route 24.

Carter stopped and faced him. What had she looked like before that Vietcong rocket mangled her features? Quite handsome in a Germanic fashion, Rankin imagined, judging from the underlying bone structure. Interesting. But by no means as interesting as Anna Turnipseed's morphology, which undoubtedly resembled that of the northeast Asian migrants to the New World.

"Which way?" Carter's voice was raw with fatigue. No doubt she'd never planned to drive this far.

"Right, my dear," Rankin answered.

"Don't call me that," she snarled.

"As you wish." Rankin let her go five miles to the east, then told her to pull off onto a power line road that struck south into the rolling grasslands. Again, no other headlights showed anywhere in the vicinity. The dried autumn grass shivered in the rising wind. "Left onto that little dirt road coming up."

"Get me stuck, Rankin, and I'll shoot you on the spot. I'll kill you right now!"

"You won't get stuck," he reassured her. But her sedan bounced a good deal as she climbed the road in low gear. They topped the crest of Yakima Ridge, and clustered lights appeared in the valley below. "Stop anywhere here," he said.

They'd come to a flat place along the ridge, and Carter circled around it, letting her lights flare out over the sparse prairie grass. As if searching the darkness for evidence of a grave.

"No, it's not what you think, Deborah."

She braked and shut off the engine. Her lights remained on. "What are you saying?"

Rankin gazed out over the floodlit installations of the Department of Energy's Hanford reservation. "Poor Elsa's down there in a secure vault. It's the best I could do for her."

Carter stared at Hanford. The strength of her hope—her all-too-human denial, really—fascinated Rankin. She'd probably made the most obvious mental connection as soon as the discovery of Willow Creek Woman was announced. But she'd refused to believe that Elsa might be beyond rescue; it wasn't human to abandon hope, so Carter hadn't.

Suddenly, a moan escaped her lips.

Except it was more tortured than a moan and soon swelled into an enraged shout. So loud she probably didn't hear the snick of the rear passenger door latch being opened. But the dome light came on as Kawatu slid into the back seat and began to curl his powerful hands around her throat.

She fired twice while spinning around in her seat.

The hot blue flashes were so near Rankin's face he was momentarily blinded. Deafening reports. A big caliber. When he could see again, two spidery bullet holes pierced the rear window, and the trunk lid—stitched by the same rounds—was bobbing up and down. The car rocked under him as if in an earthquake.

Carter and Kawatu were grappling for the pistol.

He expected Kawatu to quickly overpower her, but the woman showed a hysterical strength that made her the man's match. Rankin tried to punch her in the stomach, but one of her long legs jackknifed up and slammed his head against the side window. His skull was still throbbing when a scream made him clasp his palms to his ears.

Rankin struggled to make sense of the scream in the chaos of flailing arms. The pistol was no longer in sight. But apparently Carter had needed both hands to hang on to it, and Kawatu only one. Using his free hand, the man had gouged out Carter's right eye. His thumb was left bloody, and the ruined globe was smeared across the woman's scarred cheek.

But on the two of them fought.

Dropping his hands from his ears, Rankin searched the glove compartment for a weapon. A metal flashlight, a screwdriver, anything. But there was nothing useful inside.

Carter pounded the heel of her hand into the base of Kawatu's nose. His head snapped back, and Carter leaped over the seat at him. Their struggle looked like a violent sexual coupling in the backseat. It had the sweaty, primal energy of sex.

Rankin groped in the space between the bucket seats for the pistol, hoping that it had fallen there. No.

Carter reared back her fist. But as she hurled it at Kawatu's throat he thrust her upward with his knees. She crashed into the roof, buckling the sheet metal with a crunch. The dome light was covered by her body, and in the semidarkness the pistol roared and flashed twice more.

Then silence for two heartbeats.

Kawatu continued to press Carter's body against the roof, even though two black streams of liquid were pouring out of the woman's abdomen. "Let me down, let me down," she gasped breathlessly.

Kawatu was preparing to fire once more with Carter's pistol when Rankin shouted, "Don't shoot inside here again! We're in a metal box, for godsake!" He feared a ricochet.

"Let me down," Carter begged even more desperately.

"Do as she asks," Rankin said.

But Kawatu swung his elbow up, crushing the woman's larynx with a sound like a wishbone snapping. Even in the dim light, Rankin could see froth bubbling out of the corners of her mouth. Then she went limp.

Kawatu lowered her onto his chest and looked up at Rankin, almost sheepishly.

The anthropologist roughly took hold of him by the chin. "What took you so long?"

As always, Kawatu gave no answer. His dark eyes shone with a brutish innocence. He was of the Fore, and their ways were inexplicable to outsiders. It was enough for Rankin that, upon being herded at gun-point into the sedan by Carter, he'd seen that the trunk lid was slightly ajar. If Kawatu hadn't been inside holding it, the lid would have sprung all the way open. That knowledge had kept him from putting up a fight at the outset. That and the fact he hadn't wanted a corpse on the grounds of his estate.

"Take me home, my boy."

16

In the crime lab, Anna suggested to Emmett that they use the elevator instead of the stairs. As much as possible, she didn't want to retrace any of the steps in this building that had led to her bungled attempt to get Emmett to open up. Last night, after leaving the resin casts with the sculptor, they'd checked into a hotel in downtown Portland. An awkward moment followed when their separate room-service dinners arrived at the same time—and they traded embarrassed smiles from their doorways. She half expected him to invite her to join him, if merely out of habit. But he didn't. So she picked at her Salisbury steak alone in her room. A call later to Dr. Tischler provided no encouragement: It was time for Anna to risk a frank discussion with Emmett, even if that talk led to estrangement. She recalled gliding through the warm water of the pool at the Kah-Nee-Ta. Water, through which the past couldn't chase her. And roller coasters, too swift for memory to keep up with her. *My sexuality is finally awakening, and we're moving toward estrangement.*

The elevator doors opened on the third floor.

Stepping out, Emmett asked her, "You have the beauty pageant photo?"

Anna nodded. There was something comforting in his asking, as if they were a long-married couple jogging each other's memories over minor details. Except this wasn't minor. Anna had brought one of Elsa Dease's missing person flyers. Why did this job make personal concerns seem trivial? Maybe they were, in comparison to murder and mayhem, but she was tired of her own needs feeling like guilty pleasures.

Angela Bream was hunched over a clay head. The face under reconstruction was turned away from Anna and Emmett. "Good, you got my message," the sculptor said. "I'm farther along than I thought I'd be, though I didn't get home this morning until three."

"We appreciate the extra effort," Emmett said.

Anna's heart was pounding too fast for small talk. She didn't want to round the table. Didn't want to see. There was still hope as long as she didn't look. She found herself remembering Elsa Dease along the John Day River beside Minnie Claw. In her wing dress at Rankin's examination of John Day Man.

As Anna hesitated, Emmett took the flyer from her hand and stepped behind Bream. He scrutinized the rebuilt face, then compared it to the photo.

Anna waited for him to say that this was indeed Elsa. But, with his jaws clenched, he motioned for her to come around to him.

At last, she beheld the face.

Her first reaction was one of amazement—that within eighteen hours Angela Bream had been able to transform a fleshless, partial cranium into two-thirds of a living face. A face with animation, personality, experience even. Emmett used the flat of his hand to block off everything below Elsa's upper lip on the photo. He again made the comparison, obviously having the same problem Anna was. She'd tried to make the slight leap of perception needed to match a photograph to any secondhand likeness, be it an artist's drawing or a reconstructed skull. But couldn't. Maybe it was the false eyes, a brown similar to Elsa's but set in the sockets more shallowly than the Warm Springs woman's had been.

"Well . . . ?" Bream asked uncertainly for their verdict.

Emmett shook his head. Anna agreed: This was not a likeness of Elsa Dease. But her relief was mixed with weariness—once again, they were back to square one. "Good job," Emmett finally said to Bream. "I'd like the local FBI field office to photograph both sculptures as soon as John Day Man is completed."

"Tomorrow afternoon," the sculptor said. "I've got to sleep sometime."

"We'll get the photos out to missing persons bureaus all over North America," he said to Anna. "This face looks nothing like Spirit Cave

Man's or Buhl Woman's." His cellular rang. "Parker here . . ." He frowned as if the reception was bad, then said louder, "I can't hear you. Let me give you a land-line to dial. . . ." Bream recited her phone number, and Emmett repeated it into the cellular. Seconds later, the phone chirped like a cricket in Bream's small, glass-enclosed office. As Emmett hastened to answer it, Bream asked Anna in slight confusion, "You two expected a familiar face?"

"Yes," she admitted, "a missing person off the Warm Springs reservation. But this isn't she. Almost Hispanic, isn't it?"

"Maybe," Bream said. "If these specimens hadn't come through Dr. Rankin, I'd say they were a couple of contemporary Eurasians or mixed-blood Amerinds."

Emmett returned to Anna's side. She could see from his look that it was disturbing news. "Deborah Carter's missing. . . ." Pretending not to eavesdrop, Bream began smoothing some of Willow Creek Woman's clay with her fingers. "She missed a public meeting on a canal project yesterday evening and didn't come into work today."

"Who just phoned?" Anna asked.

"Your bureau's resident agent from Yakima. He offered to take the report, but we're closer and I think we should handle it."

• • •

A downpour was filling the Columbia Gorge, and Emmett strained into the tire mist being kicked up on Interstate 84. His wipers were at their fastest cycle, but still it was almost impossible to see. And then there was Anna. She was waiting for him to explain his mood since returning from the East. He just couldn't string the words together. He switched on the emergency light in the grille to clear the traffic out of his way on the slick freeway. "You up to interviewing Carter's assistant?" Emmett temporized. "I can drop you off at a motel in The Dalles and meet you later for dinner."

"Shut up," she said, blowing her nose into a Kleenex.

So he shut up.

Less than a minute later, she asked, "Did you have a layover in Oklahoma City on your flight back from Florida?"

He braced for the coming confrontation, his abdominal muscles tightening as if in expectation of a blow. Anna knew. However inaccurately, she had an inkling of what had happened. Had she picked up on his guilt? How was that possible? His own feelings about Saturday night had shifted from guilt to self-doubt—had Christine Kelly slept with him only to quash rumors that she might be gay? Carter's career had suffered from that accusation, and here a federal investigator was in North Carolina further dissecting the woman's life. Maybe Christine had figured that bedding him was a cheap price to pay to stay on the advancement fast track. "What would it matter if I did stay over a couple hours in Oklahoma City, Anna?"

"You tell me," she said. Two of his three ex-wives lived in Oklahoma. That's what mattered. But he wasn't about to deny anything. She would squeeze the truth out of a qualified denial like the pit from a rotten peach. "What did it, Em?" she asked with a catch in her voice that made his heart ache. "What'd I do wrong?"

"It's me."

"Something did it," she said doggedly.

His rehearsed speech flew out the window. "That night in the pool . . ."

"Yeah?"

He dropped an octave from emotion, despite himself. "We were so damn close—"

"Closer than you'll ever know." She bit her lower lip. "Go on, I'm sorry."

"I just can't go to the brink one more time like that. I can't. Not after all these months. It isn't just the sex. It's the closeness that goes before and after. I hunger for that, Anna."

"And you don't think I do too?"

Emmett spun the wheel, barely clearing a tractor-trailer that was swerving out of his way. His cellular rang. "Ignore it," he said.

"We can't." She reached inside his coat pocket for the phone. "Special Agent Turnipseed . . ."

Emmett felt as if he were being drafted helplessly down a misty gray tunnel toward the oncoming headlights of the westbound lanes. His hands gripped the steering wheel, but he didn't seem to be driving. He was being propelled forward by something beyond his control, something inexorable pushing him from behind.

"You're saying it's not identifiable?" Anna asked as he cracked his window, hoping the velvety, cool air would help ease the sensation that he was slowly suffocating. "Okay, I've got it—thank you." She returned the phone to his pocket without touching his chest. "That was the detective from Crook County S.O. Toxicology protocol's in on Gorka Bilbao. The night he was killed, he had a blood alcohol of .290." Drunk twice over, Emmett noted to himself. "Also there were traces of an unidentifiable chemical substance in his bloodstream."

The explanation for the dilation of Bilbao's eyes that night he interrupted them at dinner in the Kah-Nee-Ta. "Did they screen for all known drugs?"

"Yes—still negative, although it was probably organic. And possibly heat-sensitive, which could account for the difficulty getting a positive I.D." The call had made her get a grip on herself, and Emmett almost thought she would let their bruising discussion slide for the time being. Until she looked at him with glistening eyes once more. "So you were going to let us quietly blow over?"

"Stop it."

"Where exactly were you back East when you fell out of love with me?"

Shit. He tripped off the yelp siren for a plumber's van to get out of the left lane. "I didn't fall out of love with you, Anna."

"Then what'd you do?"

He saw no other way out. Everything else just prolonged the agony. And he owed her the truth so she wouldn't blame herself. "I slept with somebody. A woman I'd never met before. Somebody I'll never see again. It was that simple. And that stupid. I'm not going to defend what I did—" He flinched as she began punching him with her fists. Furiously, she struck his face, neck and right shoulder. He heard himself telling her to stop, but, masochistically, the blows felt good. Emptiness could be filled with pain. He concentrated on not sideswiping the cars he was passing, but finally had to pull off the interstate.

Crying now, she asked, *"Why!"*

Before he could try to answer the unanswerable, she bolted into the midday twilight of rain. He got out and ran around the front of the

Explorer to catch her. She splashed across a flooded ditch and stood under a cedar tree, clutching herself in her arms. Her hair was already wet and streaking around her neck.

The emergency light was still flashing on and off in the grille. Trotting back to the Explorer, he turned it off, then approached Anna again.

"Don't you touch me," she warned, wild-eyed. "Don't you ever touch me again!" Her tone was so delirious Emmett didn't know what to think.

Then it dawned on him.

She wasn't seeing him. She wasn't accusing Emmett Parker. It was inconceivable to him that she could feel this way about him, no matter what he'd done. "Okay, Anna. I'm going back to the car. I'll wait for you in the car." But he felt as if the heavy rain was pressing him to the muddy spot on which he stood. He couldn't move as long as her eyes were riveted on him. The right cuff of her pantsuit had ridden up over her ankle holster, but she gave no sign that she was thinking of going for her pistol. The idea that she might suddenly shoot him struck him as absurd, but he also realized that he'd do nothing to stop her. It might feel even better than her punches had.

"Get back in the car, Anna. *Please.*"

But she went on standing there, thin and childlike.

He'd stunned her. That made intuition a crock. Nothing had prepared her for the shock of his confession, and already he knew that it would be one of the biggest regrets of his life.

Then she blinked repeatedly, as if awakening from something horrific, and gave him her back.

Emmett returned to the Explorer, soaked, his knees feeling as rubbery as they did after a shooting.

She got in after a minute, and he merged into traffic again. His mouth was too dry for talk, and he didn't try to. Talk was hurtful. Anna, surprisingly, broke their silence as they neared the first exit for The Dalles. "No bottles," she whispered dully.

"What?" His voice crackled like cellophane.

"Bilbao had a high blood alcohol, and we found no bottles in or around his cabin."

Emmett gazed at her in astonishment. Unbelievable. She was really two people in a single body, one professional and one private. One resilient and one atrophied, each completely sealed off from the other. Now she'd never let him see that damaged private person again.

He didn't have a clue that she'd raised welts on his face until Carter's assistant looked at him strangely in the lobby of the Corps of Engineers headquarters. Emmett grimaced as he caught sight of himself in a mirror in the corridor. Both Anna and he were sodden and bedraggled, but Michael seemed so rattled by Carter's vanishing that he paid their appearance little mind as he ushered them into his office. Despite her dripping clothes, Anna exhibited a ghastly serenity that said that she'd already walled off their disaster on the interstate. She was in perfect control again. *But at what fucking price?*

She calmly asked Michael, "When'd you become worried about the colonel?"

"Last night, somewhat. She didn't come to a public meeting in town, but I told myself, 'Well, okay, she's been under a lot of stress lately and maybe it's just too much for her to put on a dog-and-pony show.' I covered for her. Until this morning when she didn't report to work. Around ten, I checked her house—she has me keep a key to water her plants when she's gone. Her car wasn't in the garage. I called the PD, but they had me phone the FBI agent in Yakima. You know, the guy who handled the safe bombing here."

Emmett realized that this was his best chance to probe Carter's activities of the past two weeks, but he had little enthusiasm for it. "Do you know where Colonel Carter was the evening of October nineteenth?" When Elsa disappeared.

Michael used a pencil eraser to flip through his calendar pages. "Here at the office until eleven or so."

"How do you know that?"

"We worked together on a news release. About Dr. Rankin's exam that day."

Emmett asked, "And where was she the evening of October twenty-first?"

"That was the Sunday of the bombing, right?"

"Right." And the night Gorka Bilbao had been murdered.

The aide's pencil slowed over the pages as he apparently caught on that the purpose of the interview had changed. But then he said with scarcely contained relief, "Oh, now I remember—with me. After all the firemen and cops cleared out, we had an early supper and some drinks at the Baldwin Saloon."

"How early?" Anna asked, retaking the line of questioning.

"Fourish." Michael reached for his ringing telephone. "Corps of Engineers Administration." More than enough time for Carter to have driven to Bilbao's cabin in the Ochoco Mountains. "Yes, she's right here." Michael cupped his hand over the mouthpiece. "Call for you, Ms. Turnipseed, from the U.S. Attorney." He pointed at a closed door to the side. "Take it in the colonel's office."

Emmett speculated why Anna and not he had been requested—Rankin's doing again, no doubt. It was time to set the anthropologist back on his heels. "Michael, who suggested that one of the bones be radiocarbon-dated?"

"Dr. Rankin, of course. But there was a wait while the court considered his brief."

"Then what happened?"

"Well, the approval came after a couple days, so Dr. Rankin returned here to pick a sample for the test."

"Did he say why he chose the fifth metacarpal and not some other bone?" Emmett asked.

"No, all that's out of my league. I just opened the safe for him on the colonel's orders."

"She wasn't in the room with you two?"

Michael thought about it. "Briefly. In and out. A lot was going on that day. The press in her office, waiting."

"So you actually saw Dr. Rankin take the metacarpal from the safe?"

The young man was bright enough to catch the point. "His back was to me."

"He didn't bring all the bones out onto the big table?"

"No, he said he'd just be a minute. He handed me a bone. I wrapped it up according to his instructions and shipped it off."

"Michael, where is it now?"

The aide fished his keys out of his trouser pocket and unlocked the file drawer in his desk. From it, he produced a still-sealed FedEx envelope with a UC Riverside return address. "This came yesterday. I've been so busy. What do you want me to do with it?"

• • •

Anna watched Emmett open the front door with the key Michael had given them. Then she led the way into Deborah Carter's house. Again, as in Dr. Sinclair's Victorian, a miasma of mold greeted her. The rain was loud on the shake roof, and the interior of the place felt clammy.

"I'll start with the garage," Emmett said, giving Anna a wide berth as he passed around her.

The first words from him in ten minutes. On the drive from the Corps of Engineers, she'd reported what the U.S. Attorney wanted the two of them to do—drop by Rankin's mansion this evening and explain to him why they'd gotten court permission for forensic sculptures behind his back. Anna had argued that she hadn't realized Emmett and she were to clear all moves through a civilian anthropologist. The prosecutor said they weren't expected to. Nevertheless, he asked the partners to smooth Rankin's ruffled feathers—apparently some fence-mending was in order after the U.S. Attorney had sided with Mel Brantford, the new NAGPRA monitor, in trying to block further radiocarbon dating of the remains. Emmett's only response to her had been "All right, whatever."

She sensed that he was maneuvering to keep Rankin out of the loop—but carefully, by gathering as much evidence as possible to attack his credibility. Obviously, it had made a deep impression on him that old Dr. Sinclair, himself a scientist, was suspicious of the science used to evaluate John Day Man. She herself was so heartsick it was difficult to think.

While he went through the garage—presumably for explosive materials used on the safe—Anna drifted into Carter's austere living room. She moved as if in a trance, pivoting like an automaton as she raked in details. Nothing was out of order. Nor did anything surprise her, having met the woman.

Yet, in contrast to the living room, Carter's bedroom was strikingly feminine. Frilly, lacy and soft around the edges. A scent of rose petals permeated it. The furniture chiefly consisted of a four-poster bed with muslin canopy, a dressing table and a camel-backed sofa with plush cushions. A coffee table was arrayed before the sofa, and on it were a bottle of Chivas Regal whiskey, a solitary glass and a paperback book. If a suicide note had been left behind, it would be here, Anna felt sure. The inch of liquid in the bottom of the glass looked like ice melt. No lipstick on the rim, although Anna couldn't recall having seen Carter wear any. She was respectful of the glass as potential evidence, but she saw no harm in picking up the book. *Death in Venice* by Thomas Mann. It'd been put down open to two pages, and brackets were inked around a passage:

> *The lad had just reached the gate in the*
> *railings, and he was alone. Aschenbach felt,*
> *quite simply, a wish to overtake him, to*
> *address him and have the pleasure of his*
> *reply and answering look; to put upon a*
> *blithe and friendly footing his relation with this*
> *being who all unconsciously had so greatly*
> *heightened and quickened his emotions. The*
> *lovely youth moved at a loitering—*

Enough. No more painful glimpses into Deborah Carter.

She took in the entire room once more, and as she slowly pirouetted, the ornamentation fell away, melted in her clouding eyes like the superfluity it was. The only thing at the heart of this room was loneliness. Anna's numbness momentarily deserted her, and she imagined herself thirty years from now decorating a back room like this as a retreat from failed relationships. How many by then?

"Find anything?" Emmett's voice interrupted her from the hallway.

She didn't face him. "Nothing. How about you?"

"Just an empty box of .45 caliber ammo on the workbench in the garage. And two cartridges on the cement floor. As if she or somebody loaded a magazine in a hurry."

• • •

This day will go on forever, Emmett reflected as he waited for the Lexus to come up the long driveway to meet Anna and him. The lights of Rankin's house below were bleared by the rain. Reaching over, she turned off the heater blower—their clothes were finally dry after the soaking along the interstate. She took a brush from her purse and ran it through her hair. Watching her, he realized how completely he'd succeeded in North Carolina: There was no going back, and from now on he'd be privy only to mild intimacies like the sweep of a hairbrush through her hair.

The gate opened electronically, and Kawatu exited the Lexus. He jogged to Emmett's window, which Emmett let down.

"Please park near that car there." The New Guinean indicated a U.S. Bureau of Land Management Bronco cruiser.

As Emmett did so, Kawatu turned the Lexus around so that it was pointing downhill. Then he got out and held an umbrella over the open front passenger door for Anna. "How very nice to see you again, Ms. Turnipseed."

"Thank you," she said, getting inside.

Emmett took the backseat.

Setting off for the mansion, Kawatu commented on the torrential rain, and Emmett left the chitchat to Anna, who seemed to cope with the aftermath of this atrocious day better than he did. He wanted to sleep. Go home to his Trappist cell of an apartment and sleep. The weather was probably balmy in Phoenix tonight. And, undoubtedly, his desk at the office was piled deep with accumulations since his assignment here. Momentum.

"Here we are." Kawatu stopped under the porte cochere and darted around to Anna's door. "The doctor awaits you in the library."

"I'll handle this," she said under her breath to Emmett as they passed through the foyer. Obviously, she was setting the tone for their future relations.

Tomorrow, he'd ask to be taken off this detail.

Rankin's color was up, probably from the drink in his hand. But there was also an eruption of small sores over his cheekbones and on his chin. "They're here," he announced impatiently to a lanky man in the tan and brown uniform of a BLM law enforcement ranger. For Anna's sake, Rankin rose on wobbly legs. He made introductions. The ranger was named Bill Heizer; Emmett had already learned that he patrolled the resource area encompassing both the John Day River and Willow Creek. Heizer stood on the outer hearth, rocking on his heels before the flames. He seemed ill at ease, particularly when

Rankin failed to explain his presence and instead griped to the partners, "So you two got Angela Bream busy reconstructing casts of the specimens—behind my back."

"You have a problem with that, Doctor?" Anna's inflection was so sulphurous that Rankin fell silent.

But he soon recovered his indignation. "Only that Bream couldn't make King Tut look like an Egyptian. You might've consulted with me first. I would've recommended a sculptor with far more talent."

"We're satisfied with Ms. Bream's work," Anna declared.

Rankin seemed to appraise her mood for a moment, then lowered himself into his chair. "Sit down, please. May Kawatu get you both something to drink?"

They declined.

"I've learned something you two should know concerning Colonel Carter." He cued Heizer with a nod.

"Well," the man began uncomfortably, "last summer while on night patrol, I drove up on a fed-plated sedan at Camp Watson. . . ." Emmett missed a breath. There it was: *Watson.* "I saw right off—"

"Excuse me," Anna interrupted, "but are you the ranger who found that the cavalryman's grave had been opened?"

"Yes," Heizer replied. "Anyway, the driver of the sedan had parked right on top of the old cemetery, and I advised her of the fact."

"Did you recognize the driver?" Rankin asked, falling into a staccato courtroom cadence.

"I did. Colonel Carter."

"You'd met her before?"

"Many times."

"Was there a passenger with her?"

"Yes. Elsa Dease."

"And how'd you know her?"

"We served together on an interagency committee to protect archaeological resources."

"Did either of them explain their presence at Camp Watson?"

"The colonel did all the talking," Heizer answered. "She said they were there to discuss a watershed issue."

"I'm sure it was," Rankin said dryly. "And what time of night was this?"

"Around eleven."

The anthropologist triumphantly hoisted his eyebrows at the partners. "There you have it. Now you know who propped the cavalry trooper's skeleton in your vehicle and set it afire, no doubt as a warning for you two to back off."

Anna said without fanfare, "Carter's missing."

Rankin paused. "You mean she's a fugitive." More a statement than a question.

"We don't know that," Anna said.

"Well, it's obvious she felt the noose tightening around her neck and decided to bolt while there was still time. Have you two put out a BOLO?"

"Not yet," Emmett said. In his mind, the only thing lending credence to Rankin's assertion of flight was the evidence of a .45 caliber weapon having been hastily loaded in Carter's garage. Someone like the colonel wouldn't impulsively turn to suicide. She'd work toward it in a sad, measured way, tidying up all the loose ends in her life before blasting her brains out. Carter had been either angry or frightened as she loaded that pistol.

Anna broke a second silence in the room. "Mr. Heizer . . . ?"

The ranger stepped down off the hearth apron. His calves were probably getting hot. "Yes?"

"How long have you known Dr. Rankin?"

Heizer smiled pleasantly at the anthropologist. "Oh, what, Doc, five or six years now?"

"Something like that."

"We at BLM would be lost without him—bones show up on public lands all the time, and the good doctor I.D.s them for us. Usually, at no expense to the taxpayer."

"Least I can do, my boy. And if all federal officers were as cooperative as you, I wouldn't feel the need to carry on the bulk of my work in Canada."

Anna's clear, sharp voice cut through this love feast like a knife. "When, Mr. Heizer, did you tell Dr. Rankin about your encounter with Colonel Carter and Elsa Dease at Camp Watson?"

Rankin's hands gripped the armrests of his chair in an attempt to steady them. They were shaking again.

Heizer's face darkened. "I'm not sure. Must've been recent—"

"How can that possibly matter?" Rankin interjected.

"Just a formality for my report, Doctor," she said innocently. "I might have to testify under oath how this information made its way to me." Then she peered directly at Heizer as she said, "As any defense lawyer will no doubt ask you when you first told anyone else about the encounter at Camp Watson." The ranger obviously understood that he'd just been cautioned about committing perjury. "Did you mention the encounter with Carter and Dease in your patrol log?" Public record, Emmett noted to himself.

"No," Heizer confessed. "And I don't recall when I first told Dr. Rankin about the incident."

"Then you discussed it with him more than once?" she asked relentlessly.

"I could have," the ranger hedged. "I just don't recall."

Anna stood. "Please tell Kawatu we're ready for the shuttle, Dr. Rankin." She started for the door.

Emmett followed her out. Perfect. She'd put Rankin on notice not to try to manipulate the investigation as a means of getting back at his enemies, real or imagined. Emmett had planned to do the same, but now there was no need. "You did well," he congratulated her as soon as they reached the foyer. "*Really* well."

"I don't need you to tell me that," she said without looking at him.

• • •

Sometimes you can measure the validity of a theory only by the fervor of the efforts to suppress it. The thought was a consolation to Rankin. But it also infuriated him that all his expectations had come down to a consolation, a grand subterfuge to keep his ideas alive until someone, in a more enlightened time, dusted them off and carried his hypotheses about human prehistory in the Americas to acceptance.

Kawatu, his legal heir, was not that someone.

Rankin glanced over his adopted son's work station in the laboratory in the basement of his mansion. Kawatu had tacked newspaper photographs of Special Agent Turnipseed to a corkboard over his desk. A sketch, still in progress, was reducing the structure of her face to bare bone. Where would Anna Turnipseed's skull fit into the morphological record Rankin was creating? He wasn't sure yet, but her quarter-Japanese blood might help him prove the link between Native Americans and migrants from northeast Asia fifteen thousand years ago. Turnipseed, he was convinced, uncannily resembled the prototypical Indians to arrive in the Americas, a kind of missing link that had stubbornly evaded him after a lifetime of digging. This would help explode the native myth that Indians had sprung from the Western Hemisphere like Athena from the brow of Zeus.

Hurry. Turnipseed and Parker are only a few days from putting everything together. Buy more time.

Rankin shuffled past the towering oak cabinets that occupied fully a third of his laboratory. The brass knobs to the bone drawers gleamed in the muted fluorescent light. These cases held thousands of remains now illegal for him to possess, thanks to NAGPRA. Kawatu had no real interest in these dirt-stained shards of calcium carbonate. In fact, it had taken considerable conditioning to get him to handle bones, for his fear had been great of their *maselai,* or spirits. Greed had been the carrot, and greed alone made Rankin trust his adopted son.

He unlocked a black steel door and, with effort, swung it open. Out of the blackness came the sweet odor of death. He flicked on the track lighting, and a scene of fourteen millennia ago sprang to life—the entrance to a cave in the lava flows of the Columbia Plateau. The ancient evening was painted on the far wall in soft pastels of blue and pink. Hunkered around a cook fire were five wax figures of a Paleo-Indian extended family, authentic down to their elfin size and the wispy beards on the men. They were busy butchering and roasting a dismembered human corpse. The eldest male was carrying the severed head—Caucasoid features on the death-stunned face—to a rock anvil, where an aged woman waited with a hammerstone in hand to smash the cranium and free the protein-rich brain from its shell. A naked child sucked on a ribbon of intestine that dangled from his mouth.

There had been a time when Rankin envisioned throwing open his laboratory to the public. Ensconced behind glass, his technicians would labor away at a constant stream of specimens brought in by his field teams. The pièce de résistance would have been this diorama, a lifelike illustration so all could understand how mundane the unimaginable had been. Everything would finally make perfect sense—except, perhaps, Deborah Carter's corpse wrapped in plastic just outside the ring of the little family.

Rankin slipped the obsidian knife from the rigid grasp of the adolescent male figure and used it to cut the packing tape that bound Carter up in her cocoon. The plastic spread aside, revealing her at the end of her first twenty-four hours of death. It was an irony of fate to leave a woman with a disfigured face a comely body. Carter's was flawless but for the two bullet wounds in the abdomen. Her face looked deflated in death, and the right eyelid sagged in on its empty socket.

He sensed Kawatu behind him.

And there he was, standing placidly just inside the steel door after escorting the BLM ranger up to the gate.

"You'll be going out tonight," Rankin said.

Kawatu accepted the order without expression, although his eyes were keenly alert. *Opportunistic* was probably the better word.

"I'm sorry now I had you dump the colonel's car in the river. It would've been useful for our present need."

"Present need, Father?"

"Turnipseed and Parker are moving faster than expected. Take this . . ." Rankin gave him the stone knife with edges so sharp even the most skilled knapper could seldom make one without cutting himself in the process. Kawatu waved the ebony blade back and forth in the artificial firelight, evidently taken with its multifaceted sheen. ". . . and remove her head."

Kawatu addressed the chore with no reservations. Unhesitatingly, he straddled the corpse, leaned over and began slicing. Fresh bone and cartilage were no obstacle for an instrument that had been used to butcher Columbian mammoths twice the size of modern elephants.

Rankin shifted around so that he could study his adopted son's face as he worked. Amazing, how innocent his violence seemed.

17

Nels Sward's eyes snapped open on the interior of his tent. The canvas pulsed like the walls of a womb exposed to an invasive, surgical light—dawn. Patricia's blankets had partially slid off her cot, exposing her bare shoulders. Her skin was a glacial white. She was impervious to cold. In many ways, she was coldness personified, a creature of ice with a sere passion that blew through him like a polar wind. Her occasional warmth toward him was feigned. He was convinced of it.

Sward sat up in his own cot, and his hangover found him with a skull-splitting headache. He stood with care. He'd only gone to sleep a few hours ago, after a long night of feasting and drinking. Now he'd pay for his excess until his stomach was calm enough to accept drink again.

Maybe it was time to leave Oregon. Nothing had been accomplished here. The Judeo-Christian bureaucracy had won again, and the Norse Folk Congress had been robbed of its sacred centerpieces. Sward's followers were trickling away in ones and twos. Only half those of a fortnight ago remained in camp.

Sward staggered outside in his long johns and urinated, in violation of his own sanitation rule. The portable chemical toilets were all the way across the fire circle, and he wasn't sure his bare feet could bear the frozen ground that far. As he squirted out a misty yellow arch, he rocked back on his heels to spare his tender soles. "What's wrong with me?" he asked up into the sky. Terrible and vivid dreams had racked his sleep, and now he was shivering with fever. Steam flowed off his hot skin, and he could feel the blood hammering through his arteries, its merciless swishing leaving him nauseated.

But these sensations were reduced to insignificance by the glory of the dawn. He was captivated by its colors. He could actually hear them. The scorching red sizzled like bacon in a skillet, the molten gold bubbled thickly and the celestial blue shrieked like the wind strumming a telephone wire.

He was rising.

As his hands shot out to the sides for balance, he let go of his penis, and warm piss soaked the crotch of his long johns. But he didn't mind. He could feel himself levitating. He was being sucked up into the dawn, enveloped by its singing colors. He'd lived the last twenty years of his life in the fervent hope that he might rise above his mortal existence and join the gods. Now that the moment was upon him, he couldn't believe it.

He was so incredibly happy. So fulfilled.

Then he came crashing down.

He was on his knees. The ascending sun had let go of him, and he was earthbound again. He looked all around. Something was coming. More federal cops, perhaps. They hadn't arrested him. Did that mean they intended to come back and burn him? Were he and his followers standing on the brink of another Burning Time?

Coming to his feet, he rushed back inside the tent.

He ripped through his duffel bag, flinging dirty clothes over his shoulder.

"What're you doing?" Patricia asked sleepily from her cot.

He found it. His revolver. "We're not going to be caught with our pants down this time," he explained to her. "We lost our Ancient Sister because we buried our heads in the sand. Nobody's going to just stroll into this camp and take what's rightfully ours."

She rolled over and showed him her back.

Post a guard, an authoritarian female voice told him. It had come from outside his head. The hair on the back of his neck stood: The voice was as real as Patricia's had just been.

He was rushing for the flaps with the handgun, when the straw-covered dirt floor rocked beneath him. He was pitched off his feet.

Lying stunned on his side, he looked at Patricia, expecting her to bolt upright in her cot and share his alarm.

But she went on dozing.

"Didn't you feel that?" he cried.

She grumbled for him to be quiet.

Sward rose to a crouch and stiffened for the next tremor. But nothing happened. After a minute, a bird sang out in the morning, the sound both frightening and enchanting. An omen, he felt, telling him to trust his instincts. He'd just started to relax when the earth convulsed again. Near the end wall of the tent, the straw-covered dirt floor began to bulge. Cracks radiated out from the rising deformation, making a screech like steel being torn apart.

Sward howled, trying to blot out the sound.

Finally, Patricia sat up. She tracked his gaze to the growing bulge in the dirt. It erupted into a cloud of dust and straw as a female head jutted out of the earth. Sward was peripherally aware of Patricia's scream, but it seemed unimportant—for he realized that he was beholding the goddess Frigg. Odin's wife had but one eye, and her lightning-scarred face glared at him with a cyclopean ferocity that made him feel as if every cell of his being was charged with power. *Make your woman be still!* Frigg said angrily in Swedish. Sward's mother tongue, which made him suspect that this revelation was for his benefit alone.

Patricia was balled up on her cot, stretching the tent wall outward as she tried ineffectually to shrink from Frigg. "Show respect!" Sward shouted at her.

"My God, oh my God . . . what is that thing!"

"Hush!"

But Patricia went on screaming, forcing Frigg to raise her voice: *She betrayed you, Nels, as others have betrayed and shall betray you. Trust no one, especially the wife you have held to your breast!*

Sward began to say something in Patricia's defense, but Frigg made the words evaporate before they could reach his tongue. The goddess was right, so undeniably right.

Shoot her, Frigg cried, *and join me at the right hand of Odin!*

Sward trained his revolver on Patricia's cowering figure. But hesitated.

It was she who told the authorities about the Ancient Sister!

The overpowering logic of that made everything fall into place.

Sward had never believed that Dr. Rankin told Agent Turnipseed, as some in camp had suggested. Sward had offered the anthropologist the opportunity to study the skeleton with complete freedom, something the government would never allow. It made no sense for Rankin to conspire with the authorities, putting the remains out of his and every other scientist's reach for all time.

Don't you see? Frigg asked contemptuously. *This woman wanted you arrested so she'd be free to join her Indian lover. What does the cuckold need to understand—a bolt of lightning from Thor's hammer?*

Sward brooded over the sight of her body. She wore nothing but her panties. Her partial nudity fueled his anger. He cocked the revolver's hammer, making Patricia fall silent, at last.

But only momentarily.

"What are you *doing*, Nels?"

He fired. The bullet hurled her against the tent wall and held her there for a split second. She was starting to slide down the canvas when the next bullet pinned her against it again. Sward wasn't aware of the entry wounds sprouting on her flesh, or even the repeated jumps of the gun in his hand. Just her grotesque, twitchy dance as the rounds alternately grasped and let go of her.

Finally, the hammer clicked on a spent cartridge, and Sward lowered the revolver to his side. He faced Frigg.

There are others with betrayal in their hearts, she said to him. *Reload. Destroy them before they destroy you!*

•   •   •

Anna rushed out of the Explorer even before Emmett could back into a space among the law enforcement vehicles on a knoll above the White River. Gabriel Round Dance emerged from a small group of Wasco County deputies and met her in the middle of the parking area. The tribal sergeant had phoned her at the Kah-Nee-Ta forty minutes ago, explaining only that Wasco S.O. was asking for all available mutual aid for a hostage situation at the pagan encampment. Anna scanned below. The circle of tents looked deceptively peaceful in the river valley. No sign of any people stirring. But no fires either, even though the temperature was still in the teens at 7:35 A.M.

The sergeant said, "We had an informant inside the camp. He phoned 911 by cellular, but then Sward must've taken it away."

"How many hostages?" Anna asked.

"About fifteen. That's what the informant said before he was cut off."

"Any casualties so far?"

"One possible—Sward's wife. Everybody was awakened at dawn by the sound of shots. Sward herded them all at gunpoint into the big tent. Mrs. Sward never joined them." Round Dance dipped his head at Emmett, who'd just caught up with Anna.

Parker asked, "Has a perimeter been thrown around the camp?"

"Yeah, but not much of one," the tribal sergeant admitted. "A few deputies at the base of this hill, and a Forest Service cop in the trees across the river."

Anna sized up the current: too swift and icy looking for anyone sane to attempt a crossing. Briefly, she thought she could hear a voice in the distance. But it might have been only the breeze in the junipers. She asked herself if, previously, she'd seen anything in Sward's behavior that added up to this morning's violence. But she had no answer. White paganism seemed strange but not murderous.

"We're waiting for SWAT and the hostage negotiator to arrive," Round Dance went on. "Last I heard, an ETA of about twenty minutes."

"Team's responding from The Dalles?" she asked.

"Yeah," the sergeant said.

She and Emmett exchanged a knowing look. It was purely professional, like all their dealings now: Parker had once referred to this stage of a police response as SWAT Paralysis, Patrol's psychological dependence on specialized personnel coming to the rescue.

"I've got movement," a tense voice came from a nearby car radio.

"Who's that?" Anna quietly asked Round Dance as she and everyone else turned toward the tents below.

"A deputy on the perimeter."

A tall, balding male in long johns had emerged from the largest tent. The one in which Willow Creek Woman had reposed in candlelight, Anna recalled. The distance was at least three hundred yards, but she recognized the figure in his underwear to be Nels Sward. He'd forced a heavyset, red-bearded man out of the tent with him—the guard on Willow Creek Woman's skeleton the night Rankin had summoned her to the camp. A steel-blue weapon glinted in Sward's right fist. He was shouting something at his captive. His expression was unreadable, but his taut body language promised gunplay at any moment.

"Anybody have a rifle with a scope?" Emmett asked with mounting concern.

No reply came from the gathered lawmen.

Sward raised his handgun to the other pagan's head. The fat man fell spinning to the ground, and a microsecond later the crack of the single shot rolled up to the knoll.

It was over in a blink, and Sward barged back inside the big tent, leaving the corpse sprawled in the bright morning sunlight.

Anna hurried over to the huddle of Wasco deputies. "Who's in charge?"

A corporal stepped forward, sickened by the sight of the execution. "I am, I guess. Who're you?"

"FBI. Let's get some people down there *right now.*"

"My orders are to contain the situation till SWAT arrives."

"Those orders just got superseded."

"Says who?" the corporal protested.

"Me," Anna said. "That homicide occurred on federal lands. I want a shotgun." Quickly, one was handed over. Emmett and Round Dance each nodded that they'd go down to the camp with her, and a young, sandy-haired deputy raised his hand as if in a classroom, volunteering as well. "Radio the perimeter and advise them we've got an entry team on the way," she told the corporal.

She set off at a brisk trot, resisting the compulsion to take final snapshots of everything around her. The pearly blue sky. A few high cirrus clouds wreathing over Mount Hood. It was too cold for scents to carry well, but she found the gin smell of the juniper woods nostalgic. She'd grown up among junipers. *All this acute sensibility comes from fear.* Maybe that was unfair to herself. It came from the knowledge that it was impossible to survive firefight after firefight. The odds caught up with everyone, regardless of skill or bravery, and the presence of hostages further stacked those odds against you.

She fed a shell into the chamber, but kept the shotgun on safety.

Emmett rested a hand on her shoulder, but then let go when, without turning, she began to descend a ravine carved by numerous springs.

No doubt he'd meant to tell her to use the gully for cover.

She ignored him.

The draw was frozen in the shady places, and she had to pick her way around fountains of ice that had crystallized over the springs. Someone fell with a grunt behind her. Round Dance, who was helped up by Emmett.

She halted the party. A gray-mustached deputy had risen out of the bitterbrush. She pointed with the flat of her hand toward the tents, and the cop nodded that he understood her signal.

Then she led the others on.

By this point, she could clearly hear Sward railing about something. He was carrying on in guttural Swedish. Or what she thought to be Swedish. He sounded beyond reason. She might have to kill him in the coming minutes. That made the cold seem deeper, and she ground her teeth together to keep them from chattering, although her legs continued to carry her forward at a determined jog, beating out a prayer to the spirits of this juniper forest: *Please don't let me fuck up. Not in front of Parker. He's lost the right to criticize me. . . .*

They came to the first tents.

Raising her hand, she stopped the others and went to a knee. She could see the front of the large tent, and the red-bearded corpse sprawled before it. From inside, Sward's voice went on ranting in Swedish. She decided to get behind the tent before he appeared again. Rising, she scuttled along—and immediately sensed a void of sound and motion behind her. No one was following her.

She looked back just as Emmett commanded, "Nels, stop right there!" Parker was prone behind one of the logs circling the fire ring, his handgun drawn on Sward.

Round Dance and the young deputy had backed off several yards but also had their weapons aimed at the pagan leader.

Sward had just manhandled another hostage outside—the old woman with the British accent who'd seemed to be the reigning elder of the group. Sward was using her as a shield, and Anna could see Emmett visibly gauging his chances for a quick head shot.

"Think about what you're doing, Nels," the old woman said with a surprising calm. "You're not yourself."

By feel, Anna took the shotgun off safety with trembling fingers, then began working her way around the backs of the tents. The air was icy on her sweat. Her face was bathed in it, and she couldn't seem to get enough air down her windpipe.

In English, Sward shrilled, "I'm sick and tired of Christian prejudice!"

"I understand, Nels," Emmett responded, his face creased by worry but his voice steady. "You don't have to tell a Comanche about Christian prejudice. Put down your gun and let's talk about it."

Anna crept in behind the big tent, wiped her sweaty palms on her sleeves for a surer grip on the shotgun, then plunged headfirst under the seam. Scrambling into the interior, she stood and swept the barrel over a blur of frantic people. They were sitting cross-legged in the straw. As soon as she saw no weapons, she held a forefinger to her lips. A pasty-faced woman started to clasp her legs out of relief, but Anna roughly pushed her back. That got all of them in the obedient hostage mode again, and no one tried to touch her as she threaded her way forward.

Outside, Sward bellowed, "I've had it! I refuse to suffer any more indignities because of my beliefs!"

"What indignities, Nels?" Emmett asked, sounding genuinely curious.

"Oh, you know!"

"No, I don't. Tell me about it."

"Don't cause more harm than you already have, Nels," the old woman implored. "That is our sacred oath—to cause no harm. At all cost, no harm to others."

But Sward didn't seem capable of listening to either Emmett or the pagan elder.

Through the crack in the flaps, Anna could make out his back. His silhouette and that of his hostage were framed by the dazzling sunshine. She lined her sights up on the approximate level of his heart, then waited with her forefinger in the trigger guard. *What will your weapon do?* Twelve-gauge shotgun pellets were round and slow moving, so there was a fair chance the balls wouldn't penetrate Sward's body and pass into the old woman. But Anna wasn't sure. Not at a range this close. Leaning to one side, she increased the angle of her line of fire so the pellets were more likely to deflect inside Sward's body. Even with that, she drew her bead on his left shoulder, praying that a hit there would be enough to drop him. It felt like playing billiards with human lives.

"I have had it!" Sward roared. "I have just had it with all of you!"

His tone told her that the time had come. He'd boxed himself psychologically, and there was nothing left for him to do except kill his hostage.

Anna began to squeeze the shotgun's trigger when Sward removed the muzzle of his revolver from the old woman's temple and fired the weapon against his own. As he tumbled, a spurt of blood sprayed from his head. The flow swiftly stopped, but Sward was still clutching the weapon. Anna leaped out through the flaps and seized his gun hand. She wrenched the revolver out of his spasming grasp and hurled it aside. Two shadows flickered over her. Emmett and Round Dance, still drawn on Sward. The young deputy had yanked the hostage out of the way.

"We'll take care of Sward," Emmett told her.

Pushing herself off the ground, Anna stumbled inside the tent again. She felt as if her legs were made of clay. "Where's Patricia Sward?"

"We don't know," a man with bruises on his neck replied. "But the shots seemed to come from their tent."

Anna tried to recall its location from her previous visit. No good. Her mind's eye saw only blood gushing out of Sward's head. "Where's that?"

Another pagan weakly gestured. "Three tents over."

Anna ran outside. She gulped for air even though the chill burned her lungs.

Something made her open a flap to the Sward's tent with the shotgun. She saw nothing at first. Just the puddle of sunlight she'd let in on the straw-blanketed earthen floor. She sidestepped, and a bare foot came into view. It was the color of parchment. She thought someone was beating a soft cadence on a drum in camp, until she realized that the thumping came from inside her own chest. Creeping into the tent, she smelled blood. So strong she could taste it too—like a penny on her tongue.

Patricia Sward's seminude corpse was stretched across a cot, arms and legs in twisted attitudes. There was a pattern of blood-ringed bullet holes on the tent canvas just above her. It was perfectly duplicated on her torso.

Her eyes seemed to be riveted in horror on something at the far end of the tent.

Anna told herself that the woman's gaze was no more than a trick of her rigor-frozen eyelids. But it was so insistent she found herself looking toward the back wall of the tent.

There, propped upright on the straw, was Deborah Carter's head. She could tell that it was severed because a flap of skin around the base of her neck had curled up. One eye appeared to be glaring back at Patricia Sward. The other eyelid was depressed but cracked open enough to suggest the dark cavity behind it.

Anna fumbled for the tent pole with her free hand and held on to it until a wave of dizziness passed.

• • •

Despite the murky jurisdictional issues surrounding the bloodfest at the pagan camp, the County of Wasco was able to tap all the federal and state resources it needed. FBI technicians rushed to the scene along the White River. The chief state medical examiner and two of his most experienced pathologist's assistants were flown by an air national guard helicopter to the Mid-Columbia Medical Center at The Dalles. There, in the same autopsy suite where Dr. Rankin had examined the cavalry trooper's skeleton, the threesome conducted a carnival of slicing and sawing so malodorous and gory that Emmett wasn't surprised to catch Anna's relief when an orderly told her that she had a call from Washington. Presumably FBI headquarters, but Emmett made up his mind not to ask her about it when she eventually returned.

There was already enough on his mind.

The three postmortems—the Swards and the male follower Nels

Sward had executed—had progressed to the same point: Trunk cavities had been sawn open and the vital organs exposed. The chief examiner labored over Nels Sward. If there were answers to be had, they were hidden in Sward's remains. Still, Emmett kept track of the work on all three trays. And strained to hold down the sensory input that came from watching three human vessels being methodically gutted. The scrub suit he'd been given was dotted with pink fluid, but in no way was as splattered at those worn by the examiner and his assistants.

Even to the well initiated like Emmett, it all seemed like a gross violation of the sanctity of the human form. If anyone failed to understand native revulsion for scientific evaluation, let him witness an autopsy.

Finishing a sequence of cuts with a pair of scissors, the chief examiner stepped back to give his diener room. This autopsy aide, a Hispanic with an expressionless mask for a face, lifted an entire block of organs out of Sward's gaping chest and deposited it with a plop on a small dissecting table that had been fitted over the pagan leader's legs. Now Emmett was really thankful that Anna had left the room, for the examiner cut away the intestines and handed them in a tray to the diener, who began washing them out in the sink at one end of the autopsy table.

Knowing what was coming next, Emmett took two steps back. The examiner sliced open Sward's stomach. Despite the exhaust fans whirring overhead, gastric acid immediately poisoned the air. Emmett didn't look over the pathologist's shoulder at the stomach contents. They resembled stew too much, and he liked stews. Instead, he fixated on Sward's head. It was covered by a big flap of chest skin that had been pulled back to reveal his ribs. He hoped that the bullet track wouldn't complicate the examination of the man's brain. The .38 special round hadn't exited the far side of the cranial vault, so it had careened around inside, for sure, mashing parts of the lobes into pulp. The answer to today's murderous binge might be explained by something as simple as a tumor.

Raising his acrylic face shield, the examiner asked the P.A. closest to him, "What are you finding in the way of contents?"

The younger man was bent over Patricia Sward's stomach. "Salad greens or spinach, I think."

"Brad?" the examiner inquired of the other P.A.

"Chicken and macaroni salad, mostly."

"Anything like calf brains?"

Both P.A.s answered in the negative, which made the examiner turn to Emmett. "Did all three of these people share a communal meal last night?"

"Yes, I believe so—some kind of feast." Emmett had interviewed approximately half of the survivors, leaving the other half to Anna.

"What was on the menu?"

"I don't know," Emmett admitted. He hadn't realized that their food might have forensic significance. He'd been more interested in how much Sward had had to drink—copious amounts of mead, according to his followers. "What's it matter?"

Anna had come back into the suite. She carefully averted her eyes from the cadavers as she asked, "What's wrong?"

But the examiner had crossed the chamber to the isolation refrigerator. The one in which staff never stored their lunches. He took out a large specimen container. Through its translucent sides Emmett could make out Deborah Carter's severed head. Removing it, the examiner flipped the head upside down and examined the base of the skull.

Emmett joined the pathologist. Anna was just a step behind him.

The base of the cranium had been enlarged. The examiner frowned up at the inadequate fluorescent ceiling fixtures, and Emmett handed him his penlight. "Thanks."

The little beam probed the inside of Carter's cranium—and revealed that it had been hollowed out.

"Jesus Christ!" the pathologist exclaimed. "What kind of people were these!"

• • •

On the midnight drive across The Dalles to the Wasco County sheriff's office garage, Anna felt as if she were floating between two different emotional states. One offered a curious sense of safety, curious after all that had happened since Sergeant Round Dance's call this morning. At the beginning of her treatment, Dr. Tischler had explained to Anna that people with a sexually tormented past often go into regulation-laden professions with multiple layers of structure, like the FBI or the military, even though those same jobs expose them to dangers that replicate the terrors of their childhood. A twisted coping mechanism to alleviate chronic psychic pain. *Well, at least it worked today; I'm still hanging together.* But, on the other hand, she was shaken. The universe no longer felt familiar to her. One human being had devoured the brain of another. She'd suddenly realized in the autopsy suite that this was the world of her ancestors. Whenever the Modoc heard a rumble in the sky, they'd thought of cannibalism, for the Five Thunders felled and cooked humans with lightning, then devoured them in their lodge of cumulus clouds.

Emmett, who was driving, broke her train of thought. "I'll phone Angela Bream in the morning."

"Okay." Two messages had just been forwarded to them by radio. One from 5:15 that evening to call back the sculptor. Emmett was right: No use bothering the woman this late at home; they'd already gotten word from the Portland FBI office that John Day Man's sculpture was finished and a flyer with photos of both reconstructions had been widely disseminated. The other message had been an urgent request for them to meet with the senior evidence technician, who was at the sheriff's office garage in town.

Emmett now pulled up to the electronic gate at the rear of the headquarters while Anna got out and showed her credentials to a deputy behind a greenish, bullet-resistant window in the sally port. She wondered if Emmett looked at her anymore when her back was to him.

Minutes later, they walked into the garage.

At its center was Nels and Patricia Sward's Volkswagen van, the interior disassembled and spread out over the cement floor. The FBI head technician promptly waved the partners over to a workbench on which he'd bagged and tagged articles of evidence. One item leaped out at Anna—a hunting knife atop a paper bag. "What was the name of the victim up in the Ochoco Mountains?"

"Gorka Bilbao," Anna replied.

"Don't touch the knife, but you can have a look."

Emmett let Anna go first. There was a rust-colored stain where the blade met the hilt. Dried blood, Anna surmised. And initials crudely etched into the laminated handle: *G.B.* She stood aside to let Emmett examine it. She no longer felt capable of surprise. Studying the van, she asked the technician, "Can you scrape the wheel arches for soil samples?"

"What do you have in mind?"

"Nobody saw a VW van in the Ochocos that night. It'd be nice to link it to the dirt roads in those mountains."

"What was that homicide—almost two weeks ago now?"

"Yes."

"And a couple of storms in between?"

Anna nodded.

"I'll flake some dirt off into a pillbox, but I can't promise much."

Emmett yawned. "What else do you have?"

The technician handed him a small glass vial. It too was already sealed, but Anna could see nothing inside.

"Fibers?" Emmett asked.

"Forest green," the man answered. "Probably polyester."

A spark of recognition went off behind Anna's tired eyes. That day along Tanner Creek, Deborah Carter had been wearing a forest green sweater. But the spark was quickly extinguished in a wash of exhaustion that came over her. The adrenaline that had sustained her all day was now spent.

"And finally these . . ." The technician shook several long dark brown hairs out of an envelope onto a rubber mat. "Collected from the latch that lets the rear seat fold down flat. They were all stuck in the mechanism, like some hair got caught and had to be pulled free. Anybody in mind for a DNA comparison?"

"Yes," Anna said. But enough was enough. She didn't want to imagine Elsa Dease lying dead in that backseat. She didn't want to imagine anything. She wanted oblivion.

18

There had been nothing remarkable about Nels Sward's brain—other than the track of the bullet that had ripped through his right temporal bone and imbedded in the opposite wall of his cranium. The examiner found no tumor ravaging Sward's sanity, no obvious disease capable of igniting a murderous psychotic break on a sunny autumn morning. So, as a last resort, Emmett now relied on toxicology to explain the pagan leader's rampage. But those results might be days, even weeks, in coming.

Heading back to the Kah-Nee-Ta, he and Anna had passed the abandoned camp minutes ago. Abandoned but not struck. All the tents still stood, filled with the belongings of the pagans who'd scattered for motels or home as soon as the partners finished interviewing them. The site was now ringed by yellow police tape and guarded by a reserve deputy sheriff so that the technicians could have another uncontaminated go at it in daylight.

Anna's interviews had yielded a significant fact. At the feast yesterday evening, Sward had been served his food first. By his wife, Patricia. Did that mean only she, or perhaps she and her husband, had knowledge of what was truly on the menu? It was also possible Anna and he were dealing with social pathology, that the entire Norse Folk Congress knew about Sward's cannibalism and some members had willingly feasted on Carter's remains with their high priest. Where was the rest of the colonel's corpse?

This line of speculation turned Emmett's stomach. Fortunately, the press had not been let in on the sickening detail. All he needed at this happy juncture in his life was a Manson Family–caliber media circus.

He checked on Anna.

She'd bunched up her parka and wedged it between the side of her face and the window glass. Apparently asleep. Although the glow of the dashboard instruments was too dim for him to tell for sure. Not until he'd driven miles up the Wapinitia Road and a car went by in the opposite direction did he see in the flare of the headlights that Anna's eyes were open.

There was one last thing to do. After that, he hoped he'd feel better. "Anna . . . ?"

"Yes?"

"Tomorrow, I'm going to ask to be taken off this detail." Her silence made his chest tighten. He wondered if she'd start pummeling him again. Earlier, he'd had a fantasy in which those blows had led to a heartfelt kiss. Even more. That improbable more, always dangling in front of him like an unreachable carrot. "I feel bad about leaving—"

"I wish—" She cut herself off, paused, then said with exaggerated politeness, "Sorry, I interrupted you."

"That's okay, go ahead."

"I was just going to say I wish you wouldn't do that."

Was she offering him forgiveness? If so, it was completely unexpected. He hadn't known until this moment how much he wanted her forgiveness—even as they parted.

But then she added, "One of us ought to remain onboard. For continuity."

"What do you mean?" He kept staring up the road as it climbed the last grade before Simnasho.

"That call at the hospital was from the head of the Indian Desk at headquarters in Washington," she went on casually. "I finally said yes to taking the post as her assistant. I start in two weeks."

"D.C. That'll be a big change. Feels nothing like Indian Country."

"I know, but I liked the woods and fields around Quantico."

"That's right, the academy." He slowed for a curve. "Well, congratulations. This is probably for the best." His own insincerity stung the back of his throat like bile.

"If you don't mind," she said, "I'll shove off for home in a day or two. So much to do. Find a mover. Rent out my condo."

"Anything I can do to help?" he volunteered. "I'm an expert on moving."

"No thanks. I can handle it."

Emmett suddenly switched on his high beams and leaned over the steering wheel. Then he slammed on the brakes. He was already out his door and running when Anna asked, bewildered, from behind, *"What?"*

He left the road and sprinted into the brush. A slice of moon hung overhead, but its wan light revealed no movement to him. Just the outlines of the hillside above, which took shape as his eyes adjusted. Crashing through a sumac thicket, he replayed in his mind the vision he'd just seen through the windshield. It was still starkly vivid—an emaciated woman, almost nude, her dark hair a matted tangle, darting across the road at the point where his headlights had faded into the night. So real. So breathtakingly real.

He halted to listen.

Nothing.

Anna called from twenty or thirty yards below, "Emmett!"

Her echoing voice died away in the ravines above, and he probed the silence that followed. A twig snapped out in the darkness in front of him. He rushed toward the sound, and noises from the same place told him that he'd flushed something. Thuds of hooves and the whisking of legs through the leafless branches. These sounded like the flight of a deer, and—still running—he asked himself if he'd fabricated the phantasm on the road out of something as explainable as a pair of highly reflective doe eyes.

Or had the specter transformed itself into a deer?

That's what his Comanche great-grandparents would have believed, and the muted lunar light made anything seem possible. He stumbled on what felt like an exposed root and recovered his balance without slowing. Was he dreaming? He felt awake, but this was how the sleeping brain processed horrors of the kind he'd witnessed today.

"Emmett!" Anna was still following him.

"This way," he gasped as he stopped on a stretch of soft ground, "and keep quiet." He reached into his jacket pocket for his penlight to search for this creature's tracks. Then he recalled—he hadn't reclaimed his little flashlight from the pathologist, who'd left smears of blood and bits of tissue on it while examining the empty interior of Deborah Carter's cranium.

Plunging on without waiting for Anna, he started up a ravine.

The gully was hemmed in by basalt cliffs, rock so black it seemed to absorb the wan moonlight. He felt his way with the toes of his shoes. He soon wondered if he'd chosen the right draw. No sounds above urged him on, and he began to feel like a fool. What if he came up empty-handed?

There was a clatter of stones, but it came from behind. Anna, still trailing him.

He forced himself to continue up the ravine with the thought that three people—Minnie Claw, Anna and now he—had seen *something* along this road. A presence was making itself known. But was it only to ensnare Anna and him? Ghastly pictures flickered behind his eyes. Gorka Bilbao's roasted viscera. Carter's decapitated head with its ripped-out eye. Sward blowing his brains out. What strange visions had possessed these individuals . . . before they died horribly?

A spot on one side of the ravine seemed darker than the rest of the background.

Emmett tried to control his loud huffing so that he could listen. Kneeling, he found a pebble and flung it into the deepest part of the darkness. The belated click told him that he'd found a cave, a huge bubble that had formed long ago as the basalt cooled.

Rising, he crept up the fan of rock rubble that spilled out of the opening. Its top had been worn flat, suggesting human habitation. Ancient or recent? He took his first step into the cave—and a savage feline snarl flew out at him. He slid back down the bank, protecting his throat with his left forearm and drawing his revolver. As he strained for a glimmer of eyes coming at him out of the inky dark, Anna's voice asked in alarm, "What is it?"

"Cougar, maybe. Whatever you do, guard your throat." That was usually the fatal blow from a mountain lion.

Anna turned on the flashlight she'd brought from the Explorer. Clasping it next to her pistol, she held them over her head to sweep the small cave.

It was empty.

Emmett stared in disbelief as Anna's beam again rippled over the rough walls and across the stone-littered floor of the cavity. No tracks in the black sand between the stones. Not a thing. The snarl had been so real. But only as real as the phantom crossing the road, he reminded himself.

Then he whispered, "Work your light across the back wall one more time."

"Like this?"

"Yeah."

There it was again, a jagged shadow that appeared for a split second as the light passed over a crack. Its outer edge so perfectly matched the inner contours of the wall the fracture was virtually invisible—unless it was lit from one precise angle, as Anna had just accidentally done. He took the flashlight from her and cautiously clambered up the ledge once again. Approaching the fracture from the side, he noticed a crude straw of dried cheatgrass and pine needles spilling out of the eight-inch oblique passageway. It widened slightly, but he had no hope of squeezing his frame through.

There was no need.

Elsa Dease cowered in the widest part of the recess, shuddering as she glared up at the light. There were hollows in her filthy face from hunger. Her frayed white sweater was stained with what looked like berry juice. She snarled viciously, baring her incisors at the penetration of her lair of the past two weeks.

Then Anna saw too. "Oh no." She depressed the light in Emmett's grasp so that it wasn't shining directly at Elsa, and stepped in front of him. "Elsa?" she asked gently.

Another blood-curdling snarl.

"Elsa, I want to help you."

• • •

"Stand aside, Round Dance," Tennyson Paulina said as he barged past the tribal sergeant and threw open the door on the sedated young woman and her mother. Gabriel Round Dance did nothing to stop

Paulina, and Anna scanned the Warm Springs Hospital corridor for Emmett, who'd momentarily left to return a phone call. Vernita Dease glowered up from bedside at the intrusion, and Elsa twitched with fright through her Thorazine haze. Anna started to take down the Paiute cowboy from behind, but he spun on her as if he had eyes in the back of his head and said with beer breath, "I'll just be a minute, Turnipseed, so let's not everybody get up on their hind legs."

"What do you want?"

"A word with the Deases."

Anna decided to give Paulina exactly a minute before throwing a wristlock on him. She'd just learned from Round Dance that all the Paiute suspects in Bilbao's murder had been released from the Crook County facility this morning for lack of evidence. "Any objections, Vernita?" she asked.

"Let him talk," the Shaker woman said.

"Thanks." Paulina turned to Elsa, who appeared to be comprehending none of this. Her condition visibly pained him. "Sweetheart, I had me a dream in jail. Kept havin' it each night till everythin' was made clear to me. I saw this whole nightmare, from the first Ancient One being torn out of the riverbank, to you half out of your mind in a cave." The Paiute inhaled deeply to control himself. Uneasily, Anna remembered her own dream of the hummingbird outside a cave, trying to keep her from discovering Elsa's corpse. "So now that I see everythin' for what it is," Paulina continued, "I promise you I'll make it all right. I'll throw down a line of blood these demons can't cross. They'll never come after you again, darlin'." He shrugged at Anna. "That's it. I'm finished."

"You better watch how you make things right," she warned, "unless you want to wind up back in jail."

Without another word, he about-faced and strode bowlegged down the corridor.

"You hear me, Paulina?"

•   •   •

It was 2:00 A.M., but Emmett now felt no hesitation in calling Angela Bream at home. Three hours ago, the forensic sculptor had left a second message for Anna or him to contact her right away. "Hello," the woman answered groggily.

"Ms. Bream, this is Emmett Parker."

Instantly, her voice sounded awake. "Listen, somebody phoned me this morning about the flyer."

"Why didn't that person contact Turnipseed or me?" Only their names were listed on the bulletin, although the number for the state crime lab had been included.

"The Mountie was afraid of stirring things up over nothing and wanted more information before phoning you."

"Mountie, you say?"

"Royal Canadian Mounted Police in British Columbia. He asked me if I had the rest of John Day Man's face done yet, and I explained it'd never be completed—not without finding the mandible. You mind a little intuition?"

"Never been more open to it in my life." Emmett tossed his empty coffee cup into the wastebasket under the nurses' station desk.

"This guy strongly reacted to the reconstruction. In my experience, when somebody reacts like this, he *knew* the subject."

Emmett's pulse quickened. "How can I reach him?"

Bream gave him the number of the RCMP substation in the town of Nanaimo on Vancouver Island. "He's night watch supervisor, so he should be available now."

Minutes later, Emmett was explaining himself to a corporal. ". . . So I hope you can appreciate our urgency in following up on any and all leads."

"Well," the Mountie said defensively, "I didn't call the FBI because I wasn't ready to go out on a limb over this." He pronounced the word *out* as if it hurt his mouth a little to say it. He also sounded middle-aged and cautious by nature. "Federal-to-federal stuff can't be handled at my level without clearance. What're you again, Parker?"

"A criminal investigator for the Bureau of Indian Affairs, U.S. Department of the Interior."

"You yourself First Nations?" Canadian political correctness for Native American.

"Yeah, Comanche. How about this, Corporal—tell me what you know. I'll keep it under my hat until you can route the information through proper channels to the Seattle office of the FBI. I won't act on it until Seattle officially breaks the news to me."

Silence. Which discouraged Emmett until the corporal dampened his voice to confide, "I swear the face belongs to Nathan Creech, a member of the Nootka tribe up here."

"You're sure? It's just a partial sculpture."

"I'm sure, Parker. I took Creech's mugshot from his arrest file and compared it to the picture on your flyer. It's uncanny. Same eyes and nose."

"Okay, make sure the photo gets routed upstairs too. What's Creech's arrest record consist of?"

"Trespassing. Political activism, mostly. He was a royal pain in the ass to the timber industry and archaeology projects up here—until he dropped out of sight six months ago."

John Day Man had some Caucasoid characteristics; everyone from Dr. Sinclair to Angela Bream to Thaddeus Rankin agreed on that. "Is Creech a full-blood Nootka?"

"No, his mother was white. Why?"

• • •

When, after twenty minutes, Emmett didn't return to Elsa's room, Anna left Vernita at her bedside. The mother was clasping her daughter's hand in both of hers, praying. Anna went outside to the front steps of the hospital for some fresh air—poor Elsa had added to a day of vile smells by vomiting on Anna's blouse while Emmett and she helped hold the thrashing young woman down during the emergency room doctor's examination.

Gabriel Round Dance sat on a planter, backdropped by the lights of the tribal capital. He'd excused himself for a cigarette some minutes ago. In addition to the need for air, Anna had wanted to talk to the Wasco sergeant. She hadn't liked the way Round Dance let Paulina blow right past him into Elsa's room. What had Gorka Bilbao shouted at the sergeant the night the Dodge diesel had forced him off White-horse Rapids Road? *You don't fool me, Round Dance. You Wascos are just too chickenshit to tangle with Tennyson Paulina. That Paiute's got the power over you fish-eaters, and you know it too!* If she'd been less tired, she might have framed her question with greater diplomacy. Or maybe it was the time in her life for assertiveness in everything. "Why do you always handle Paulina with kid gloves?"

The sergeant didn't answer.

Anna needled him with a long silence. The night was cold. But the cold felt pure. Clean.

Finally, Round Dance crushed his cigarette under his boot sole and gestured at the metallic glint on his Tuffy jacket. "You know, my dad wore this same badge."

"Did he?" Anna asked to keep the fragile conversation alive.

The sergeant nodded. "Never talked much about the job. Never talked much about anything." A bittersweet chuckle. "I wish he'd told me the way things really are for a cop. You slap on a Sam Browne belt, mount up and ride out to do justice. Except to make justice work you've got to make decisions. Decide this person is right and that person is wrong. Piss folks off, no matter what you do."

"A policeman's lot everywhere . . . right, Gabriel?"

"You and Parker never worked a reservation full-time, correct?"

"Correct."

"You two work like white cops. In and out. Do your thing and go home to suburbia. I can never get away. So everybody I piss off I see day in and day out. At the market. The gas station. The hospital. Standing there, giving me the evil eye."

Then it hit her. Bilbao had known about Round Dance's fears. "You mean, wondering if somebody you've pissed off might try to witch you?"

"Hell yes," he said angrily. "My father at age fifty-five was in perfect health. Not a single problem, according to his department physical six months before."

"Six months before what?"

"His heart exploded in his chest." Round Dance faced her. "I talked to the coroner. My dad's heart was in shreds, like tissue paper. Now, a reasonable man, and I think of myself as a reasonable man, would look for a scientific explanation and be satisfied with it. But I also remember that the winter before his death, my dad arrested Tennyson Paulina's grandfather for stealing a horse in the South End. Old Man Paulina got six months in the tribal jail. It was all over the rez, how that crazy old witch was going to use bad power to get even. How he was going to hatch tiny snakes in my father's heart to eat away at it. What would you believe, Turnipseed?"

She honestly didn't know. But the interrogator in her glimpsed an opportunity that wouldn't come again. "You saw that Dodge pickup go past on Whitehorse Rapids Road, didn't you?"

Round Dance sighed. "Washington tags," he admitted after a moment. "The license plate bulb was out, so I couldn't read the numbers. But I recognized the state. And I knew Tennyson has Paiute kin on the Yakima rez up in Washington."

So Bilbao had been right on target—Round Dance feared that Paulina was behind the ramming attack of the big pickup on the fossil hunter. "Year of the Dodge?"

"I don't know—current model. Maybe last year's. It looked new."

"The night Parker's and my vehicle was torched . . ."

"Yeah?"

"Why were you headed away from the lodge instead of responding to the arson call?"

Round Dance exhaled. "Does any of this really matter?"

"Yes. And why'd you meet with Nels Sward at a motel in The Dalles?" Anna asked seamlessly.

Round Dance stood, and Anna expected him to walk away.

Today, during the assembly-line interviews of the Norse pagans, one of them had mentioned in passing that Round Dance had met with Nels Sward at the motel in The Dalles—weeks before the move to the camp along the White River. The pagan hadn't known what was discussed between the two men.

"Shit." Shaking his head, Round Dance looked out across the lights of his capital. "Wascos are supposed to be the most modern Indians on this goddamned confederated rez. I've got a degree in political science from Corvallis. And most of the college grads here are Wasco, you know that . . . ?"

Anna just waited for him to go on.

"So the question is, why'd I believe that a white sorcerer could have greater power than a Paiute one? I really don't know. I can't explain the feeling, not rationally. Are whites better at magic than Indians? You got me, Turnipseed. But somehow, when Sward started poking around

Warm Springs, asking about folks who might have the power, it just felt like a chance to get even with the Paulinas."

"I understand," Anna conceded.

"Do you really? Because I sure as hell don't."

"What did Sward want to know about Paulina?"

"How his magic worked."

Anna noticed Emmett coming through the lobby toward them. "How does it work, Gabriel?"

"I don't have a clue. I'm not Paiute. Except it does. Why else would Elsa go off the deep end? And Sward kill Colonel Carter before shooting himself in the head? After he pulled the trigger, that was my first thought—Paulina did it to him. Paulina has the greater power. We're all puppets on his strings, whether we know it or not."

Emmett held open the door for her. "Doctor'll talk to us now."

Anna asked Round Dance, "Want to join us?"

"Nope," the sergeant said dismally. "A white doctor has nothing to tell me I don't already know."

• • •

The emergency room physician looked adolescent to Emmett. Probably fresh out of residency, working off his federal loan. But he sounded knowledgeable enough as he leaned back in his swivel chair and rattled off Elsa's vitals. Her blood pressure was elevated, but that was probably due to her mental state more than anything else. She was malnourished enough to have acidosis, reduced alkalinity of the blood and body tissues due to a lack of nutrients. However, she was not dehydrated, as the physician might have expected.

"There's a creek in the canyon below the cave she was holing up in," Emmett explained. "I think she went out after dark to drink. That must've been when she was sighted crossing the road."

"I see," the doctor said. "Does she have a history of emotional problems?"

Emmett was surprised that, with Vernita present in the hospital, they were being asked to divulge information about the young woman. "Did you know Elsa before tonight?"

"Only through articles in *Spilyay Tymoo*," the doctor said, referring to *Coyote News,* the tribal newspaper. "She always seemed like the belle of the ball to me."

"Haven't you discussed Elsa's background with her mother?"

"Tried. The woman won't open up to me. She just says she won't question God's gift to her. Her daughter died and came back to life, just like some kind of Indian prophet she named."

John Slocum.

"Whatever problems Elsa may have had," Anna finally answered, "I don't see how they led to her abandoning her car in the middle of the night and hiding in a cave for two weeks."

"All right, next possibility—does Elsa have a history of drug abuse?"

Anna glanced to Emmett. "Unknown, but I don't think so," he said. "She went through the University of Oregon. Gainfully employed here on the rez—"

"What are you saying, Doctor?" Anna interrupted. "That drugs could explain this?"

"Look, this wouldn't be the first time I've treated apparently responsible people on this reservation for ingesting hallucinogens. Has something to do with some kind of mystical quest."

"Spirit quest," Anna clarified. "And only mild hallucinogens are used for spiritual purposes. If at all. Most often, an altered state of consciousness is achieved through fasting or exercise."

Emmett asked, "Could there still be traces of a chemical substance in Elsa's bloodstream two weeks after she took it?" He was recalling the toxicology report on Gorka Bilbao—the unidentifiable chemical substance found in his blood.

"I'm not sure," the doctor said. "I'll ask the toxicologist to pay particular attention to the possibility."

And cross-reference the findings with those from Nels Sward, Emmett made another mental note. But would either Elsa or Sward have taken a hallucinogen that threatened a psychotic break with reality? Many such substances were psychomimetic, capable of producing the symptoms displayed by psychotics and paranoids. Had both Dease and Sward, of their own volition, individually taken the same dangerous drug—and then somehow overdosed on it? That was the Teflon coating the gears of Emmett's fatigue-numbed mind, making it impossible for the all-encompassing solution of Sward as the orchestrator of this to stick. He also had the sense that things would be clearer if only Anna and he were freely communicating.

But maybe that interplay of ideas no longer mattered.

The head FBI technician was mining the Swards' van for physical evidence that continued to stack up against the pagan leader. And nothing counted like physical evidence.

Emmett saw that Anna's color had gone sallow. The doctor noticed too, for he asked her, "You feeling all right, Ms. Turnipseed?"

"Just tired." Her voice sounded frail.

The wall clock read 3:35. Emmett rose. "Let's call it a night." They could pick up the reins tomorrow. Together, perhaps.

19

Anna had already been awake two hours when the senior FBI evidence technician phoned at 10:00 A.M. He'd just wrapped up his work on the Swards' van in The Dalles. *No wonder law enforcement people die prematurely, if only from chronic sleep deprivation.* Having only gotten four hours herself, she hoped her life in Washington would be less grueling.

The serology report was in on the knife with the initials *G.B.*: The blood residue found on the blade matched Gorka Bilbao's group—O. Confirmation by the DNA lab that the blood was positively the fossil hunter's would take more time, but the technician was pleased. He was sure he had the murder weapon in at least one of the homicides. Found under the driver's seat in Nels Sward's van.

Spurts of physical evidence against the late pagan leader were becoming a flood, and this trend dovetailed with Emmett's growing doubts about the authenticity of the two sets of remains. Almost miraculously, Sward and his wife had found Willow Creek Woman. Did that mean that they'd also arranged for Bilbao to discover the male specimen? Sward had demanded a forensic sculpture of John Day Man long before Emmett and she asked the court for the same thing. Was that only because he'd planted a modern Caucasoid skull? He'd also threatened to file a complaint with their superiors when Emmett and she refused to help him. But never had. Why?

Anna resisted being sucked back into the investigation. It was time to make a clean break. She was leaving as soon as a rental car was delivered from Madras. It would arrive before 11:00, she'd been promised by the clerk over the phone. On to Portland International Airport, a flight to Las Vegas at 6:00 P.M., followed by a temporary resumption of her old life for two weeks and then off to Washington, D.C.

And a future looming like a black hole before her.

She was closing the zipper to her carry-on bag when a rap at the door made her jump.

Damn. She knew she couldn't go without saying goodbye to Emmett, but she'd hoped that fate would intervene. No chance of that now. And it'd be tacky of her not to try to say something, even though she had no idea what that something might be.

She unlatched the deadbolt on Emmett. His eyes were raw looking from sleeplessness, but his suit looked fresh. "Heard your phone ring," he said, stepping past her into the room. "Anything up?"

"Yes, there's a match—Bilbao's blood type and the dried residue on the knife found in Sward's van."

Emmett nodded as if that were a given already. "Thought we'd drop by the hospital—" Then he noticed her luggage on the bed. "You're going today?"

"As soon as my rental car arrives from Madras."

"You don't even want me to take you to the airport?" For the first time in her memory, there was a catch in his voice.

"You've got better things to do than chauffeur me to Portland."

"I suppose." He sank into one of the chairs at the table. As if he suddenly needed to sit. "You might want to take a look at this." He'd taken two pages from his coat pocket.

"What?"

"Nathan Creech's mug shot and John Day Man's flyer with Bream's sculpture."

She didn't approach the table. This case swallowed up everything, including the only foreseeable possibility for her own happiness. She had nothing left to give it. "They look alike?" she asked disinterestedly.

"Dead on, just like the Mountie said."

She finished up packing, inwardly running through a mental list of last-minute details. She'd told Emmett everything Round Dance had said to her about the Dodge diesel. And this morning, before the evidence tech called, she'd phoned the Yakima FBI resident, asking him to assist Emmett until the U.S. Attorney and both bureaus decided how to reconstitute the task force. "Listen," she said, "if you need anything, you can—"

"Didn't keep the peace very well, did we?" He tried to smile, but the effort faltered, and she was terrified for a moment that he might cry—she'd never seen him like this. "Especially between ourselves."

"I guess not."

"Well, we both get an A for effort." Then, yawning as if none of this mattered, he heaved himself up out of the chair. But his nonchalant look crumbled as he passed close to her. And when he stopped just inside the door, he didn't face her. "I don't know why I did what I did back in North Carolina," he said quietly. "At first, I thought I did. But I don't. And now I'd give anything for the answer."

Then he was gone.

•   •   •

Vernita Dease shot up from the bedside chair as Emmett cracked open the door to Elsa's hospital room. "My daughter's sleeping," she whispered.

"How is she today?"

Vernita looked pleased. "Better, the doctor thinks. She remembers something about her drive back from The Dalles that night."

"Like what?"

"Coffee at Starbucks. Don't ask me why she remembers just that and nothing else. But everybody here thinks it's a good sign."

Emmett gave the woman's arm a reassuring touch. "Sorry for the interruption." Coffee at Starbucks with Thaddeus Rankin, a confrontation between science and native tradition Anna and he had witnessed like a silent movie from the tavern across the street. He pivoted and almost bumped into the juvenile-looking doctor. "Morning, Doc."

"Morning."

This, Emmett realized, was the physician who, according to Anna, had treated Dr. Rankin the night of his collapse at the pagan camp. In the coming days, he wanted to challenge the anthropologist with what Dr. Sinclair believed about John Day Man—the bones were green, not ancient. And his own questions about the fifth metacarpal Rankin had chosen to be radiocarbon-dated. After this interrogation, he didn't want Rankin's attorney to bitch that the BIA had held a sick man's feet to the flames. "Can we have a word in private?"

"Let me check on Elsa," the doctor said, "and I'll meet you in my office."

There was a pillow and a blanket on the sofa in the stuffy cubicle, so Emmett took the chair opposite the desk. He began his wait by trying to think of ways to get the physician to violate the doctor-patient privilege, but as the seconds ticked by he wrestled with a ridiculous urge to go back to the Kah-Nee-Ta and catch Anna before she left. He dreaded his eventual return to the lodge, lying down alone and hearing the silence on the other side of the wall. Thankfully, the doctor rescued him from his own impulsiveness by coming into the office just when Emmett was taking hold of the armrests to rise. The young man gestured at his bedding on the couch. "Three days on and three off. What's it like in the rest of the world?"

"You don't want to know," Emmett said. "Understand you treated Dr. Rankin here—what, a week ago?"

"That's right," the young man replied, his guard going up. "Has that become a law enforcement concern?"

"Might be," Emmett hedged. "In terms of his support to the investigation. I'm about to ask for his help in a big way. All I want to know before I impose on Dr. Rankin—how ill is he? How advanced is his Parkinson's disease?"

The doctor began shuffling papers, and Emmett surmised that he'd just been dismissed for crossing the line. But then the man cleared his throat. "Dr. Rankin doesn't have Parkinson's. Alzheimer's was my first guess, but he doesn't suffer from that either. Your partner gave me the clue that helped solve this, so I suppose I can divulge it to you."

"How's that?"

"Agent Turnipseed told me he stamped his feet before he passed out. That symptom steered me in the right direction. Next I sent a vial of Dr. Rankin's blood to the U.S. Department of Agriculture. They've got an experimental screening for cattle, but it's in the process of being modified for humans."

"You just lost me, Doctor."

"The USDA test confirmed that Dr. Rankin has an infectious protein disease."

Emmett sat up. "What's that?"

"The most common form in the Western world is mad cow disease, bovine spongiform encephalopathy, which humans can contract by eating infected beef, especially cow brains. As a matter of fact, when I phoned Dr. Rankin with the lab results, he admitted enjoying some steak tartare in London years ago while on a lecture tour. He argued that it'd been over a decade ago, and I'm afraid I had to break the bad news to him. Incubation periods for these diseases can be as long as thirty years. Maybe longer, given host genetics and other factors. So little's known about them."

"These diseases," Emmett said, stressing the plural.

"In sheep it's called scrapie. In humans, Creutzfeldt-Jakob disease—that's what killed George Balanchine, the ballet choreographer. When transmitted by human flesh, as bizarre as that sounds, it's called kuru. Though, that's grown increasingly rare in the one place it occurs—Papua New Guinea, where the government clamped down on the cannibalism of one particular tribe. . . ." He began going through the papers on his desk again, this time obviously in search of something.

"The Fore," Emmett said, his neck and shoulder muscles tensing as an epiphany began to tighten down the confusion of the past weeks.

"Uh, right . . . how'd you know that?"

Emmett stood and parted the venetian blinds with his fingers. "Surprising the useless detail you pick up in my line of work." From here, he could just make out the tribal police headquarters. "What causes the infection, a virus?"

"Something called a prion. It slowly crystallizes the protein in brain cells, rotting the organ until it looks like a sponge. That's why the condition's called *spongiform* encephalopathy."

"And the symptoms, other than foot stamping?" Emmett sat again—but on the edge of the chair. He suddenly had a very full day ahead of him.

"Gradual loss of coordination. Slurred speech. Shaking of the extremities. *Kuru* means 'to tremble' in the Fore language, though it'd be more accurate to say that Dr. Rankin's suffering from CJD, not kuru with its cannibalistic association."

"Of course," Emmett said dryly.

"As the nervous system degenerates, the trembling becomes less controllable. Dementia develops, raving belligerence toward others. This can resemble paranoid schizophrenia, and gross psychopathology follows in a few cases. Then death. There's no cure."

"How long does Rankin have?" Emmett asked.

"He told me he's had symptoms for nearly two years now. CJD sufferers seldom last more than thirty months after the onset of the disease."

The doctor's phone rang, and Emmett got up and excused himself.

Out in the parking lot, he paused while inserting the key in the Explorer's lock. He thought of heading north to the Kah-Nee-Ta. To convince Anna to remain here at least for a few days. He'd use this new information about Rankin as inducement. But, starting the engine a moment later, he saw the dash clock. It was after 11:00. She was already gone. The perfume she wore to mask the smells of homicide still lingered in the interior. Desert lavender, mostly. He hung his head for a minute. *Well, at least when you divorce the FBI, you get to keep the car.*

Then he drove across Warm Springs to the police building.

Gabriel Round Dance stuffed a sheaf of papers into the pencil drawer of his desk as Emmett burst into his office. "So you saw a spirit pickup truck behind Gorka Bilbao on Whitehorse Rapids Road," Parker declared, slamming the door behind him.

The sergeant froze for a full three seconds, then took the computer printout from his drawer and tossed it across the desk to Emmett. "We see what we're conditioned to see. That's basic behaviorism."

"So what'd you see that night?"

"Nobody behind the wheel of the Dodge. Just like Bilbao did. Was it imagination or fact? What do you think, Parker?"

Emmett broke eye contact with Round Dance to scan the face page of the printout. State of Washington Department of Motor Vehicles. A list of registered owners for the latest three years of Dodge diesel pickups. As he began reading, Round Dance said petulantly, "Page nineteen, midway down."

It leaped out at Emmett: *Kawatu Rankin, 22935 Rattlesnake Road, Klickitat Valley.* He'd expected the Dodge to come back registered to

Dr. Rankin himself, but this made even more sense. The anthropologist had mentioned that Kawatu had his own place, and Emmett had
never seen anything but the Lexus four-wheel drive on the estate
grounds. He had to settle down to keep thinking clearly. But it was
tough. Breaks in cases came with the same speed and volume as breaks
in dams.

"You going up there?" Round Dance asked.

"Yes."

"Want me to tag along?"

Emmett debated letting the man redeem himself, but an Oregon
tribal cop a hundred miles out of his jurisdiction in Washington State
would be more trouble than help. "No," he finally said, "BIA has the
run of the whole country. You don't."

"Then let me arrange a backup for you with the Klickitat County
sheriff's office."

An even more troubling offer. Emmett wanted a discreet look at
Kawatu's place, and if the deputies arrived there before he did, all was
blown. "Tell you what, I've got a cellular. If I don't check in with your
office by seven this evening, roll some help out to Rattlesnake Road."

Round Dance nodded.

"When'd you decide that the Dodge pickup was real?" Emmett
asked.

"Don't know that I have."

Emmett broke off a searching stare and turned. He was to the door
when the sergeant delayed him. "Parker?"

"Yeah?"

"You think I'm nuts?"

"No. You just respect your own fear. After what happened to your
daddy, I understand that. But I don't get this—why'd you hold back
on Turnipseed and me about the truck?"

"You're outsiders," Round Dance said impassively.

•　•　•

A call came from valet parking—Anna's rental car was waiting for
her at the entrance to the lodge. Forty minutes later than promised.
She carried her bags outside and was locking up the room when the

telephone rang again. She decided to let it go. Maybe it was Emmett, and she wasn't up to another wrenching farewell. But it could be the Indian Desk at FBI headquarters—her new supervisor had a line on an affordable rental just across the Potomac from Washington in Arlington.

"Turnipseed."

"Good morning, Anna," Thaddeus Rankin said. "I *believe* it's still morning."

She checked her wristwatch—morning for another twenty minutes. His slightly sloppy speech and aimless greeting made her suspect that he was drunk. "Good morning."

"The discoveries about Nels Sward—*wow.*"

"Yes, they've surprised all of us." Although tempted, she didn't ask the anthropologist how he'd learned about these discoveries. From the U.S. Attorney in Portland or the medical examiner who'd supervised the autopsies on the pagans, it no longer mattered. She wanted out. She'd detested coming back through a door she'd just locked.

"They've more than surprised me, I must admit. They've thrown me for a loop."

"In what way?"

"I don't want to discuss this over the telephone. Would you and Mr. Parker be so kind as to join me for dinner, say at seven tonight?"

"Sorry, Doctor, I'm on my way to the airport right now. I've taken a post with the Indian Desk at national headquarters."

"What's this?"

He sounded so flabbergasted she said sarcastically, "I was sure you knew."

"I had no idea . . ." Then he rebounded, smoothly but for his intoxicated speech, "How marvelous for you. A big promotion?"

"I'll be the assistant director."

"Grand. And Mr. Parker will remain here?"

"Yes, until the case is closed."

"Is that imminent, Anna?"

"I don't know. You'll have to ask Emmett."

A momentary silence. "Well, would you mind extending my invitation for dinner to Mr. Parker?"

"I'm afraid I won't be seeing him again." She hoped that she'd said this without any apparent emotion. "I was already out the door when you rang."

"What time does your flight leave?"

"Six."

"Then I absolutely must meet with you before you go."

"Why, Doctor?"

His breath gusted in the receiver. "I now have reason to believe both skeletons might be hoaxes."

"Say that again."

"You heard me. As much as this disappoints me, the truth's the truth. Sward may have planted both sets. Plus added a few bones of genuine antiquity—Asian or Middle Eastern—to the mix. I may have helped his cause by choosing one of these older bones."

"The fifth metacarpal."

"Yes. Metacarpals are pretty much alike, so one of them is a good choice for radiocarbon dating. That's because, unavoidably, the bone's destroyed by the test. Sward must've known this. Now, with your help, I'd like to prepare a brief asking the court for a chemical assay on that metacarpal and other bones from John Day Man."

Anna didn't know what to say. This was precisely what Emmett wanted at this point. And, potentially, Thaddeus Rankin was twice the ally Dr. Sinclair was. The brief could be her parting gift to Emmett, to soften the jagged edges of their rift. She needed that. Something unexpected had happened along that rainy interstate last Wednesday, something Dr. Tischler had long urged her to do—she'd confronted her father, if rather strangely through the proxy of Emmett Parker, and told John Turnipseed never to touch her again. Even from the grave. Since then, her anger felt different. Manageable, maybe. Even toward Emmett, as well.

She rechecked her watch.

It'd take no more than two hours to reach Portland International. She'd planned to sit around the airport as an alternative to spending the bulk of the day with Emmett. "Expect me in about ninety minutes, Doctor."

"Thank you, my dear."

• • •

The Klickitat Valley lay north of the river behind the desolate and
wind-blasted Columbia Hills. According to the topographical map,
the dirt extension of Rattlesnake Road was less than two miles from
Rankin's estate. Yet not even a jeep trail cut directly through the hills
from the Columbia basin, and Emmett had to drive ten roundabout
miles via U.S. 97 to reach Kawatu Rankin's neighborhood.

As the numbers on the widely scattered mailboxes got closer to
22935, he pulled off into a corral deserted for the winter and parked
the Explorer behind a cattle chute.

A bone-chilling gale was blowing out of the north. It whipped
Emmett's tie over his shoulder as he glassed Kawatu's cottage with bin-
oculars. The shingle-sided house lacked a garage, and no Dodge diesel
was parked outside. Nor was movement visible through any of the
windows. The cottage sat on several brushy acres, and the closest
neighbor was a quarter mile away. Two poplars stood like golden pil-
lars on either side of the driveway, their fall foliage in stunning contrast to the drab house and surrounding barrens.

Avoiding the road, Emmett set off on foot for Kawatu's mini-estate.

In the distance, a rooster tail of dust rose off a side street from a
UPS truck making deliveries. The wind had dried out the land since
the last rain, and nothing could move on these unpaved country lanes
without raising dust. Advance warning, Emmett realized, if Kawatu
returned.

He wanted a quick look inside the place. If anything looked
promising, he'd then request a search warrant as if he'd never been inside. His probable cause was on shaky grounds. While it was now clear
that Kawatu had tried to splatter Gorka Bilbao all over Whitehorse
Rapids Road, the judge would dismiss the value of that crucial link because the fossil hunter's blood had been found on the knife inside Nels
Sward's van. Too much had happened these past two and a half weeks,
too much evidence had been manipulated for Emmett to trust in that
knife.

Approaching the house from the rear, he saw a pair of locks on the
back door, one of them a commercial-grade deadbolt. He knocked.
If Kawatu appeared unexpectedly, Emmett planned to say that he

thought he'd heard someone in the backyard. But a minute came and went with no answer. He went over to a window, moistened his dusty-tasting palms on his tongue, flattened them against the glass and lifted the sliding panel up and out of its frame. He rested the panel inside the room, then crawled through the opening. A bedroom, although it took him a moment to realize that. There were no beds, nightstands or dressers, just boxes and crates stacked everywhere, pyramids rising from the shag carpet, altarlike piles standing in the corners. Van Heusen shirts and Fruit of the Loom underwear still packaged. Belt sanders and power drills and airless paint sprayers, brand new in the boxes. Canned goods, especially candied yams and Spam.

Emmett listened to the household. No sound except the hum of the refrigerator. He wiped his palm prints off the window glass with his handkerchief, put the panel back in its frame and slid it shut.

Then he ran his eyes over the accumulated plunder.

Rankin had rescued an eleven-year-old Kawatu from a jail in Port Moresby. The boy had become an adept thief, he'd said. Had the grown Kawatu gone on thieving in America without his mentor's knowledge, or—given the size of this stockpile—branched out into fencing stolen property for local burglars?

A receipt caught Emmett's eye. It was taped to a wet-dry vacuum box. From the Wal-Mart in The Dalles, dated three months ago.

Stolen goods didn't come with receipts.

Emmett slipped into the living room. Here there were even more intricately stacked piles of goods. Shotguns and rifles in their plush-lined cases, so clean it was obvious that they'd never been fired. Braun coffeemakers. Knives of every description.

Emmett glanced up.

Hanging from the ceiling fan on a monofilament fishing line was a toy-sized effigy of a pickup truck, woven from what appeared to be dried palm fronds. It rotated in the stir from Emmett's entry.

At last, this warehouse of unused merchandise made sense.

These weren't material goods, not figuratively, even though Kawatu had re-created a virtual Kmart inside his home. They were the seeds of riches, things emblematic of the prosperity the man desired for him-self. Much like the figure of a deer or an antelope pecked into a rock by a Paleo-Indian hunter—to show the spirits what he wanted.

Emmett had first heard about cargo cults in an anthropology course at Oklahoma State. Astounded by the mountains of cargo brought to New Guinea by U.S. troops during the Second World War, the natives could not fathom the industrial-agricultural base that had produced those goods. Instead, they decided that this wealth had been created by their ancestral gods for them, but whites, crafty and deceitful conjurers that they were, had siphoned off the riches for their own use. Some tribesmen built replicas of general stores they'd seen in Port Moresby, put locks on the doors as white men did and waited for the gods to fill these places with goods. In the highlands, they cleared mock airstrips and wove effigies of Dakota transports in the hope that this would stimulate the gods to airlift them cargo that wouldn't be intercepted by white men.

Kawatu's variation on this magic had worked. He'd fashioned a Dodge pickup from palm fronds, and the ancestral spirits had seen fit to give him one.

Emmett moved on.

The second bedroom was also crammed with cargo. Sports equipment: basketballs, boomerangs, diving masks and flippers. Kawatu had left a narrow aisle that led to a chaise longue cushion spread out on the carpet. His bed. An old U.S. Army blanket, olive drab in color, was his only bedding. A World War II memento Kawatu had brought with him from New Guinea to his new home in the Kingdom of Cargo?

In the kitchen, the first thing to catch Emmett's eye was a vine twining up a bamboo trellis out of one of the sinks, which had been filled with potting soil. This tangle of jade-colored growth pressed against the window glass, straining with a tropical hunger for the sunlight beyond. It had managed to set forth yellow blooms, some of which had matured into seed pods. Although exotic looking, the plant resembled morning glory, which had psychoactive properties, so he twisted off one of the pods and pocketed it. For later testing—and comparison with the unidentifiable chemical substance found in Bilbao's blood, plus anything in Elsa's and Nels Sward's panels.

He instantly recognized a gadget on the drainboard. From the legal wiretaps he'd conducted through the years. It was a dropout relay, used so a tap is actuated only when the telephone is lifted off the hook. It had no purpose on Kawatu's own phone, but meant that he had acquired specialized gear to tap the phones of others. What had Paulina asked Emmett that morning in the tribal jail? *You tappin' my phone?*

The message light was blinking on the answering machine.

Emmett threaded his way through boxes of pots and pans, Dutch ovens. He touched the play button on the machine, and an automated voice declared that this call had come in at 2:35—fifteen minutes ago: "Come back to the house at once. I'm expecting a visitor." The caller didn't identify himself, yet Emmett had no doubt he was Thaddeus Rankin, sounding slightly tipsy.

The "at once" suggested that Rankin expected Kawatu to be home soon.

Quickly, Emmett examined the rest of the kitchen. A crate of Thunderbird wine lay on the floor under the table. The dividers showed that there had once been twelve bottles inside. Just three remained. Emmett took out a fifth. Half empty. Curiously, the other two bottles were full but their plastic cap seals had been broken.

The refrigerator was filled with unfamiliar fruits and vegetables. Dark, misshapen tubers. Fat red bananas. And in the freezer was a frosted-over box that took up the entire compartment. Emmett wiped away some ice crystals with the heel of his hand, and letters appeared:

MITE, MIL

He vigorously rubbed the entire end of the box:

DYNAMITE, MILITARY, M1
(MEDIUM VELOCITY)
MANUFACTURED UNDER U.S. ARMY CORPS OF ENGINEERS
CONTRACT #4912-663-21-6023

He stood perfectly still in an effort to control his excitement. Military dynamite had been the variety of explosive used on the safe in The Dalles headquarters.

Like a dam breaking.

His mind racing now, he tried to think of a way to seize this evidence without having to resort to a search warrant. There was no way he'd leave this bonanza to be rehidden by Kawatu, which meant bolstering his probable cause with a reason to have immediately entered the house. The bottles of wine. What had Anna said after that nightmare in the squall on Interstate 84? *Bilbao had a high blood alcohol, and we found no bottles in or around his cabin.* Was the case of Thunderbird in plain view from outside through the overgrown kitchen window? No. Using his foot, Emmett scooted the crate over so that it conceivably was.

Still, this wasn't enough to justify his warrantless entry.

He was looking around for something else, when the window suddenly vibrated.

The wind was howling, and Emmett gave the steady vibration no thought—until he realized that a window creaks in a gale, not vibrates. He peeked through the foliage of the vine. A Dodge pickup was barreling dustily down a dirt road that came out of the Columbia Hills. The timbre of its diesel engine was shaking the window.

Kawatu drove past the west side of his own house and presumably turned right onto Rattlesnake Road to reach his driveway.

Emmett didn't see—he was already running for the bedroom he'd broken into minutes ago. He had no key to unlock either of the deadbolted doors in the kitchen and the living room. Throwing open the window, he dove out, his chest taking the punishment of the metal track on the sill. He reclosed the window with his fingernails, then sprinted through a shower of golden poplar leaves, keeping the house to his back as the engine noise died out front.

• • •

When Kawatu failed to meet Anna at the gate on the bluff above the mansion, she got out of the rental car and pressed the intercom speaker button.

"Yes, Anna," Rankin's voice promptly responded.

"Should I wait for Kawatu, Doctor?"

"No. He's out and about. . . ." Rankin gave her a code to be entered on the pushbutton digits. An unusual act of trust, she thought, for a man who previously had let no one but Kawatu drive down to the mansion. "Meet me in the library, my dear."

The gate glided open, and she hurried back to the car. The wind whistled through the wrought-iron fence staves, and there were white-caps on the gray-green waters of the Columbia below. She started down the long driveway as the gate clanked shut behind her. Mount Hood was already throwing a conical blue shadow across the basin, reminding her to make this visit brief. But she didn't regret coming. Closure had always revolved around the skeletons, somehow, and now even Rankin doubted them.

Still, a tingle on the back of her neck cautioned her to take this one step at a time. She didn't trust Rankin. Nor did she quite know what to make of this titanic shift in his attitude toward the remains.

She dabbed the backs of her earlobes with perfume—the house reeked of ancient death, and more than anything she dreaded those funereal odors.

Parking under the porte cochere, she opened the car door but then pulled it shut again—a tumbleweed had invaded the immaculate grounds and skipped past the side window. She made sure her pant leg covered her pistol in its ankle holster.

The entry was unlocked, as Rankin had intimated.

An unpleasant sweetness was added to the usual stench. Maybe it was the anthropologist himself, something given off by his palsied body as it slowly broke down. "Doctor, I'm here," she called out.

"This way, Anna," his voice led her on.

There were visible wet spots on the Persian runner in the corridor.

Rankin was waiting for her in his fireside chair, dressed in field khakis. He failed to rise when she entered the library, but raised a drink to toast her. The ulcerated sores on his face had spread since their last meeting, adding to the picture of physical decline and decay. "Here's to the conquering heroine on her way to bigger and better things."

"Hopefully." She sat on the same sofa Emmett and she had shared.

"Something to drink, Anna?"

"Not now, thanks."

"Splendid news about Elsa."

"Yes, it is."

He sounded soberer than he had on the phone. But the scotch and soda in his grasp probably meant that he hadn't slowed down since his call to her. "Where's the fifth metacarpal now?" he asked while mention of Elsa Dease still hung in the air.

"I don't know," she lied. Over the protests of Mel Brantford, the NAGPRA monitor, Emmett had shipped it to the Portland FBI office for safekeeping—until a potential homicide investigation was ruled out.

"What do you mean *you don't know?*" Rankin asked.

He probably had information that could expose her lie, but she held her ground and quietly stared back at him. In that instant, it became clear to her why she'd come. She wanted to look Rankin squarely in the eye when she said the following. "I don't know how important the metacarpal is to the investigation any longer."

Rankin blinked twice, then hid his expression behind his glass. "I don't understand," he said, after swallowing. "An assay will expose the hoax, if the bones of the same skeleton have different chemical compositions. I thought you and Parker would jump at this chance."

"Too late."

"In what way, my dear?"

"We're ready to ask the court for DNA testing on John Day Man."

"Without the mandible?"

"I'm no expert, but I understand that the chances of finding intact collagen increase with the freshness of the remains."

Rankin shut his eyes for a moment. "This presumes you have a subject for comparison."

"We do."

"Who?"

Rising, Anna took from her jacket the two pages Emmett had left on the table in her room. She gave them to Rankin. His gaze fixed on Nathan Creech's mug shot. Then on the flyer with the photo of John Day Man's sculpture. He focused on the face. Only when the papers fell from his grasp and fluttered to the floor did Anna realize the risk she'd taken in coming. For once, he looked stunned. He took hold of his cane as if he meant to rise and come at her. But he kneaded the crook in his trembling hands and glared at her with an incongruous smile that was cut short by a fierce twitch of his head. "You and Mr. Parker seem to have leapfrogged ahead of me."

• • •

For thirty minutes, Emmett waited out in the brush for Kawatu to obey Rankin's phone message. Finally, the man drove off toward U.S. 97 in his Dodge diesel, and Emmett jogged back to the Explorer. He accelerated up into the Columbia Hills along the unpaved road Kawatu had just descended. Less than a half mile along it, a gate barred further progress. A sign read:

NO TRESPASSING
DANGER!
PELIGRO!

Entry on foot was discouraged by a chain-link fence that evidently ringed the site. It was topped with razor wire, although in places the mesh drooped on its poles.

Emmett threw the Explorer into reverse and backed down the road to the first wide spot. Parking, he got out and cut across a grassy slope to a stretch of fence line that wasn't visible from the gate. There was no other way around the enclosure. Kawatu's tire tracks never left the road. And they continued past the padlocked gate onto the grounds. Whatever his interest had been in this place, it had been inside.

Emmett found what he was looking for—a gully recently cut by rainwater under the fence. He crawled through the tight space, grimacing at what this did to his last clean suit.

Shielding his eyes with a hand, he stood still a few seconds to get his bearings.

Some kind of grit was being eddied around by the strong wind. Volcanic cinders, Emmett realized, feeling their bite on his cheeks. There were red and black heaps of them along the ridge the site occupied. Trudging over these grainy dunes, he saw no buildings or anything else that might have been of interest to Kawatu. But the airborne cinders made seeing difficult. The Columbia River appeared intermittently to the south, as did Rankin's mansion.

All at once, the earth collapsed beneath him. Like the sand draining out of an hourglass. The funneling cinders tugged at his lower legs.

He'd already sunk down to his knees when he flung himself backward. He landed with a grunt on a firmer ground. Between his outstretched shoes, a V-shaped cut opened on a huge hole. Then he understood. Blind, he'd stumbled up to the lip of a wide pit, and a slab of sheer wall had given under his weight. He scrambled back several more feet before the entire side of the pit caved in and carried him down.

A cinder mine.

In the West, volcanic cinders were preferred over salt as a spread for winter roads. Some prospector had found a pocket of them on this basaltic ridge.

What, if anything, was Kawatu using the site for?

Emmett began circumventing the pit. Cautiously now.

A rickety-looking hoisting apparatus tilted over the rim, seemingly ready to tumble inside at the slightest nudge. The winch barrel had disintegrated, littering the cinders with fist-sized ball bearings. When the mine was in operation, this machinery had provided access to and from the diggings below, but now Emmett trusted neither it nor the frayed cable that plunged out of sight into the depths.

But, as a blast of grit ebbed, he saw that an orange nylon rope ladder had been dropped over the wall opposite him. It looked fairly new. Rounding the last few yards to that wall, he came upon two wooden pallets that had been lashed together to form a kind of pier out to the crumbly lip—and the top of the ladder.

Still, even from the outermost pallet, he couldn't see most of the floor of the pit, which led him to believe that the miners had undercut the walls, cobbing out a flask-shaped cavity.

But, at last, he had no doubt that Kawatu had used the ladder recently, for his tracks coming and going from the pallets showed as fresh divots in the cinders.

That settled it.

Emmett had to see what was below.

His stomach knotted as he inched over the side. The ladder swayed under his feet. He tried to loosen his death grip on the rungs, so his hands wouldn't knot up. But the wind spun him around, and he held on with all his might as he gazed straight up to ward off an onslaught of vertigo.

The sky was the color of ashes.

To get going again, he told himself the wind would have less effect on the flimsy-feeling ladder the lower he got.

Downward he crept.

Off to the left, he noticed a scored line in the pit wall, as if something had rubbed against the cinders. The chafing bite of a rope as an object was lowered to the bottom?

He twisted around and, risking another rush of dizziness, peered directly down. In the middle of the floor of the pit were the rusted remains of ore buckets, metal drums and a mucking machine. As he'd suspected, the walls had been undercut, creating recesses that were completely out of sight from above.

The wind began whipping him around again. Wildly.

A steel spike had been hammered into the cinders, and he was reaching for this obvious handhold when a glint of monofilament line made him freeze. He traced it from the spike, across the pit and to the black mouth of a little cove in the far wall. He believed that he could see something pointed shining in the midst of that darkness.

What if the gale slammed him into the spike on his ascent?

Hanging on to the ladder with one hand, he unfastened his belt, stripped off his holstered .357 magnum and wedged the weapon in the back of his waistband. Then he ripped off the belt and, as lightly as he could, looped the buckle over the head of the spike. Easing down the bucking ladder as far as he could go and still reach the tip of his belt, he paused. And thought a moment. What if the trip wire connected to an explosive? Unlikely. Kawatu wouldn't want to blow to smithereens whatever he was concealing below.

So Emmett gave a yank on his belt.

A wicked-sounding whisk was followed by a thud into the wall.

He looked up. Two feet above his head a shaft was imbedded in the cinders. Clambering up several rungs, he pried it out—the projectile from a speargun. A lethal-looking point probably guaranteed to penetrate the toughest shark's skin. He stuck it back in the wall, then looked across the pit at the cove in which the gun was concealed. The monofilament line had formed part of a tension release mechanism attached to the trigger. A skillful booby trap.

Kawatu was a man of many talents.

Emmett's hands finally cramped, and his belt, weighed down by the freed spike caught in the buckle, slid through his fingers. He leaned over and tried to snatch it. But it was no good. The chunk of iron clanged loudly against one of the metal barrels below, and instantly there was a deafening rustle. A wave of flapping noises welled up toward Emmett, and he hugged the wall as man-sized bats hovered in the pit, kept by the high winds from breaking out into the sky above. They hissed strangely at him. He expected them to squeak, trying to locate the walls in their day blindness. But then one swept close, and he noticed the obscenely red head. It was featherless. And the bird's talons were yellow.

A vulture.

He had disturbed a flock of turkey vultures, large birds with wing spans of six feet.

That meant only one thing—there was carrion in the bottom of the pit.

At last, a solitary buzzard braved the full force of the wind. When its delicate wing bones weren't snapped, the others swooped up, rocking from side to side in their ungainly way of flight, and left Emmett clinging weakly to the rope ladder. He took a minute to stop shaking, then went the rest of the way to the floor of the pit.

Nothing lay in the recess before him, so he turned with his heart in his throat.

The cavern reminded him of one of those limestone sinkholes in Central America down which sacrificial victims had been hurled. The presence of a skeleton added immeasurably to the impression.

He closed slowly on it, wary of more booby traps.

The skeleton was chest-down on a bed of cinders in the deepest recess. A flat stone had been placed on the back of the neck and the mid-joint of each of the extremities—Emmett could only guess that these weights were intended to keep the vultures from completely dismembering the remains and flying off with body parts. Through an undercurrent of shock, he recalled the little-believed report of the Wishram Heights woman who'd seen a buzzard on her kitchen windowsill with a human ear in its beak. Wishram Heights was less than five miles from here.

He lifted the stone off the victim's neck. It had protected the top of the scalp from the ferocious scavenging—a flock of vultures could pick all the flesh off a body in a few hours. Dark brown hair mixed with gray. A middle-aged individual. Carefully, he turned the head, but the cranium snapped off at the first vertebra. Revulsion made him want to drop the head, but he held on to it, all the while his eyes fixed on Tennyson Paulina's face. The dry wind had given the Paiute cowboy's skin the texture of old leather, and the whites of his eyes had gone brown from exposure to the air. But some of the living man's expression survived in the self-amused curl of his lips. He seemed to be trying to peer up at the bullet hole in his forehead. It'd been tattooed by gunpowder—he'd been shot at close range.

Emmett put down the head and stood back from the remains.

Another early observation had been dismissed out of hand. The round puncture in John Day Man's tibia, which Rankin had brusquely explained as the possible work of a scavenging rodent. In reality, the mark was from the beak of a turkey vulture.

As of this moment, Dr. Thaddeus Rankin was out of the court-recognized-expert business.

Emmett eased down on his heels to think.

Anna had seen Paulina last night at the hospital, half in the bag and ranting drunkenly that he'd had a vision or a dream in jail. What had Anna said he told an uncomprehending Elsa? *I promise you I'll make it all right. I'll throw down a line of blood these demons can't cross.* Whether his medicine was bogus or not was superfluous now. Somehow, the Paiute shaman had zeroed in on Rankin, gone after him late last night or early this morning. But the anthropologist had bested him. Nothing was more dangerous than a dying man. Now Paulina was in much the same state Nathan Creech had been when the Canadian Indian's bones had been hoisted out of this charnel pit for further doctoring to make them look ancient. That was it—Rankin was transforming his enemies into archaeological specimens that supported his pet theories. Willow Creek Woman—whoever she one day might prove to be—had been defleshed here as well. How many others? Only Rankin and his osteological technician knew for sure.

Another thing was for certain—Paulina's modern bullet wound would be bashed out with a stone axe or some other period weapon that made his fatal injury consistent with a bygone time.

This was a factory in which history was fabricated.

Standing, Emmett moved out into the stronger light at the middle of the pit's floor. The afternoon was growing late. As he found his belt, threaded his holster through it and put them back on, his mind was filled with the logistics of taking down Rankin and Kawatu. How fast could the FBI resident get down here from Yakima? Maybe it'd be better to rely on a combined force of Klickitat deputies and federal rangers assigned to the Corps of Engineers installations. They were closer.

He turned for the ladder—and saw that it was gone.

His surprise was brief. Scarcely a moment's hesitation followed before he drew his revolver. Over its phosphorescence-tipped sights, he scanned the entire rim. No one showed. His cellular phone. Keeping his eyes trained above, he dug out the phone and flicked on the power by feel. Only then did he glance at the screen.

No service.

Something flew down at him. He easily avoided the object—until it ricocheted off one of the ore buckets and hurtled back at him at a crazy angle. A ball bearing.

He shifted around for a glimpse of Kawatu. He had no doubt that the New Guinean was his attacker. What had alerted him to Emmett's presence? Dust rising from the road that led to the site? Or something out of place inside his cottage? The man didn't reveal himself, not even when he lobbed another steel ball down into the pit. It whirred past Emmett's face and crunched through a badly oxidized drum.

"I've phoned the sheriff's office," he calmly announced, backing into the same recess where Paulina's skeleton lay shining in the dusk. "They're on the way here."

No response, just the wind skirling over the top of the pit.

Three or four balls came down at once, ringing off the mucking machine and glancing around the bottom of the pit like cannon shots. Emmett made himself as small as he could, but there was no safe place in this hole. One lucky hit could crush his skull like an eggshell.

The cable. It snaked down limply from the hoisting apparatus on the surface. Time had begun to unravel the individual strands. But its two-inch thickness had been designed to bear the weight of tons of cinders, so Emmett was willing to gamble that it would support a 190-

pound man. He darted around the circumference of the pit, staying close to the wall as more iron hailstones rained down on him.

Reaching the cable, he holstered his revolver, spat into his palms and prepared to lunge out of the way if the entire coil came tumbling down. Then he gave the line a heave. The slack came out, and the anchoring held.

He started climbing.

He was twenty feet off the ground when Kawatu reared into sight and hurled another bearing. The ball bounced painfully off Emmett's hip, but he managed to wrap an ankle around the line to keep from falling. He also brought out his revolver and fired once at Kawatu's last position. The man had vanished again, but Emmett mostly wanted to keep his head down.

The shot reverberated in the pit.

When these echoes faded, a chilling sound drifted from above—the groan of failing metal. Emmett jammed his .357 into his holster and clutched the cable with all his strength. The rust powder gave him a firm purchase on it. But he was still sliding downward. The cable itself was slipping. He pulled furiously, hand over hand, for the top. Almost there, he craned his neck for an upward glance.

Kawatu stood beside the hoisting works, looming over him. He had no visible weapons. Emmett was fumbling for his revolver when the cable shuddered and dropped a full foot before snapping to a halt. He gave up going for his handgun and held on.

The cable screeched through its pulley, and he slid down another foot. He was at least forty feet off the bottom. The height of a four-story building. Even if he survived the fall, he had no chance if he lay at the bottom with two shattered legs. No water or food. It was a myth that vultures restricted their diet to carrion. They would attack the helpless as well, and their beaks were as sharp as scalpels.

Incredibly, Kawatu offered a helping hand. "Throw away your gun, and I will save you."

Emmett paused with his hands on the grips of the revolver. Never in fourteen years had he given up his weapon. But the hoisting works went on groaning.

"Quickly, man," Kawatu urged.

The .357 plummeted from Emmett's grasp. He reached up, and the man took hold of him in the same split second the cable became weightless. Off to Emmett's left, the winch assembly fell away in a blur. He was only dimly aware of the crash below, for as soon as his shoes touched the surface he prepared to take on Kawatu.

But before Emmett could regain his balance and disengage his right hand, the man swung a metal pipe around into the side of his head.

A black stain spread from the point of impact and darkened his brain.

20

As soon as Anna could leave the mansion without raising the anthropologist's suspicions, she would phone Emmett. The thought of seeing Parker again no longer troubled her. In fact, she had to meet with him, for only he would understand the significance of Rankin's reaction when she'd handed him Nathan Creech's mug shot and the photo of John Day Man's sculpture. It'd been a visible punch to his solar plexus, one from which he had yet to recover, for since then there was a different pitch to his voice. Higher, thinner. "You and Mr. Parker haven't disappointed me with your thoroughness."

Anna kept her composure, although there was a growing tightness in the pit of her stomach. Was Rankin inching toward an admission?

But then he retreated into a sulking paranoia. "I really don't understand why people must work so hard to discredit me, Anna. Is the truth that daunting?"

"I'm sorry, Doctor—it's almost four. I've got to get going to make that flight." Even though she now had no intention of leaving Oregon tonight.

"I wish I could just fly away." Rankin hoisted himself to his feet on his cane. She thought she had a clean exit until he added, "Come a moment, Anna, I want you to meet my father." She gave her wristwatch a conspicuous glance, but he protested, "Humor an old man, my dear. Won't take but a minute."

Perhaps it was too soon after Rankin's recoiling at Creech's mug shot to go. She might also be witnessing a complete mental breakdown.

From it, a wealth of self-incriminating statements might spring. She relented with a slight nod.

He led the way. There was a new quality to his gait, a rigidity of his legs that made his halting steps seem Frankensteinian.

They came into a room with vaulting windows. He opened the blinds, but the winter light did little to dispel the gloom. A putrid sweetness so pervaded the stagnant reaches of the big house she half-wondered if Rankin had his father's remains on exhibit. But, thankfully, only native artifacts filled the room. They looked Melanesian to her.

Through the windows she had a view of the driveway and the gate far above. Except for those up on Highway 14, no vehicles were in sight. Headlights were coming on against the dusk. Still, the prospect of Kawatu's arrival made her uneasy.

She turned.

The portrait of a white man in his late forties hung over the mantel. A forgettable face except for his emphatic eyes. Rankin had inherited them. "Father," he addressed the oil as if it were a living being, "may I present Ms. Anna Turnipseed. Anna, Mr. Herbert Rankin."

She was in no mood for make-believe. "Your father was an anthropologist too?"

"Yes. But Papa was a complete innocent, and he had no idea he was playing the most dangerous game in the world. . . ." Rankin paused, no doubt waiting for Anna to ask.

She finally did so if only to hasten the next opportunity for her departure—the seconds in this house now pricked her like needles. "And that game?"

"To discover the true origins of mankind. You have no friends, Anna, when you venture into the human past, seeking the truth. Ask all the greats—Darwin, Wallace, Leakey. Human beings guard nothing as tenaciously as their sacred fantasies about their origins. . . ." He smiled. "Oh, I see the question burning in your heart, Anna—*Why do you hate native peoples so much you must deny them the comfort of their beliefs?*" His head began jerking, and he fisted his ponytail to steady it. "Not so. I've always admired your most basic beliefs." Letting go of his hair, he gestured at the portrait. "Unlike my father, who to his dying day was a product of his own culture, I could take off the blinders of

Western conventionality. I'm one up on Papa, Anna, though I'm paying for it with my life."

"I don't understand," she said.

"There's a saying in my business: 'The field anthropologist must always save a white linen suit for the trip home.' Well, I burned that suit one afternoon in the highlands of New Guinea. . . ." He hobbled over to a chair, and she alertly shifted to keep track of him, even though the half turn put the windows to her back. "It was at a funeral feast for an elderly woman who'd been my principal informant among the Fore. She'd died of kuru. . . ." He looked sharply at Anna. "Ever heard of it?"

She shook her head.

"A terrible infectious disease," he said. "Used to decimate the Fore, nearly extinguished them as a tribe. Kawatu's own mother perished of it. . . ." Anna kept a blank face as he blithely went on about protein in the brain and cerebellar dysfunction. Previously, Rankin had claimed to Emmett and her that Kawatu's prostitute mother died of syphilis. What else might he let slip in the coming minutes? She was now glad that she had stayed, for he no longer seemed capable of weaving his cover stories into a coherent whole. "And, before my eyes, Anna," he continued, "my informant's kinfolk broke out the knives and carved up that fine old woman until no piece of her flesh was larger than a walnut. Her sisters began passing out these morsels on platters of banana leaves. This was all done with the piety of a Catholic priest dispensing the host to the faithful. Her closest kin were served first, and they received the choicest parts. The brain's highly valued, so you can imagine my astonishment when I was honored with a lightly steamed piece of cortex." He sat.

"And you ate it," Anna said with revulsion.

"Of course I ate it. Nobody knew how kuru was transmitted in those days. And, putting any health concern aside, I was being offered eucharistic bread in the holiest rite of a people I'd come to love. Do you honestly think I would have refused this signal honor? I was *wontok,* one-talk in pidgin, one of them who talked their talk and walked their walk, not just another white anthro with a steno pad and a tape recorder. I was *connected.* Isn't that what all you modern Amerinds hunger for? To be connected again?"

Something in his unblinking eyes made her think of her pistol in its ankle holster, but she waited. It was too soon to think about taking him down. She expected Rankin to incriminate himself at any second. Closure seemed only a breath away, and there was an element of greed in this business, as in all others. But not for profit. For learning the secrets that made a prosecution possible. And to achieve that, you sometimes had to risk body and soul, either exercising a kind of reasonable recklessness or walking away empty-handed.

She was walking away from Oregon with so little, she needed this.

"Ask me, Anna."

Her mouth was dry. "Ask you what?"

"What tasting this forbidden fruit was like."

She couldn't.

"The bit of brain was restless on my tongue," he went on anyway. "As if it were still charged with synaptic energy. But I chewed, swallowed—and was energized, Anna. Suddenly, I was brimming with the boundless power of life. All the primal forces in that fine old woman had passed into me and the others there, and I felt her presence inside me. Pulsating. Palpitating. Everything the Fore believed about endocannibalism was true. It wasn't superstitious claptrap. They'd grasped the great, enduring truth about mankind—we evolved out of a murderous mix of conflicting races. Murder is our essence. Our inheritance. And nothing celebrates murder like cannibalism." He stared beyond her, out onto his grounds, as if reliving that distant feast.

She could no more take her eyes off him than if he were a coiled rattlesnake. "You said you're paying for that experience with your life?"

"Yes, I'm dying, Anna." He stood. "Come, I want you to meet a friend of mine. We recently patched up our differences, and nothing is more pleasing than burying the hatchet with an old friend."

Anna didn't move. Was this another introduction on the order of the one he'd just made to his father? Was his diseased mind now inhabiting a world entirely of his own design, surrounded by obliging relatives and friends? Regardless, she had yet to hear him say the thing that would enable her to end this grotesque theatrical. Once she heard these words, she'd take Rankin down herself. She felt she no longer needed Emmett. *Now prove it to yourself.*

"Come, come," Rankin said.

She had a weapon, and he apparently had none—there were no bulges in the pockets of his khakis. She followed him out to double aluminum doors at the far end of the main corridor. He opened them on an elevator car. They stepped inside, and he punched a button marked *B*. As they started down, Anna said nonconfrontationally, "You told Emmett and me Kawatu's mother died of syphilis."

Unfazed, he peered up at his own reflection in the mirror on the ceiling of the car. "Did I?"

"Yes."

"I've said so many things these past months, Anna. One of the luxuries of dying is that you no longer have to worry about what you have to say to whom."

The door whisked open on total darkness, and Anna heard Rankin step out. She didn't emerge until banks of fluorescent lights started coming on. The anthropologist waited at the wall switches for her. "There. No bogeymen."

An expansive laboratory began with an open area of autopsy trays and workbenches and faded into several aisles of towering cabinets at the rear. She realized that this basement was not only the source of the smell she'd caught on her two previous visits—a fetid medley of dry rot, musty earth and mold—it was also the origin of a cloying stench that had sifted upstairs.

She noticed a bulletin board—with a newspaper photograph of her on it, plus freehand sketches of crania. "Why do you have my picture?" she demanded, although a chill went down her spine.

"You're remarkable . . . prototypical. Consider this all to be a compliment, Anna."

Rankin had just said that he was no longer worried about what he said. She decided it was time to test this. She wasn't sure how long she'd been sitting on this question, only that it had been taking shape for days. "What did you put in Elsa Dease's coffee at Starbucks?"

Rankin had set off for the back of the laboratory, but now he made a half circle and regarded Anna with a slight tilt to his head. "Elsa has a marvelous Caucasoid bone structure. It's nothing more than a coincidence of hybridized genetics found in mixed-blood people, but I'm convinced she resembles a young woman of the first wave of migration to the New World. The Caucasoid pioneers typified by John Day Man and Willow Creek Woman. You, Anna, with your Japanese blood, re-semble the second and later wave from which modern Indians are de-scended. I look into your face, and I see the missing piece to a great puzzle about human migration."

"Why'd you poison Elsa?" More adamantly.

"Why?" Rankin sighed. "Human behavior isn't random. But it's often unpredictable." He resumed his stiff-legged walk toward the back.

How had Elsa been unpredictable? The only thing that came to Anna's mind was the woman's suggestion at the conclusion of Rankin's examination of John Day Man that the remains be made available to other scientists to evaluate his cannibalism claim. Anna had written off Elsa's outburst as a flash of temper, but apparently Rankin had foreseen danger to himself in it. Anna quick-stepped to catch up with him, checking the lab benches for any weapons he might use. Atop some were flasks and beakers filled with chemicals. Once before, she'd had ether splashed in her face, and didn't want to repeat the eye-scorching experience. They walked past a bottle cart holding two cylinders of liquid nitrogen. Rankin paid neither the glass containers nor the tanks any attention.

"What'd Elsa do to upset you?" she asked.

"She threatened to expose my cryptograms to the future."

"What cryptograms?"

"Have patience, my dear."

"And what'd you give Bilbao to drink that showed up on his blood panel? Emmett and I found no bottles up at his cabin."

"Patience," he said less agreeably.

They'd come to the ten-foot-high cabinets, which seemed to arch over her. They gave off an almost imperceptible hum, a buzzing rest-lessness that she could only liken to beehive boxes. And it was colder here than in the rest of the basement. The kind of suffocating cold that left you depressed. She yanked open a drawer. Earth-stained bones. Another drawer. More bones. Names of tribes were in the label holders. A huge collection of native remains in flagrant violation of NAGPRA. The sight of so many disjointed skeletons made her skin crawl—this felt like cracking open crematorium doors at Auschwitz.

Why had Rankin let a federal officer come down here? Was he throwing in the towel? Did he now want to be stopped?

They passed sheets of plywood painted black. She suspected that windows lay behind them.

Rankin unlocked a steel door with a key. "Gorka Bilbao had a loose tongue. I knew he'd talk to Parker and you, so I had Kawatu shadow him in his pickup truck."

"And later you had Kawatu torture and kill him."

"Let's not belabor this, Anna. My illness made me sloppy, otherwise you'd still be at a complete loss. I was merely defending myself every step of the way. Everyone attacks me. The most recent attack came early this morning, when that Paiute charlatan broke into the house and bloodied up the place."

"What're you talking about?"

"The Paiute gashed his arm with a knife and smeared his blood around my corridor so I'd have to pass through his power. To weaken my own powers, I suppose, before he tried to finish me off. Thank God Kawatu had come to work early."

Then it hit her. "What've you done to Tennyson Paulina?"

"In due course, Anna," Rankin said. "All in due course. It's become so very tiresome."

Maybe he wanted to be arrested. Maybe he'd wearied of this nightmare of his own doing. "You'll have to come away with me," she said.

"Understood." He ran his palm over the door. Affectionately. "Before NAGPRA ushered in a new Dark Age, I hoped to open this exhibit to the public. Give them an authentic glimpse into our benighted human past. One element was lacking, though, until a few days ago. The smell . . ."

Anna stood back.

"Fortunately, kuru doesn't affect my muscle strength." Winking at her, Rankin swung the heavy door open.

For an instant, the daylight was so convincing she believed she was looking outside, into some secret grotto in his garden. Then she noticed the track lighting along the ceiling. And the lifelike human figures gathered stock-still around a fire ring in an artificial cave. Diminutive native people in a tableau, butchering game, feasting on it.

Then out wafted a puff of air so foul Anna covered her nose and mouth with a hand. Still, her eyes watered from the bite of caustic vapors.

Rankin seemed oblivious to the stench. "You have company," he announced into the cave. "I believe you remember Anna Turnipseed . . . don't you, *Deborah?*"

Anna looked back to what—at a side-glance—she'd taken to be the carcass of an animal. It was a headless human torso. Female. Badly decomposed. One of the Indian figures was gnawing on a blue-black arm. Anna's stomach curdled, but she stifled a retch as she pulled her pistol from her ankle holster. She drew down on Rankin. "Let me see your hands, right now!"

Rankin didn't seem to hear her. "I apologize for the odor. We dipped the body parts in paraffin, but still—"

"Show me your hands!"

A shadow stretched down one of the aisles between two bone-storage cabinets. It flitted around Anna's feet and disappeared again. She reeled that way. Nothing. She checked back on Rankin. He was no longer in sight, but he hadn't gotten around her. She was sure of it. If anything, he'd withdrawn into the diorama.

A drawer full of bones rolled out several inches, startling her. Had she failed to fully close it? It was labeled: *Modoc.* No time to think about that, for someone else was in the laboratory. The scuff of a shoe sole came from a few aisles over. She sidestepped toward the last position of the sound, holding her pistol before her with both hands.

Kawatu was down here. Close by.

The lights went out.

Automatically, she took a step back, then went motionless, relying completely on her ears for warning.

"Anna . . . ?" Rankin's voice drifted to her from some distant corner of the laboratory. She pressed her back against the drawers, preparing for a rush from either the left or the right. "Can you hear me, my dear?"

Somehow, the darkness made the stench even more revolting. She fought another gag reflex. How could Rankin move through it as if he were in a perfume factory?

"I arranged for you and Parker to come here, you know," Rankin said. "Consider it a compliment. You two were my litmus test. If you could be convinced of their authenticity, my cryptograms to the future were safe." That was it: His messages with hidden significance were John Day Man and Willow Creek Woman. "Now I only hope Parker's less prescient than you, Anna. I saw it from the beginning—you're the more gifted investigator, although you lack his megalomaniacal self-confidence." Rankin fell silent for a moment. "I'm tired, you know. I've been temporarily bested by my detractors. My cartouche, my royal seal, has been chiseled off all the monuments raised in my honor. Still, death has no sting. My cryptograms will redeem me. Would you care to join them? It's an enormous honor to bear the truth to posterity."

Her hands were slick with sweat, but she refused to take either of them from her pistol for even an instant. She vowed not to wind up as Deborah Carter had. She'd keep her wits about her no matter what happened in the coming minutes, no matter how many horrors Rankin hurled at her in this charnel dungeon.

Something crashed against the tiled floor and clattered as it seemingly disintegrated into a thousand pieces. Some of these sharp bits bounced against her shins. She spun toward the clamor, her forefinger bearing down on her trigger. But she didn't fire. No target. Only blackness confronted her, although the jarring sound itself had flooded her eyeballs with swirling specks of light that only now were beginning to fade.

She took a step forward, and her right shoe crushed something into grit. Bone. Kawatu had strewn bones over the floor to tell him of her movements.

Another crash made her freeze. She came within a hairsbreadth of firing her pistol by reflex. She wanted badly to start shooting if only to relieve her tension, but sensed that once begun the impulse wouldn't be satisfied until she'd emptied her clip. And for what? The second crash had come from completely across the lab.

Kawatu was whisking around the basement like a ghost.

"Soon we shall be bones, you and I, Anna," Rankin's otherworldly voice went on. "And there will be no one after to study us. No one to say who we were and what we did. No one to resurrect our songs and our superstitions. Ponder our tools. And the benign ignorance of the universe will be pestered no more by science." He chuckled wistfully. "Is that what you really want? Not I, my dear. I want to be poked and prodded, chemically assayed and carbon-dated. But more so, I want my ideas to live forever. The NAGPRA reactionaries will rebury John Day Man and Willow Creek Woman so no one will ever find them again, but that will not be the death of Thaddeus Rankin's ideas. They shall rise from the ashes and spread their wings once again—if only because they were so unfairly suppressed in this time. Some inquisitive mind yet unborn will ask, *What great discovery was quashed when a number of rare skeletons were put back in the ground at the beginning of the twenty-first century?* And the search will continue. Continue to culmination. Isn't it ironic that sometimes the truth must be salted away in deceit?"

Stairs.

The elevator could become a death trap for her, but she recalled a door marked Exit off to one side of it. She skimmed her shoes along the floor, so as not to bring her soles down on the crusty, brittle remains. But still there was bone dust everywhere, and each skating motion made a noise like sandpaper being scraped. Still, she continued toward where she believed the door lay.

"Anna, talk to me. There will be more than enough silence after you're gone. Let's fill our last minutes together with friendly discourse. No more silence, dear girl."

Yes, she abruptly decided.

She had come to one of the lab benches. She swept her arm over its top. Then, while the clangor of broken glass and wash of spilled chemicals still echoed in the basement, she ran blindly for the door. Something hooked her ankle and sent her sprawling. She landed chin-first, and her pistol rattled across the floor and away from her. She groped for it. Her search widened into the spaces under the autopsy tables. Something cut the heel of her right hand. Shattered glass. The death stench was now overpowered by ethanol and other smarting chemicals she couldn't identify.

She was on the verge of abandoning her 9mm and making directly for her rental car when a shaft of light spanned the length of the floor.

Her pistol lay within reach. Seizing it, she looked up just as the elevator doors slid shut and the blackness returned.

A sliver of light in the door seam went out from bottom to top as the car climbed upstairs.

Before the darkness, she'd glimpsed Kawatu in the elevator. His next move was obvious—to trap her downstairs.

21

Emmett's eyes startled open. But the patterns of light and shadow surrounding him swam in kaleidoscopic circles that made him want to puke. He touched the left side of his head—and flinched from the pressure of his own fingers.

He was breathing. He started there.

And he was prone.

His fractured consciousness could bear only one discovery at a time.

His inner wrists were rubbing together. He tried to pull his hands apart, but they were shackled with nylon tie-straps. This minimal exertion left him hyperventilating. He decided that the only sensible thing to do was to creep back down the well of darkness from which he'd risen. But there was a reason not to go under again, wasn't there? He just couldn't pluck it out of the confusion that filled his skull like wet concrete.

Remember.

He'd been bounced through the windy night. A big star had hung low in the sky. The eastern or western sky—what time had it been? What time was it now? He'd been agonizingly cold. Lying in the open, then, exposed to the elements. A cold he hadn't fully shaken, for he was still shivering. The bed of a pickup truck. The throaty obbligato of a diesel engine being run at high speed. A stop. Being jostled from the back of the pickup into another vehicle, which was intoxicatingly warm. Enclosed, then.

Emmett sat up. And the top of his head seemed to lift off in a dazzling sunburst of pain.

Groaning, he slowly recovered from this hasty movement.

And as soon as he recovered, he comprehended. He was in the cargo area of Thaddeus Rankin's Lexus sport utility. Kawatu had switched vehicles somewhere—that's why the Dodge diesel pickup had never appeared on the estate grounds. Gingerly, Emmett swiveled his head for a look forward. The driver's seat was empty, and the engine wasn't running. Kawatu was nowhere in sight. The four-wheel drive was parked beneath the porte cochere at the entrance to Rankin's mansion.

Emmett checked the ignition. The keys were missing.

That meant the New Guinean had gone inside the house to see Rankin. Emmett realized that his fate was being decided by the twosome as he wallowed in a cerebral fog.

He tried to open the Lexus's rear hatch, but it was locked from the dashboard or from outside.

Swinging his legs around to climb over the backseat, he found that his ankles, like his wrists, were bound with flexible tie-straps. Flailing and chafing were useless—the ties were as strong as steel. His shoes and socks were gone. Frisking himself with his elbows and fettered hands, he discovered that his cell phone, keys, pocketknife and wallet had all been taken as well.

His revolver, he suddenly recalled, was at the bottom of the cinder pit.

Clamping his teeth together to keep from biting his tongue, he tumbled over the back of the seat. His upper body tobogganed into the floor, and once more his head exploded with fireworks, immobilizing him. His consciousness went on and off like house lights during a thunderstorm. *Don't go out . . . don't go out.*

Kawatu could be expected back at any second, and Emmett doubted that he'd bring word of a reprieve. Probably the only question in the man's mind had been how to dispose of the federal officer, a big enough issue for him to seek Rankin's advice.

Emmett pushed open a rear passenger door. The wind slammed it shut again. Too weak to fight the northerly, he squirmed across the seat to the opposite door. It faced the brightly lit entrance to the mansion, but he shoved anyway.

This door stayed open.

He slid outside like a sack of coal, striking his shoulder against the pavement so hard he blacked out. Maybe not more than a few seconds. But he came to with an even greater urgency to get away. Into the surrounding night.

But first he had to free his limbs.

Crawling to the back of the Lexus, he hooked his hands over the tailpipe. The stink of scorched skin filled his nostrils as the hot tube fried the sides of his wrists. But then he smelled molten nylon, and his hands dropped free as the tie-strap drizzled in two. Rubbing his burns, he shifted onto his back and draped his ankles over the exhaust pipe. More blistering agony. But his ankles parted.

Standing, he studied the house. The front door was shut, and there was no sign of Kawatu. A sedan was parked in front of the Lexus, a Ford with a rental company sticker.

Who else was here? Somebody who might help him?

Not likely, he decided.

He staggered out onto the lawn to plan his next move under cover of darkness. The bristly turf felt like ice crystals under his bare soles. He crouched down on one knee, shuddering from the cold that was now trapped inside his marrow. The driveway was lit by landscaping fixtures all the way up to Highway 14, making it a gauntlet.

Were headlights slowing near the gate?

Emmett couldn't tell: His vision had improved somewhat, but everything in the distance was still a watery blur. He made up his mind not to go for the highway. He was too far from the closest reservation to count on anyone stopping for a shoeless, disheveled Indian.

He grunted as he rose unsteadily to his full height, his head screaming for him to lie still again, and struck out for the barren terrain to the east. How long would his feet stand up to the shoals of coral-sharp basalt that plunged all the way down to the river? His toes were already numb. But his bigger worry was the lack of vegetation beyond the estate fence, other than shin-high dry grass. No place to hide. And he had little doubt that a man reared in the wilds of New Guinea would be a skilled tracker.

The fact became glaringly obvious to Emmett—he couldn't outdistance Kawatu on foot.

He about-faced and lumbered back to the Lexus. He found a tool kit under the front seat, took out the tire iron and used its pointed end to pry the panel cover off the steering column. The inner workings looked nothing like those of the old Chevrolet he'd hot-wired as a teenager in the parking lot of his Catholic Indian boarding school. Back then he'd connected a brown wire to a purple one, and the engine had coughed to life. Now he was confronted by a thick bundle of at least thirty wires.

Maybe the Ford would be simpler.

He shambled ahead to the rental car and ducked inside. As with the Lexus, no keys had been left in the ignition. He sat limp in the driver's seat for a few seconds, waiting for the fireball inside his head to subside. So he could see, let alone think.

Footfalls.

He could hear footfalls approaching. Flopping down across the seats, he listened. Someone was chuffing for breath as he neared the house at a dead run. The semienclosed space of the porte cochere scrambled these sounds into overlapping echoes, and Emmett couldn't tell where the runner was headed.

Silence.

Emmett looked out again. The runner had vanished. Had it been Kawatu returning to the mansion after preparing a grave for Emmett Parker out on the grounds? If so, why hadn't he glanced into the cargo area of the Lexus and noticed that his captive was missing?

The front door to the mansion was now ajar.

Emmett bent over to wrench the panel off the steering column. Good—only eight wires, but none were brown or purple. Something distracted him, made him sit up again and sniff the Ford's interior.

Perfume.

He sat without moving a muscle, not wanting to believe, not trusting his nose. Desert lavender. Finally, turning around, he saw both a carry-on and a garment bag in the backseat. He unzipped the garment bag—and beheld a blue FBI windbreaker.

Christ Almighty.

Trying to make sense of this was futile. Anna was inside the house with Rankin and Kawatu. Everything got down to that. And the only reason the New Guinean had failed to reappear in the last several minutes was because he and the anthropologist were dealing with her.

Glass tinkled, and Emmett instinctively pulled his head down into his shoulders. After a moment, he took stock of the Ford's windows. They were intact. But the breakage had been close by.

He got out of the sedan and rushed half-tripping toward the mansion's entrance, holding the tire iron like a club.

• • •

There was a small rectangular window in the door. Beyond it, just enough light spilled down from the landing above to show Anna that the compartment was the stairwell. But the knob was locked. Frantically, she moved on to the elevator, felt the wall for the button. She pushed it. No whine of hoist cables followed, no rattle of counterweights inside the shaft.

She pressed again, harder. Nothing.

Finally, she found the switches that Rankin had used to illuminate the lab. She jiggled all of them, but the lights didn't come on.

Meanwhile, behind her, the anthropologist could be heard prowling the basement, his voice never coming from quite the same place out in the vastness. "Anna, my dear," he asked with an unnerving civility, "where are you . . . ?"

She orbited him along the walls, feeling caged, knowing that Rankin had sealed all the exits in anticipation of her visit. But why had Kawatu broken off hunting for her and gone upstairs? To work the electrical circuit breakers and keep her in the dark no matter where she went?

She halted after a fruitless, bumbling search for another door leading out—kicking herself for not having paid more attention to her surroundings upon arrival in the lab. Emmett. Her mind had been consumed by the separation with Emmett, as much as that now chagrined her.

Hunkering down, she peered out into the darkness, trying to catch movement.

A bone popped as a shoe pulverized it. Rankin was on the move somewhere near the cabinets. He said, "Anna, I'd like to give you the honor of becoming my last cryptogram to the future. Your indignity will be brief—NAGPRA shall see to that."

She was tempted to challenge him over how he planned to get away with killing her, but she already had an inkling: Rankin had managed to explain Deborah Carter's death to the apparent satisfaction of law enforcement. Pagans were made-to-order scapegoats, and she suspected that one of Sward's followers would be framed for her own murder.

But it's not going to come to that.

Windows.

From her two prior visits, she recalled transomlike basement windows. The panes had been painted over. She groped her way to a sink counter on the outer wall, clambered up on it—and blundered into one of the basins. Toppling, she pitched face-first down the length of the counter, smashing beakers and scattering metal utensils with her outstretched arms.

She sprawled dazed on the surface for only a heartbeat before rising again.

This time, she'd managed to hang on to her pistol.

Flipping it around in her hand, she used the butt as a hammer to strike the wall above her head. Twice, she tapped against plaster. Then, as she sidestepped along the counter, the pistol butt punched through a pane of glass. Streaks of light hatched from the break. She enlarged it, and a solid band of yellow streamed in from the porte cochere. This light also brought the security bars into stark relief. She'd remembered the windows but forgotten the bars covering them.

Then she saw Emmett.

She had to bite off an exhilarated shout—Rankin was still stalking her. Parker staggered from her rental car toward the front door of the house. Two things helped her choke down her joy: He wobbled as if he could barely keep upright. And, to her back, another bone was crushed underfoot.

Spinning around, she came face-to-face with Thaddeus Rankin.

He loomed so large in her pistol sights it took her a second to realize that he was still fifteen feet away, frozen in the shaft of light from the shattered window. His ponytail had come undone, and his long white hair framed his pustulated face. His jaw muscles quivered obscenely under the ulcerated skin. In one fist was an obsidian knife, gleaming as blackly as his eyes, and in the other a short-barreled revolver. He was aiming the muzzle at the floor, and Anna was still out of the reach of his blade. "Please remain where you are, my dear. I prefer not to use firearms. It's laborious to disguise bullet damage in a specimen that's allegedly ancient."

"Drop your weapons!" she barked at him.

"Do you finally understand what I had to do? Fight fire with fire, Anna. I've used NAGPRA's own power against itself. My native detractors love nothing better than reburying evidence, so it's only fitting that I used the act to bury these specimens beyond the reach of forensic science, forever. You and Parker are quite correct—John Day Man is Nathan Creech, who was half Nootka and half white. I'd gone to British Columbia to escape ceaseless interventions against my digs, but Creech shut me down there too."

"And Willow Creek Woman?" Anna asked, despite herself.

"A Zuni bitch of mixed blood who closed down my excavation in New Mexico. That site would've definitely proved the existence of both interracial warfare and cannibalism in prehistoric North America."

"What'd you use to drug Elsa and the others?"

Rankin shook his head as if she'd disappointed him. "Fear itself is the greatest hallucinogen. Never forget that. Fear can make you see and feel anything, *anything*."

She hovered on the brink of shooting him. But would it amount to suicide-by-cop? Clearly, he was willing to die at any time. Thanks to NAGPRA, he trusted that John Day Man and Willow Creek Woman would go back in the ground, never to be analyzed again. He could die in peace because he had faith some future anthropologist would believe that Thaddeus Rankin had been onto something momentous— only to be cheated out of confirmation by his enemies.

Kill him before he gets off a shot!

"Drop your weapons, Rankin!"

He refused. But she couldn't summarily execute him, even though there seemed to be no soul behind his glassy eyes, only a loathsome hunger. "I just want a taste, my dear. No indignity, I promise." He took a rigid stride toward her.

"Freeze!"

"What a joy to feel what you feel . . . believe what you believe . . ." Rankin stepped toward her again. "I want you inside me for the journey out of this corrupt old body." He drifted into her shadow, but his eyes continued to shine up at her. A third step, and he was now close enough to plunge the stone knife into her groin.

That was it.

Her pistol jumped twice in her grasp, and Rankin disappeared behind the powder flashes. The twin blasts covered any sound of his falling. Anna leaned to the side, trying to catch sight of him again, but nothing showed in the fan of faint light on the floor—except a splattering of deep maroon blood.

She leaped off the counter, then leaned forward, straining for his indistinct silhouette among the lab benches. The cone of light spilling through the broken window only seemed to intensify the blackness in the rest of the basement.

She realized that she was backlit, a perfect target. While crossing into the shadows, she examined the blood spatters. The tapered ends of the drops pointed in the direction the wounded Rankin had fled. Toward the rear of the lab. She didn't want to fight this out in that hideous mock cave, gagging on the foulness of Deborah Carter's rotting flesh. And she was almost willing to wait for Emmett to reach her. Surely, he must have heard the gunshots.

But another part of her refused to rely on Parker ever again: *You can do this alone . . . you can do this.*

She advanced between the benches, sweeping her pistol back and forth. She felt something slippery under her shoes. Pooled liquid. Genuflecting, she touched her fingers to the cool stuff and brought it up to her nose.

Ethanol. Alcohol.

Ten paces later, she nearly slipped on more liquid. This felt viscid. Sticky. And it smelled metallic. Blood. The splatters definitely tended toward the cave. Rankin had retreated into his lair. To bleed out and die? Or had he been dying for so many years now his virtual corpse possessed a kind of zombie invulnerability?

Something about the cabinets slowed her steps.

Instead of faintly humming, as before, the bone repositories seemed to be rattling in agitation. A vibration from the forced-air heating system? But the heat wasn't running, for the area surrounding the cabinets was now even more intensely cold. *Rankin . . . focus only on Rankin.*

She covered her nose and mouth with her free hand to approach the open steel door to the diorama. Still, the stench reached down her windpipe and made her gag. The blood trail had petered out, but she sensed Rankin waiting inside with his own handgun.

A light came on behind her.

Reeling, she drew down on the open elevator car at the opposite end of the basement. The doors had whisked back, and Anna had a dim, chaotic view of a tall and muscular figure with raven hair charging out into the darkness with his revolver drawn.

Pressed flat against the wall behind him was Thaddeus Rankin, in faint relief, as unmoving as a statue.

She cried, *"Behind you, Emmett!"*

But Rankin's obsidian knife plunged into the raven-haired figure's back, and he crumpled to the floor.

Running, Anna fired once—purposely high, trying to divert Rankin from his attack without accidentally hitting Emmett. But the anthropologist went on slashing and hacking, so viciously the two men seemed to be enveloped in a pink haze. A cackling sound rose above the awful thudding of the knife—Rankin's laughter. He laughed convulsively as his right arm rose and fell again and again, thrusting and thrusting. His savagery seemed inexhaustible, feeding on its own fury.

Too far, you'll never reach Emmett in time.

Anna steadied her elbows on a bench top and carefully squeezed off a shot at Rankin's head.

She missed.

Emmett was now taking the ripping blows like a sandbag.

She sprinted headlong at Rankin.

But, blood-splattered, grinning, he scuttled back into the elevator car. He hit a button with the heel of his red-stained hand, and the doors shut. Leaving Anna in total darkness. Even the weak light from outside had now been extinguished.

• • •

Emmett tottered through the front door and made straightaway for the library, where Rankin conducted all his public business.

The room was empty. Where, then, had he taken Anna?

And why?

He wanted to cry out for her, but that might force Rankin's hand. Instead, he went to the desk and traded the tire iron for a stiletto-like letter opener. He tried the telephone, but the line was dead.

A sharp click came to him from somewhere out in the house.

The lights in the library and corridor leading to it went off. His presence had been noted, and someone was manipulating the circuit breakers. Kawatu, most likely. Emmett recalled seeing a box of matches among the desk appointments. He fished for it, grabbed it and dropped it in his shirt pocket.

"Parker . . . ?" an accentless voice inquired tentatively from the hallway.

Emmett held his tongue. It wasn't the New Guinean. And probably not Rankin. Somebody else in the anthropologist's employ, like a rent-a-cop? There was a security firm sign on the front gate.

"Hello, can you hear me?" The voice was farther along the corridor this time. Familiar sounding, but not familiar enough for Emmett to answer. His ears were ringing at the excruciatingly high pitch of a dentist's drill, and everything he heard was muffled and distorted by this inner sound. He shrank from the flashlight beam that bobbed along the Persian runner in the hall. He backtracked to the desk and knelt behind it. The beam methodically probed the library. It settled on the desk, stayed there for what seemed an eternity, so long Emmett got ready to spring up and hurl the letter opener at the holder.

But then the light swept down the hall.

Emmett never caught sight of the man.

Within seconds, an electrical drone mimicked the ringing in his ears, although at a lower pitch. But it was definitely outside his head. Machinery operating, an elevator maybe.

Emmett rushed to follow: The man might lead him to Anna.

But the end of the hallway was silent by the time he reached it. He struck a match. The flame showed him elevator doors. He shoved the letter opener into the crack to see if they might give. If he got inside, he might be able to use the escape hatch in the roof of the car, to pounce on Rankin and his hirelings. But the blade bent, and the doors didn't budge. The match guttered out, and Emmett lit another to search the hall.

Stairs. Every elevator was backed up by stairs.

His second match went out, but not before he tested the knob to a door. It was unlocked. He was nudging the door open when it flew out of his grasp. He lurched forward and was met by an onrushing force that closed like talons around his throat. It drove him back into the corridor. He extended his left arm behind him to take the brunt of the fall, but his skull bashed against the floor with such velocity that lightning forked through his brain. He realized that fingers were digging into his windpipe. Breath was gusting into his face—he was grappling with a human being, although at first the force had seemed inhuman.

Emmett flexed his fist—the letter opener was still in it.

Yet he must have telegraphed its presence by tensing his hand, for his attacker abruptly let go of his throat and began trying to wrench the opener away from him.

"Let go of the knife," Kawatu whispered, "and I won't hurt you."

"Where's Anna?"

"With the doctor in the basement."

"Is she dead?"

"I don't know."

Kawatu's tone of unconcern so infuriated Emmett he slammed his left forearm into the man's jaw. The New Guinean recoiled, but then raked his clawed fingers across Emmett's cheek, going after his eyes. Emmett twisted his face to the side and clenched his eyelids as tightly as he could. His grip on the letter opener was weakening, while Kawatu's strength seemed to be increasing. Emmett tried to join both his hands around the hilt, but Kawatu pinioned his left wrist.

Two muffled gunshot reports came from under the floor.

Emmett bucked frantically, trying to whip Kawatu off his chest, but every exertion now brought on sunbursts inside his head that took him to the edge of consciousness. He couldn't pass out. Even a grayout would cost him his life. And Anna's. The shots had sounded like 9mm rounds.

Another pistol report thumped below.

And then one more, after a pause. She was either shooting blindly or her pistol had been taken from her.

Emmett shoved his free hand under Kawatu's chin and pushed with all his remaining strength. The New Guinean didn't budge. "Stop fighting, Mr. Parker," he urged. There seemed to be no anger in the man, just a calm resolve to deal with troublesome prey. He let go of Emmett's wrist and struck him in the chest.

More fire flashed behind Emmett's eyes. Astonishingly, in its wake he could actually see Kawatu. Using a knee, the man was pinning Emmett's hand that held the opener—and staring down the corridor with a look of surprise. Emmett glanced in the same direction. There, the elevator doors had opened, flooding the hall with the foggy light he'd assumed to be the product of his swollen brain.

Rankin crawled out of the car on his side. He was holding a bloody handkerchief to his left hip with one hand and brandishing a snub-nosed revolver with the other. His khaki pants were drenched in blood, and his face was chalk white. "Turnipseed shot me," he said, his voice shuddery from shock. "Let's get on with it, my boy."

Although his expression remained impassive, Kawatu took Rankin's words as a cue for him to stop toying with his prey. He slid a large, blocky-looking pistol from his waistband and jabbed the muzzle between Emmett's eyes. Seeing the big bore descend on him, he believed it to be .45 caliber. The kind of ammunition Deborah Carter had spilled around her garage. He tried not to drift, but concentrating on anything was finally impossible. Nor would his leaden arms obey the impulses of his short-circuiting nerves.

Rankin asked, "How many more police are in the house?"

"I don't understand," Kawatu replied.

"Other than Parker and Turnipseed, are there cops in here?"

That visibly puzzled Kawatu. "None I know of, sir. Why?"

"No matter." Rankin winced as a rivulet of blood bubbled out from under his sopping handkerchief. He kneaded a corner of the cloth into a point and rammed it into the bullet hole. "It had to end this way, I suppose."

"Shall I . . . ?" Kawatu asked.

Spray my brains all over this corridor, he means. Emmett reached down deep inside, searching for one last reserve of energy. But his body felt like a tub of putty.

"Don't kill him," Rankin told Kawatu. "We need him to deal with Turnipseed below."

Emmett chuckled thickly.

"What, Parker?" Rankin asked.

Emmett shook his head as much as the pressure of the muzzle allowed. His feelings defied explanation. He'd never known such an improbable happiness. Anna lived. And was kicking the shit out of her enemies.

"Pacify him," Rankin ordered Kawatu.

The bore left the sweaty spot between Emmett's eyes, and the butt promptly swung back at his temple. The same side of his head Kawatu had struck before, Emmett noted with an odd sense of detachment as the blackness came pouring in again like warm tar.

• • •

In the darkness, Anna touched the corpse only once. To feel a carotid artery in the neck to see if there was yet a pulse. There was none. He was gone. The seemingly indestructible lay destroyed. She waited with a panicky expectation for her feelings to run away with her. But rage, grief, terror—these all compressed down into a hard clarity of purpose—*Get the bastards.*

Rising, she began putting her defenses in order.

Rankin, if he still lived, and Kawatu wouldn't leave her at liberty in the basement. Even her limited freedom of movement was a danger to them. The New Guinean would come down after her, probably sooner rather than later, and she'd be ready for him.

She would kill Kawatu, then Rankin.

She rummaged around in the darkness until she located an autopsy tray. It was heavy, possibly even bolted to the floor, but she heaved the table over with a loud crash, then scooted it around so the top faced both the elevator and the stairwell door at a slight angle. To deflect bullets.

How many cartridges did she have left?

She'd fired a total of four times at Rankin. Her pistol held fourteen rounds in the magazine and one in the chamber. Eleven cartridges remaining, then.

All you need is one, Emmett's voice coached—but she brushed it aside before her loss consumed her. There was more than enough time for that later. *Concentrate on the here and now—and live as long as you can. The dead cannot exact vengeance.* She nurtured the deep, dark calm within her. It was stronger than anger, more pliable than fear. Life had never seemed simpler.

She cleared the bench immediately behind her of the flasks and beakers and possibly volatile chemicals they contained. The heaviest she set down beside her, removed the lid and smelled the liquid. More ethanol.

Then she knelt behind the autopsy tray and waited.

Rankin wanted her dead, no matter what. Another set of remains to present to NAGPRA so they could be locked away for eternity. She saw no reason to negotiate with him, other than to buy time. And time was on Rankin's side.

She heard a squeak of cables, and then the elevator doors parted on human figures. Anna aimed for the middle of them, frantically trying to make sense of the inconceivable. For a horrifying moment, as her eyes darted spasmodically from figure to figure, she wondered if she was losing her mind. Had Rankin slipped her something after all? Kawatu was propping up Emmett Parker, who was semiconscious. His head lolled onto a shoulder, and blood seeped from a temple. The New Guinean lifted Emmett's face by jamming the muzzle of a pistol under his chin.

Instantly, Anna looked to the body on the floor in front of the elevator. The now unknown man had come to rest on his back, civilian clothes gashed and ripped by the obsidian knife Rankin had dropped in the blood that had pooled around the corpse. Enough of the face showed for Anna to recognize Gabriel Round Dance, bug-eyed in death.

She wasn't losing her mind. And Emmett was alive. But she smothered the spark of elation before it distracted her. "Drop the gun, Kawatu!" she ordered.

"That would be my suggestion to you, Anna." Using his cane, Rankin sidled out from behind Emmett and his assistant. One entire pant leg was wet with blood, she observed with satisfaction, although she'd been aiming at the middle of his torso. He still gripped his small revolver, which he used to gesture at the corpse. "Who was my assailant?"

"You murdered Sergeant Round Dance."

"Pity," Rankin sighed. "A full-blooded Wasco, just another Amerind. Of no interest to science. Please, Anna . . ." He abruptly doubled over in pain, but then came up smiling as if the wrenching spasm had only been a trifle. "Please, enough pandemonium. Put down your weapon, and let's talk about this like civilized people. . . ." He was crafty enough not to use force of argument. He had no argument that might appeal to her. Instead, he was relying entirely on tone, a warm and reasonable one. "Personally, I'm of a mind to phone the Klickitat sheriff's office and let the chips fall where they will. But my adopted son is of the opinion that the situation can be salvaged by disposing of Round Dance, Parker and you." She shifted for a shot at him, but the anthropologist crept back behind his human shields. "By chance, Anna, did you arrange for Round Dance to back you up here?"

Anna didn't know why Round Dance had been miles outside his jurisdiction. But was it unwise to admit this to Rankin? Was he worried about more law enforcement on the way? His question meant that the Wasco sergeant and Emmett hadn't come here together. So more backup could be just minutes behind. But would Kawatu execute Emmett if he felt hemmed in?

"You're not getting away, Rankin," she finally said.

"Don't be surly, Anna." He peeked around Kawatu's arm. "But you have come to hate me, haven't you?" *With every fiber of my being, you son of a bitch.* "I hope you now hate me enough to understand the appeal of exocannibalism. The tactile pleasure of punishing me with your teeth, of breaking my body down piece by piece in the acid cement mixer of your gut. In the brainstem, the neural circuits for oral and genital gratification are like twin wires in the same power cord." He paused. "Kawatu, kindly shoot Parker in ten seconds."

The New Guinean gave an obedient nod, and his lips began pursing to a steady, one-second beat.

Anna counted to herself. *Nine . . .* She emptied her mind, wanting nothing to get in the way of her coming reaction. *Six . . .* Sweat dribbled out of an armpit and ran icily down her ribs, but she ignored the sensation. *Four . . .* On the third beat, she grabbed the jar of ethanol and hurled it just beyond Round Dance's body. It shattered against the floor, and the alcohol slopped around the feet of the three men in the elevator.

Kawatu withdrew deeper into the car, dragging Emmett with him.

The fumes wafted out to Anna, clouding her vision. "One spark from a muzzle," she announced, blinking back the sting of tears, "and we'll all fry!"

"Push forward, my boy!" Rankin shouted. "Out of here, quickly!"

Hugging Emmett close to him, Kawatu advanced, firing from the hip as soon as he was clear of the car. Anna didn't wait to see if his bullets glanced off the stainless steel of the autopsy tray. She ran backwards, watching for even a momentary chance to return fire without hitting Emmett. Yet not more than an inch of Kawatu's face or body showed to either side of Parker's slumping shape. He shot every two or three strides, and Anna could hear the bullets imbed in the bone cabinets behind her.

A high-pressure hiss made her turn around. She flinched as something tubular launched off the floor past her and careened among the lab benches. A liquid nitrogen cylinder, punctured by one of Kawatu's rounds. It rocketed around the lab like an unknotted balloon, smashing flasks and spilling more chemicals, before playing itself out among the cabinets.

Anna scrambled back on her heels, struggling to get a bead on Kawatu through the blinding vapors. Overhead, the ventilation system automatically whirred on.

Although still in Kawatu's clutches, Emmett opened his eyes. Anna thought she saw him mouth the word *shoot!*

But she had another idea.

With Kawatu rushing toward her, she stooped, touched the muzzle of her pistol to the edge of a large wet circle on the floor—and fired. *Whoosh!* The flames were invisible but they brushed her cheeks like a torrid breath. She heard her eyebrows singe.

Kawatu recoiled, letting go of Emmett, who sank to his knees in the now semitransparent flash fire. Anna shot once on the fly, taking no time to see if she'd struck Kawatu. Her arms closed around Emmett's waist, and she rolled with him out of the reach of the flames. His clothes were burning in patches. She beat out the flames with her free hand, then spun back toward Kawatu and lined up her sights on him.

He was ringed by waist-high blue and green flames. Had he dropped his pistol? He wasn't holding it. He'd stripped off his shirt and was using it to fight the fire. "No, no!" he shouted as the tide of fire spread and began igniting the wooden lab benches. He seemed oblivious to Anna, even to the bullet hole in his left shoulder. Fiery tendrils licked at his pants and curled around his legs. His only concern was the fire; he flailed madly at it with his shirt. The sleeves unraveled into sparks, and soon he seemed to be battling the fire with nothing more than a handful of flame.

The ceiling sprinklers sputtered to life, and he grinned up into this artificial rain as if it promised salvation. However, the spray only added steam to the chemically fed fire. One by one, the hoses to the Bunsen burners burst, and six-foot-long jets of blue whipped back and forth like dancing cobras.

Kawatu went back to beating the flames, trying to save his inheritance.

Anna looked for Rankin. Nowhere in sight. But the elevator doors were still open. She began dragging Emmett across the glass-littered floor toward them. Any glimmer of awareness in his eyes had gone out again, and he was dead weight in her arms.

Arching his back, Kawatu cried out. His pants were now engulfed, but he reached behind and pried the pistol from his waistband. The smoking gunmetal was too hot for him to handle, and the weapon squirted out of his grasp. The ammunition cooked off like firecrackers, but Kawatu ignored the violent popping as he strode toward Anna and Emmett. Flames wrapped around him, seemingly flowing from his skin now, but his face showed nothing but a cold hatred as he moved toward her—she who was the cause of all this.

She fired.

Kawatu kept coming on.

Again, she pulled the trigger.

He stumbled slightly, gurgled something in pidgin that sounded like an oath, but refused to go down. He reached out for her with a burning arm, his subcutaneous fat dripping off the muscles in driblets of fire.

She cranked off another round, more wildly than before, not knowing if she was even close to the mark.

He teetered on the balls of his feet in the same split second that fire seemed to burst from his head. His hair crisped, and a shrill, inhuman scream was ripped from his lungs. Collapsing, he vanished in the hottest part of the fire.

Which continued to spread.

Anna seized hold of Emmett's shirt collar again and pulled. "Come on, Parker. Help me, dammit!" He didn't stir.

But then she saw Rankin standing behind a ghostly sheet of flame. "Don't be obstinate, Anna," he said to her over his revolver. "Time to die . . . time to throw yourself on this bone heap we call the world."

She swung her muzzle toward him, but with the sickening knowledge that he had the drop on her. As soon as she fired, she sprawled over Emmett, protecting him. If Rankin had gotten off a round, its report was lost in the crump of another container of alcohol igniting. The roiling flash of heat gave her the adrenaline to drag Emmett two yards closer to the elevator. Through the shimmering, aurora-like flames, she saw Rankin slinking back into the aisle between two bone cabinets.

A strange warble rose above the sounds of the burning lab. Kawatu's corpse giving up its pent-up breath? No. It sounded like the cry of a bird. Air was rushing in the broken window. Was that the cause of the trilling, mournful call—the night gushing through the sawtooth-edged window frame to fill the vacuum being created by the fire?

Anna glanced back at Rankin—as a cabinet tottered and crashed at a tilt against the one across the aisle from it. The drawers rolled open, showering the passageway with bones, a cascade of rattling bones that poured over Rankin. He stumbled. His feet shot out from under him on the fibulas and tibias, all slick from the sprinklers, and he landed on his back with a loud crunch. Skulls hurtled down with such force he threw his arms over his head until the avalanche of Indian remains spent itself to a trickle.

Anna saw that he still held his revolver.

As the birdlike screech grew louder, the blaze inched toward him. He attempted to rise, but the loss of blood was weakening him at last. Clutching his leg wound, he gazed listlessly into the approaching fire. But as the heat drew close, it proved too hellish to endure. Again, Rankin struggled to rise, but the mound of skeletons was so unstable he kept slipping. He began to kick an opening down to the solid footing of the floor, but more bones poured into the space he managed to clear.

Anna continued lumbering with Emmett toward the elevator.

Rankin gasped. Wicked little tongues of flame were flickering up through the pile, scorching him in fits and starts. He fell into a kind of desperate, clumsy backstroke, but the disarticulated skeletons seemed to absorb his thrashing and hold him fast. His floundering became wild, almost pointless, and the bones lower in the mound glowed orange with heat.

Rankin raised his fist. In it was the snub-nosed handgun. He pointed it at Anna, and she fumbled to return fire. Nothing. The slide to her 9mm was open, and the trigger was dead: She'd emptied her magazine against Kawatu without realizing it.

Rankin howled with glee at her helplessness. "Time to die, Anna!"

But above him, a mid-level drawer, partially cracked, rolled fully open at that moment. Bones tumbled out of it, including skulls, and Rankin's gun hand was driven down into his lap. He stiffened as a fireball mushroomed up out of the bone pile and sheathed his entire body in flames.

The warble was replaced by Rankin's wailing scream.

Looking away, Anna dragged Emmett past Round Dance's body and into the elevator. She closed the door on the inferno. The control panel was smoking, and the alarm in the car was yelping. She pressed the button for the ground floor.

The car didn't rise.

She batted all the buttons. And was rewarded only with the light in the car bumping off.

Please . . . help us . . . help us.

On that, the light returned, cables whined, and the car ascended. There was no safety until both of them were outside, as thick smoke was wreathing through the mansion, but she lingered a few seconds in the corridor on the ground floor to gather her strength for the last haul. While she lay there winded, her left hand throbbing from second-degree burns, Emmett said, punch-drunk, "You missed your flight."

"Shut up, Parker."

22

Anna stayed on at the Kah-Nee-Ta while Emmett recovered at the Mid-Columbia Medical Center in The Dalles. Ostensibly, her reason for remaining in Oregon and not taking the post waiting for her at the FBI's Indian Desk in Washington was to wrap up any loose ends for Emmett. And every few days, she dutifully reported to him at the hospital. One evening, she told him that Elsa Dease was much improved. On another, she brought the lab report on the seedpod Emmett had picked from the vine growing in Kawatu's kitchen—tropical wood rose. While the seeds were a mild hallucinogen chemically related to LSD, they alone could not have produced the psychotic breaks experienced by Elsa and Nels Sward, according to the toxicologist. Those lapses into insanity continued to defy explanation for everyone except Minnie Claw. The Sahaptin elder firmly believed that all the events of these past weeks had been the work of the hundreds of *skeps* in Rankin's bone cabinets, struggling to free themselves.

Anna was able to explain why Gabriel Round Dance had shown up unexpectedly at Rankin's mansion. A touch of amnesia had made Emmett forget Round Dance's promise to check on him at Kawatu's cottage that afternoon. Assisted by Klickitat County deputies, the sergeant located the FBI Explorer near the cinder pit. But, as a tribal officer and a stranger, he'd not been able to persuade the local cops—who were great admirers of Thaddeus Rankin—that the forensic anthropologist might be behind Emmett's disappearance. So he'd gone on alone to the estate, scaled the fence—and died, trying to help Parker.

That hurt.

Everything hurt, including Emmett's head, but nothing more so than the endless questions raised by his enforced introspection in the hospital. He asked himself if a personal reason might be delaying Anna from heading east. He never brought up the subject to her, as if the mere mention of her plans might jinx his hopes, and was heartened each time she appeared in the doorway to his private suite.

Her lightly burned left hand healed quickly. His bone-bruised skull and swollen brain took much longer.

Finally, after three weeks, he was released. She picked him up and drove him down to the Kah-Nee-Ta, where she'd already checked him in to the room adjoining hers. For two days, as she busily closed out the investigation, he watched her for a sign that she was about to go. The wait became so emotionally grueling he felt the need to talk to someone objective.

And now, at last, the phone rang in Anna's room.

It seemed plausible to him that the caller might have mistaken the message he'd just left with the answering service, so he rapped on the connecting door. "Anna . . . ?"

No response.

He jiggled the knob in frustration while the phone went on ringing, and was surprised to find the door unlocked. How long had this been the case? He was annoyed with himself for reading so much into so little lately. It smacked of a dependency that shamed him.

Anna's clothes were spread neatly over her bed, even her undergarments, and he paused while lifting the receiver to listen for the shower running. It wasn't. "Emmett Parker here. Doctor . . . ?"

"I'm not a doctor," a female voice noted. "I'm trying to reach Anna Turnipseed."

"Don't know where she is right now. This is her partner. May I take a message?"

"Please. This is Janeen Dull Knife with the Indian Desk in D.C. Would you have her phone me at home right away?"

"Sure." His heart was pounding. Ridiculously fast. As if this were the biggest thing in his life.

Dull Knife gave him the number, and Emmett dutifully jotted it down for Anna's sake. "Got it."

"And . . ." The FBI supervisor's voice thinned off into uncertainty.

"Yes?"

"Tell her she really ought to reconsider."

"Reconsider what?" Emmett asked.

But Special-Agent-in-Charge Dull Knife put up her guard. "Just have her phone me right away."

"Will do." Emmett hung up and placed the note on the bed near her clothes. But then he saw that he'd laid it too close to her bra and panties, so he moved it to a more respectful place. After this, he slammed his right fist into his left palm—with a burst of unbridled happiness. Which he promptly reined in. Again, was he reading too much into some murky signal? No, he decided. Anna wasn't going to Washington. Eyes misting with relief, he paced around her room. His skull began to ache, but he was too hopeful to let anything bother him.

Where the hell is she?

He checked the bathroom—empty, then rushed to the window on a hunch. The swimming pool lights had been extinguished, but a head was breaking the surface. Last evening, while he lay on his bed watching a college football game with the sound off, he'd heard her go out and return an hour later, only to immediately run her shower.

Each night after dinner was she venturing out to the pool?

The phone in his room rang, and he raced through the connecting door to answer it. "Doctor Tischler?"

"Yes, Emmett. How are you?"

"Okay." An absurd lie. He'd never been less okay.

The psychiatrist said, "I must say I was surprised to get your message."

"I'm surprised with myself I called you." He took a moment to make sure he had his composure. "I screwed up with Anna. Bad."

"Tell me about it." There was just enough sarcasm in the psychiatrist's inflection to make it clear that Anna had already discussed North Carolina with her. Apparently, Dr. Tischler recognized her unprofessional lapse, for she quickly amended, "Tell me exactly what you feel you screwed up, Emmett."

He frowned. "You know what I did, so let's start there."

Silence, then: "Okay, that's where we'll start. What do you have to say?"

"I need to know *why* I did it."

"It wasn't just for the sexual release?"

"No."

"Come on, Emmett—"

"Let me put this in perspective for you. I've been married three times."

"I know." Another dash of sarcasm.

But Emmett went on, "And each of those three times I had no outside relations until wives one, two and three had agreed to the separation."

"Interesting." Ice clinked in a glass on Tischler's side. "So the one-night stand back East was a departure from your normal behavior? Don't bullshit me now, Emmett."

"Absolutely a departure," he said fervently. "And the fact I did something like this to Anna is driving me nuts."

"You love her?"

"Yeah." His voice cracked, and he gritted his teeth in embarrassment.

Dr. Tischler asked, "You're a recovering alcoholic, aren't you?"

"Yes."

"Have you started drinking again over this?"

"No, why?"

"Interesting."

"You already said that."

"But it's true. Your self-esteem hasn't suffered. In fact, it may have been reinforced by the infidelity. You're a tough nut to crack, Emmett. Tough enough for me to have done some reading on the Comanche. As a people, you're big on saving face—am I correct?"

Emmett grunted assent. He didn't feel like discussing the complexities of tribal social interaction.

"You were saving face," Dr. Tischler flatly declared. "Being Comanche."

"Pardon?"

"Most partners of abuse victims feel victimized."

"By what?"

"Circumstances beyond their control. By their partner's abuser, even though the abuser might be long absent. It's convoluted, but the mind-set can run something like this: You wonder why Anna didn't find a way to end the abuse. That leads to the misconception she collaborated with her abuser. The next fanciful leap is, 'She cheated on me with her father.' It seems suspiciously possible because the past refuses to give her any peace."

Instantly, he recognized something in the scenario, but said, "That'd be irrational of me."

"Tell me about it," Dr. Tischler said.

"I wasn't playing tit for tat, Doctor." Although, all in all, North Carolina felt very much like tit for tat to him.

"Weren't you? Anna's been trying your patience. To the limit, I'd imagine. It's almost impossible for a sexually active male to constantly postpone his own needs. Maybe you wanted to give her a reason to be patient and forgiving with you. You can't maintain face and be willingly victimized at the same time. Otherwise your resentment would poison the relationship. Now that you've saved face, you believe you can go on with Anna."

"Is that it?"

Dr. Tischler chuckled. "Hell, I don't know, Emmett. People are a mystery to me. Aren't they to you?" Before he could respond, she added, "All this might be beside the point to Anna."

"What do you mean?"

"Is she there with you now?"

"No, she's swimming, I think."

"Ah," Dr. Tischler said significantly.

"Are you trying to tell me something?"

"Yes—I think we've had a breakthrough, Emmett. I look forward to our next session. Good night." Then the raspberry-like dial tone was filling his ear. Staring through the window at the darkened pool beyond, he hung up.

Trunks.

He flung open the top dresser drawer and began searching for his swimsuit. He felt completely out of control. What had Anna said to him on one of her visits to the hospital? It'd been in reference to the cabinet that had tottered over Rankin's head, the loose pile of Indian bones that had ensnared him. The Klickitat fire chief had attributed the toppling of the cabinet to a draft created by the firestorm raging inside the basement, or even to a bullet-struck liquid nitrogen tank that had sailed around the lab. But Anna wasn't convinced. *We're not as free as we think we are,* she'd said to Emmett. *Maybe the old folks have it right—we're often in the hands of forces beyond our understanding.*

So, against his better judgment, he stripped off his clothes, hopped one leg at a time into his suit and headed down to the pool in order to humiliate himself. The temperature was in the twenties, and the cement was doubtlessly cold. But he had no sensation below his knees. He was floating on expectation.

Anna was doing laps.

He padded out onto the end of the diving board and sat, although he had to tense his muscles to keep from shivering. His dangling legs startled her as she swam under him. She backed off with a splash and treaded water to look up at him, then stroked her sleek hair back from her face.

"What do you want?" she asked.

A lot of replies came to mind. But only one approached the truth. "You."

She visibly thought about it, and he prepared himself for crushing disappointment. He deserved to be disappointed. *Come on, piss me off so I can go on with my life.*

But after a long moment, she said, "You'll have to catch me this time, Em."

Then she darted under the surface and streaked for the far end of the pool.

He dove in after her.